Surrender

Surrender

G.R. Thomas

*To my dearest husband, Chris,
thank you for supporting me, without question,
in a passion that is completely self-indulgent.*

Prologue

Syracuse 212 BC

The stench of the narrow, dusty streets made Lucius wish for the battlefields more than ever. The smell of human waste rolled his stomach until bile coated the back of his throat. It gnawed at him more than seeing the entrails of a dead soldier. His protracted reposting under General Marcellus was nothing short of mind-numbing. Running meaningless errands for that tyrant not only left his body lacking its former battle strength, but had driven him to the evils of too much wine and women for the lack of adventure. He grimaced with disgust at himself as he wiped strands of amber hair and sweat from his brow with the back of a battle-scarred hand.

He smoothed down his leather tunic after a wind gust and re-adjusted his beloved sword around his waist. A gift for bravery; his thumb rolled across the top of the hilt as he made the last turn into a small cobbled street, barely two soldiers wide. The effort of dragging his right leg with any semblance of dignity slowed him down considerably. A damned injury that saw his last battle a career-ending one. Lucius resented this lameness and ground his teeth in an almost permanent scowl. Barely twenty-five, he struggled to sustain his young family on his paltry wage on the outskirts of Rome. The pressure to provide well for them was immense. He could envisage the look of shame on his late father's face when he stared into a looking glass during his morning ablutions. This extra job though, bringing in the old rogue, Archimedes, would see an extra one hundred denari in his eager hands.

Yet to lay eyes upon his two-year-old daughter, the monetary reward was all that pushed Lucius to accept such menial tasks so far beneath a centurion of his standing. He growled to himself, but pushed on towards his destination.

Lucius arrived at the ramshackle frontage, stopping to rub the ache from his temples before he announced himself. Frustrated, he kicked out at a stray dog, sniffing for a scrap of food. Headaches had plagued him of late. None of the poultices had worked, not even an entire night's worth of drinking could dull the pain. He'd resorted to Vitriola recently, using far too much of his precious wage to acquire the addictive tonic. It worked somewhat, but left him with nightmares of hellish proportions.

"Be damned with it, pull yourself together!" Lucius muttered to no one but himself as the dog returned, its skinny frame desperate for anything. This time Lucius relented, and gave it a quick scratch behind its ear and a small morsel of hardened cheese from his money pouch. Smiling at the rancid creature, he removed his helmet and ran his hands through the nearby water spout to cool his himself. A garish mythical face, with a leaden pipe for a tongue, precious liquid trickled refreshingly across his palms. Replacing his helmet, Lucius made a quick prayer, the horrid clay face drawing his fear of the Gods to the forefront of his mind. Satisfied that Mars would protect him, Lucius straightened his back, squared his shoulders, and banged upon the outer door with a firmly clenched fist.

"Archimedes of Syracuse, General Marcellus requests your presence today."

A shiver ran through him, despite the unforgiving dry summer heat. No answer. It was no surprise; the old man notoriously resented the Romans. Lucius smiled wryly and banged again with the same result.

With the hilt of his sword, he snapped the locked handle from a weathered wooden door and entered a modest courtyard. Chickens darted frantically out of his way, clucking indignantly as Lucius crossed the dirty space littered with tools, wood and rusted metal remnants. He stood at the base of a set of stairs, drawing his attention up towards the living quarters. Lucius wrapped a hand around the balustrade.

"I call upon you one last time, Archimedes. Present yourself, old man. Your council is sought by the great Roman Empire. You will be well rewarded for your efforts." Lucius' knuckles cracked on the wobbly balustrade; his patience wore thin. His mouth formed an even tighter line.

Hurried footsteps alerted his attention to the obvious. Archimedes was not going to play nice. The footsteps transitioned into the thud of heavy and hasty dashing about, echoing down from the second story of the derelict home. Despite his cumbersome limp, Lucius took the rickety, greying stairs two by two. He burst through the front door in a matter of seconds. He stopped to take stock of his surroundings. A stinking, ramshackle living space crammed with scroll-covered tables. Lucius' peasant-born brain couldn't make sense of the etchings of machines and numbers that lined the walls. He grimaced, but the complicated drawings were well beyond his education.

He listened carefully for more movement; caught sight of a picture that drew him in for reasons he could not explain. A hastily sketched circular object. Three circles, one within the other, with regular rectangular protrusions around the outer circle. Beneath the strange image, someone had scrawled some kind of mathematical calculations. Running his fingers gently across the parchment, Lucius clutched his head as that unwelcome ache suddenly pierced mercilessly through his skull again. A quick guilty nip of Vitriola placated him temporarily. He carefully placed the valuable vial safely back in his pouch, where it rattled against his last coins. Hand preparedly on his sword, Lucius deftly advanced through the mess.

A small side table lay askew, olive oil glugged slowly from an upturned urn. A handful of olives rolled amongst breadcrumbs along an uneven floor. With the stealth of a wild cat, Lucius stepped carefully around these to avoid making a sound. A muffled grunt issued from beyond a still swinging curtain, drawn across the entrance to the far room where the light was dimmest.

Unsheathing his sword, eyes narrowed, Lucius reached out with the well-forged length of steel, the tip hooked the tattered material and peeled it aside. Sunlight spilled through a small dirty window. Within the modest space knelt a hunched figure. The aged fellow was caught in the act, hammering a floorboard down with the hasty tap of a mallet.

"Leave me alone, there is nothing here for you, Roman," Archimedes grumbled, not giving Lucius the decency of even looking at him.

"Stand up old man. You are to present yourself this day to General Marcellus. He seeks your battle smarts. He offers you a great reward to share your weaponry knowledge with the Roman Empire."

"Never. I help the people of Syracuse, not those murderous beasts!" Archimedes refused to look at Lucius.

"Treason will cost you your life, old man. Don't be foolish," Lucius responded with a strain in his voice, the searing pain crushed his head. His vision faded in and out, his patience rapidly diminished, his fists clenched repeatedly.

"A mere humble life I will gladly give." Archimedes, turned on his knees, now looking up to Lucius with a defiant, tight-lipped expression.

Overcome, Lucius leaned into the wall, his voice strained, an octave higher than normal.

"Just give it to me!" he yelled.

"Give you what? Is it not me that you are wanting?" Archimedes asked quizzically, his brows raised in feigned innocence; his jowls hid a faint smile.

"You know what I want. You've hidden it, now give it to me!" Lucius clawed impatiently at his splitting headache, glaring down at the elderly man, his eyes bloodshot.

"What is wrong with your voice Centurion?" Fear now peppered Archimedes' thin voice. He scuttled backwards. He knew he had quickly pushed this predator too far.

Lucius stumbled again, leaning heavily on his sword, the tip splintered into the floor.

"You will fear more than death if you don't give me the Kaladai!"

Archimedes eyes shot wide at the bold demand coming from the imposing soldier, unintentionally indicating he knew what the centurion was talking about. Accidently, Archimedes had revealed that he knew exactly who he was dealing with. Stupidly, he glanced momentarily at the floor before flinging the mallet hard at Lucius. The crude tool bounced pathetically off Lucius' gleaming metal breast plate.

"Foolish human!" Lucius pulled wildly at his hair; he flung his helmet to the ground with a thud. The voice, his voice, was not his own. He felt like he was sinking, deep and lost within himself whilst something else was rising out.

"Argh! What… what is …happening? Beloved Mars… protect me!"

Luminous sweat poured down Lucius' face, fluid pooled blindingly in his eyes. Grinding a fist in his eye sockets, the last of the brave centurion's resolve gave way as he saw blood on the back of his hand. Lucius gave in with a deep, resigned sigh. Defeated, he sank back into the depths of his mind and let go. Lucius' body stepped menacingly forward, but Lucius himself, the brave and noble centurion, was now gone.

The imposing figure glared down at Archimedes, who knew his time was up.

The voice was now sweetly feminine, but it dripped with the venom of a viper.

"Did I not give you the fire of God? Weapons that could have made even *you* a God on this sickly rock! Did I not entrust you, Archimedes, with the wisdom of knowledge no human should ever know? And you reward me with consorting with my enemy?"

"I-I know not what you mean!" Archimedes backed hard up against the wall, eyes watering in fear, yet his jaw remained firm, clinging to every morsel of bravery that he could muster. He was proud and would take his dignity to the afterlife, not give it up to a traitorous monster.

"Oh, don't play with me now. You have betrayed me to them, used my wisdom and power for yourself. Was it not to be the other way around, dear friend? Were you not supposed to serve me in return? My feelings are hurt, Archimedes."

The coyness of the female voice frightened Archimedes even more. She was now more vicious than she had been when they'd first met, when he was a mere lad. Once taken by her immense beauty and charms, and without the foresight of maturity and wisdom, Archimedes had agreed to things he should never have.

Lucius dropped his lip in a womanly pout, his expression one of hurt. He toyed with his razor-sharp sword, dragging it back and forth across the floor. The scraping sound bored into Archimedes' resolve. The old scholar relented. His body quivered.

"I thought we were kindred? Lovers, in fact? Do you not recall those nights, my darling?" Lucius questioned, leaning into him, patting at Archimedes' arthritic hands.

Archimedes swallowed multiple times; mouth dry from the horror of what he knew was coming. Lucius straightened, imposingly tall, smiling maliciously as the sword moved like a pendulum of intimidation. Eventually, Archimedes found a small amount of spittle, licked his cracked, thin lips, and responded in a measured tone. With one bony hand holding himself steady against the wall, he pointed accusingly with his other.

"What you desire is not right. I am wiser now about your agenda than all those years ago. Back then, I was young, foolish, and greedy. I was driven by pride and manly desires. I have wizened to you and your selfish cravings. You are worse than the Daimon." Archimedes spat in disgust at Lucius' feet, "I have chosen to help those that wish to preserve what is good and whole. You tricked me once, but no more!"

Lucius stared wistfully at the quivering old man before he shoved him out of the way with a forceful kick to the chest. A sadistic smile split his face as the old man fell. Archimedes stiffly recovered with a groan, pulling a white stone hanging around his neck; he began to chant.

"Pray all you want; they can't help you now!" Lucius hissed.

Archimedes prayed harder; Lucius raised his sword and brought it down. With a sickening crack and squelch, it pierced the chanting scholar from collar bone to pelvis, pinning him to the floor. Archimedes gurgled a last breath as blood bubbled from his slack mouth. He managed the slightest of defiant smiles at remaining silent in the face of his enemy before the light left his grey eyes. Archimedes slumped; his body slid further into the sword.

"Ugh, now I'm all dirty!" Lucius took a step back, annoyed and satisfied all at once, he wiped arterial spray from his hands. Slick with blood, he moved into the soft sunshine by the window and peeled off his clothes, one piece at a time, until he stood naked in the burning afternoon light. One last scream from the all but lost human soul escaped from within as Lucius' body changed. It quivered and shimmered, skittering in and out of focus. His face elongated, then snapped back multiple times as the centurion form faded away. A tall, ethereal female appeared in its place.

Anjou'elle stretched luxuriously, relieved to be back in her own body. She looked innocently over her shoulder at the vertical corpse. Twirling her ebony locks, she laughed a sweet, feminine trill as the sunlight caught in the white streaks of the waist-long hair. Her black-rimmed blue eyes sparkled like gemstones.

"Oops. So, sorry," she smiled nonchalantly at Archimedes; his body stuck in a grotesque pose around the steel blade.

Kneeling and comfortable in her own nakedness, Anjou'elle's arm lit up, white hot. A crackle of electric energy burst from her palm. A handful of floorboards were left in cinders. Her eyes lit up with delight, glowing inhumanly. Reaching in, she found it for a second time. The last time was immensely more difficult. Sinking the ship on its way to Rhodes had taken so much effort that both she and her sibling had needed months of rest. The first Kaladai sat rusting away on the sea floor. This time was delightfully easier, as she pulled out an oily sack wrapped around her heavy, circular prize.

"Will they never learn?" Anjou'elle scorched the metallic object with bursts of her elemental power until it melted into a useless iron puddle.

She stood, stretched her nakedness towards the sun, and screamed maniacally through the window.

"This world belongs to me!" She glanced back at the cooling corpse. "Did you hear that, old man? Oh" she pouted, "…sorry, you can't, you're dead!" Her laugh trilled like birds in springtime.

"How about you, oh great Creator? Have you not enough to tend up there?" Anjou'elle giggled girlishly as she looked skyward, daring an answer from I'el. Unsurprised with His ignorance, she shrugged and sighed, almost bored with it all, before vanishing in a blinding flash, her victorious cry trailed behind like the shriek of a witch.

Within seconds, another figure materialised into form, in the same fashion that the evil one had departed. He reached sorrowfully down, long white hair hung as heavily as the sadness of his expression. He shook his head.

"Will this never end?" Uriel shook his head as he placed a gentle glowing palm across Archimedes' heart.

"May the blessings of I'el and all of A'vean be upon you, loyal friend. My soul is heavy with your pain. This is not a death befitting you. You shall be rewarded for your sacrifice." Uriel shut the old man's dull eyes, then placed his white-hot hands across Archimedes' slackened brow. Uriel closed his eyes to concentrate.

"I see what you have seen. Forgive us, that we asked so much of you. She will pay dearly in time, as will her vile sister. Now, move on and await your place in A'vean, dear friend." Uriel drew out the still shocked soul of Archimedes and turned to the luminescent presence behind him.

"Rach'ael, please take extra care of this one."

"With honour Uriel," she nodded respectfully, azure eyes sparkling brightly as she stretched out a slim, translucent hand to Archimedes' soul.

"Come dearest kindred, I will accompany you to a place of peace," Rach'ael said. She smiled warmly at the loyal human.

"Be off with you. Journey well." Uriel raised a hand in farewell.

The apparition looked back at the Uriel. Archimedes bowed.

"I am sorry that you must start again," Archimedes lamented.

"Another will come and we shall continue. Your plans at least are with me. What is done is done. Iel's puzzle will, in time, be solved. Until then, the Watchers must wait as they have humbly done for so long. Now, be in peace," Uriel answered with a nod and a smile.

With that, Archimedes ascended to the Middle Realm with Rach'ael, a Keeper of Souls. Uriel took the secret plans extracted from Archimedes' memories. How long would he have to wait this time for the right human mind to help the Watchers of A'vean?

Chapter One

Mould, thick and sickening stained each breath. Musty air pricked at my senses before I was conscious enough to open my eyes. Something soft and scratchy pressed into my cheek. I lay frozen in a state of fear and confusion. I was relieved, as I emerged from the fog of sleep, that I could wriggle ten fingers and ten toes. At least part of me was intact. I opened one eye just a crack. I was resting on a lumpy pillow and a very uncomfortable bed.

Darkness.

I remained still and quiet as my vision adjusted.

Click.

A door creaked open. I shut my eye again and held my breath, trying to control the panic of not knowing where I was.

What the hell had just happened?

I attempted to fake sleep whilst straining every other sense to find out what was going on. My spine burned instinctively, a raw reminder of my new and unpredictable power.

Deep breath in, deep breath out, repeat.

Keep it cool Soph. My thoughts raced and my senses kicked into overdrive; taking in every smell, sound and whisper of movement.

I had to work out what was going on before my whacked-out angelic body put on its own light show.

Ashes and spice. No!

I bit my lip to stifle the cry that wanted to escape. Silently approaching me, I noticed the softest footfalls that a human would not sense. The rhythmic beat of another's heart pulsed in my ears; the vibrations quickened with increasing intensity, and finally the added tang of sweat thickened in the air. That nervousness matched my anxiety.

He was here. His presence was all too quickly and heavily by my side. The bed dipped under his weight. He drew in a long breath, then exhaled, until the tension seemed to recede from him. Rhythmic breaths, cool and teasing, cooled the heat of my cheek. He leaned over me. He inhaled my scent as though I were a dog. Anger rose in my chest; I swallowed it away as silently as I could.

A hand ran softly down the length of my hair, stopping and starting; hesitating. The pin-prickling reaction on my arm reflected the revulsion and betrayal that was welling up inside me. I stiffened ever so slightly, holding back the nausea he stirred within me. I groaned and breathed out languidly as though I remained in a state of restless sleep.

He drew back quickly, his weight lifted from the bed, although his scent lingered… intoxicatingly. I berated myself for even noticing it. There was the rustle of a plastic bag. I cracked an eye open again, peering through strands of loose hair that curtained my face.

Slightly parted drapes across a small window revealed his broad silhouette. The moonlight cast an eerie incandescence across the room. A red and blue glow flashed on and off repeatedly against his sculpted body, highlighting unhealed, garish wounds. The sight caused the realisation that I seemed to have no wounds. I wasn't sore anywhere, even after the beating I'd received from Yeqon at Stonehenge. My face surely should have been sore after the eye-watering punches? *Who had healed me?* My armour was gone too! Just my flimsy clothes and bare skin separated him and me. I felt goosebumps rise at the thought that someone had touched me while I was unconscious.

Returning my attention to him, I noticed a large gash across his abdomen. It glistened with recently clotted blood. Hints of a bluish swelling over his face shone in the neon flashes. He brushed his hair out of his face; the bandage was still on his arm from the wound Jude had inflicted when they were training at the Katoika sanctuary. As though just noticing it, he slowly unwrapped the cloth and discarded it on the floor. Momentarily preoccupied, he inspected the silvery scar along his forearm before scratching at his wrist and fiddling with what looked like a bracelet.

A shout came from somewhere outside, drawing both our attentions to the conversation. It was in Spanish, yet I understood it as clearly as though it were English. *Strange.*

"Eh, Cesare, you see that weirdo in room twelve? He's up to somethin' man. Get rid of him. You're weird enough for the both of us. We don't need strangers causing trouble."

"Who you callin' a weirdo?" said a younger voice. There was laughter before car wheels crunched to a gravelly stop outside. The laughter faded.

"Let's crack some juice, Raf. We'll keep an eye on the weirdos on the cctv." Footsteps receded as new voices followed the slamming of a car door.

"I told you we took the wrong exit!" a woman moaned.

"Will you just let it go? I'll get the bags; you go see about a room!"

A child whined.

"Too cheap to fly. We could've been there in an hour. But no, you had to do a road trip!"

More crying.

"This place looks like a crack house. Bloody hell, Mark, someone will probably mug us while we sleep in this place!"

"A bad paint job means nothing. God, you sound like your mother. It's just for one night, for Christ's sake, just go check in!" the man said.

"You promised me better than this," the woman snapped.

"I promised you love… stop being a snob," he answered.

"Prick," she snapped again.

Footsteps clicked quickly away; the child screamed louder.

The man grumbled to himself as he slammed a car door shut. As he swore repeatedly to himself, the sound of suitcases wheeling away accompanied him.

So, I was in some sort of run-down motel and people were speaking English and Spanish. The arguing couple had distinctly American accents. *Where the hell was I?* I wanted to go home. Where was that exactly, though? I didn't know anymore. Enl'iel, Brennan, and Jaz crossed my thoughts. I wished Koi was here to help me out. The memories of Stonehenge came flooding back. My Ben, my sweet Ben, he'd deceived me. He was a devil in disguise, literally, and he was right here. My captor, my betrayer.

There was more rustling in the room. I snuck another look at him.

"I know you're awake," Ben said.

I held my breath.

"Are you hungry?"

What? Am I hungry? Of all things, I wasn't expecting room service from this murdering, double-crossing bastard. My cheeks burned with anger. Since the charade of sleep was over, I sat up slowly, double-checking for injuries, whilst fully aware of his position every single second. Thankfully, everything really was intact as I realised a new and usual feeling towards Ben…. hatred. It felt sour and heavy in my gut.

I shuffled backwards until my back hit the bedhead. Grabbing a pillow, I cuddled it to my chest as though it was some sort of protective barrier. I narrowed my eyes, watching his every measured move. Ben quietly studied whatever was outside the small window, biting into an apple. Every casual crunch he took stoked the rage in my stomach into an inferno like I'd never felt before. My face glowed of its own accord as the mark of A'vean scorched across my right cheek. Its light revealed Ben's face more clearly. I didn't fight the reflex, allowing this new body of mine to protect itself. Yep, it really was Ben, or whoever or whatever he was. My heart ached with the betrayal.

Deep breath in, deep breath out, repeat.

Think, Soph. Think! I wondered hard and fast on a get out quick plan.

"Don't do that. You'll have those damn humans back sniffing around. If that happens, I'll have to get rid of them and I know you don't want that." Ben's voice was flat. *Crunch, annoying crunch.* He bit down to the core of the apple.

More death. I couldn't deal with that, especially right now, and he knew it. Ben knew me all too well, perhaps better than I knew myself, and that gave him a vastly unfair advantage. I knew nothing about him, when only a day ago I thought of him as my... My fists clenched in frustration and pushed the thoughts away until my nails clawed into the lumpy pillow. I exhaled slowly and quieted my face down to nothing more than a simmering pulse that barely lit the space in front of my nose.

Through clenched teeth, I whispered, "How could you?" I sounded even less like the old me than ever before. I didn't know who I was anymore. Was I the soft-hearted, forgiving healer, or the supernatural angel who felt like her humanness was fading with every outburst of anger? I was a mess.

Silence. Ben shuffled his feet, took another bite, then threw the core carelessly to the ground.

"Look at me," I demanded quietly.

I sensed his pulse quicken, heard the blood rush through his veins. Ashes and spice overwhelmed the air I breathed.

"Who the hell are you?" My voice dripped with acidic accusation. The only giveaway of my fear was the quiver of my lips as I hissed out the words.

More silence.

"What the hell are you?" My tone increased in volume. My eyes stung.

He looked at me. His eyes, God, they were so wrong. Where had that beautiful emerald gone?

"Answer me, damn it!" I snapped. Anger set a tremor in my hands. Frustration had me white-knuckling the innocent pillow.

"I am no one," Ben finally conceded, his tone unemotional and flat.

"What the hell kind of answer is that? What are you? Are you the same as me?"

"I'm nothing compared to you," he whispered.

I was confused. He'd kidnapped me at Stonehenge under the threat of Yeqon and his horde of Daimon, the traitorous Watchers-turned-demonic army, hell-bent on destruction. Now, we were holed up in a skanky motel and he was all coy. It was beyond insane and completely unnerving.

"What have you done, Ben?"

Silence again.

"What did you do to…" I gulped back a sob. "What did you do to Jaz?"

"She's safe."

"What?"

"I would never hurt her." His gaze was back at the window. The neon lights flashed on and off, on and off.

Relief teased me, if that *was* the truth. But how could I believe anything from his lying mouth? Anger and confusion blended into a headache of epic proportions.

"But it's okay to hurt me?"

"I haven't hurt you." Ben pulled the curtains closed slightly, still keeping a watch outside through a crack. "You talk too much, Soph." Hearing him say my name so casually and familiarly was an assault.

"What? You expect me to be happy and silent that you've kidnapped me?"

"It would be easier to tolerate, yes."

"Tolerate! Ugh! You pig! Tell me where we are! Let me go, damn it!" I wanted to get off the bed, to run, my muscles coiled and ready to spring, but I was unsure what move he might make. He looked frightening. The blue-red neon glow across his scarred torso emphasised his size and strength; a life and experience I wasn't aware of. I'd never realised just how large and strong Ben actually was. It had always been his eyes that had drawn me in. His beautiful green eyes and humbled charm. *Ugh! What a naïve fool I'd been!* The thought echoed repeatedly through my scattered thoughts. The attraction I'd suppressed for so long was marred now by his clenched jaw, the unpredictable nature of whatever he was, and what his intentions might be. My heart was sinking. That suppressed emotional mess just got messier. Love and hate exploded like a supernova in my heart, leaving a black hole behind.

His nostrils flared as he maintained his silent vigil by the window. I glanced around the small room some more.

A frayed sombrero hung on the opposite wall. A faded print dangled askew with the words, *Hola, Benvenido!* underneath it. 11:23 pm December 26th glowed in a lime green on the bedside clock. I'd lost days! How many? Five days! Panic set in again. I didn't know what had happened. How was I unable to remember five whole days?

What had he done to me?

"Where are we, Ben?" His name felt like poison as I tried desperately to keep fear from my voice. I needed to keep some semblance of control. I had to keep him thinking that I could or should be a threat. Hell, I knew I was a threat. I knew I could hold my own to a point. I'd learned that by now from my training with Lorcan and Koi. What I didn't know was Ben, and what he could do, and that left me unsure of myself and my next move.

"Northern Mexico."

"What?" A chill prickled the back of my neck.

"I brought you here so I could think."

"Think! What about? How you're going to kill me? Hand me over to those monsters? All while pretending to be my friend for so many years. Pretending to …." I gulped. Unwelcome tears arrived. They undermined my forced calmness. I clenched my fists tighter in silent frustration until my nails bit into my palms through the fabric of the pillow.

He continued to search for whatever he was looking for through that damned window.

"I thought we… you and me… and you're just a… just a liar. A liar and a freaking evil angel or …God…whatever!" I desperately sucked back those unfaithful tears of hurt, wiping them with the back of my hand, not wanting to show my all too evident weakness. I hated tears now; betraying, weak, useless tears.

He stared at me once more with those horrendous, blackened eyes. My vision, despite the cloudiness of my grief, had now adjusted to the dark so well that I could see him perfectly clearly, every beautiful, untrustworthy inch of him. I had my own built-in night vision too, it seemed. His nostrils flared and lips tightened as he bit back something he wanted to say.

"What are you going to do with me? Tell me the truth, enough lies. Don't you at least owe me that?"

"You're the Earth-born Angel. I'm supposed to bring you to the Empyrean realm, to Yeqon."

An involuntary shiver ran through me.

"The hell you will!" I wanted to scream at the top of my lungs, but kept my voice as calm as possible. Speaking through clenched teeth was remarkably helpful with this.

There was no chance he was taking me anywhere. In reflex, I deliberately quickened my breathing, encouraging that simmering burn in my spine. The burn that promised everything that was possible with this new body. The energy flowed freely, but felt strange; like tasting a meal you loved with a new spice added that made it slightly unpleasant. I drew on it anyway, as hard as I could. Sliding off the bed, I headed for the door, watching what his next move would be. My wings begged to be free, my pulse raced, and my back ached to release them.

"Don't do this, Soph, I swear you'll regret it!" He sounded so calm, so very Ben.

"Don't you *dare* tell me what to do. Get away from me!" My hand was in front of my body, aimed at him in warning. I'd unleash whatever I had at him, despite it being him, despite every conflicting feeling churning beneath my skin.

He made a slight move in my direction.

I released a surprisingly weak, sputtering shot of electrical energy at his feet. The arcs of power flew from my fingertips but fizzled away quickly. Despite the disappointing lack of firepower, the room still lit up like a theme park as he dodged my ammunition with ease.

"Stop it, damn you!" Ben pushed away from the window, flexing his arms and clenching his fists through his hair.

A half dozen more useless shots left my hands as I inched closer to the door. He stood his ground, not retaliating, just dodging the onslaught with annoying ease and looking increasingly pissed off.

Changing tactic, I drew on memories of the Katoika Sanctuary back in Strensham, willing myself to transfer there ASAP. Ben inched my way, knitting his brows, mouth tight, his face as dark as I'd ever seen it. Those eyes, those frightening black-rimmed eyes undermined my bravado. It was hard to tell if it was rage or something else. I felt myself fade in and out a little as I concentrated on the training room and Koi, Lorcan, anyone. The pull of the transfer attempt in my gut was weak, more of a tickle. The memory wouldn't stay clear enough in my mind to lock onto the cosmic force that should have pulled me away to freedom.

As Ben made it to within a few feet of me, I threw everything I had at him in self-preservation. My wings were finally emerging, albeit weakly. The veins in my arms glowed white hot, but I just didn't seem to have the same oomph as usual. The atmosphere felt heavy and empty.

"Back off!" I finally landed a shot to his arm, the uninjured one. He rubbed it quizzically, as though marvelling at the effect it had, which apparently wasn't much. He then quickly advanced to within a foot of me, the door and freedom.

"Don't make me stop you, Soph," he growled. His eyes bored into mine.

"Just try, traitor!" I snapped, my lips peeled back over my teeth like a cornered animal. I couldn't stop the tremble that took hold of them.

"Hey, what's going on in there? Raf, call the cops. I want these freaks outta here!" The voice was right outside as someone started banging on the door. My back felt the force of the thuds. I thought I heard a gun hammer being cocked into place.

"Whatever you're doin' in there, you're goin' down, man! We don't need your trouble here. Get out now, it's either the cops or my boys… your choice."

We both seemed to stop and hold our breaths.

"Damn it!" Ben punched the wall to the left of me, leaving a gaping hole in the filthy, nineteen seventies style paper-lined plaster.

"I warned you. You're forcing my hand." He grabbed for me.

"What the…stop, don't touch me!" I wasn't quick enough to defend myself.

Ben moved like lightning and was an inch from me before I could draw another breath. I fumbled around uselessly for the door handle and, as I did so, he threw something at me. The bolt of red light caught my wrist, cuffing it to the wooden handle. I yanked at it, only to feel the sting of its iron embrace as it glued my hand to the door.

"I will not warn you again," Ben said, way too close for comfort. He seemed to hesitate a moment, and that's when I tried to punch his face with my free hand. My arm only made it halfway when he cuffed that one to the door with another flash of red. He then grabbed my shoulders, pinning my body against the door, between him and whatever was outside. I was completely incapacitated. The glaring of my mark burned hard through the inches between us, highlighting every line of his face. Every pained angle showed the strain of whatever he was up to. His ebony hair was now peppered with wisps of white, and those eyes… they were just… they were just like Yeqon's. He leaned against me with his bruised and battered chest. Despite my every effort to wriggle free, he had me pushed up against his warm skin, so close that I could feel his rapid, familiar pulse pound against me.

"I hate you; I hate you so much!" I'd never uttered that ugly word to another living creature.

His breath rolled over my hair and down my neck, soft and calm again.

"I know you do. But I have to do this."

"No, you don't."

"This started long before you were even a thought." His face was too close. I turned mine away, looking at the floor.

Nausea bubbled up like it had in the past. It was only then that I realised I had been feeling sick whenever I was near him, ever since the incident at the hospital. As I'd been quickening, my instincts had sensed Ben's darkness. I stopped wriggling. It was pointless. I quickly figured I'd save my energy for a later opportunity to escape, hopefully without feeling like I was about to hurl.

We stood in momentary silence, uncomfortable silence. The only sounds were his very measured breathing and the intermittent threats from the people outside. In the brief quiet, the heat of his skin, his sweet scent, my heart quickened for the wrong reason. I felt disgusted with myself. His hand cradled my head, in a sort of embrace against the mountainous musculature, keeping me still and under his control.

Ashes and spice. Damn it to hell Sophia! He's the enemy!

I tried focusing on the nausea, thinking it would be preferable at that moment to my pathetic hormonal ambush. But his other arm then pulled me in closer. Immense heat emerged behind his back, the glow of his own wings chasing away the darkness of the night. My hands were suddenly free of the shackles, yet felt as useless as if they'd remained bound. I couldn't think. My breath caught in my throat.

"I'll never forgive you for this."

"I don't deserve forgiveness." His tone seemed strangely defeated. It tugged a small corner of my heart. I kicked that part of myself that always wanted to bloody help. I squashed it down hard and locked it away. What was going on? Was he doing this under duress? He'd certainly seemed to be bullied by those revolting creatures back at the Henge. They'd beaten him to a pulp. Did it matter? *No.* He was evil and a liar. I struggled again as I felt a change in the air. He was just too strong.

If he could have pulled me any closer, we would have been sharing the same skin. I could barely breathe now. My heart was surely about to explode.

"Shh." Ben's mouth grazed my ear, a chill coursed down my neck. I nearly groaned. *Oh, my God, Soph!* The glow of his emerging wings warmed me. Their duskiness reminded my hormones he was, in fact, a devil. The room sizzled with their power, making the hairs on my arms erect. I was momentarily and pathetically numb. Common sense and feelings raged a futile internal battle. His proximity was insufferable.

The surrounding air shimmered, warping in and out of focus. I felt a slight pull in my gut as his wings fully enveloped me.

No, please no!

"How could you do this, Ben? How could you do it to me?"

Tears pooled in my lashes. They flooded down my cheeks, dripping across his battered skin. He jolted back, as though my tears were poison, like they stung. His breath caught, his body stiffened, and his wings faltered for the tiniest of seconds as he pulled me in tighter again. I was sure, as he leaned his head down onto mine, that I felt a tear from him drip down onto my shoulder.

"I do what needs to be done, Sophia. Now be quiet."

The pull strengthened in my gut. We were transferring. The last day that I remembered flashed wildly through my mind, ending with *that* kiss. The room disappeared as the aggressive banging on the door continued, then faded into nothingness.

I couldn't get that kiss out of my mind. The taste of his lips on mine as the blackness of space replaced the musty motel room. I was disgusted with myself that I'd felt such passion, such desire for someone, for something so purely evil. What did that make me? Who did that make me?

My vision faded, his grip on me tighter than ever.

"Damn you, Sophia!"

Chapter Two

After a whirlwind of light and dark rushing towards me, I came to an ungraceful thud on a dry, rocky surface, and thankfully, out of Ben's embrace. I rolled away, backed up, crouched low to the ground, and scanned for threats. A silken night sky spangled with stars, untouched by city lights, glimmered in smears of white and orange. Their reach didn't stand a chance against a deep and thick darkness that surrounded me. The moon tried too, but the baroness of night sucked her blue hue away.

Tepid air clung to my skin as I tentatively turned around, searching for wherever the hell I was… searching for him.

I felt his presence before I saw him. Ben's statue-still frame stood quietly, a few feet away in the shadows of the night. His unfathomable eyes stared down at me in the most pained of ways. With anger re-surging, I instinctively tried to throw a bolt of energy at him. A sparkler would have had more impact. My power sizzled and crackled pathetically away into nothing but a faint glow on my fingertips. I gazed quizzically at my hands.

"What the?"

"It doesn't work out here unless you actually know what you're doing… and you don't." There was a cockiness in his tone. I was reaching pissed off again really quickly.

Ben smiled smugly as he launched a small burning bolt behind me, setting a tumbleweed alight. I dodged, slipped on the sandy ground and fell, quickly launching back up into a defensive stance. Ben's brief light show highlighted a desolate space of red sand and rocks around us. The purple outline of mountains bared down upon us in the distance. Something howled not too far away.

"Where are we *now*?" I ground out the words, dusted myself off, readying for whatever was coming next. The air was cooling; my blood was boiling. His stare was heavy. Even when I looked away, I could feel it linger on me like a touch.

"We're still in Mexico," he answered.

"Well, what are we doing out here? It looks like the desert! Going to knock me off out here where no one will find my body? Leave me for the wildlife to snack on?"

"They'd break their teeth on your bones. You're an angel. Diamond bones, remember?"

"Smart, aren't you?" I laughed. "Well, what then?" I was looking for any sign of rescue or escape. Nothing.

Where was everyone?

"I'm trying to decide what to do with you," he said.

"You have no right to decide anything about me!" I snapped back, hoping to sound confident, but I was shaking and my voice hitched. He paid me no attention.

Ben paced back and forth, pulling something from the waist of his pants. He began spinning a small weapon across his palm. The point of metal glinted under the intensity of the starlight.

"And you think better out here?" I stretched my arms out. "Does the wilderness help your conscience? Do you even have one?"

He remained frustratingly quiet.

I stamped my foot, energy sizzled on my fingertips. "Are you thinking of taking me home at all?" I was wondering what he was going to do with that length of silver.

"We could have stayed back there," he thumbed in the direction of the motel, I assumed.

"But no, you had to go have a hissy fit and attract the locals."

"Hissy fit! You're a pig!" My fingers sizzled again.

"I've been called worse. Just sit and shut up for two seconds so I can think, and tone down your temper or worse things than me will show up." Ben melted away into the darkness.

My fingers curled back in on themselves; I peered over my shoulder. *God, what else could be after me?*

I followed Ben's silhouette quite a distance as he walked away, hands in his pockets like a broody teenager. Unfortunately, the limits of my night vision revealed itself after about a hundred meters, and he disappeared into the inky blackness.

Despite my utter hatred of him, suddenly being alone in some part of the Mexican desert had my nerves on the brink of utter panic. I crossed my arms to stop the onset of shivering. It wasn't the air temperature; I was scared to death as I stared wide-eyed around this unknown place. *Pitch black.* I dared not light up any more than a hand span in front of me, lest I drew out something more sinister. It was the only thing he said that I believed. That said, I apparently had a power outage anyway, so I was up the proverbial creek if anything jumped out of the shadows.

My heart raced; it rushed in my temples. My breaths were too fast, too loud.

Deep breath in, deep breath out. Repeat.

Despite knowing I could survive without air, it didn't mean that fear didn't stoke my survival drive. I struggled to calm myself.

Something scurried behind me. I turned to find nothing. Another howl serenaded the utter silence of the night. *Coyotes?* I imagined all manner of beasts drooling for a midnight feast. If only my beautiful, smelly old Shadow were here, he'd protect me. A lump formed in my throat at the memory of his dreadful death. Crouched down, I was ready to run. I could see clearly enough in the darkness to make a run for it, but there was a glaring problem. It was pure, scary darkness out there. And where would I run?

Another scratching sound behind me had me in an immediate sprint, anyway. I ran anywhere but where I'd been. There was nothing but rocks and weeds to follow. The air was dry and empty. I'd never felt such nothingness before. My imagination was in overdrive; I was sure something was following me. All the slithering of unpleasant things and the pitter-patter of unidentified creatures set my energy flowing. I reacted instinctively and blindly threw out weak sputters of whatever I could draw out of the empty air. Useless sparkles fizzled away in every direction. I didn't want to draw attention to myself, but what else could I do? Just wait to be overcome or eaten… or worse?

I had to risk using the elements available to me in this weird void. The E'lan was like an echo of itself, barely anything palpable in the ether to grasp onto. I tripped and fell, spitting out a mouthful of bone-dry dirt whilst rolling into a quick ball and back up into a defensive crouch, looking wildly about for whatever was out there.

Footsteps.

Wide eyed, I searched for the source.

"Are you actually trying to get us found? Believe me Soph, there are much worse things out here than cougars and rattle snakes. Quit the fireworks show. I already told you that your powers won't work out here, now cut it out!" Fear coloured his tone and unsettled me more.

"I'll quit when you let me go."

"Not happening."

"Bastard."

He put a hand across his heart and gasped sarcastically.

"Technically, you're wrong. My parents were officially married when I was born," Ben chuckled. I was livid.

"Traitor!"

No response.

"You make me sick… literally!"

He snorted in the shadows, as though that amused him.

"Coward!"

He flew at me. We slammed hard into the ground. We rolled a few times through the bite of the sand before coming to a stop, Ben on top of me. For a moment, we stared hard at each other, gasping for breath. His pulse near mine, his smell leached on my skin. Nausea clung for control again.

"Never, ever call me that!" Ben's mouth hovered inches from mine. His breath was heavy and ragged with anger. His arms and legs corralled my body, but he didn't touch an inch of me. Some sick part of me wanted him to, and I hated myself for allowing the thought.

The malevolent blackness of his eyes undid my courage, and my stomach turned to jelly. As though reading my mind, Ben suddenly changed them back to the emerald that they once were, before they flickered to a new and unfamiliar black-ringed blue. It hurt and confused me even more to see that. He briefly looked more than ever like *my* Ben. My guts clenched; tears pricked the back of my eyes. My heart hurt.

I didn't understand this strange biological magic of his, or what it meant. The Watchers and Eudaimonians could mask their eyes to hide in the human world, but this flickering between fully black spheres and almost normal eyes was a ghastly and demonic step up from that.

I had nothing; no clever retort or bravado. His proximity left me slack-jawed and vulnerable. I blinked my eyes clear. All I could manage was to meet that frightening gaze without allowing another tear of weakness to escape.

Ben stared a moment longer, deeper into my unrelenting defiance, then pushed away from me with an annoyed grunt. He dusted his hands off against his thighs. I quickly scrambled up. I kept my distance… and my mouth shut. A wind picked up, cleared the sky of scattered clouds. Moonlight spilled brighter across the landscape. It paled his complexion, deepening the dark circles under his eyes.

"Save your energy, Soph. We're in the Zone de Silencio. It's below the gateway to the Empyrean Realm," he said and pointed casually above his head as though I was supposed to actually see something other than empty space. My look of confusion prompted him to go into more detail.

"Yeqon's realm sucks all the elemental energy from the immediate area. That's why your power won't work. That's why the locals can't get their cars and computers to work. That's why planes fail and compasses go haywire. Our realm is like a vacuum for energy. So, show a little intelligence and accept you can't do anything more than Jaz could out here. I know how to work around this place, you don't," he smiled smugly, shook his head and looked above at things I couldn't see.

Dejection set in with that verbal slap in the face. No power, no allies, no clue. I was a weak angel at best in this place. Without my full strength, out here in the wilderness against him, I was nothing more than a mere human, as he had so blatantly pointed out.

Ben returned to a brooding silence as he apparently decided my fate. His gaze darted frequently between the sky, me, and the mountains in the distance. His hands raked obsessively through his hair. My own thoughts raced as well. I concluded that at the minimum, perhaps I could keep him talking for long enough that, if anyone was looking for me, they might just happen upon us before he dragged me to Hell, literally.

"So, what's this realm then? Where exactly do you think you're taking me?"

"I'm trying to think, be quiet, will you?" He paced faster.

"At least give me the decency of telling me something about the last place I'll draw a breath!"

His head snapped up. I thought I saw a flash of pain cross his expression.

He recovered quickly, clenched his jaw and ran his hands through his hair more angrily. He drew a deep breath and let it out slowly.

"It's where we've lived for the past, I don't know, forever, waiting for you."

"You mean where the Unseen live? Yeqon?"

"Pretty much," he nodded and paced in circles. My skin chilled. Defiance fizzled; my knees wanted to give way.

"You *can't* take me there! *Please* Ben?" I stepped closer to him, hands steepled under my chin. Strangely, he stepped away from me.

"Please, we were friends once. Please don't do this. If there's any part of you that was real with me, please listen to that person, that friend, *that* Ben?"

He growled, fisted his hair and pulled hard. His arms fell slack. He studied me in a strange, strained way. He then turned away and blended back into the shadows of the night. "Stay put. I'll bind you if you try to run again, so just sit down and be quiet for five damned minutes!"

Wind pushed at me, dirt swirled along with it, biting into my flesh. My mouth was dry. I licked my cracked lips, watched him weave in and out of the shadows, arguing with himself.

I thought maybe some part of him might be real, might remember the connection we'd shared, the friendship, the… whatever it was. Maybe not. I squatted down, head in my hands.

Was there a word to describe the cataclysm of emotions I was feeling in that moment? I could go from zero to a hundred in a nanosecond, and that could encompass every conceivable emotion all at once. How could one feel love, loss, fear and rage all at once and not lose the plot? My thoughts were a blur. Is that what the betrayal of a loved one does to a person? Completely screw with your brain until you are a hot mess ready to explode? A few weeks ago, I knew me; I knew who I was, and I knew where I was going. I knew where my heart's desires lay, albeit in secret. Well, I thought I knew, but now my lovely life had spiralled into this chaos. My thoughts grew into a seething anger at myself for being such a fool. Throw a little humiliation into the mix and, well, there you go. I was just the catch! *God, I needed an Eccles cake.* I thought randomly of Eilir's special treats, something that could not betray me. This was how messed up I'd become. Alone in the desert of Mexico, kidnapped, literally powerless, stalked by a Daimon, and here I was wishing for a sweet pastry!

Just as I collapsed onto my butt, head in my hands and contemplating my lack of options, there was sudden shouting in the distance, accompanied by the revving of a gutsy-sounding engine.

Spotlights crested a hill not too far away as someone shouted in a heavy Hispanic voice.

"This is private property. Get the hell outta here! Take your weapons before we do!"

The vehicle advanced quickly, followed by shouts and a few gunshots that blew dust up around me, scarily close. I scrambled up to run, but not before I was back in Ben's heavy embrace. His wings alight and closing fast around us. He held me close, his heart thudded frantically, in a race of its own.

"Damn you to Hell, Soph. They've bloody tracked us out here because of you. I told you to not to use your power. Now I've got no choice!"

"What…?" I didn't get to finish my question as we zapped out again.

Chapter Three

Heat punched my face as, once again, light broke through the darkness of the transfer. Humidity had sweat immediately beading down my back as I quickly took in my new surroundings. The clear night sky was gone. A feeling of claustrophobia set in.

I pushed away from Ben the very moment I garnered the strength, slipping onto my backside as I did so. He didn't resist, letting me fall painfully onto sharp rubble.

He'd turned his back on my humiliation and thrown up a light orb, giving the small cave an uninviting orange hue. Its light didn't chase away enough of the foreboding shadows. I dared not take my eyes from Ben as I pulled myself up, rubbing at the sorest parts. A few painful scratches bled down my feet, staining my toes red.

Ben squatted down, hunched over, fingertips digging into his temples. He still looked every bit like Ben. It was in the angle of his face, the way he ran those hands through his hair; every little nuance that used to catch my breath. Yet I knew he wasn't Ben. Ben was a figment of my imagination.

I was exhausted. It hit me like an avalanche. When had I last eaten? Slept properly? Did it really matter? Was I just a dead girl walking? I was parched; the heat was stifling. Exhausted, I flopped back to the ground feeling disoriented and defeated.

"I'm thirsty."

He sighed into his hands.

"Do you have any water?"

Ben shuffled about, kicked a rock with his bare foot hard enough that it smashed loudly against a wall veiled in shadow. He stood, stretched his arms out behind him and shook them out. He glanced back at me over his shoulder. His blue eyes, ringed with that awful blackness, drew me in a moment longer than necessary with a shard of hope, before he disappeared into the shadows again. The scent of ashes and spice lingered.

"Please?" My voice trailed off into a whisper, "Don't leave me!"

His heavy footsteps faded in the distance.

The orb light my only company, I shuffled back into a corner of the barren cave, too scared to follow him into the darkness; into the unknown. I didn't know where I was, but it certainly didn't feel like any place I wanted to venture out into on my own. Despair set in way too quickly. I hugged my knees into my chest and looked around the uninviting space.

Earth-born angel! Saviour! What a joke you are right now, Soph! How could I possibly get out of this situation? I was lost, alone, with no power and at the mercy of him.

After a time, I forced my attention onto something other than despair because, to be honest, that wasn't getting me anywhere either. Taking in the immediate surroundings for clues, I swept the oven-like cave for anything that might help me end this nightmare. The red hue of the walls reminded me of central Australia. Everything was ochre, the rocks, the dust, but the smell of the air was sulphurous. I pinched my nose against it. A faint whistle, like a breeze squeezing through the cracks of a rattling window, was the only sound.

Other than that, I found myself in a bare space the size of a modest living room. The shadows that I didn't want to venture into seemed deep and uninviting. There was nothing of significance that might provide me a clue to where I was, or a means of escape. I slumped back into a hunch under the light of the orb; my only friend.

Something crunched in the distance. Footsteps were closing in. It pulled me from my self-absorbed pity party. I jumped up and shuffled away to the farthest corner of the space, which really wasn't far at all. There was nowhere to hide other than those shadows. Was it Yeqon? Had Ben gone to get him? Was he literally delivering me to the Devil?

My face glowed a small, pathetic light with fright. Every hair strained on edge as the footsteps drew nearer. I bit my lip in frantic thought, tasted the thickness of my blood. I tried fruitlessly to draw out my wings. A useless tingle was all I could manage, and only halfway up my spine. My imaginary, calming waterfall didn't seem to work here. Nothing worked. *Damn it!*

As the footsteps closed in, I searched frantically for anything I could use as a weapon. My pockets no longer concealed that handy diamond dagger, just the useless crackle of the scrolls still hidden away.

"Come on! Think!" Pulling at my hair in frustration, I remembered Koi's wise words that there were times you just had to use whatever was at your disposal, even a rock. With the first moment of luck in far too long, I found a football sized rock a few feet away. Heavy in my hands, I edged to the mouth of the tunnel opening and stood off to the side, out of the view of whomever or whatever was coming. With the rocky weapon poised high over my head, I felt a small sense of bravado return. I held my breath as the footsteps became achingly close. The opal pendant hummed against my chest as though encouraging me.

Deep breath in, deep breath out, repeat.

My cheeks burned with terrifying anticipation as the footsteps stopped somewhere just short of the entrance, hidden in darkness, as though they knew to be cautious. I was certain whoever was there would hear the wild thrashing behind my rib cage and give my plan away.

The footsteps continued, then paused again, just short of where I was hiding. A sigh. More footsteps. *Crunch, crunch.* A large silhouette emerged around the corner. I lunged, screaming as I thrust the rock hard into its head. A bright flash illuminated the scene. Something struck me, propelling me across the darkness. A loud crash underpinned my cry of pain.

"Shit! Look what you made me do! Calm the hell down, Soph! Mother of…" Ben's voice faded.

I blinked away a near concussion and my vision cleared. Ben kicked at what looked like shards of clay, rubbing his head in apparent pain.

"That was your water, now you'll have none," he growled and grimaced, pressing bloody fingers against his head. I felt a thrill that I'd got the better of him for a moment, and was vastly relieved it wasn't Yeqon.

The wet patch of earth a mere few feet away was torturous as I helplessly watched the water absorb into the dust. My throat was immediately a million times drier for the sight. Ben must have noticed me licking at my cracked lips and eyeing off the spill that was already bone dry.

"If you want more, stop attacking me!" He rubbed at the back of his head one last time. I noticed his injuries everywhere else remained raw, as though they were just inflicted.

I laughed to myself, "Well, isn't that an ironic request since you've attacked me! Not to mention the minor issue of kidnapping."

He continued to rub his blood-soaked head, but strangely didn't heal it. Blood dripped from the rock. The injury must have been deep, but he wasn't going to admit it. Only now did I noticed Ben moved gingerly, and without sudden movements, as though in constant pain. Extensive bruising covered his abdomen, and a crimson gash swept up through his navel and around his side, as if someone had sliced him with a giant talon.

"You've not healed yourself. Why?" I dusted myself off, standing as far away as the space and shadows allowed.

"I enjoy the pain," he answered sarcastically.

"Then why are you rubbing your head? Seems like it bothers you?" Satisfaction at this surprised me. I didn't like this vindictive, emerging quality in myself.

"Doesn't mean I ask for it!"

"I'd say you asked for it with a flashing neon sign."

He glared at me; his eyes flashed green, blue, then jet. He turned as if to leave. I panicked again.

"Wait! Please, can I have some more water?" I stepped forward, reaching out for mercy. It was an impossible balance of not succumbing to him, trying to being strong, yet also needing to be compliant so I could get what I needed and delay whatever his plans were. And, to be honest, I was terrified.

Ben paused.

"You'll have to wait now. It wasn't easy to get without being questioned."

He was barely a foot away. I studied Ben as much as I dared, taking in everything I could, trying to figure him out. He glanced my way multiple times as he kicked the shards of the water pot away; his eyes hooked me with every fleeting glance.

"So, who are you? Is Ben even your name?" I licked my sore lips, aching for some moisture. The insufferable heat was sucking everything from me.

"Sit," he said as he ran his hand through his hair, in that classical Ben habit. He paced back and forth before stopping at the opposite side of the cave. The edge of his body blurred in the shadows.

I complied, not wanting to turn him off sharing anything that might help me form an escape plan. Anything that might help delay Yeqon.

Ben sat on an out-cropping of rock opposite and flung another orb to the ceiling. It was a mesmerising sight the way those circles of light emerged out of his palm, spinning into existence, before being hoisted into the air where they hung as though gravity was mere fiction.

I could see him more clearly. His eyes struck me again, but it was the ring of black around them that caused me to shudder inside. That small hue of darkness took from his beauty, adding nothing less than imminent danger to his expression; to the entirety of who he was. Did it hint at the Daimon lurking inside? *What are you?*

That saying, *'the eyes are the windows to the soul'*, struck me. Did that relate here? Were his eyes the window to his demonic soul?

"How do you do that?" I pointed towards him, "You know… with your eyes?"

He looked at the ground.

"They were solid black when you kidnapped me. Now they almost look normal again."

Ben looked up; his expression a hybrid of pained and benign. A fleeting touch of shame seemed to bleed through.

Good, he should be ashamed.

He looked away, then back to me, and the rings were gone; his eyes restored to their previous enticing green before they settled in an opalescent blue. *Just like mine.* This unsettled me even more because he looked like Ben, a battered and bruised Ben. It tugged my heart until I reacquainted myself with the reality of where I was. *Where exactly am I?* As though he could read my thoughts, Ben spoke.

"We are safe for now."

"Safe! I'd hardly call this place safe!" I measured my tone, not wanting to put him offside again. The more I could glean from him, the better. It was hard though, as fear, hate and instinct fogged my mind and reasoning. I found it almost impossible to stick with one emotion for more than a few seconds.

"Be grateful. You could've already been dead by now." Ben cocked an eyebrow at me.

I balled my fists; my nails dug into the palms again. Rage blossomed.

"Grateful!" I struggled to match his blandness. Utter confusion locked my jaw. Standing, I rubbed my palms angrily together. They stung mercilessly. I begged my power to listen. Ben remained seated, all too calmly, which infuriated and frightened me even more.

Deep breath in, deep breath, repeat.

Calm down Soph, control, you need control.

I couldn't refrain from a shaky tirade. Fear consumed me. I was angry. I was everything all at once, and I must have missed the handbook of *'How to deal with being a Daimon's hostage.'* I pointed accusingly at him.

"You should be grateful that I can't use my power because otherwise I would blast you into another realm!" I wasn't sure I even knew how to do that, but it felt good to say.

Pace, breathe in, pace, breathe out, pace…. stay calm.

"Tell me, *who* the hell are you? You're not Ben. At least tell me one damned truth. If I'm about to die, don't I at least get to know that?" While my muscles strained to repress the simmering rage, he too battled those black rings that seemed to pulse around the blue and green that flashed repeatedly. A muscle twitched along his jawline.

"You want some truth? Really?" He tilted his head, a half-smile pulled colour into his face.

"At the minimum, but my freedom would be better." I held his stare, only just. I wanted so much to never see that darkness again.

Standing carefully, splinting his abdomen with his hands, Ben slowly closed the distance between us until we were inches apart. We stared each other down, nose to nose. His breath fanned my skin. His beautiful, warm, betraying breath. It lasted only seconds, yet felt an eternity. I broke the tension first, stepped away, not sure if I needed space in case he attacked. There was no telling what he was going to do. What was going on, or who he was, remained a mystery.

"The name my mother whispered into my ear was Nik'ael," his voice was suddenly gentle; sentimental. His face softened at the memory; his eyes settled back to blue.

"Nik'ael? That's what they called you at Stonehenge," I recalled. It was a strange, yet beautiful name, like all the Watchers and Eudaimonians I now called my family. But not him.

"So why do you go by Ben?'

He hesitated, chewed his lip, his attention never leaving me. Shrugging his shoulders, he explained, "It honours a friend, brutally slaughtered by his own kindred, *my* kindred." Ben's mouth tightened at the thought, then softened once more. His eyes misted, a flush crawled up his neck.

"His name was Aben'ziel, a brave warrior." His eyes flashed fully black, then back to black-rimmed blue. They bored into me; I held my ground and didn't break his gaze despite the need to run, to be anywhere but there.

"Why do you keep changing your eyes? Is that even what you really look like?" I asked.

He smirked; the blue of his eyes sparkled. The pallor of his skin warmed a little more and that flush reached his cheeks.

"So many questions, like always, Soph."

He seemed amused. *Damn him*!

"How could you possibly conceal yourself from Nan, I mean, Enl'iel? She could read anyone's energy." For a moment, I felt less frightened of him; more intrigued to know of how he managed the incredible deception. Like when I was discovering who I was, a curiosity eclipsed the fear of the unknown to understand it.

"Hmm!" Ben's dimples stressed the breadth of his amused smile. It made my heart flutter. I hated myself, swallowed hard; looked more defiantly at him to hide my despicable emotions. He smiled a little deeper. Did he know? Could he? My cheeks flushed, but thankfully, he said nothing of it.

"That has been very challenging. Enl'iel is powerful despite her youth. I suppose it's her bloodline that carries such strength. She nearly had me back at the Strensham sanctuary, you know. She couldn't quite put her angelic finger on it, though, when she was helping me with the injury that bloody Jude gave me."

He glanced at the wound on his arm that I'd helped to heal; a mere silvery scar the only evidence of it. "It took every ounce of my energy to subdue my aura that day."

I remembered how grey Ben had been when we were trying to heal the sword wound that he'd received in combat training. I thought he had been in shock; in reality, he was struggling to hide the Daimon that he was.

"That's why you looked so sick?"

His mark glowed brightly across his face, the swirling white tendrils of energy highlighting the squareness of his jaw. He regarded me quietly, offering a mere nod of acknowledgement.

"You're… like me?"

He quirked an eyebrow in response to my question.

"No one is like you, Soph." Ben's face darkened, as though he'd mentioned something he shouldn't have.

The intense connection and the baring of his mark made the hot air hotter. My heart raced and my face burned like lava. I don't know why, but I reached out to touch his face. He drew in a sharp breath, watching my every move. Realising how close we were, I quickly withdrew my hand but wasn't able to take my eyes from the mesmerising energy pulsing softly from the swirls of his mark. He bit his lower lip, leaning into me a little further. I was so confused. My hands trembled, so I wrung them until the knuckles whitened. I felt drawn to him and repulsed all at once. I was exposed and vulnerable. As though sensing the turmoil, he closed the gap further, and I looked back up. He reached out, ghosted his fingers down my cheek and across my mark. His touch was fire. He drew in a quiet breath.

"Don't!" I shoved his hand away, my fingers getting caught in a beaded bracelet around his wrist. It snapped, the beads bounced across the ground, rolling in a hundred different directions. Whatever the moment between us was, it instantly disintegrated.

"What have you done?" he roared and shoved me roughly away, scrambling on the floor, desperately trying to collect every bead.

"No, no. Neren'iel, no!" Ben sobbed. His cheeks flamed as he frantically scooped up the few beads he could find, red dust sieved through his fingers.

"I'm sorry, Neren'iel, forgive me," he whimpered. He raked his hands through his hair. Dusty streaks coated its blackness. Hanging his head low, Ben slumped to the ground.

What was this?

He looked more vulnerable than me for a moment, as lost and bereft as I was. Instead of feeling happy about it, I felt the sharpness of his pain as keenly as if it were my own. How could a devil, a Daimon, a monster, feel pain? Was there some part of him that was still good? I knelt, watching curiously as he still scrambled fruitlessly in the dust.

"Sorry, I didn't mean to break it." I reached for a lonely bead that rested by my toes, picking it up to pass to him.

He turned on me and snapped. "You *don't* know what you've done!"

He stood and loomed ominously over me. I shrank back, small and insignificant; my guts churned.

No, there was no goodness in him.

"Leave this cave at your peril," he hissed through his teeth. His red-rimmed eyes brimmed with tears. He stormed out, leaving me confused and alone, scrambling for even one clue as to how I was to get out of this Hell.

The pounding became steadily heavier and faster as Jaz put every effort into each kick and punch. Sweat glistened across her pale frame, like the crystals that peppered the walls of the underground cavern. Her mouth a tight, white line, her eyes focused, each movement precise and deliberate. In between grunts of effort; her constant stream of expletives had many a spectator raising their eyebrows, unused to such language in the world of the Watchers and Eudaimonians. They left her be though; they felt her agony.

The hessian sack fared less well than expected under the efforts of an untrained human. Sand plumed out in small puffs, sticking to the moistness of her prominent, flushed cheekbones. Jaz was gaunt from an absent appetite since the attack at Stonehenge. No one really felt much like eating, or anything else, other than engaging in intense training and reconnaissance, since Sophia was taken. The losses at Salisbury had been hard. It had taken days to officiate the rites of mourning, escorting human souls to the Middle Realm and farewelling the Watcher and Eudaimonian souls at the Cavern of Souls. Enl'iel had barely drawn breath for the amount of work to be done. Healing the injured and keeping a watchful eye on the ever-unpredictable Jaz had her constantly on the go. Even Brennan had failed to smile for days on end.

Yet, this initial feeling of shock and defeat was rapidly replaced with an impossibly strong resurgence of determination to outwit Yeqon. The drive to rescue Sophia remained paramount in everyone's mind. After the week of healing and remembrance ceremonies, the underground sanctuary of Katoika, under the thousand-year-old church in the little town of Strensham, England, was back to near full force, training its warriors around the clock. Jaz was now one of them.

Her pixie-faced grimace hardened into a ferocious attack on the training dummy, slowed only after Kristen yanked the ear buds from Jaz' ears. The classical music blared melancholy, rhythmic notes as they dangled over her shoulders. Jaz stopped and glared angrily at Kristen. With shaking, fatigued hands, she grappled with the fiddly white cords, attempting to put them back in.

"It's time to rest, yes?" Kristen suggested. She was weary of holding the punching bag, but more worried about Jaz, who was so intensely focused on destroying the poor sack.

"Just a bit longer. His face is so bloody clear in my mind!" Jaz puffed out her cheeks as she delivered yet another uppercut, so very hard that sand poured from a new hole she'd made. Jaz' knuckles bled through the bandages that were wrapped supportively around her hands. Kristen smiled at the sheer determination; her admiration inched up a little each day for the fellow human. However, Kristen's concern for Jaz' state of mind overrode this admiration at the moment. Kristen's eyes were soft with worry as Jaz barraged into the sack again.

"Not… my… fucking… brother… lying… pig!" Jaz chanted as she round-housed the bag with her bare feet.

"Jaz, pl…"

"Shut up and hold the damn bag, Frenchie!"

Kristen complied with a resigned sigh as her body took the force of Jaz' anger. The language or attitude did not offend her. Kristen felt sorry for the poor girl. Such betrayal warranted intense emotion, that much she understood. She couldn't imagine her own brother, Thomas, turning on her, deceiving her as Ben had done to Jaz.

"Not… my… brother!" Jaz spat. She blinked away tears, wiped her face along her arm and checked if anyone had noticed the weakness before continuing her routine. Jaz repeated the verses of the vengeful mantra she'd begun days ago. It had evolved from a hysterical crying marathon after waking from the sudden transfer Ben put her through. No one knew why he had unexpectedly sent her from the battlefield back to the safety of the sanctuary. No one understood why, after revealing himself to be in league with the Unseen, that he'd spared her life.

"Not… my…" Jaz was coaxed gently back from the sack, and those rare tears flowed as Enl'iel gathered her up into an embrace. Kristen leaned forward, resting her hands on her thighs, catching her own breath. She smiled weakly at Enl'iel with thanks for the reprieve.

"Enough now, Jasmine dear. Enough. You are going to exhaust yourself and poor Kristen, too. What good will you be to Sophia if that happens? Come. Eat and rest. If you have a decent meal tonight, you can train again tomorrow, okay?" Enl'iel rubbed her hand lovingly across Jaz' mess of hair that was now punctuated with an unusual streak of white through her fringe. An elemental scar from the transfer was the conclusion that Enl'iel and the Alchemae healers had settled upon.

"I can't stop; I need to be strong. I need to find them. I want to help!" Jaz' body shook. Enl'iel unwound Jaz' fists, calming her with each soft word she spoke.

"And so you shall, my dear. You have great strength of heart, but you're near skeletal. You must feed your body and your soul. Jude will never allow you to join the warriors if you do not care for your complete self," Enl'iel smiled and patted Jaz' hand. "Besides, you're worrying poor Brennan to near ascendance. He couldn't have you fade away on him. He's so very fond of you. You know he is taking Sophia's kidnapping on board as his own singular responsibility? He hasn't annoyed anyone for days, not even Jude!" Enl'iel's smile was weak with the worry she had for Brennan as well, but the mere mention of his name helped.

Jaz couldn't repress the tug of her own smile. She sniffed her tears away. "Thanks, Enl'iel."

Jaz relaxed, pulled away from Enl'iel, regaining her personal space. She wiped her eyes and peered self-consciously around the training room. Her attention fell upon someone by the wall of gleaming armour. Jude was cross-armed, emotionless, and glaring intensely in her direction. He'd pulled her out of her bed that morning days ago and practically shaken her out of hysteria when the memories of Stonehenge flooded her. Realising her adopted brother had in fact been a traitor, a Daimon concealed among them for twenty years, had caused Jaz to be inconsolable and violent. Walls were punched, glasses smashed, hair was pulled. Ben was her only family, making it the ultimate betrayal, a lifetime of lies. Jude had literally picked her up, held her out in front of him and given her two options: buck up and fight, or leave and never look back.

Anger flamed across her chest as she pinned his stare. Humiliation fanned the heat as well.

She couldn't leave. She couldn't run off into the real world and live knowing what she knew, leaving everyone who meant everything to her behind to face the Daimon and not know what happened. Jaz didn't know how to fight with anything other than words and her fists, so she took up his offer. She immediately began training to fight with the Watchers of A'vean.

Blinking away the emotive reverie, Jaz pulled herself back together, pulling her eyes from his cool blue ones as Enl'iel tried to draw her away from the training room.

"Okay, okay, hands off! I'll eat, I'll rest. I'll even drink one of your disgusting teas, but please, let me train?" Jaz' expression pleading.

"Agreed, Jaz." Enl'iel's soft smile calmed everyone; even the fire in Jaz.

"In fact," Enl'iel's eyebrows raised wistfully, "I have a very nice new brew that stimulates the appetite. It's a sad circumstance that I just can't seem to improve the flavour though," she mused as she walked Jaz towards the showers.

"You've got to watch that one, Jude. She's a grenade ready to explode," Thomas said as he hoisted a mace back onto the wall, nesting it neatly amongst the others. Jude took a thoughtful, deep breath, stretching out his arms overhead after his own work out. He settled them behind his head and leant back between two swords and an axe head.

"Yes, but that's what makes her so appealing. She's got grunt and loyalty. She will be a good fit for your company," Jude responded. His eyes trailed Jaz until she disappeared from the arena.

"Perhaps she will, until she gets someone killed with her impulsiveness," Thomas retorted, unimpressed.

"She'll be fine with time. There's something about her." Jude's mark glowed ever so slightly across his cheek. His eyes were hard with concentration as he tried to work out the gutsy girl.

"Something about her? Other than her filthy mouth?" Thomas laughed to himself. "Merde, she makes us sound like kittens!" He finished clipping up another two swords to the shiny wall.

"Well, a foul tongue can be trained out of her!" Jude glanced down at Thomas with a wry smile! "Kittens! You wound me. Rottweilers, at least Thomas! Give me some credit!" A rare rumble of laughter reached the back of Jude's throat, only a twinkle of humour making it to his eyes.

"Too true, you can drop one with the best of them!" Thomas slapped Jude across the back and laughed too, but Jude was already back to his standard, stony expression.

"There's a fire in her soul. I saw it the day she arrived in London," Jude said as he pushed off the wall, calling back to Thomas without looking back.

"Have her fitted for armour tomorrow. Weapons and the offensive will be her strength. She's certainly offensive to me! I'll start training her myself as soon as she has gained weight and physical strength."

Chapter Five

Huddled in the fading light of the slowly dying orb, rolling one of the beads between my fingers, I couldn't think of him as anything other than Ben. I didn't know a Nik'ael; that was someone I didn't want to know. It had been confusing enough coming to terms with the name Enl'iel when she morphed from my Nan into what she truly was, a hybrid of a Watcher and a human, a Eudaimonian. Too much concealing had been going on by too many people. Brennan, Cael, even my beloved horse Grey, who had revealed himself to be some sort of Pegasus. Ben would just have to stay Ben. The dirty, lying scumbag devil, Ben.

I wondered who this Neren'iel person was that he seemed so distraught about. He'd been so stony and controlled until this name came up. Was it the person who had given him the bracelet? Clearly, it must have been immensely important. He was distraught when I accidentally snapped it from his wrist. The small brown bead between my fingers was quite worn, no longer a perfect, round ball. Was it from someone he'd loved, or who'd loved him? In that instant, I felt an intense, unexpected rush of jealousy flush my cheeks. Disgusted at myself, I flung the bead as hard as I could, hearing it shatter in the shadows. My physical strength was at least intact.

"Stupid girl!" I snapped at myself.

"She is not happy."

I nearly jumped out of my skin as a scratchy voice echoed, unseen, from the shadows.

I jumped up, crouched defensively, stared hard into every corner of space, seeing nothing.

"Who's there?"

"Why is she sad?"

"Show yourself!" Fear whipped at my heart at the sound of the faceless voice.

"She is mad. She is mad and sad."

"Who are you?" My voice wavered. "If that's you Ben, it's not funny." I tried to hide that damned fear, but my breath was thready, my emotions laid all too bare.

"Ben? Who is Ben? Tell us."

"Stop it. Who's there?" I squinted at the shadows; nothing.

A breeze rushed past me; it ruffled through my hair. I spun, looking for the source in the ever-growing darkness as the orb of light lost its bite. I backed up against a wall, eyes desperate and wide. There was such nothingness in this place that even the shadows felt like they sapped my energy. I saw nothing, not a silhouette, nothing at all.

"No one is there." The creepy voice was closer, yet no more visible. Left or right, I saw nothing, but I most definitely felt something. A ghostly coldness washed across me, like a cool current in the ocean. My skin turned to ice.

"Who is it, damn it!" I edged along the wall.

"We are no one."

"Stop talking in riddles!"

"She is impatient, disappointing. No one has lots to tell."

Invisible fingers grabbed at my hand. I yanked them up out of the way, holding them close to my chest. Chills coursed along my spine as my mark tried to glow, its light spilled only inches into the growing dark. I worked frantically on my wings, breaking an even heavier sweat than the humidity of the cave brought on all too easily. They merely sputtered and receded back into my spine.

"Damn this place!" I kicked out, flinging debris into the air.

"This is the place of the Damned already," the voice snickered with amusement.

"She wants to know things, yes?"

"Yes, I want to know things. Just show yourself and stop playing games!"

The orb light suddenly popped and disappeared. I was now in the kingdom of creepiness.

Thump, thump, ker-thump.

My heart was in my throat. I edged the other way, wondering if it was the way to the tunnel, to wherever Ben had gone.

"She wants to know how to escape?"

My eyes strained in the darkness, to no avail.

Night vision! Where the hell are you now?

"Yes, of course I do! Are you here to help or play games?" I demanded. My fake bravado didn't even fool me.

"Games, we like to play games. She plays games, she gets answers."

"What?" I searched more frantically, and finally, probably through the sheer intensity of fear, my night vision kicked in. It drenched a few feet in front of me, just as a steady wind swirled out of nowhere. In the dusky light, the breeze sucked specks of dust up into a mini vortex. The twister danced and swirled in front of me, gathering more dust and momentum until it was almost opaque. A spinning wall of ochre moved rhythmically a few feet in front of my frozen position.

After a few moments, the wall of dirt took shape, billowing in and out as it fought to emerge into something. The sound was like that of walking on gravel as it writhed and swirled before settling into a singular shape. The silhouette of a face oozed from within it as the rest stretched out into the form of a small body, gnarled and hunched over. Transfixed at the odd sight, I stared down at what seemed a small, elderly man. It looked up at me, blinking its sandy eyelids almost inquisitively, as though I fascinated it. My guard relaxed a little, my face glowed brighter, and I could see the strange creature more clearly, but kept my distance.

"What are you?"

"She is beautiful," it said with a dusty grin, head lilted to one side.

I inched a little further along the wall.

"She will not be harmed by us. The danger lies out there, not within." It pointed toward the mouth of the tunnel with a crooked, gritty finger. "She can escape if she plays with us," it said, raising a gravelly eyebrow.

My gut said no, my desire to escape said yes.

"How do I escape? If you're not here to hurt me, will you help me?" I suddenly felt a glimmer of hope ignite.

"Will she play?"

Impatient, I snapped at the creature, "Yes, damn it, just tell me what to do!"

Unaffected, it responded calmly. "She will give us a memory," it said as it shuffled back slightly.

"A memory? What do you mean?"

"What is to you, a memory, is to us, energy." It rubbed its small hands together, rolling them; hopeful. It was strange the way it referred to itself in the plural.

"What kind of memory?"

"The best kind. Of love," it smiled toothlessly.

Not thinking of anything other than escape, the idea of sharing a memory seemed a small thing to give for potential freedom.

"How do I give you a memory?"

It rubbed its dusty little hands back and forth in gleeful anticipation.

"She agrees to offer a memory?"

"What does it involve?"

"She holds hands with us, that is all," it answered, dust drizzled from its face as it blinked faster with the excitement. I thought briefly, illogically and desperately upon the pros and cons.

"Yes, yes, okay. Just get on with it before he gets back!" I snapped again, worried an opportunity could be lost.

"Yes. We do not want to see him. Bad, bad!" The creature of dust shuffled around and then took a step closer to me. I recoiled a little.

"She does not need to be scared. We will not harm her. She gives us her hand." It reached out expectantly, smiling almost innocently through hanging jowls, dripping dusty drool.

I hesitantly offered my hand; it snapped it into its grasp like lightning. The rough, supernatural palms rolled gently over mine; a greedy look now replaced the innocent one.

"She is strong. Mm, mm, just what we've been waiting for."

Suddenly scared, I tried to pull my hand back, but its grip turned to stone, moulding around my hand like a vise.

"She made a bargain. She must pay," it said.

"No, I changed my…" My head flung back. My mind flooded with a million visions, all of my memories rushing past. A slide show of my life. They flickered forward, stopped then moved on. It was this creature, filing through my mind, looking at my private memories, waiting to find just the right one. It stopped on my sixteenth birthday. I could hear myself laughing as I swung on the rope, letting myself go at just the right moment. I was airborne a mere few seconds before I splashed into the muddy waters of the Murray River. Emerging to the surface, Ben caught hold of me, swimming us both back to the shore. We had a water fight along the way, slipping in the mud as we crashed to the ground under eucalypt trees, scorching sun striping our skin through the branches. We were laughing hysterically in exhaustive fun. As I lay catching my breath, Ben's fingers wound around mine, his laughter slowly waned to slower, nervous breaths. I looked at our hands at the same moment that he had. We locked eyes, my heart flipped.

"No! You can't take that!" I yelled, forcing my eyes open from the unwelcome breach.

"Yes, yes, this is the one. Love. Love. The power of love is what we need." Its grip tightened.

My head snapped back again. The creature was trying to pull this memory from my subconscious.

"Argh, no! Stop!" I slammed against the wall, rock bit into my skin, my entire body trembled as I fought it.

"She wants freedom; she must pay a price," it laughed cruelly.

I yanked my hand, desperately trying to free myself. The creature's claws were solid. I was stuck. The pulling feeling in my mind was nauseating, my insides felt like they were being sucked by a vacuum. Ben and I appeared again, fading from my thoughts. That innocent memory, full of hope and promise, began to elongate and flicker, draining away.

"No, please" I sobbed.

An explosive crack and a flash of light filled the cave. I slipped down the wall, my hand suddenly free. I cowered away as the creature screamed. It arched its back, spun around, returned to a vortex of dust before it collapsed to the ground. Its screams of betrayal faded and disappeared into the stinking shadows. A new floating light appeared above my head. Ben stood over me, arms crossed.

"Meeting the locals so soon?" He wore a smug, amused expression.

Apparently, he was over his temper tantrum.

"Did you do that?"

"If I didn't do that, who knows what kind of dribbling mess you'd be in, Soph?"

"What was that thing?" I said as I got up, keeping a safe distance between us after our last exchange.

He laughed lightly, shook his head, "You were doing a deal with something you didn't even know? I didn't realise you were that naïve, Soph." I hated the way he called me Soph, as though we were still all buddy, buddy.

"How the hell am I meant to know what anything is?" I shrugged; arms wide. "What was it then? Are you going to fill me in, or are you enjoying this game you're playing?"

"This is *no* game, trust me." Ben's eyes cooled, but remained mainly blue. He itched his wrist where the bracelet had been. There was a welted rash, a bead-shaped inflammation. I held my tongue, not wanting to cause another incident so soon.

"It's an Asmodai. They feed on memories and emotion. It's the only way they can take any physical form, which is what they desire most. I promise you, a horde of those in flesh and blood is not a party! They're nasty little things that hitched a ride from Satanos long ago. They can take one or all of your memories, leaving you nothing but a vegetable. Whatever it was offering, it wasn't worth it."

"And you're safer than that thing?"

"Than that? Yes."

"Then take me home. It was offering me freedom. I'm not free. Show me you're better than that thing."

He ignored me and placed a wooden plate at my feet.

"Eat."

A shiny red apple, a rough-looking wedge of bread and what looked like braised onions and leeks garnished the dish. My mouth watered for the mere fact it was something edible, but I made no move towards it.

"Don't waste it."

"It's probably poisoned." I shoved it away with my toes.

"Well, what would the point of that be? Yeqon wants you alive, so that he can kill you." Ben had this kind of smart-arsed expression on his face, yet his voice seemed to catch. "Just eat. It's been days since you ate. You need to feed the energy that drains your mortal body. Did they not at least teach you that?" His tone seemed resigned to the dog's breakfast that had been my introduction to who and what I really was. I couldn't recall my last meal, and my stomach betrayed me with a loud grumble. I pressed against it, but it roared a little harder.

My attention darted between the food and Ben. His revelation made annoying, perfect sense. I'd had a ravenous appetite since my body had evolved from human to supernatural, back in the living room of my little home in the Dandenong Ranges. I longed desperately for that place, for the stillness, the quiet; for my beautiful Shadow and Grey, both now gone. I swallowed away the bitterness that clawed the dryness of my throat.

I wanted that food but forced myself to hold off, watching Ben's every unpredictable movement.

He turned his back, knelt and felt around on the ground, running his hand along the gravel. "Hmm…" Ben swiped a bit of dust away, pressed his ear to the ground, and seemed to listen.

He stood, threw a barrage of short bursts of energy into the ground. Dust plumed around him; the stink of the cave worsened. The barrage of energy blasts sounded like a jackhammer. When he'd finished, a spring of water bubbled up into the small hole he'd created. He bowed in a sarcastic way.

"You have food and fresh water now," he said and turned to leave. "Wait!"

Ben stopped, turned back to me, "What now?"

His jaw feathered, his fingers tapped his thighs, as though he was impatient to be somewhere. His injuries remained unhealed. The gash across the ripples of his stomach glistened with fresh blood.

"Where are you going?"

Ben rubbed his hand across his face, wincing, a swelling, inflamed across the back of his hand.

"Just eat," he sighed.

I kicked out at the plate again, scattering the food everywhere.

"God! Ben!" I scrunched fistfuls of my hair. "Just tell me what's going on!"

I calmed myself as quickly as the outburst had appeared, letting my shoulders slump.

"Please, Ben?" My lips trembled, "I'm scared."

Ashes and spice overcame the stench of the air. His breaths hastened. The orb light betrayed a moistening in his eyes. Nostrils flared; mouth thin. Ben glanced over at the food I'd wasted and raised his eyes back to mine. They were black as night.

"I'm going to bargain for your life."

Chapter Six

"I'm just beside myself, Brennan. How could I have been so fooled?" A handkerchief sopped up the diamond-like tears streaming down Enl'iel's flushed cheeks. The powerful arms enveloping her gave little solace.

"Enl'iel, we were all fooled," Brennan said as he ran his hand gently along the length of her hair.

"It's pride, you know?" Enl'iel sniffed. "I thought too much of myself. I'd hidden her away, protected her from it all, but I was too comfortable, and that clouded my judgement." She dabbed her eyes and twirled the pendant around her neck as she leaned into Brennan.

"His power is unique and no one in living memory has ever laid eyes upon the Unknown One. All we have is the Keeper's silhouette of him on the sanctuary wall back in Australia, and it certainly didn't look like Ben." Brennan's brows furrowed; his jaw muscles worked overtime. "He sure as hell sucked me in and I'm just a tad older than you!" Brennan shook his head, planted another kiss on Enl'iel's hair. "Man, I'd love to zap his arse!"

"Oh Bren, I'm the one who failed her," Enl'iel sobbed and pressed a hand over his heart. She looked imploringly into Brennan's eyes. "My one job was to protect her, and I literally invited the devil himself into our home, repeatedly," she cried harder. Fresh tears filled her pale lashes. "Oh, and poor Esme," Enl'iel's words hitched. "Ben and Belial killed my beautiful, dear Esme." She leaned deep into Brennan's chest and wept quietly. They huddled upon a faded lounge in the library of the Katoika sanctuary, both in shock at the kidnapping of Sophia.

Brennan took over the tear dabbing. They sat in silence for a while. Only Enl'iel's occasional sniff sliced the heavy solitude. The light orbs seemed to lull with her emotion, dimming the room and then brightening again.

"I knew there was something distinctly off balance when Jude wounded his arm during training. When Sophia and I were healing Ben, his blood had bothered me. The colour, the smell, but I'd put it down to the effects a chromious blade might have upon a human." She bit her lip, twirled her pendant a little faster. "I thought it was the fact that he'd touched an element not of this world that made the blood react that way." She dropped the pendant; anger pinned her brows together. "It was his camouflage. How could I not see through his deceit when it was right in front of me, running down his arm, dripping all over me? It was on my skin and I didn't feel its power!" Enl'iel clenched her jaw; yet pain still tugged at her lips.

"You're too hard on yourself." Brennan gathered her hair down her back, plaiting it into a single, pure white strand. He pulled a few stems of lavender from a nearby vase and threaded them lovingly through the braid. Enl'iel calmed a little, Brennan pulled her back into his side, placing a quick kiss on her temple. The gauntness of Enl'iel's emotions reflected on Brennan's face. Pain and failure clawed through his guts, but he masked it as she looked to him for support.

"Her welfare sat upon all our shoulders. We were in the Stasis room too when you treated him. None of us detected his concealment. Hell, I lived down the road from him and felt none of his negative energy. He's clearly extremely powerful." Brennan kissed Enl'iel's cheek, lingering a little longer. "Don't worry, Li Li, we'll find her. Soph is strong, and I think she realises it more than she lets on. We just need to get some intel before we can take the offensive. Koi and Ged are pretty sure he took her straight to the Empyrean realm. It's the only place they could hide her from Lorcan's tracking."

"Then she's dead already!" Enl'iel's tears thickened. She fell back into Brennan's embrace.

"I don't know about that." Brennan gulped back a sob and sniffed. His arm clenched a little firmer around her shoulder. Twenty perfectly aligned white scars along his biceps shimmered as he rubbed her arm.

"We don't even know if she retrieved Enoch's clue. I lost sight of her when she followed those Keepers into the Avon River. We can only hope that she got caught before she found anything. Soph's no good dead to them unless they have all that's needed to control the portal. Even then, they *have* to realise by now that they can't open it without her being alive. Ben had to have worked that out during all his spying." Brennan quieted for a moment, then sat up straighter, holding Enl'iel out in front of him. He looked deep into her eyes, tilted her chin up.

"Anyway, I have a little hope. Ben, or whoever the hell he is, sent Jaz back here. Why would he do that? His loyalties have divided. I'm sure of it, and that gives us a glimmer of hope. If he were as black-hearted as the rest of the Daimon, he would have either killed Jaz or left her to die. She would've been an easy meal for Lilith. He must have a soft spot for Jaz. If he's attached to her, for whatever reason, perhaps he has a weakness for Soph, too? He certainly made himself look in love with her over the years, even if he was stalking her. Surely you didn't miss all those puppy dog eyes between them both?"

Enl'iel nodded. "I didn't miss any of it." She leaned back into him, a slender hand resting back over his heart, the beat of it calming. She watched his chest rise and fall, listened to the breath rush in and out. His life force, his smell, the feel of his skin. It strengthened her and reminded her she was not alone in her darkest hour.

"Jaz, I could almost understand Ben having an attachment to her. If the story of how he found her is even true, but Sophia was his mission, Brennan. How could he love Sophia when she is nothing more than a means to an end for them? He wouldn't dare betray Yeqon. No one does and survives." Her fingers curled into his chest.

Brennan kissed the top of her head. He recounted the day Sophia had told him about her new friend Jaz and her adoptive brother Ben. Apparently, he'd saved Jaz from the house fire that had engulfed her home and her parents. Jaz had confirmed that Ben had literally pulled her from the flames. A question mark was now left over the rest of their story, though. No one had ever met their supposedly deceased adoptive parents. Were they even real, or worse, did someone dispose of them?

"No matter his intent now or then, Ben is a traitor and if we apprehend him, we will deal with him as such," a weary voice interrupted Brennan's thoughts. Both he and Enl'iel sat up to see Gedz'iel, who had arrived with an unnerving silence. The skill of stealth was his calling card. Koi, Kea and the Eloi council entered the room after Gedz'iel, one by one, with the static sizzle of transference.

"Man, you nearly scared the angel out of me Ged!" Brennan rose, quickly washing the goofy smile from his face, seeing Gedz'iel's reaction to his misplaced humour. He ran a hand through his silvery hair, greeting the leaders of the Watchers with a sufficiently humble bow. Gedz'iel acknowledged him with a stern raise of his brow. The five Eloi inclined their heads, letting their marks glow in kinship.

"I'll be the first to knock the wind out of the bastard when we find him," Brennan declared to the grim-faced group.

"The line shall be long, Brennan, but protocol must come first. May I also add, there is little of what I would call an angel left within you, young one, a little too much human, actually!" Pathos spoke calmly. A smile cracked the hardness of his steely glare. All the others, short of Gedz'iel, succumbed to a brief laugh at Brennan's expense. Brennan smiled and performed an exaggerated bow, typically making light of things. Pathos quickly regained a stony expression.

"When Ben, now revealed to us as Nik'ael, the Unknown Daimon, the traitor, stands before us, he will yield all that he knows before his judgment is passed," Pathos said.

"Until then, we continue our relocation to Turkey. Katoika is no longer safe. From the hidden ruins of Derinkuyu, we shall continue training and begin the search for Sophia. Lorcan has mustered his best apprentices and is leading us in tracking her energy signature. They have already started their search at Stonehenge. I am thankful to you, Koi, for the foresight of choosing Lorcan to help with her training. His connection to her will be the stronger for it," Gedz'iel said.

Koi acknowledged the compliment with a humble nod of his head. Enl'iel sobbed.

"Enl'iel, this is no time to weaken. I know you burden yourself with what has happened. She was all of ours to protect. The weight is upon us all. We all suffer the loss. We need your skills as a healer and protector now more than ever. Are you able to preserve the young and the injured whilst we hunt? Brennan shall stay with warriors of his choice to guard you all," Gedz'iel's tone was always softer than normal with her.

Enl'iel dabbed her eyes a last time and patted down her clothing. A quick pinch to her cheeks gave her a healthy blush, and a return to her usual poise and confident countenance. Her mark glowed across her cheek.

"Yes, your Grace," she bowed. "I am, and always will be ready. I am perfectly capable of protecting our most vulnerable." She inclined her head.

"I have no doubt of that," Gedz'iel smiled softly at her, before continuing his orders.

"Brennan, as much as you are an impeccable warrior, you are an even better guard as evidenced by watching over Sophia along with Cael and Kea for all those years. You are to remain with Enl'iel and protect the rest of our family when they arrive in Turkey."

Brennan nodded, "Of course." Disappointment coloured his eyes, the desire to poke a demon with something sharp at the forefront of his mind.

Gedz'iel spoke further, his wings fanned like hands emphasizing his words.

"As expected, Yeqon is keeping a low profile for now, lest he draw us to wherever he has seconded Sophia. Consequently, we must hunt them down. I do not doubt he will try to cause havoc in the human world, forcing our hand and dividing our loyalty to protect Sophia as well as humans. This will be a difficult balance should it occur. Until we understand his tactics, though, we proceed with an offensive search. The Eloi will each lead one squadron. We want to come in at Yeqon from every angle. Lorcan will appoint a tracker to each squad under the leadership of the Eloi. I believe he shall work closely with you, Pathos, as you were his teacher once?" Gedz'iel asked.

Pathos nodded. "Indeed, Lorcan has long since not required my tutorship, but we work well together. We understand each other's movements innately. "He will shadow me, and we will assign the other trackers to squads based on skill and need," Pathos said.

"Very well. I shall skim the edge of the Empyrean realm this evening with Koi, joining Lorcan for any leads, then return him to you. Lorcan scouts as we speak. There unfortunately is no trace of Sophia as yet," Gedz'iel said. "You will take your brothers to Derinkuyu and perform a final security check with Jude. Assess the local township, ensure that the population are safe. I do not wish to lead us and our human brethren into anything unexpected. I am hoping the Daimon have long forgotten this old fortress."

"As you wish," Pathos responded. "Initial reports are that Derinkuyu remains abandoned. My brothers and I shall assess for any daemonic energy signatures. We shall clear the way for the safe arrival of everyone. All shall be well," Pathos answered with a reverent nod for both himself and the ever-silent Theus, Serail, Matias, and Amais, who completed the Eloi council. They all transferred away without hesitation, a nanosecond of bright light, the crack of a whip, and they were gone.

"Am I to look in on Nevşehir, or do you wish me to stay underground, Master Gedz'iel?" asked Brennan in an unusually respectful tone.

"Yes, after we arrive and confirm our supplies, I want you to stay within the bounds of the sanctuary and on the very deepest levels. Despite your ridiculous quirks, of all those here, I trust you implicitly with the care of the next generation," Gedz'iel said.

Brennan seemed surprised at the compliment, widening his eyes, throwing a quick wink back at Enl'iel.

"*Until* then," Gedz'iel grumbled, his patience with Brennan lost already. "Escort Enl'iel and the Alchemae with the young and ill to the upper level, where they shall stay well-guarded. When you are confident it is safe to transfer to Turkey, do so. I want Cael there as soon as possible. He heals well, by the grace of I'el. With Lorcan hunting and Jude on his own, his battle smarts would be of significant benefit when he is well enough. If the Alchemae feel safe in the fortified rooms of Derinkuyu, they will stay fully focused on his intensive recovery. I believe Cael will be at least able to offer guidance and intel from his time protecting Sophia in Australia. Also, I want you to assist both Jude and Kea with the final preparations for their departure. The sooner they leave, the better."

Brennan withheld his standard groan at having to be in Jude's presence. He knew better on this occasion.

"Leave no trace of us here, Brennan. Not a weapon nor a stone as evidence we have been here. Disable the Zythros stone, Jude will need to assist you with that. Seal the human entrance under the church. Enl'iel, ensure the Alchemae have all they need to set up an immediate and working Stasis room. We cannot count on when our first injured will come in once we join Lorcan in the search. Jude has prepared and checked all the battle armour and weapons, despite human-sitting young Jasmine. I commend his patience." Gedz'iel arched his brows, shook his head. A rare show of emotion. He straightened his posture. "Watch that girl, both of you." He pointed at both Enl'iel and Brennan. "There is something about her that even I cannot put my finger on, but I am certain she will be more trouble than worth."

"Jaz sure is testing Jude's limits, and those goal posts weren't too wide to begin with!" Brennan chuckled.

"Hmmm, well, watch her. She's a distraction, at best, and distractions are dangerous. We tolerate her for Sophia's benefit only, not our own. I will return before dawn." Gedz'iel blinked out. The room dropped into an absolute silence. The orbs floating overhead flickered over Enl'iel and Brennan. They stood in silence a moment, considering the enormity of the task ahead.

"Well, it's just you and me and this whole damn place to organise," Brennan said as he swept Enl'iel up in his arms. Angst shadowed his face momentarily; he pulled her close; safe.

"It's overwhelming, Brennan. I just hope we aren't too late. Can we get to Sophia in time? Has this all been for nothing?" She snuggled into him.

"Li Li, we've fought an eternity. We've worn Yeqon down. He is desperate, but not dumb. He will soon realise he can't kill Sophia, and that is all the advantage we need." Brennan kissed her cheek, drank in the smell of her… just in case.

"By the blessings of I'el, I hope you are right," Enl'iel sighed. "I know I'm so young, and have experienced so little compared to all of you, but I'm so very weary of the fighting. The death, the fear, the unknown. I long for peace for me, for you, and for Sophia."

"One-day sweet Li Li, one day soon we will all have freedom from all of this." Brennan spun slowly, "I'el shall forgive us and restore us to our homeland. No more hiding, no more shame or pretending to be anything other than what we are and…" A small glint shone in his deep blue eyes. "We shall be free to have more time for this." He kissed her passionately as they transferred together out of the dusty library below the crumbling church on the hill.

Chapter
Seven

"Stand down!" Yeqon demanded. The mountain rumbled along with the command. The imposing leader of the Damned threw a goblet to the scorched ground. It splintered into a hundred pieces. His scarred chest heaved with rage.

"Or what, Yeqon? You'll set your lap dog, Nik'ael, upon me? You may as well hand him your weapon and let him sink it into your chest! He has betrayed us, yet you sit there waiting for him to return at his leisure with the girl. It has been nearly three sunsets over the mountain, yet where is he?" Asbel matched Yeqon's stare with a defiant sneer. Orbs materialised across his palms, ready to defend himself.

"You are asking for a death sentence, Asbel. Stop before it is too late," Kasadya said, stepping into the fray. He pressed a calloused hand against Asbel's heaving chest, holding him back, only just. Kasadya extinguished the orbs with a small pulse of energy before Asbel completely lost his senses.

The great mountain of Tartarus thundered its disapproval in the background, spewing ash from its lofty heights as the five figures glared at each other atop the pumice stone ledge.

"Stop, brother. Do you not see it too? Our leader has weakened; we should hunt the traitor down as we speak. Every minute we spend on this wasteland of a world scourges my soul. Is the rest of eternity here not frightful enough for you?" Asbel snapped at his sibling with a growl.

"Silence! Both of you! Test me, will you? Challenge me if you dare! I am in full control of Nik'ael. He is exactly where I want him. He is in our realm as we speak. Indeed, he has fallen and hides the Earth-born, but does that not give us advantage? He will do anything for her, to protect her. He will yield to my will, remaining a valiant agent, to stop me slicing the life from her, including extracting all the information we need to get her to open the portal gates to A'vean. I've witnessed first-hand that her constitution is surprisingly strong. She will not fold as easily as we expected. She would endure torture, it is certain, to protect her secrets." Yeqon paced, tapping a dagger against the back of his hand. A pulse bounded in his temple, sweat glistened in his beard.

"But she played her hand too easily at Stonehenge, revealing her weakness all too willingly. Her vulnerability is as Nik'ael's, that of the heart." A vindictive smile split the hate in his face. "Their fondness of each other is their undoing. If I threaten Nik'ael, if I threaten her, and anyone else of significance to them, they both will yield to my will. So, wait I will, until I feel the time is right," Yeqon pointed the dagger. "*YOU!* Asbel, have no faith. *YOU!* Asbel, betray me more by your lack of faith. *I AM YOUR GOD!*"

All stood in stillness, the mountain as well. Froth settled in the corners of Yeqon's mouth, his nostrils flared, his eyes landed on each one of the Unseen. They all took a step back, yet Asbel held his ground defiantly.

Yeqon struck Asbel across the face with the hilt of the dagger. Asbel fell hard, teetering on the sharp ledge of pumice. Plum blood sprayed across his face from the fractured nose and spilt lip. The others dared not help him. Asbel slowly stood, his lips slick and swollen. He backed away, spitting in Yeqon's direction. Kasadya stepped between the two, eyes wide at Asbel's insubordination. His hand held his brother back from adding fuel to his emotional fire.

"Next time, Tartarus will be your final resting place, body and soul!" Yeqon slackened his stance and quieted his voice. The blackness of his eyes faded back to a faint shimmer of the once opalescent blue they used to be. The occasional flicker of red shot across his irises. For a moment Yeqon stood in silence, glaring at his subordinates as the insufferable, sulphuric air blew gently through his ashen hair. His beauty shone through, hiding the evil of his heart, the ultimate weapon.

"Lilith, come," Yeqon called. The lanky woman with sunset eyes appeared from behind the carcass of a boab tree. She snaked herself around him.

"Let us retire and wait for Nik'ael. It is time to eat and rest." Yeqon kissed her hungrily before pointing her toward the blood-soaked Asbel. Her eyes lit like a child seeing sweets.

"Oh, I am starving, my love!" Lilith cooed, clapping her slender hands.

"Good. Tonight, Asbel will feed you," Yeqon laughed deeply.

"No! Master, please?" Asbel cried. His pride evaporated as he rapidly tried to heal himself of his injuries. He backed away from the seductress as she licked her plump red lips and bared her razor-sharp canines. The others mirrored the look of horror on Asbel's face. The dishonour was unprecedented.

"Lilith feeds best on blood rich with emotion. Tonight, your arrogance will fill her well. Be grateful she cannot suck the life from you, my brother, merely your dignity. Challenge me again and I will throw you to our children whose hunger never tires." Yeqon smiled vindictively.

In a blur, Lilith descended upon the neck of the insolent Asbel, who, with no other recourse, offered himself up to the foul mother of all vampires.

Alone again, my emotions were a dizzying yo-yo. The cave walls felt like they were pressing in on me one minute, the next, I was trying to concoct an escape plan. *What was going on?* What was Ben up to? Was he my enemy? Yes, he felt very much an enemy; he looked like an enemy, especially when his eyes turned to that horrifying blackness. He killed Esme; I had to remind myself of this awful fact. Instantly, my heart hardened against him. Whatever his conflict was, it didn't matter to me, but I wondered with a flicker of hope if I could use it to my advantage.

Succumbing finally to the growls of my stomach, I relented and plucked a piece of coarse bread from the floor, dusting it off where it lay by the spring of water Ben had conjured from the ground. I inspected the bread thoroughly, prodding and smelling it for any sign of poison. It seemed ok, despite looking like knobbly cardboard. I took a small bite; it tasted even worse than it looked. It had the gritty texture of dirt, but it immediately quelled the angry protests of my stomach.

As I chewed, a pulsing feeling irritated my chest. I placed my hand worriedly under my throat, feeling a vibration emanating from the necklace I'd retrieved from Queen Elizabeth Woodville's grave; my grandmother. It was emitting a strong, rhythmic resonance. Plucking it up, I looked down to see the opal glowing varying shades of colour.

It was a mystery, but just holding onto it gave me a small feeling of hope. The veins in my arm fluoresced whilst it was between my fingertips. *Curious.* Besides this small glimmer of positivity, I still did not know what was going on… about anything. I'd lost track of time. The last thing I knew, it was December twenty-first. Now… well, days had flown by. I felt completely displaced in time, space, and reality. As I held onto that humming little opal, I wondered if it was nearer to my birthday. New Year's Day I'd be twenty-one, and apparently have all my power fully developed. The closer I was to that, the closer I might be to having a chance at escape, if I survived long enough. Then I remembered I couldn't find the E'lan in this place. What good were supernatural powers that were out of charge? My shoulders slumped with the realisation that perhaps this was it, this was my end?

The jewel continued its incessant pulsing, becoming stronger. My stomach still grumbled. I poked through the food, avoided the pungent smelling onions that were a little too dirt covered and finished the bread. *This could be your last meal.* It tasted sourer than ever.

Thirst remained torturous. I crawled my sweaty self to the small dark pool of water Ben had left behind. It looked okay. There was no apparent funky smell about it. I reached tentatively in, grabbed a handful. It was cold and clear as it trickled through my fingers. I rushed handfuls to my lips. The cool liquid immediately soothed the parching ache in my throat. I splashed some over my face and down my arms, washing away some of the sticky sweat and dirt. After having my fill, I sat, somewhat sated, and gazed at the rippling water as it slowly returned to stillness. I leaned in, saw my reflection, as clear as the finest mirror.

White hair, grimy and matted; it curtained my shoulders as I studied myself intently. *Strength, find your strength.* The reflection was still so very unfamiliar.

I ran my fingers along my mark of A'vean. The pretty white swirls looped and coiled and tingled under my fingertips. My strength was inside; I felt it, but I had to master it, to drag it out. My appearance had nothing to do with who I was and what I could achieve. *How could I use that inner power here?* As I studied myself, memories floated through my mind. Images of loved ones left behind, fortunately untouched by that wicked little Asmodai. I settled somewhat uncomfortably on that memory of Ben, Jaz and I on holiday that summer so impossibly long ago. The Asmodai had really wanted that memory.

It was a precious recollection, a joyous memory, now tainted with a terrible truth. My eyes glazed across the pool, recalling more of my past. I smiled as I thought of the first time my newly coloured rainbow hair had been on public display. Ruffled playfully by Ben, fussed on by Jaz, and admired by everyone. I concentrated hard on that pleasant feeling. Fun, acceptance, family. The necklace thrummed a little harder. I didn't let tears come through; I widened my eyes, allowed that memory to emerge fully as though I was really there. My focus was on the colours, the smells, and the wonderful emotion of simpler times. My smile deepened, despite the horrendous circumstances I found myself in.

I shivered and snapped out of the reverie, worried something was approaching. I turned to check the cave; the orb still glowed a somewhat comforting light. Nothing. No one was there. Hand on my heart, relieved, I looked back at the water to take another scoop. Shocked, I let out a gasp. I glanced around almost guiltily, then back into the water. I ran my hand all over my face, up onto the top of my head, then slowly down through my hair. Again, I turned around, making sure. My hand slid through my hair, ending with a tight fistful of it. I couldn't believe the reflection, so I brought the handful of hair up so I could see it with my own eyes.

Blue, pink, green, and purple laced through my trembling fingers. I peered back into the reflection, swirled my fingers through the water, erasing the image, and waited. The water settled once more. There it was, my hair, restored to its former rainbow state.

Chapter
Nine

The brush slid slowly through a thick mane of short black hair, stopping briefly at the white streak, before continuing on until every last knot was eradicated. Sweat was replaced by the earthy aroma of cedar and lavender oils that Enl'iel insisted was to be combed protectively thought the strands. What was once gelled within an inch of its life, now hung limp and glossy across Jaz' shoulders. Jaz regarded her reflection as though looking upon a stranger. Smooth pale skin, free of any adornment. The eyes that looked back seemed blank, not really understanding anything they had seen. Those deep green eyes were wide and frightened.

Jaz picked up the small nib of eye charcoal that Kristen had scrounged for her from somewhere. She wasn't half bad amongst this strange lot, and she was human, so that meant a tick in Jaz' book of people to potentially trust. Jaz drew the colour smoothly across her eyelids. She gave it a gothic smudge with a practised sweep of her finger. Eyeing off her handiwork, she suddenly didn't like what she saw. She drew it on thicker, this time on the lower lids as well. *There, that's it*, she thought. *No, no it isn't, not anymore!*

"Fuck!" Jaz ruffled her hair and flung the charcoal across her room. It landed on the four-poster bed near a small backpack, zipped full, ready for the move. She stared at the pack a moment; her lips pressed thin. Jaz thought of everything else she could be doing, then she thought about Sophia. Jaz shook selfish thoughts from her mind, found a hair tie and pulled her hair up into a small tight pony tail. It only got in the way when you were trying to fight, and that's all she'd been focused on since she'd woken up surrounded by the weird fairy-like medics. She'd developed quite the reputation, swatting them away every time they insisted on threading herbs and flowers through her hair for her *'own good'*. She smirked at the memory. Grabbing a towel, she moistened the end with the last of the water from a cup and scrubbed the make-up away.

"What God-forsaken hell-hole are they taking you to now?" she asked her non-responsive reflection before yanking the bag from the bed, letting a pillow to fall to the ground. She kicked the pillow aside and finished the last sip of a cup of tea, only because she was thirsty for something hot and they didn't have double shot espresso. Jaz placed the empty cup on top of her toast crusts. She still hated the crust.

The door creaked open without a knock. She turned around accusingly, her instant go-to emotion.

"Do you have any understanding of the word privacy?" she glowered at Jude who filled the threshold of her room. Half-naked, *of course,* and annoyingly, it had her pulse racing. She deliberately threw him a disgusted expression.

"I'm barely decent, Freak. Get out!"

"Honestly, do you think I care if I catch you in your underwear? I have better things to worry about, like finding Sophia and kicking some Daimon arse!"

He leaned into the doorframe, arms crossed, a lock of white hair draped across his chest, fallen from his thick braid.

"Besides, *Human,* I'd hardly describe you as ever being decent!" His conceited expression made her pursed lips whiten all the more.

Still not used to the fact that none of these otherworldly angels seemed at all taken by her physical seductiveness, Jaz felt offence at his lack of interest of her in her underwear. It just seemed like her one and only power was gone.

"Wait in the corridor Freak, I'll be out when I'm ready!" She pointed for him to leave with an impressive scowl. He barely reacted, which pissed her off even further. She was so screwed up right now with what she wanted and what she needed, her mind a scramble, but the one thing she was clear about was that she had to find Sophia.

Jude smiled; his right eye twitched as he stared at her. He left without protest. He really liked getting under her skin.

Jaz ruffled through her bag and quickly dressed.

"Okay sister, you can do this," she coached her reflection one last time. She headed out the door, rubbing absentmindedly at the precious bracelet with the small white stone that Sophia had given her.

"You know you look so much nicer without make up," Enl'iel complimented Jaz as she entered the training room. Jaz immediately distanced herself from Jude who pretended not to notice her. He packed up neatly ordered weaponry, facing his back to her.

"Yeah well, no one to impress anymore," Jaz answered blandly.

"It's the spirit we see and love Jasmine, not the adornment on the outside. One day you will appreciate this too, you will see." Enl'iel caressed Jaz' hair. "Here, I found a small pack of instant coffee up in the manor. Eilir always keeps a stash of this and that. Drink up. When we get to Turkey you should be in better spirits. I've not been there myself for a long time, but Brennan promises me they make wonderful coffee, if that's your thing," she said and passed Jaz a small mug.

"Oh God, thanks, I so need this!" Jaz gratefully took the cup and sipped the unsweetened brew. Through the steamed it, she studied her surrounds.

The enormous room slowly filled with all those yet to evacuate the sanctuary. The chromious-lined walls glittered with the reflections of the orbs that floated in neat order high along the roof top. They lit the space like a warm summer afternoon.

A small tug on Jaz' leg had her looking down at the beaming face of Av'ael.

"Oh, hey pipsqueak!"

A pair of milky eyes gazed up adoringly, accompanied by a toothy smile.

"Pretty Jazzie!" Av'ael squeezed onto her leg in a tight hug.

"Will you find my friend, Sophia?"

Jaz paused mid sip, "Er, you bet kid. I'll find her, don't you worry." she patted Av'ael's head awkwardly. Av'ael's hair was intricately braided with lavender sprigs, making her look like she'd just stepped from a page of A Midsummer Night's Dream. Jaz pulled her hand away, rubbed it on her pants.

"Please find her. I need to tell her a secret," Av'ael said through a funnelled her hand over her mouth to emphasize the whisper and secrecy.

"Well, what is it? I'll tell her when I see her." Jaz started losing interest, the billowing crowds hooking her attention. Av'ael tugged at her leg again.

"Jazzie, the man tells me things in my dreams and I have to tell Sophia!" Av'ael tugged Jaz' pants again.

"The who?"

"The man with the big swirly eyes. He makes me laugh," Av'ael said, giggling behind her hand.

Jaz was about to fob her off when she remembered that Av'ael had somehow helped them connect the dots with one of the scrolls. She'd had some crazy dream and built a little stone replica that clued them into the fact that it was Stonehenge they needed to go to. One of the artefacts Sophia needed to hunt down was hidden somewhere there. All from a dream. Pulling her sour attitude in on a tight leash, Jaz knelt, took Av'ael's hands in hers.

"Okay kid, you keep that little secret and I promise Sophia will come home. You can tell her all about your dreams, okay?"

Av'ael clapped and jumped up and down with excitement just as her name was called.

"Come Av'ael, it is time for us to leave now. Say goodbye to your friend." Her mother smiled cautiously at Jaz. Av'ael gave Jaz a tight squeeze before running off to her mother.

Jaz stood up, slurping at her cup only to find she'd already finished. "Ugh!" She placed the cup on the ground as she noticed some movement amongst the large gathering.

People were starting to leave in small groups.

In a somewhat stunted conversation, Jude had explained to her the previous evening why they were relocating. She wasn't arguing, she didn't want to run into any more of the beasts she'd come across. The zombie-like Rogues and the drug-addled Afflicted had her stomach churn at the thought… and then there was Ben. Her fake brother, the one who'd cared for her for so long. The dirty dog had betrayed her and everyone else. She didn't want to come face to face with any of them – yet. But soon, she clasped her hands together, her knuckles whitened, soon she would be strong enough and she could join the human fighters. She would hunt those bastards down. For this reason, being forced across the globe again was something she was willing to endure, purely as a means to an end.

"Hey! Mini Princess, enough skiving. Get over here and help," Brennan called. Jaz hadn't noticed both he and Lorcan's return whilst she'd been chatting to Av'ael.

Helping Jude pack weapons wasn't on her list of fun things to do, but with Brennan and Lorcan present, she made her way through the sea of bodies to help.

"You're looking less *corpse* today. I like that on you!" Brennan joked as he pulled her into a hug.

Jaz took it for a moment, then pushed him away, "Yeah well, opinions are best kept to themselves, especially in the morning."

Brennan smiled wider at her bitchiness. "I really like her," he said to no one in particular.

"Mind your mouth, Jasmine," Jude grumbled.

"Freak."

"Oh, come on, are we putting up with this for another day?" Lorcan moaned, "Pull your head in and grow up, Human!"

"The name's Jaz," she smirked at Lorcan. Her hand flung up, but a swift move by Brennan curled her middle finger back down.

"When you show respect, I'll use your name. Take a cue from Sophia," Lorcan answered and continued packing. "Do I need to worry about you as well as Daimon causing havoc while I'm searching for *your* best friend?" Lorcan scowled at her, no hint of humour unlike his brother, Brennan.

Taken aback for a moment, Jaz was more overcome by the immediate heaviness that weighed upon her heart. It had been what… five whole minutes since she'd thought of Soph, wondering if she was dead or alive? The thought knocked the wind from her. She clutched her chest; the pain was all too real. The smart retort she was going to sting Lorcan with died in her throat.

"Sorry, Lorcan." Jaz rarely conceded to anyone.

"It's fine," Lorcan dismissed her with a wave of his hand. "Just keep some perspective kid, okay?"

Jaz forced a smile in his direction. It wasn't returned.

"Hurry up, we need to move out ASAP," Jude snapped as he passed Jaz a box of weapons. They stacked them on a large stone platform. Jude then interrogated Brennan in an equally impatient tone. "Brennan, have you secured the church entrance?" His voice strained with the effort of sounding any semblance of polite.

"Done. It won't be opening any time soon. The staircase has been dismantled, and I've left some keepers at the veil. If anything makes it through to the main entry, I'll be alerted immediately," Brennan answered, "Not to mention its arse will be blasted off!"

Jude regarded Brennan blandly, then glared at Lorcan, no words needed.

"I've disengaged the Zythros stone," Lorcan said.

"Good, saves me yet another job. We can leave as soon as Koi gives the word," Jude said and kept packing.

"What, no thanks for me?" Brennan quipped as he helped Jaz hoist a heavy box up to the platform where Enl'iel was waiting. Brennan quickly grabbed another box, avoiding a potential nose bleed from Jude, whose fists were glowing.

"What's with you two, anyway?" Jaz asked as they made their way up the steps of the platform. She'd noticed Jude still clenching his fists, eyeing off Brennan like a piece of fresh meat. When he'd seen Jaz catch his anger, he'd left to follow Lorcan to where Kristen and Thomas were mustering the last of the human troops.

"Ah, that's a long story Mini Princess," Brennan chuckled and shrugged. "Let's just say we're not best buds anymore and leave it at that."

"Shit, what the fuck did you do?" Jaz questioned; her gossip antennas were suddenly humming.

"Mini Princesses really should use nicer language," Brennan answered, then ruffled her hair. She shoved him away, disappointed.

"Here you go Li, Li. One washed, mended and packed human ready to go. Just gonna check in with the Alchemae to see if they need any help." Brennan looked down at Jaz, uncharacteristically serious, "No more argy-bargy with Jude or my bro while I'm gone!" He deposited Jaz with Enl'iel, a stern pointed finger waving between Jaz' bright green eyes, before he blinked out in a quick white flash.

"What have you done to upset Brennan, young lady?" Enl'iel asked, an amused smile warming her face.

"Uh, I don't know what his deal is?" Jaz shrugged. "I just asked him what the problem was between him and Freak over there… I mean Jude."

"Oh, I see," Enl'iel arched her brows, smothering a smile with a shake of her head. "Well, that's one of those skeletons in the closet I'm afraid. It's a rather gargantuan sore point for Brennan, so best not press him on it. Okay?" Enl'iel asked.

"Well, don't we all have seem to have those these days?" Jaz thought briefly of her parents. Her last memory of her mother was terrifying and as vivid now as it was the day it happened. Jaz had found her mother screaming, her skin bubbling like roast pork, engulfed in flames.

Jaz shook her head to rid the ugly memory; there were a lot of those these days, especially since Stonehenge.

Heat and light suddenly surrounded them both as Gedz'iel and the Eloi council arrived. Jaz protectively shielded her eyes, already aware of the danger. The first rule of thumb for a human working with Watchers; be prepared at all times for their arrival and departure via transference. She was already attuning to the static buzz in the air that preceded the approaching transfer of someone. It was surprisingly easy for her to notice. The hair on her neck stood each time the build-up of energy was close by. This was, so far, the only piece of good advice from Jude that she'd appreciated. That remained her own secret though, as she wasn't going to give him a molecule of satisfaction, not a thankyou… nothing.

"Your Grace," Enl'iel greeted Gedz'iel. Jaz moved behind her and kept her mouth shut.

"We have a development. Sophia's energy signature has been picked up," Gedz'iel said.

Jaz slipped out from behind Enl'iel, her attention firmly on the imposing Gedz'iel. Her heart beat faster, her mouth open. She wanted to ask more, but bit her lip.

"Oh, thank the heavens, where?" Enl'iel clapped her hands to her heart.

"Northern Mexico."

"Oh no!" Enl'iel's hands flew to her mouth, tears welled in her wide eyes.

"What do you mean, 'Oh no'? Isn't that a good thing, that we have a lead?" Jaz asked, as she became aware of Lorcan's presence behind her. Her heart beat faster, a nervous shake took hold of her hands.

Lorcan mumbled to himself, "I didn't want to be right on this one."

Gedz'iel met Jaz' hopeful eyes. His impatience at her unwanted interruption knit his brows together.

"Yes, it is a lead young one, yet it is not at all encouraging. This place where Sophia has left her elemental signature, it is at the entrance of the Empyrean realm. The Daimon realm. The place she will die."

Chapter Ten

Mouth agape, I stared incredulously at my reflection. Slowly, my stunned expression curved into a smile. I admired my multi-coloured hair. I could change my appearance. I looked exactly like the old me, before the world turned inside out. My heart hammered with the realisation that I wasn't as powerless as Ben had led me to believe. This new evidence of his deceit hardened my view of him even further.

"There's a way out," I whispered. I prodded my face and twirled coloured strands through my fingers. *Escape!*

As though the horrid place knew of my thoughts, there was a sudden rumble in the ground and an explosion somewhere in the distance. I ducked for cover as dust sprayed overhead. Coughing, I stayed down until I realised I was safe, and the ground settled once more.

Picking rubble from my hair, the thought of actual escape swirled through my mind. The opal hummed harder as though encouraging me. I touched it and wondered how could I use this concealment talent to my advantage? Could I alter my image well enough, convincingly enough, to find a way out of this place, wherever it was? I quickly realised there was only one way to find out. Waltzing around looking like my old self was not going to get me anywhere quickly. I had to try to morph my features into someone, or something insignificant, but what?

A Daimon, a Rogue? I rubbed the goose bumps that prickled my skin at the thought. *Ugh!*

I wasn't sure I could stomach the mental image of one of them long enough to even try.

First thing was first, I had to see what exactly I was capable of, just in case it was merely a fluke. That would be an awful cosmic joke. I looked up to the dark ceiling.

"C'mon, are you finally going to give me a break?"

I stared into the thick darkness of the tunnel and listened.

Silence.

Nothing but the hum of the light orb; I was alone. For now, at least, I had the opportunity to see what I was capable of.

First, I tried my wings. No amount of grimacing, twisting and puffing would bring those babies out to say hello. That was deflating to say the least. Flying would be handy, even though I was far from proficient, a little airborne activity could prove to be advantageous in the great escape. To my surprise, my mark glowed quite easily with the mere thought of drawing some power from within myself. Its warmth seared across my cheek and was a whole lot more comforting than previously. When it came to searching for the E'lan however, the positive energy in the atmosphere… nothing. Still, only small white and blue arcs of electrical energy danced across my palms, like the dying flickers of a light bulb about to expire.

It was like all the times I'd tried to help Ben start a motorbike engine that had unexpectedly died. The countless hours he had taught me all about the workings of the motor engine had once upon a time, been cherished memories. All those seemingly innocent teenage years; encounters that were just a job for him; tainted memories. I scrunched my palms in frustration, wondering how Ben used his power so easily, when to me, the air was like a vacuum. Then again, he wasn't me, he was a Daimon, and I supposed Daimon had other means of power.

Bad power. Turning back to the mirror of water, I relaxed and hoped for the best.

Deep breath in, deep breath out, repeat.

Eyes closed tight, I imagined whiteness, pure clean whiteness and I let it drape down over me, like a fresh, clean sheet. A shiver slid through me, and when I opened my eyes, my smile broadened even further. There it was, white hair again, replacing the rainbow mane.

"I can do it!" I clasped my hands into a jubilant clap.

"Do what?"

I nearly hit the roof. Scrambling up, I found Ben towering over me. *How had he snuck up on me like that?*

"Do what, I asked?" His eyes did a quick sweep of the space, and then suspiciously all over me. Violation was all I felt as he inspected me like chattel. *You have no right!* I thought.

With a defiant edge to my voice, I answered, "Force myself to stomach that food… and you!"

"I don't believe you, was that Asmodai here again?" He took a step closer, tilting his head curiously.

"Was it making you promises it can't possibly keep? It'll only lead you straight to Yeqon anyway. Those creatures never give, they just take." Ben's stare was intense, probing me for a truth I wouldn't concede. I held my head high, giving him my best *'try me'* look. He sighed, rubbing an unusual eruption of stubble across his normally smooth chin. He backed off and took a seat on a rock, running his hand through his hair again. He looked exhausted.

He didn't press for anymore explanation, but rather, he seemed more relaxed while I was back on high alert, feeling damned lucky that I'd changed my hair back before he'd returned.

"What day is it?" I asked, "I don't even know what day it is."

"Why does it matter, Soph?"

"You don't get to call me Soph. My friends and family call me that."

"Okay then, why does it matter what day it is… Earth-born?"

I bristled inwardly. I could only imagine the words Jaz would use to describe him now.

"I suppose it doesn't matter, other than wondering if I'll make it to twenty-one, just a small important detail for me before I'm sacrificed."

Ben's face hardened, the darkness under his eyes deepened. He worked his jaw, took a deep breath and ran his palm through his hair again. God, I hated that. *God, I loved that.*

"Up here, it's no particular time or day. The sky rises and falls, but time is nothing. This place is an illusion. A reflection of Earth, the negative of it. Hence the fun weather and welcoming aroma," he said as he swept his hand out like a weather man.

I almost giggled, but clenched my jaw and swallowed it down. It must have been nerves. How could he make light of anything? God, this erratic behaviour of his, the confusing thoughts rushing through my mind, it was almost impossible to think straight.

"Down there," he pointed to the ground, indicating the actual real Earth, I'd assumed. "It's December thirtieth."

He must have seen the surprise in my face, and the fact that my mind was suddenly racing.

"Yes, it's your birthday tomorrow. And no, I haven't baked." Ben leaned on his knees, fingers steepled against his face. He actually smiled at his little joke. My teeth ground, I looked away. *Pig*

"Best you stay here rather than whatever it is you're up to. If you move outside this cave, you'll be limp at Yeqon's feet before you could draw a single breath."

Why did he care?

I quickly processed what he said, realising how much time had passed. I'd slept what…once…twice since I arrived in this rocky prison.

"How can over a week have passed?"

"Obviously your psynostris has kicked in. You won't need to sleep much anymore," he said. He scratched the welts on his wrist some more.

Why inspecting my hands was of any help understanding this revelation made no sense, but I looked at them anyway, trying to ascertain any physical change that may show evidence of this new ability. Sleeping once a week just didn't compute in my logical former-nurse mind. I was slightly alarmed. It felt like I'd really lost time, and it was deeply unsettling. On the other hand, considering where I was, a lack of exhaustion could come in handy.

"So why do you keep coming back? Each time I see you, I think it's my death knell."

Ben leaned back against the wall and stared lazily up at the roof, resting his hands limply on his lap. He sighed, tiredness slackened his face, but he maintained a steely scrutiny in my direction.

"A few years ago, I would have done exactly as Yeqon asked, instantly and without question. I've done some bad things Soph, for him… for me. But now, he's power hungry and lost his sense for the greed of it. He's taking the prophecy too literally. *I* know you don't have to actually die to fulfil it." His expression softened a little, he massaged his temples. "I want the portal open to our home as much as anyone, but Yeqon has enjoyed an eternity of bloodletting that's left him with an almost insatiable lust for death. All of them have it, no thanks to Lilith. Trust me, be grateful you're here, with me," he said and leaned forward, resting his head in his hands.

"Lilith… that… that woman at Stonehenge?" It gave me chills. Her blazing eyes seared into my mind. She had actually bitten into Yeqon's neck. The memory was not welcome in the slightest.

"Not many have ever seen her… well not seen her and survived that is. She's the most evasive and dangerous woman in human history. I bet you know about Eve though"

"Lilith is the one Eve seemed to take the fall for," I finished his sentence.

"Pretty much. You've been listening. Only way to survive."

"Tell me more about her," I asked, feeling knowledge about her would be vastly helpful to my survival.

"She's no concern of yours. That is, unless you don't listen to me and end up with Yeqon. She's his queen."

"I got that from what I saw back at Stonehenge. So, I'd say she's very much a concern of mine!"

"Well do as you're told then, and she won't get her cannibal jaws into you!"

My blood chilled.

"Do as I'm told? Let me go, Ben! Take me home, or are you just going to screw with me until I go mad, holed up in here, not knowing what's going to happen to me? Maybe I'd rather take my chances out there?" I pointed dramatically to the sinister looking exit.

Ben was up in a flash, breathing heavily, the veins in his neck bounced with the rage of his pulse. He seemed to be struggling to keep his pupils from dilating fully black again. There was just a small seam of blue left. His buttons were so easy to push, his reactions completely unpredictable. He seemed unsettled, unsure; quite like myself. I backed up against the opposite wall as he advanced in my direction. He grabbed my jaw, tipping my face up to his. He searched deep into my eyes, looking for what, I had no clue. His breath spilled warm over my skin; he was uncomfortably close. He leaned closer, resting his forehead on mine. *God, he smelled good.* Our noses were almost touching. I closed my eyes, my hands splayed behind me, they itched to reach forwards.

Ashes and spice infused into my senses. Ben drew a long, slow breath. I held my own trying to banish him from sight, smell… touch. He drew back. I opened my eyes to find his boring into mine.

For moments that seemed like hours, he looked long and deep into my eyes, the only sound being our collective heartbeats thundering in my head.

"You will be *my* death!" he whispered across my fiery skin. I swallowed hard. His lips quivered in a tight line.

"Come with me." Ben yanked me unceremoniously into that uninviting black tunnel.

Chapter Eleven

I couldn't possible sweat any more than I already was, yet the atmosphere in the menacing tunnel demanded more and more. Even breathing felt uncomfortable, the air was thick and stifling. Shafts of steam spewed up sporadically from invisible jets in the floor. Helpless in the darkness, Ben pulled me along quickly. I stumbled unwillingly beside him.

"Stop, please? What are you doing? Let me go!"

His grip was iron, I struggled with all my strength, but his eclipsed mine. *For now.*

He didn't respond to my constant protests; he just pulled me further into the menacing darkness. The ground underfoot became soft and squelchy, oozing between my toes, churning my stomach in an instant for the worry of what I was running through. My hair unpeeled itself from the sweat of my skin as a putrid breeze picked up somewhere ahead of us. The sulphurous gale moaned, like a patient in pain. A distant, thunder-like rumble added its regular sinister beat. The hairs on my arms, neck… everywhere, stood to attention as I was relentlessly dragged headlong into something that felt so very, very bad.

Wisps of static snapped in the air ahead, breaking the blackness with flashes of red and green, but it was not E'lan, at least not the one I knew. It was dark and evil as it whipped teasingly at my skin. The atmosphere became heavier and impossibly hotter. Sizzling electrons of energy coalesced into floating iridescent sheets of evil power, the further we went.

"For God's sake, Ben, I get it, don't go leave the cave, alright just let me go!" I twisted and broke free, falling heavily into the sludge… my escape not so easy as I slipped around in the foulness. Glued into the pungent substance, I was never so glad that it was dark.

A white glow appeared in front of me. Ben's face, eerily shadowed, inches from mine. His mark glowed brighter, his eyes thankfully, more blue than black.

"Okay then, stay here." He faded, then disappeared. It was deathly quiet, bar the stomach rolling breeze. I sat stunned for a moment. He'd left me in the dark… again.

"Are you just going to leave me here then?" I called quietly, not knowing what else could be lurking around me. I called a tiny spark to my mark; my night vision was useless again. The darkness was darker than dark, if that's even possible. I could just see my hand in front of my face. There was an uncomfortable, prickling feeling beneath my skin.

Looking back and forth, listening for danger, I wondered desperately what my best course of action was. I already knew the least dangerous option I should take. As much as it irritated me to admit, it seemed Ben *was* the safest option at present. *What an irony.* I grit my teeth.

"Ugh! Fine! Help me then, will you?"

"Ask nicely." Ben was close. I was startled at the close proximity of his voice in the darkness. It unnerved me, his stealth and concealment and my complete lack of self-protection.

How often had he watched me and I didn't know it?

"What?" I snapped.

"Say please." His breath ran across my skin.

"You are such a pig!"

Silence. More silence. My heart thundered, yet I could smell him. *Ashes and spice.* He was impossible close… perfectly invisible.

"Fine. *Please*, will you help me?"

Ben was playing games with me. I wanted so bad to punch his lights out. I never thought that phrase would ever come out of my mouth about anyone.

"You seem like you know it all Earth-born. Find your own way back then, or stop complaining and you can stay with me." He remained a ghost no matter how hard I searched for him.

"So, what do you want then?" his whisper was so close I felt his lips brush my ear.

"I want to go home," I said, and never had I felt anything more deeply to be true.

He moved swiftly about me. I felt the ripples of his energy in the air, yet I had no sense of direction or which way he was coming from next.

Ashes and spice

"It's me or Yeqon for now. Do you *want* me?" His face lit up right in front of mine again, his stealth was incredible. Nose to nose, he tipped his head to the side, his eyes hooded and dark, but not with blackness. The way he asked that question was intimidation and enticement; fear and desire wrapped up into one smouldering, breathy temptation.

I hesitated.

"Well, *do you want me*, Sophia?"

"Stop it!"

"Stop what? I'm merely asking you what you want!" His eyes smiled, flickering with invitation behind his glow, something that made my heart squirm and race all at once.

"Stop playing games. Get me out of this place!"

The heaviness of the air was starting to make me dizzy; I felt a little breathless, or was it the annoying effect he was having upon me? Ben leaned in closer, his cheek grazed mine, setting my skin on fire. He whispered in my ear.

"Then, take my hand." His fingers ignited my arm as his hand ran down it until they found mine. The touch of his skin dissolved my resolve, and I hated myself.

Resentfully, I opened my palm, wanting to be out of the horrid tunnel. His fingers twined in mine. Warm, strong and soft.

Danger in disguise

His grip was gentle as he helped me up. He'd flipped his switch with his face in darkness again. Ben seemed to be able to navigate this place without the need for light, that was even more unsettling.

His pulse beat erratically, the odd missed beat fluttered against my palm as his blood surged through his body. His pace was quick but cautious. He stopped every so often, as if listening for something. Each time, his energy became heavier, and his pulse pounded all the faster. He emanated fear, and that whipped my own fear a little harder. This guy seemed as emotionally screwed up as I was. It felt like being in a cage with a beaten down lion who was equally as scared and deadly… and that made him highly unpredictable.

I kept my attention clear and my mark at a dull glow. The light was just enough to see the silvery scars that slashed Ben's back. They cut through his wing apertures. He also had a collection of straight white lines neatly positioned across his right shoulder. Just like Brennan and the others.

I followed him begrudgingly; a strained silence between us. We hurried on in this way until the quiet was broken by an unwelcome, raspy voice.

"She shouldn't go with the bad Watcher; she should listen to us."

A bright streak of electrical energy bounced off the walls ahead of us. It ended with a scream.

"We are hurt! We cannot help her if we are hurt. Protect us pretty lady, if you wish to escape! Kill the Watcher, kill the Watcher!"

Another blast from Ben, another blood curdling scream and the Asmodai was gone.

"You killed it?"

"It's already dead, can't kill it. In fact, I'm not sure you could even classify them as ever having been a living thing. They're just foul accidents of nature. I just switched it off for a while," he said.

His fingers wrapped a little tighter around mine as he turned back to me, his face alight once more. He tilted my chin and looked deep into my eyes, no shame in his stare. After a moment of searching for some unknown thing, he spoke urgently, and way too close.

"That thing will get you killed. I've already told you once. And this is the reason… it will lead you out here." He whipped back around and yanked me forward.

As though appearing from thin air, I found myself quite suddenly at the mouth of the ghastly tunnel. The welcome relief was temporary as I gazed across a new horror. Darkness dissipated into a blood-red dawn. Pinpricks of starlight across an indigo sky faded, giving way to a fiery glow. My nostrils flared.

"You get used to the smell," Ben said. He dropped my hand, "This is the Empyrean realm, home of the Unseen and all the Daimon." He crossed his arms and leaned back against the edge of the cave, "I suppose you could call it my home." He sneered at the horizon, kicked a rock down the steep incline we stood upon. He didn't seem too house-proud, and I couldn't blame him.

"This is not where the newly awakened want to find themselves alone, trust me. You're like fresh meat in a wolf's den out there."

I crossed my arms, tried to quell the shiver that clung to my insides. I didn't want him to see my fear.

An eerie morning sky emerged from the night, revealing a sprawling desert landscape. An endless horizon of mountains, ochre sand and sparse shrubs dotted with rocks, boulders and wide cracks in the earth. It looked as barren as I imagined Mars might be.

"It's not as deserted as it looks, don't let what you see, or don't see, fool you. You're looking with the eyes of innocence," he said, as though reading my thoughts.

I hugged tighter around my waist. I scanned the panorama more carefully. There was no one and nothing. It was just an endless, foul-smelling desert. He was a liar, I reminded myself.

"This place is pure evil, and evil lives on one thing alone." Ben looked at me, one brow quirked up, "Can you guess what that is?"

I shook my head, not sure I wanted to know.

"Positive energy. You would be breakfast, lunch and dinner out there, and then dessert when Yeqon got his hands on you."

I kept a stony, defiant face. I wouldn't let him know how deeply scared I was, I couldn't. Ben already had so much advantage over me, I'd given him even more in the tunnel.

"So, are you staying with me?" He put his hand on my bare shoulder, looking down at me, almost condescendingly.

"I can look after myself!" I shook away his fiery touch and made to walk away, expecting to be hauled instantly back.

He let me go. I looked back, confused, still waiting for him to tackle me back into the cave.

"See how far you get then, Earth-born." Ben's smugness fanned my rage. Despite my earlier ban on him using my name, *'Earth-born'* really grated at me. I didn't like him speaking to me as though I was a stranger, a third person, an object. Yet, I supposed I was a stranger, a means to an end, and it was hard to get used to the fact that we were worlds apart now. I turned away, and began my defiant, extremely stupid adventure.

If you ignored the fact that this was the Daimon realm, the fact that it seemed endless with no signs pointing to home, the fact that somewhere out there, Yeqon was baying for my blood, the place didn't actually look *that* bad, it just smelled it. It resembled the Australian outback suffering a hangover after a really bad night out. With this thread-bare positive thinking at the forefront of my mind, I resolved to show Ben up, to find my way out. One glance back at him galvanized my false bravado into action, any common sense had long gone. Cross-armed and smiling, he seemed more amused than dangerous. I could still feel his hands on my skin and smell his scent. *You damn fool Soph!*

Mouth clenched; I turned my back on him with a defiant finality and carefully picked my way down a small, but steep incline. Upended twice, or 'A over H' as Alfie liked to describe an impressive stumble, I was forced to walk sideways across the unstable surface. Shale as slippery as ice was sharp as glass underfoot. Stinging blood spots sprouted around my toes, but I bit back the pain. Ben wouldn't see me succumb.

Despite the wind whipping up a more morose howl, the heat under the strange pulsing sun was instantly overwhelming. I glanced back, eyes shielded with my hand. Ben was watching me, patient as ever, arms still folded. I must have been a good football oval length from him before I noticed anything of interest.

An avenue of huge tree carcasses emerged in a mirage-like haze, leading off towards a raised platform of rock. Underneath the platform was a collection of tall blackened stones in perfect alignment, not unlike Stonehenge. They seemed smooth, shiny, and well-kept; that was very different to Stonehenge. Far beyond that structure, regaled a huge pointed mountain, shrouded in plumes of dull grey smoke.

I wouldn't head in that direction if I was you.

"Get outta my head!" I yelled at Ben, yet worry clawed in my gut. I heeded his advice only because that direction felt like it could lead to bad things. Frankly, everything here could and probably would lead to bad things. I turned the other way and trudged onwards. The mountain grumbled behind me. Vast expanses of drab nothingness lay ahead, the hellish heat lashed my back.

I started to run; still, Ben left me alone. Large cracks webbed the ground. Jumping over them with ease, some were a few feet wide, others a meter or two, I was surprised with my athleticism. That victorious feeling however, was overridden by the strange, howling breeze rushing up from within the fissures. It set my pace faster. I was sure I heard cries for help deep within them. I must have been a good kilometre now. I could barely see Ben. His face a blur, but I knew his eyes were glued to me.

Now, look around you, actually look!

"I said, stay out of my …."

I felt something brush past me. Spinning around, I saw nothing. Heart thundering, heat scorched up my spine and face reflexively, it stopped at just that though, a burn. No wings, no power. A useless tease of what I couldn't do. The necklace pulsed, I clutched it, wishing for a turn of luck, stopping and surveying around me. I rubbed my soul stone bracelet, the one given to me by Enl'iel. Hoping for some comfort, but I got nothing. Zilch, nada; a pathetic void. I couldn't feel the E'lan, there wasn't one positive ion to grasp onto.

I ran on, eyes wider than ever. More things touched me, invisible things. Scratchy mutterings tormented me in the farthest reaches of my mind. After hurdling another large crevice, I found a Sophia-sized rock and slid down behind it, catching my breath and reigning in panicked thoughts.

What the Hell are you doing Soph? How are you going to get yourself out of this?

Wiping the torrent of sweat from my face, I glanced around, one hand clutched to my pendant, the other clung to the rock as though they were talismans of protection.

Deep breath in, deep breath out, repeat.

I don't know if that worked anymore, anxiety was a toxic best friend I couldn't seem to kick to the kerb.

Chewing my bottom lip, thinking of my family and all those who needed me, I forced myself to concentrate, to see with more than my eyes, looking for something… anything. The same calmness that helped me conceal my appearance was called for. An almighty ask in the current situation.

I punched fear in the face and forced my eyes closed to concentrate. I called on that calming waterfall that allowed me to settle.

Unseen things repeatedly touched and tugged at me, forcing me to break that concentration a number of times, yet I saw nothing each time my eyes flew open. I was being played again, and I needed to know by what.

"Show yourselves you worthless cowards," I called with a shake in my voice. I squeezed my eyes tighter, hand on that thrumming pendant so firmly I worried it might break. Desperately ignoring the horrid pokes and prods by invisible things, my mind eventually receded into a calmer place, away from fear and anger, a place I wished I could stay.

It was the sounds that came first, sailing in on that nasty wind.

Whispers, quiet and savage mutterings erupted into a symphony of horror. Scary, unfriendly murmurings from spectral sources that felt way to close. I opened my eyes slowly, my hands pressed against my face, squinting through the gaps of my fingers. Expecting to see a world of poltergeist things, it remained a cacophony of nasty suggestions and shouts, both near and far.

I didn't know how long I had until Ben got sick of playing his games with me, so I had to find a way out, or at least a hiding place, and quick. Trying to block out the voices so I could think on my next move, I let my eyes sort of glaze over, as though in a stare. That's when the *'real'* realm began to reveal itself in all its horror.

The haze on the horizon melted into a mirage of liquid silver. The atmosphere lobbed in and out of focus. Shapes flickered in my peripheral vision. Shadows. *Lots* of shadows. My nerves were on the precipice of *'let's completely freak out!'* I had to keep it together though, I had to be strong, I had to beat him. I concentrated on the movement of these new additions to the landscape as they flitted here and there, or, were they really there at all? Was it the heat? Was it the fear? Was I imagining it all? Blinking and refocusing, they seemed gone. *Phew!*

Slowly standing up, I edged around the rock, the necklace still in my grasp. I assumed that it was the heat getting to me. There was nothing there but dust and rocks and stench.

No, you naïve fool! Instinct screamed at me. There *was* something. Smudgy blurs of movement came back into focus. Small, tall, wide and skinny, all moving suspiciously and closer to me. As I rounded the opposite side of the rock, my eyes really began to see. The smudges became opaque, flitting all directions. With a suddenness I wasn't prepared for, the reality of this bizarre unreality hit me.

These shadows slowly revealed themselves, and they weren't shadows at all. They were, well, I wasn't sure right then, but they looked like apparitions, ghosts, monsters of every kind of nightmare a kid wakes up screaming about.

These *things* seemed busy with a multitude of tasks. Strange creatures, human-like but gnarled and disfigured, rushing around haphazardly, some pulling bushels of plants from the ground, placing them into baskets, others engaged in violent fights. Teeth and bones, there were a lot of those. Snapping and snarling and guttural conversations crossed the distance between them and me. Unfortunately, there was no sign post that said, *please exit here*.

Luckily, they seemed oblivious to me, until I had that exact thought. As though a war siren sounded, the air slowed into a molasses-like freezing of time. Every single entity in the vicinity stopped and looked in my direction. Mouth agape, hands splayed against the rock behind me, I froze too, "Holy shit!"

Snarls and growls, howls and hoots ensued as they threw their work baskets aside, ceased their fights and cautiously made their way towards me, one gnarled foot at a time. Talons scraped across the ground, drool glistened, wings beat in threat, and every one of them pierced me with the blackest of eyes. One of them, a small one, had my fullest attention. It was the Asmodai from the cave. An evil grainy grin that led the horde in their slow procession.

"She should have taken our bargain," he said. His hands rolled with gleeful anticipation. Grains of sand drizzled from his mouth onto the parched ground. Barely human visages, some surely couldn't ever have been mortal. Grotesque features, inch long incisors glistening within gaping mouths, incongruent with normality. Blackened orifices replaced eyes, yet they saw me all the better for it. Some made the Rogues look almost pleasant. I dashed around the rock to find I was surrounded on every side with everything you could imagine lived in Hell.

"Fresh meat!"

"Mine!"

Bile burned my throat.

I crouched low and kept a watch in every direction. There was no opening for escape. My wings; I tried to get them out, they seemed to emerge then sunk straight back within my back.

"Shit, shit, shit!" *It can't end like this!* The pendant pulsed wildly, as though it too, understood the imminent danger.

A sudden scuffle broke out right in front of me. These things fought for dibs on me. The supernatural melee grew, they seemed attracted to the ethereal bloody gore the fight drew. A head rolled my way and dissipated into nothingness as something else screeched bloody murder. More joined in the bloodbath, yet still, most were focused entirely on me, panting and drooling in anticipation. The fight was only buying me time as they wondered who was going to be challenged next. They seemed to be eyeing each other off.

"Want to come back now?"

I flinched, punching out behind me, only to have my wrist caught in Ben's hand. The creatures screamed and backed away when he appeared, huge wings of light waved behind him. His power and light forced the creatures into retreat. The entertainment of the gory fight less interesting now that Ben stood high above them, glowering down at them, me as his prize, not theirs.

"You see now? You're vulnerable out here."

I yanked my hand from his.

"Well, aren't you just so satisfied?" I retorted, yet secretly I was relieved more than I could admit. He was enjoying his game, yet I didn't want to be out here for one more second. I noticed the creatures had resumed their business, distancing themselves. The Asmodai watched me thoughtfully though, its sandy, slitted eyes glowered from atop a rock a few feet away. A nasty little gargoyle. Ragged baskets, now full of what looked like onions and leeks, were carried away by teams of the creatures back towards the avenue of trees. It appeared now, every bit like a workforce getting back to business. Some were entering and exiting from the crevices in the ground, glancing wearily back at us. This place was teeming with '*life*'.

"Just get me out of here!" I hated doing it, but I moved a little closer to Ben. He smiled ever so slightly, enjoying his stupid victory.

In the blink of an eye, he pulled me into his chest and I was yanked back into blackness again.

Chapter Twelve

"So, I can't have a weapon because I'm not a freaking alien? That's kind of bigoted don't you think?" Jaz smart-mouthed to Brennan as he sheathed his chromious dagger, shoving it into the waist of his pants.

"That would be yes, Mini Princess, but not because you're human, because you're you!" Brennan smiled and ruffled her un-brushed hair. She shoved him away, a look of hurt masked by purse-lipped sass.

"What?" Jaz challenged him as they packed the last bag onto the plane.

"You and that temper of yours need to earn a carry-on weapon. I don't want to be wearing a dagger tiara just because I pissed you off!" Brennan wound her right up and enjoyed every second.

"Nice, Brennan," Kea said, shaking her head as laughed.

"Brennan, leave her alone. He's just teasing you, Jasmine." Enl'iel rested a motherly arm around Jaz who seemed to accept it less reluctantly than usual.

"You need a great deal more training before it is safe for you to carry a serious weapon. Training of body *and* soul, that is, remember? Just like Sophia. Do not be offended. It's much like when you trained as a nurse. You weren't just let out wild onto the hospital wards with an arm full of syringes. You worked under strict guidance until you were thoroughly assessed as being competent. This is the same, but different. You understand?" Enl'iel raised her eyebrows, awaiting an answer.

"Why are you always so sensible?" Jaz grumbled, "But what if I'm ambushed by… I don't know, one of those things? How do I protect myself?"

"That is what I'm here for, to protect you," Jude's deep murmur made Jaz jump as he quietly appeared behind her.

"Will you *stop* creeping up on me like that, Freak?" Jaz' eyes travelled angrily all the way up to his hard expression, a light blush pinking her cheeks.

"If you can't hear me approaching, you won't know when a Daimon is about to rip your head off from behind, either," Jude said.

"Freak!" Unable to hide the fear in her eyes, Jaz flashed him her best pissed off expression and a middle finger for dessert.

Enl'iel stepped between them, "Come now children, no fighting!" She smiled, amused, yet she hadn't missed the way Jaz looked at Jude. Jaz' self-righteous indignation was peppered with something that just could not and should not be there. Enl'iel took Jaz' hand and led her onto the private jet, along with Brennan, Kea and Koi, and a large contingent of their non-ethereal family.

Koi approached, having largely left Jaz alone, he guided her to her seat. He smiled warmly.

"Jasmine, unlike Sophia, the fire in you cripples your ability to be rational, to be safe. You have so much rage, it defines you, and that will not see you to a good end. The sooner you can find calmness, the sooner you will find your true strength. You are Sophia's opposite in every way, other than the love and loyalty that burns vigorously in your soul." Koi bowed to Jaz. Words momentarily escaped her.

Koi then focused on Jude.

"Please remind yourself, Jude, that she is not one of us. Compassion will be what binds you two together. Let go of your anger, you are just like her." Koi smiled, scratched his head and made his way to the back of the A380 to help the other humans settle aboard. His words left Jaz confused and Jude grinding his teeth. Jude's facial mark flared, the swirls around his right eye luminescent. He ran his hand angrily through his perfectly kept length of alabaster hair.

"I'd rather be bound to Lilith!" Jude growled.

Jaz' mouth opened.

"And with that, we will say our goodbyes," Enl'iel interrupted before Jaz could put her oversized foot in it again. Enl'iel waved to Jude. "Travel safely, Jude."

He nodded, conceding to her peace making.

"I'll see you at Derinkuyu, Enl'iel," Jude said as he descended back onto the tarmac of the private airstrip. A fresh dusting of snow fell upon his bare shoulders.

"Thank you, Jude, take care of yourself. We will see you in the morning." Enl'iel waved down at him from the door. He nodded and transferred out in a nanosecond of bright light.

As the plane taxied away, the stars twinkled unhindered across the evening sky. The moon cast a soft glow across Jaz' cheeks. She watched the earth fall away as she absentmindedly thumbed the white stone in the silver bracelet. Her body relaxed; her eyes slowly closed. Enl'iel watched this angry young girl with increasing interest. The soul stone was secretly helping to calm the hurt within Jaz' tortured soul, yet that fire was still so strong. Enl'iel wanted to know what it was and how to harness it to help Jaz, rather than it slowly breaking her down.

"We really have to watch her, Brennan. She's one breath short of an explosion."

"Too true, Li Li." Brennan wrapped his arm around Enl'iel, pulling her head onto his shoulder as they sat across from Jaz, watching her intently, wondering when and where that fire might ignite.

A vast mountain range came into view as the plane dipped below the cloud line. Jaz stared wide-eyed at another new horizon, blanketed in snow, and as strange as any she'd seen in her short life.

"Looks pretty barren," she mumbled to no one in particular. A far from impressed look deepened the dark circles beneath her eyes.

"Whatever, s'pose we'll be back in dungeons again, anyway. Probably with no T.V. this time too." Jaz blew a tangle of hair out of her face as she stretched out her arms, looking around as she stood to do the same for her legs. It was a huge plane, packed full of people, human people mixed with the supernatural. They all looked normal, that was what was strange, just a plane full of regular looking Joes heading to a new headquarters. *To plan a fight to the death with Daimon, Rogues and other God-awful creatures to find Soph.*

Jaz snickered in resigned amusement at the twist her life had taken. *Hell, I've always liked a bit of action,* she thought. She took the last gulp of cola from the now warm can, grimacing with disgust. Brennan caught her attention from across the aisle. He looked decidedly uncomfortable squeezing his massive frame out of the standard cattle class seat.

"The things we… do for you… oh crap… Earth dwellers." He retrieved an upturned bottle from the floor, wiping down his pants to dry them of the spilled water with a brief glow from his palm.

"Sorry dude, wasn't my calling in life, but hey, here we are!" Jaz couldn't help smiling at his awkwardness.

"Yeah, well, this is no way to fly, I can tell you." Brennan stretched; his head bent to avoid the ceiling. "That out there, some good old times were had down there, Mini Princess." He pointed out the window as the plane rapidly descended towards a small airport runway. Amber lights blinked as they beckoned the plane in.

"Where exactly are we?" Jaz asked as Brennan squished in next to her, forcing her to retake her own seat.

"The coolest place in Turkey. Seat belt for landing Mini Princess, can't be too careful." He leaned over her and clicked the buckle into place. For the first time, a man leaned into her body and her reaction wasn't to grope him from head to toe. Her lack of interest surprised her.

As though he could sense her thoughts, Brennan quipped, "Don't get too excited there now, Jaz, I'm taken!" He winked at her with his sparkling blues.

Her cheeks flushed as he settled back into the seat next to her.

"Not with a ten-foot barge pole buddy." She leaned against the window to put as much distance as possible between them.

Brennan clutched his heart, "You've mortally wounded me!"

She couldn't help herself and laughed.

"You're such an idiot!" Jaz emphasised this with a playful elbow into his arm.

"A badge I carry with honour."

She studied Brennan covertly as he fiddled awkwardly with his own seatbelt. An air of calm flooded her. She took in his shiny white hair, the deep valleys of musculature down his arms, regarding him with admiration and nothing else. Her shoulders slumped, relaxed. Her fingers finally uncurled out of the almost permanent fists they'd been in since Sophia had been taken. Jaz ran her hands through her hair, blowing out a puff of breath, regaining her composure as Brennan wriggled to find some sort of comfortable position.

"We're close to our destination. Great coffee waiting for us." He clapped his hands together in anticipation.

"Where exactly are we going in Turkey?"

"Nevşehir. We land there, then roll out to one of the ancient sanctuaries. They've been abandoned since the great flood receded. Jude's checking out which one is the most secure. There's a few here around the Cappadocian countryside. These are some of the oldest inhabited areas on Earth. Spent some fine times here with the ancient civilisations. That's part of the reason we're in it big time with the Old Man!" he pointed towards the sky. "Too much "frivolity" as Enl'iel puts it!" Brennan exaggerated the word with finger quotes. "There used to be a big trade route underground, lots of coming and going. The tunnels go all the way to Scotland in some areas." A reminiscent glow coloured his cheeks. Leaning across Jaz, Brennan studied the approaching landscape with a wistful smile.

"Yeah, okay, so why are we *here* in particular?" Jaz asked, elbowing him out of her space.

Brennan snapped out of what seemed a particularly amusing memory, refocusing on the impatient girl beside him.

"Safety Jaz. Safety from Ben." He patted her hand gently and nodded firmly, as though to emphasise the point.

Jaz swallowed hard, gripping the armrests, white-knuckled again as anger re-surged. She held on tight as the plane came in to land. Again, for one of the few times in her life, Jaz had no smart retort or comment, just disbelief moistening her eyes. She blinked the feeling away as quickly as it appeared. With a slight flare of her nostrils and a quiver on the tip of her chin, Jaz reclaimed her standard *'back-the-hell-off'* expression.

As the thud of the tires hitting the icy tarmac yanked Jaz back and forward in her seat, the warmth of Brennan's hand on hers pulled her eyes up to his. Red-rimmed again with the threat of unwelcome tears, the innocent little girl buried deep inside implored him for answers without a single word.

"I know Mini Princess, I know."

Chapter Thirteen

"Just get it over with Ben, or take me home! How long is this going to go on for? Are you actually trying to help me, kill me, or save your own skin?"

Cross-armed and mad as hell, I found myself back in the cave by the pool of water. I bent down, scrubbing black sludge from my hands before scooping up a refreshing mouthful, throwing handfuls over my head to cool off. Noting my plain reflection, remembering what had happened the last time I looked deep into this little oasis, that flicker of hope burned brighter alongside my anger. I just needed some time alone again.

A loud smack followed that thought, along with the crumbling sound of rocks breaking. My attention snapped back to Ben. His fist was a bloody mess, the slender fingers bent at sickening angles. My jaw dropped in shock and disgust. He looked to the ceiling, neck muscles straining; he screamed deeply, loudly; from the very centre of his soul. His cheeks were crimson with emotion. His fully black eyes once more found mine. I backed away to the wall. Droplets of blood oozing from his hand drummed onto the ground in time with a new panic in my heart. His smug amusement had vanished into unadulterated and sudden anger. *We were the same in a totally dysfunctional way.*

"*You!* You stand there and so easily judge me and make your demands?" Ben's voice was deceptively calm, low, calculated; yet his chin quivered with the effort of self-control. The blackness of his eyes glistened in the corners.

"Ben… I…"

"*Don't* speak!" He ran his uninjured fingers through his hair. This time, the act didn't quicken my heart. The silence was thick as he averted his attention to his injuries. He pulled his disfigured fingers back into alignment with sickening cracks. He groaned with every move, but he didn't hesitate through the pain. His hands were plum and swollen with a thick coating of dust. He shook his head, mumbling incoherently to himself through his macabre act. Fear overwhelmed me, it truly shadowed me. I glanced hopefully at that water and back again. *Have I run out of time?*

He looked up slowly.

"Yes Sophia, I've deceived you. Yes Sophia, I've taken you away. But what *you* don't realise…."

His breaths deepened as he closed the distance between us. Sweat poured down his neck, glistening all the way down the ripples of his stomach, still purple with slowly healing wounds. He reached me all too soon and stood silently over me. I held my breath. He was so powerful. His menacing strength and unknown intentions held me frozen against the wall. I kept my head held high, though; I would not let him completely win this psychological warfare by falling into a dribbling mess.

"Are you done with your little show?" I blurted, then bit my lip to keep my mouth shut.

He leaned in, his entire body blacked out the rest of the cave. Good hand curled in a fist against the wall right next to my face, he moved to within inches of me. With the injured hand, he ran a blood caked finger slowly down my face, from my eye to chin. That same finger tipped my face up to his, forcing me to look at him. His right cheek was enveloped by glowing coils of energy framing his unnatural, searching eyes. I felt that energy. It was both warm and cold, light and dark. His indecisive glare flickered from black to blue and then back again. Turmoil and anger rolled from him.

"What you don't realise…" Ben leaned in closer again, his lips just centimetres from mine. I couldn't breathe.

"I could have taken you to him anytime, at any point."

His face angled slowly from side to side. He inspected every inch of my face, still running that finger softly over my mark, which was screaming from within. The burn was pain and pleasure; I was in an emotional hell. His eyes locked onto mine, settling back to the black-ringed blue.

"I could have killed you any time, or turned you over to Yeqon. Anything I wanted, really, and yet, I haven't." He cradled my chin between thumb and finger, tipping higher, so that his lips rested upon my chin. His touch was fire, it was danger. Ashes and spice punctuated the air with the metallic tang of blood.

"I have protected you from him, from everything." His breaths were ragged.

If his mouth was any closer to mine…

I could barely breathe as I placed my hands against his chest in an ineffectual effort to push him away. I wanted to run and stay, all at once. He gasped with the touch of my hands on his bare skin.

Soph, you idiot…stop…now…fight!

I tried to turn my face away again, his grip tightened even with the obvious pain it caused him.

He brought his face down, his mouth hovered above mine. A tear cut through the heat of my skin, but it wasn't mine. "I've betrayed more than myself protecting you." Ben's breath warmed my lips, his other hand caressed my face until both hands cupped my head. Common sense screamed for me to do something, but I was paralysed by his erratic behaviour, and the utter rebellious turmoil in my chest. His thumbs rubbed small circles across my cheeks. His voice, thick and husky, wavered as he spoke.

"You are my mission, my vengeance, my downfall."

I think I stopped breathing.

Just as his lips ghosted mine, he pushed himself away, clawing his hands into his head. He screamed again. Rage, pure and unadulterated.

"No!" he cried. Crouching low, the emotional roar should have woken the dead, every muscle of his body strained though his pain. Eventually, he stilled into an unnerving silence. His heaving sobs stopped. I remained frozen to the spot, an unwilling spectator. The fire of his lips still lingered on my own.

He reached out to something on the ground with his good hand and picked it up. A small, brown bead. Ben rolled it around between thumb and finger for a few seconds, then stood up, slowly turning back to me. His face was darker than ever. The cave closed in.

"*This* is why I've done the things I've done!" He held that little bead up for me to see.

"I'm owed retribution for Neren'iel, for her murder!" A sparkling tear slid down his cheek from eyes that brimmed red and angry.

"I…"

"I *said*, don't speak!" Ben growled through his teeth. He closed the space between us once more, nostrils flaring.

"This is *all* I ever really needed to remind me where my path lay." He held the bead inches from my face.

"You will *never, ever* understand what I have lost. More than Neren'iel, more than just myself." He closed his eyes and took a deep breath.

"I've lost you too." Ben searched my eyes for answers. How could he possibly expect me to have any concept of what he was going through? His eyes raged every colour of the spectrum until solidifying back into darkness. The colour of the Daimon that lurked deep inside. He was giving in to it.

Before I could react, Ben pulled me tight into his chest. The familiar pull in my gut of an imminent transfer hit me like a blow. Everything went dark. The next stop, I knew, was death.

The tangy odour of raw onions and waste hit me before I regained my bearings. The stench made me gag and my eyes water. This place was an assault on every possible sense. Ben's fingers clawed around my biceps. Blinking rapidly to clear the stinging stream, I emerged from the transference to find myself being pulled along another dingy, subterranean corridor. It was lit with sconces of flickering fire, a rough floor riddled with cracks had me trip and dodge beside him. Orange light glowed between the fissures that seemed very much to be lava flowing beneath. It would explain the burn underfoot. The wall lights sizzled and cracked, spitting out orange and green sparks.

"Ben… please?"

Flashes from what occurred in the cave spun through my mind. My lips warmed; my heart froze. He was going to kiss me! *What the hell?* Now it felt like he was going to kill me. Confusion reigned in my world; a melting pot of emotional chaos.

This is more than just you Soph, this is about everyone else. Get over yourself. I lashed myself with my thoughts, trying to pull myself together.

He pulled harder, his pace quickened, bringing my attention back to my surroundings all too clearly. Distant screams, bloodcurdling ones, instantly alerted my senses that I was desperately closer to a very bad end.

"Ben…where…?"

Each time I spoke he yanked the breath out of me, pulling harder and faster. We rounded a corner, descending into the depths of I didn't know what. It was as though he was scared to stop, as though it would challenge the decision he'd come to if he had the chance to think again.

"Ben, what are you doing?" I shrieked, as I finally strung enough words together. I twisted my body but there was no pulling away from him. His grip was iron. The ground underfoot rumbled.

Ben uttered not a single word, not a sound. His grasp tightened almost painfully. He started to a run. I was forced to match it, or get dragged along instead. He repeatedly glanced behind us as though we were running from something. The ground became increasingly sharp as the fissures widened; sulphurous vapours jettisoned up. The tunnel narrowed and sloped sharply down, like a spiral.

"Please, Ben. I'm sorry for insulting you. Don't do this! We can fix this! Come back with me and make amends!"

He jerked me each time I spoke, as if to shut me up.

I couldn't get through to him. He was switched off to me completely. Panic was again quelling any semblance of bravery. Regrets were already emerging about how I should have handled him. The essence of who I was becoming caused such confusion. I needed to adapt to my ever-changing life and destiny. I needed to surrender myself to the circumstance and allow instinct to override all that I knew before. That was so much easier to say than achieve. I needed to get over clinging onto the old me, and fast. How do you change who you are as a person though, just to survive?

Because I was still clinging to someone that was no more, I had confused myself and had failed to stand my ground. I wasn't a badass like Jaz, I never would be, but I needed to be sure of myself, just like Jaz always had been. I was a mess of what I truly was and what I thought I needed to be. Somewhere, those two had met in the middle in that cave and blew up in my face. Now I was here.

The tunnel darkened as the flickering fires along the walls lessened. The smell, it was indescribable. I gagged through it. This was a very bad place. I couldn't say I'd ever known what good Karma felt like, but this place was thick with all kinds of what I would call bad Karma. There wasn't a single positive element, not one little atom of goodness in the atmosphere. After hearing a bloodcurdling scream, I managed a surprisingly effective punch to the side Ben's face, allowing me to pull free for a moment. Unfortunately, he had me back in his control in seconds, shoving me against the wall.

Holding my hands against my chest inside one strong fist, wincing from the cut I'd opened on his cheek, Ben's horrid eyes bored into mine. He wiped one of his fingers through the blood oozing from his face. It sparkled like mine, but his oozed dark and viscous. He wiped a smear across my cheek.

"We are the same, you and I." Ben's eyes flashed green, then blue, then black again.

I was in a full body tremble, mouth glued shut and unable to avert my eyes from his. His nostrils flared, he turned and pulled me along again.

"It's best if you don't struggle. It will be quicker that way." His voice was defeated, resigned, very un-Ben. My blood turned to ice. I searched frantically for some form of weapon as I was dragged ever deeper into the hot, sulphurous earth. I clawed at the enclosing walls. I drew on anger rather than fear, making him work ever harder to get me wherever he was going. I couldn't just give in, despite my abject horror. I frantically pulled and punched and kicked at him as he dragged me further into the unknown. He was prepared for my onslaught, easily dodging and weaving my flailing limbs.

"You bastard!" I finally cried. I lashed out again and again, with every bit of strength I had. "You'll go to Hell for this!"

I finally landed another cracking punch across the same cheek bone, splitting the skin right open. He turned on me again.

"Can't you see? I'm already in Hell! I've lived it for ten thousand years!" Ben yelled through his teeth; his fist punched his heart. It trembled over whatever was broken inside. After regaining his composure, he kicked open a door behind me that I hadn't noticed at all.

"In!" He gestured the way ahead. He'd given up on who or what he ever was, or had been. Another small corridor stretched out ahead. Small rooms lined its length. They appeared to be cells. Bars of some kind of red energy imprisoned a multitude of horrendous creatures. Some appeared human, some barely animal. Some seemed a mixture of both. Others were horrifyingly spectral. What they all had in common though, was the way they became agitated and excited when they saw me. Hooting and growling, licking of lips that made me cringe.

"Oh, just a taste?"

"I'll have more than a taste!" A cackle of snorting laughter followed as they drove each other into a blood frenzy, stomping the floor and clawing at the walls.

Ben threw a shot of energy through the bars of the second one to speak out of turn, cutting him down. Dead, I think. I didn't know if they were dead or alive to begin with, but it looked pretty dead now, grotesquely sliced in two with oozing fluids draining away into the floor. My stomach churned, I looked away. That stopped them all. They backed away into the dark corners of their cells.

Ben opened a large wooden door at the end and shoved me unceremoniously inside. His hand glowed, he waved it from ceiling to floor, drawing out a set of those red jail bars. They hummed ominously, not unlike Koi's red orbs.

Glaring at me, eyes flashing, chest heaving and glistening with sweat, not another word passed his tightly pressed lips.

"Please, Ben. Don't do this?" I pleaded.

In a lightening swift move, he slammed the arched door shut, leaving me in a depressive darkness but for the faint glow and crackle of those insidious beams of imprisonment.

As the sound of that door thundering shut reverberated through my mind, I slumped to the ground. *Despair. Disbelief.* Dry grit had given way to a wet, stinking sludge seeping through my fingers, wicking up my pants. It seemed to pull me down like quick sand. My stomach felt like it was sinking away with an encroaching loss of hope that lurked in the background. How could I pull myself out of this?

I ran the previous hours through my mind again and again. Had I been the wrong measure of passive and aggressive to Ben? Would anything have really mattered? I feared my attempts at standing up to him had pushed him over the edge, yet I couldn't remain weak, playing the innocent victim. I had a duty to stand my ground, not only for myself but for everyone else, and now I was mad as hell. I'd play his stupid game, whatever it took. Angry wasn't me, but for the second time in my life, since Esme had died, I fanned an anger burning inside me. It was so foreign and unexpected, but it came with an emboldening strength. I recalled Koi telling me in training that emotions were a weakness. He also said that I could use them to my advantage, to draw out strength. It all seemed too little, too late though. I just hadn't had enough time to train and learn enough before this was all rammed straight in my face.

Now, because of my weakness, my humanness, I'd pushed the last little glimmer of goodness from whomever Ben was. Something had snapped in him back at the cave. I'd almost believed he was going to let me go. He'd wavered for days in handing me over to Yeqon. He'd fed and protected me, albeit as a prisoner, but that's what had bolstered me to be stronger with him. My attempt to flee outside, had that done it? Was it the bracelet or the memories of this Neren'iel person? Now, it seemed a done deal, he was going to throw me to *the* devil. There was no doubt in my mind. I could feel it. The nasty edge to the atmosphere, the nothingness, the existence of those revolting creatures beyond the door meant only one thing… I was a step closer to Yeqon… to my end.

My head felt heavy with the weight of it all. I grasped my temples with mud-caked hands, leaning forward onto my knees. I suddenly wished for sleep, to forget, to hideaway from reality, but I couldn't sleep anymore, well, not like a normal person anyway. Psynostris had kicked in, full force. I think I'd only slept once since I'd been abducted. And how long ago had that been? A week or more now? I laid down in the warm sludge, gazing up into the hazy darkness of the claustrophobic space. The red bars sizzled nastily, every muscle ached, yet my mark glowed strong. *Useless bloody thing!* I needed fire power, not a night light.

Deep breath in, deep breath out, repeat.

I let my eyes fall shut, sweeping my memories for something comforting to take me away from the malevolence. Immediately, I settled on Esme.

"Oh Esme, I wish you were here," I sobbed, grabbing at my pendant which still pulsed in time with the sombre beat of my heart. My beautiful Esme always knew how to make me feel better. As though she knew I needed her, from the depths of my memories I could hear the sweet sound of her soft voice singing the indigenous lullaby that she soothed me with as a child. I hummed it shakily to begin with, then with more force, drowning out the sounds beyond the door.

I repeated the sweet song about a goanna a couple of times before my voice faded away, allowing the silence to reign. I contemplated my life to this point. Had I done enough? Had I tried hard enough? The image of Esme's body crumpled and falling through the abyss at Belial's feet gave me the answer I was looking for. *No,* I hadn't done enough. I hadn't tried hard enough in the short time I'd lived this new life. I hadn't learned enough, hadn't tested my limits enough. I had to stop thinking and start acting. Esme had done enough, she'd given the ultimate, her life. If she could give her life protecting us, then I could give more and I would. Pushing up with a disgusting squelch, I inspected the foul cell for anything that could point towards an escape. Nothing but darkness, rough rock and a slimy floor.

Some sort of fluid dribbled down from the roof. Beads of whatever it was emerged from a thin crack in the ceiling, along with hisses of steam. Each glistening droplet meandered down the wall, ending with a rhythmic plop into a puddle by the side of the buzzing cell bars. Those menacing red rods immediately caught my attention. They ran with a mesmerising fluidity, like lava contained within a clear tube. Despite this appearance, no heat emanated from them. They hugged the doorway closely enough that only a paper-thin person could squeeze between them. Now and then, they stuttered like static electricity. Intrigued, I tested one bar with the tip of a finger. I was sliding down the far wall before I could register the painful slam to my spine, a singed fingertip for a souvenir.

Okay then, I won't do that again!

After sucking on my finger and rubbing the ache from my back, I went back to the ever-growing puddle, happily avoiding the unfriendly bars. The smell of the fluid was far from inviting. I wouldn't be quenching my thirst with it. However, it conveniently offered the same reflective surface that the fresh water had done back in the cave.

Peering at my filthy reflection, I ran my equally dirty hands across the hem of my pants and rubbed them together in tentative anticipation. Closing my eyes and willing myself to the least form of hysteria, I stared calmly back down at the reflection. I concentrated as hard as I could. Plucking out an image from my memories, I focused on it to the point of a migraine, waiting patiently, willing it to emerge. My eyes shut tight.

"Come on!"

My heart skipped an uncomfortable beat or two as I shivered, forcing my eyes open. Everything around me seemed disappointingly the same, unchanged.

"Crap!" I was about to rollover into a sulk again, yet, as I ran my hands over my face in defeat, I realised everything felt very different. Heart now racing, I sat forward on my knees and peered back down into the dark pool. My fingers slid along the slimy edges. Quelling a scream of excitement, I covered my mouth in shock before prodding all over my face, leaving mud spots everywhere.

Jaz stared back at me. I had a plan.

Chapter Fourteen

Jaz repositioned her heavy backpack as her allocated group made their way up the steep, ancient street of Nevşehir in search of coffee and safety. Sophia's diamond dagger rattled in dull thuds against her water bottle inside the bag. Enl'iel had recovered it during the salvage clean up at Stonehenge. She'd wrapped it in muslin, giving it to Jaz to return personally to Sophia when they found her. Jaz knew it was a gesture, a mere beacon of hope to keep her going, yet she relished each moment she could look at it, to feel it, to keep a connection with her best friend. Jaz was under strict orders to protect it, not use it under any circumstances; she was a mere human, after all, as Jude had pointed out more than once. Jaz respected that, though; she was smart enough to know when she was out of her depth, so she clung tighter to the shoulder straps as the exceptional group of ethereal and mortal troops ascended the hill.

With a little time to kill, the current consensus after touchdown was to fuel their stomachs before anything else.

"Always was one to take his damned time," Brennan puffed intricate breath patterns in the frigid air as he complained about Jude taking too long. "That fat-head should've had the place sorted by now."

His teasing delighted Jaz. Laughing had been rare since Sophia disappeared.

"And that thoroughness has always kept us safe, Brennan," Enl'iel responded sternly.

"Until the Henge. He wasn't ahead of the game there, was he?" Brennan replied, annoyed.

"Brennan!" Enl'iel stopped and pulled him aside. Everyone else moved on ahead. "That's not fair of you. Someone close betrayed us. We were all fooled." There was a distinct edge of annoyance in her voice. Enl'iel pushed him to keep walking, not wanting to draw too much attention from the locals.

"That would be my brother. Former brother! Biggest arse ever!" Jaz grumbled, no longer smiling.

"He fooled everyone. He is obviously a powerful and ancient soul," Enl'iel added before Jaz piped in again.

"He's just a complete dick. Don't you dare repeat that I said this, but you might want to cop Jude a break, Bren? If Ben fooled me, you guys seriously had no chance!" Jaz huffed. Enl'iel balked at the language, her eyes wide. Jaz' expression was indignant.

"Okay ladies, stand down." Brennan put up his hands in defence.

"Defending the mountain of a brute now, are we Mini Princess? Times are a-changing!" He ruffled her hair. She elbowed him away with a grimace.

"You can stop with the princess crap, too. I'm no princess," she grumbled.

"That is something we all can agree on!" Thomas said as he pushed past them, moving on ahead with his companions as they arrived at their destination.

"Watch it, Frenchy!" snapped Jaz. Brennan put a hand across her mouth at the entrance to a small coffee shop before she could put her foot in it any further.

Wedged between an internet café and a traditional carpet weaver, the inviting smell of strong coffee and sweets had them all rolling through the door without hesitation.

"God, this place smells fucking amazing!" Jaz exclaimed as she eyed the colourful dwelling with awe, a thick roasted aroma instantly lifting her mood.

"My mouth is watering already," Brennan added as they headed towards cosy, rear seating booths.

"Whilst I normally prefer tea, Jasmine, I can highly recommend the pistachio coffee. It's quite unique," Enl'iel commented, a gentle hand pressed to Jaz' back.

Enl'iel smiled and waved towards Kristen, Thomas and their group, who had already settled amongst several low tables surrounded by comfy, brightly coloured floor cushions. Enl'iel's' stomach growled.

"Oh my, excuse me. It has been a while since I last ate!" She blushed as she grabbed at her waist. Brennan snuggled down with her on a large, gold-embroidered red cushion as a man and woman approached in equally colourful robes.

"Merhaba." The man bowed politely to them all. His smile settled on Jaz. The woman quietly smiled as well. Their brown eyes flashed briefly opalescent blue, then back to brown. Enl'iel and Brennan bowed their heads in acknowledgment of their kindred.

Jaz eyed the couple dubiously.

"It means hello. Welcome to Nevşehir, dear Jasmine. We have heard many lovely things about you. Please, relax and eat." The man smiled deeply. Bronzed wrinkles cushioned his eyes.

Coffee was upon them in small delicate cups before anyone could say another word, as were platters of sweet and savoury delights.

Jaz' eyes bulged. "Wow!" She grabbed a handful of Baklava instead of the cheese and spinach gozleme and lentil soup pots, "Oh, yum!" she garbled around a mouthful of walnuts and pastry.

"Just a shot of your best with this and I'm sweet!" Jaz winked as the kindly lady poured her a cup of the potent brew with a smile. Jaz winced with her first sip. "Woah! Good stuff! I won't sleep for a week!"

"You are supposed to sip it dear, not gulp it like instant coffee!" Enl'iel giggled as she picked up a gold-rimmed cup and mimicked a delicate sip before turning her attention back to their hosts.

"Thank you, Ahmet, Elmas. Your hospitality is wonderful, as always."

Ahmet responded, smiling warmly at both Enl'iel and Brennan, "It is so good to see you both again. It has been too long."

"Much too long," Elmas added as she readjusted her richly coloured headscarf. "These bodies grow older too quickly. I fear our time will come sooner than yours to move on. You must visit us more often!" Her smile broadened. "You will find your accommodations well stocked. Jude has already sent for your supplies." Elmas inclined her head towards Enl'iel.

"Thank you Elmas, and yes," Enl'iel replied, "It has been much too long. Perhaps fifty or sixty years wouldn't you…" The front doorbell tinkled, interrupting them. Jaz looked up as she was dipping a finger into her cup, licking the sweet, sludgy remains from her little finger.

Jude filled the door frame and took in the surrounds like a well-trained commando. He offered a K'ufili to Ahmet and Elmas who came to greet him. His voice reached the rear of the cafe.

"Thank you once more for your exemplary preparedness." Jude kissed Elma's hand before he turned his attention to the party in the back.

With his broad chest barely covered in a light coat, purely to fit in with the local populace, his eyes fell on Jaz in seconds. She nearly dropped her cup as he moved towards their table with three loping strides.

"Enl'iel," Jude greeted her politely before he glowered towards Brennan. Jude's eyes flickered between which emotion to use, settling on professional over personal, yet his voice remained tight and blunt.

"Brennan. Everything is safe for now. The Derinkuyu caves unfortunately remain inadequately secure for my liking. I'm uncertain if Ben knew about them when the filthy scum was hiding among us. Koi and I have prepared the Kaymakli caves a little further out. The number of tourists visiting should add an element of confusion for the Daimon. It should interfere with any elemental power we might use, at least during daylight hours. The locals are unaware of the deepest dwellings below the first eight levels, which will be good coverage for us. The secluded entrance remains secure and well away from the sight of the local populace. I have prepared these accommodations with enough supplies to ready ourselves for war and protect our young. I have prepared a training room, accounted for all the weapons, and stocked the cellars with food and water. The Alchemae await you, Enl'iel." He nodded respectfully.

Enl'iel smiled broadly at his report. "And the old Zythros stone?" she enquired further.

"Koi is activating it with Lorcan. He has reanimated some dormant Keepers who are tending the stone as we speak. They are quite ancient and will take some time waking, so it will not be ready for some time yet. So, communications and transference will have to remain localised until then."

"Thank you, Jude. You are well prepared as always. You humble me. And yes, you are correct in suspecting that Ben may know more than we realise. He has had twenty years and then some to gather his intel. I feel the weight of his deceit heavily. We just can't know what he has discovered. If we…. *when* we find Sophia, we will have somewhere safe to hide her at least, and figure out this confounded game of I'el's." Enl'iel toyed with her empty cup as she pondered the troublesome thoughts.

Jude nodded silently and stood back from the small table.

"Come on then, you can come with me. Time to train you properly before you kill yourself or one of us." Jude extended a hand to Jaz, wriggling his fingers impatiently.

Jaz looked wide-eyed at Brennan and Enl'iel, unsure of what to do.

"Go on. We will be with you shortly," Enl'iel encouraged her. "Jude will take good care of you, won't you?" Enl'iel glared at him expectantly.

"Like a baby." Jude's mouth curled in a half smile as he waited for Jaz.

With a glance back at her table buddies, Jaz grabbed her bag and grimaced, but took Jude's hand, allowing him to lead her from the coffee shop. As the bell tinkled once more, Enl'iel looked to Brennan and whispered with a shake of her delicate face.

"Oh dear."

"Oh shit, more like it!" Brennan cursed.

"That is a problem, isn't it?" Thomas had appeared at their table, "I hope Jude has better strength this time around."

"I'll make sure of it," answered Brennan as he shook his head. His gaze followed the two mismatched figures as they disappeared past the frosted windows,

"I'll make sure he doesn't mess up twice."

Chapter Fifteen

Without the escape of sleep, I endured what felt like endless hours, trapped, listening to the frightening howls outside, whilst trying to hatch some sort of workable, even slightly realistic escape plan.

After a thorough inspection of every square inch of the cell, I concluded there was only one way out, and that was through the door. Those evil bars were a problem though. What was I to do about those after the nasty shock they'd given me? I tried countless times to draw on E'lan. I felt a nothingness beyond description. Not one positive vibration permeated this disgusting place, other than the reassuring pulse of my necklace and the comfort of the soul stone in my bracelet, both of which I fiddled with incessantly. I would have to rely on what I had on hand, so back to the plan I'd been forming before Ben dragged me from the cave.

With the scrolls crackling and humming away in my leg pocket, I settled by the pungent pool. As best as the situation would let me, I invited distraction to settle over my mind. Focusing on the drip, drip, drip of the pool's source of replenishment. It helped to drown out the howls outside; my mind removed itself from the immediate space with a surprising ease.

Deep breath in, deep breath out, repeat.

I gazed deep into my reflection, my vision slowly glazed over, allowing every muscle to relax. Within this mind retreat, I could file back through something familiar, to something I knew inside out, to something that spoke of home and safety and strength. I concentrated hard on that image of Jaz, focusing on every detail of her pixie face. The deliberately placed hand-scrunched dark hair, the sea green of her eyes and the milkiness of her skin. Most importantly, that constantly over-glossed pout. I felt myself smile at the thought. It took a few minutes of cementing that image into the forefront of my mind when a pins and needles-like wave washed over me. The not-so-pleasant feeling had my eyes open instantly as I checked back over the watery surface.

"Yes!" I whispered. My fingers curled into fists of victory.

Jaz reflected up at me from the inky mirror, as clear and present as if it were really her hiding beneath the surface. My arms had paled and thinned, my hair shortened and darkened to ebony. Eyes as green as Ben's once were, glittered back at me. I marvelled at my concealment, immediately understanding how Ben had fooled us all. Probing every inch of my soft, new face, I spoke to myself for reassurance and to ignore the sad crooning that was ramping up outside.

"Fire power or not, you're gonna get out of here one way or another, Soph!"

As the hours passed, under the crimson glow of my prison bars, I practised concealing myself into as many people as I could. Each appearance became easier, more fluid. Now, all I needed was the face of someone, or something that wouldn't stand out. Something from this place. Something from Hell.

As the pains of hunger gnawed, the red beams evaporated with a sizzling pop, jolting me out of day-dreaming about giant scones with lashings of blackberry jam and cream. Quickly checking I'd returned to my own appearance, I scurried away from the doorway. I pressed against the wall in the furthest part of the small space, slightly hidden in shadow as the door screeched open. As I held my breath and waited for Ben to drag me to my death, I was surprised to see a willowy woman, pale and sickly looking. Her dull, grey eyes found me immediately. She regarded me solemnly and wordlessly placed a chunky wooden plate on the ground. As if I were a leper, she slid it across to me with her bare foot. Her toes were bloodied, and her entire body screamed for a bath at the minimum, or a blood transfusion at best. A pitcher and wooden cup were placed just nearby. I didn't move a muscle as we watched each other suspiciously for a few moments. Realising my opportunity, I scanned her every feature quickly, as did she with me. There seemed intrigue, not malice in the way she studied me, gesturing to the plate with her bony hand before she abruptly turned and disappeared, the red beams reforming rapidly, resuming their teasing hum.

"They're feeding me? Fattening me up for slaughter! This just gets better by the minute. Do you see this I'el?" I gestured to the plate, laughing at the roof with disgust.

Once again, I inspected the dish, which consisted of braised onions and tough-looking bread. I thought of it as *'Stale Artisan Rustic a la Carte'* to make it seem more palatable. I poked at it.

"What's with all the onions?" I wrinkled my nose, pushing the tepid mush as my stomach growled angrily. Against my better judgement, I put a small pinch of it on my tongue. It was surprisingly sweet with an appealing caramelised flavour.

"Hmm! I suppose even Daimon have to eat," I said to me, myself and I. I sniffed the jug before deciding the water seemed safe too. After just enough to quell my hunger and thirst, I shoved it all away and returned to the watery mirror.

Beginning slowly, but increasingly more confident with each success, I morphed myself back and forth into the Afflicted woman who'd served the meal. After satisfying myself I could change swiftly into the garish appearance, I got to work on my dinner plate. Smashing it easily in half, I began sharpening it into a nasty point against the rocky wall. *What have you become Soph? Fashioning a shiv!*

Whoever came through that door next would meet an Afflicted woman with a weapon. I only hoped it wasn't Yeqon. The sharpening didn't take long before I was satisfied that the former plate was at least somewhat lethal. I was surprised though, that it seemed to tire me as I scraped the tip into a perfect needle point of sharpness. My arms felt strangely heavy from the labour, then something twigged.

"Oh no! Not now!"

My eyes instantly hooded; a tide of sleep crashed over me like a wave. My first sleep since developing Psynostris had to come now? That weekly sleeping session had crap, potentially deadly timing. I crawled sloth-like to the farthest corner, shoved the wooden blade underneath me and faced the doorway as sleep took over. My last thoughts were wondering if I would actually wake up again, or would I be slaughtered in my dreams.

Chapter
Sixteen

"Um, I'm not going down there!" Jaz backed away from Jude as he urged her to follow him down a narrow, crescent-shaped crack in the earth.

"You put me in a Mercedes Benz for twenty kilometres and then expect me to crawl down a hole in the ground in the middle of nowhere! What the hell is wrong with you people?" Jaz crossed her arms; her defiance was barely convincing.

"I'm sure you of all people have ingratiated yourself into worse accommodations!" Jude eyed her up and down accusingly.

"Oh, you're going there, are you? You know *nothing* about me, Freak!" A little bird appeared on her hand right about where her middle finger was.

"I know you more than you know yourself. Just get down there." Jude's mouth tightened as he pointed to the jagged opening.

"You pretentious pig…." Jude swiftly cut her off, keeping his voice low and deadly.

"Do you *want* to help Sophia? *Your* friend?" He raised an impatient eyebrow.

"Of course I do, Freak!" she retorted.

"Then either you follow me right now, or I'll carry you kicking and screaming. Your choice."

They stared each other down for a few seconds. Jude reached into a pocket, retrieving his favourite dagger. He began flicking the short, decorative blade up and down on his palm as he waited on her response. The blade shimmered under the overcast sunlight. Jaz weighed up her choices as she shivered under a light fall of snow and icy wind. Jude, unaffected, completely bare-chested now, just kept spinning the weapon, smugger with each chatter of Jaz' teeth.

"Oh, for fu… ugh… God damn it!" Jaz huffed and stamped her feet as she stared back over the surrounding landscape. Barren, rocky coldness, or follow him? She had zero choice, and she knew it, but stubbornness meant she was compelled to make every effort as difficult as possible for him. She pouted as she took a step down the rocky crevasse, unwillingly grabbing Jude's hand for balance.

"That would be, I'el damn it, and that's very disrespectful." Jude pocketed the dagger and invited her to add any further insults to his deity with a disapproving glare. Jaz remained too focused on the darkness he was guiding her into to let her mouth run away with itself any further. Picking her way carefully through the rubble, she gripped resentfully but firmly to his hand.

"You know, it's not normal for a girl to follow some strange dude into a dark hole in the ground."

"Are you calling me strange?"

"Entirely."

They left the conversation at that for a while as the steep and slippery entryway took up all of Jaz' concentration.

After descending for many uncomfortably quiet minutes, the Kaymakli caves revealed themselves quickly and elaborately. Jaz' face lit up with wonder as Jude expanded his wings, lighting the way ahead.

A labyrinth of smooth, arched corridors spread out in a myriad of directions. It was cool, quiet, and seemed very deserted. The walls sparkled as though covered in a light dusting of glitter. She thought she even saw some of these sparkles move and grow as they walked past.

Seeing her expression, Jude spoke, a little softer this time.

"This is Kaymakli. One of the safe havens we made for humans when this part of the earth flooded. It is rich with our elemental power." He poked the wall nearby. A vibrant green crystal emerged to meet the touch of his skin. Jaz' expression was priceless as he repeated the gesture until he had created a star-shaped outline of emeralds. A smile threatened to emerge as he noticed her awe, and he prodded a little more at the walls.

As though the place were in a slumber and slowly awakening, streams of precious gems of all colours erupted quietly and beautifully as though drawn out by his presence. Seeing the wonder in her face as she ran her hands along the living beauty, Jude moved them along a little quicker, not wanting to dwell upon things he shouldn't.

"This is not where we will be staying. For security, we will go another twenty stories down. You can either walk it or I can fly you down. We are safe enough now from Daimon picking up my energy signature." Jude flapped his wings and stretched them out wider.

"You really like to show off how big your…ah… wings are?" Jaz' cheeks blossomed; she sneered, trying to hide her embarrassment.

Jude squinted his eyes at her, repressing a smile.

"You shouldn't admire what you cannot have," he said, enjoying her reaction. He went in for a little more, "Besides, haven't you been taught to keep your eyes off a Watcher's wings? You could be blinded in an instant if I need to light up to full power."

"I've seen bigger and better buddy. I'm not scared of your big fairy wings!" Jaz looked him up and down, crossed her arms and laughed.

Jude simmered; his amusement dissipated. Humouring mortals was not his forte, he was done with playing. A light orb erupted upon his hand, he threw it like a baseball into the distance, where it floated obediently, lighting up a myriad of tunnels ahead.

He offered Jaz his hand, "Are you accepting my help? It's a long way down."

"I think I'll be okay, buddy, I have legs you know!" Jaz flashed her palm to keep the distance between them. She pursed her lips and immediately looked somewhat disappointed with her choice.

"Fine. Your pain to endure. Let's go. The others are on their way. We all have work to do, so don't lag."

Through corridor after corridor, they walked quickly and silently. Jude produced perfectly spherical orbs of warm light at regular intervals. It spilled into the darkness, lighting the way ahead like a landing strip. Crystals continued to emerge for every step Jude took, even the roofline took on the appearance of the night sky as jewels twinkled through the earth.

Evidence of previous inhabitants revealed itself the deeper they went. Discarded pottery and shards of this and that littered the floor. They passed what looked like an ancient bedroom with moth-eaten rugs and blankets under a thick layer of time.

"Not much for housekeeping, are you?"

"No one has lived here for thousands of years, Human. Don't worry though, I've got a nice spot prepared for you," he chuckled. "With a door, and a lock." The suggestion startled her smart mouth quiet, and they continued for around half an hour until her legs burned. Jaz halted, leaned against a wall, rubbing the ache from her calves as the descent sharply steepened.

"Need help?"

"No!" She grimaced in frustration, now realising that perhaps she should have joined Sophia on the running track and improved her fitness.

"Sure?"

Jaz glanced up from tending the cramps, "Keep going, I'm not an invalid!" Jaz flicked her hands towards Jude, shooing him away.

"Fine," Jude sped off at a much faster pace. As he turned this way and that, down a more complicated route of tunnels, Jaz was forced to run to catch up with him. If she lost sight of him, she would be completely screwed.

"You're doing this on purpose!" She yelled, then mumbled to herself, "Smart-arsed freak!"

"Slow down, will you?" Jaz called with greater effort, her breath was getting tight, her legs jelly, "Cut it out…slow…down!" The pitch of her voice heightened as he seemed to disappear more quickly around each new turn.

"You said you weren't an invalid," Jude's voice echoed back, he was far enough away now that she could only see the faint glow of his wings.

Jaz jogged harder, but seemed to move slower, wincing as the burn engulfed her legs.

"You're… enjoying… this!" she huffed through her exhausted breaths.

"You bet I am, Human!" His voice was faint, and then he disappeared.

"Shit!" Jaz stopped, leaned onto her thighs, gasping for breath. "Shit, fuck!" Turning this way and that, she assessed her surroundings. The light glow of the closest orb only lit the immediate area in front of her. A myriad of dark tunnels ran in different directions, leaving her helpless for choice. "You bastard!" she gasped, her breath slowly easing. The cramps in her legs remained. Jaz had no clue which way to go. Looking for footprints in the rubble, finding nothing, she kicked out in annoyance and screamed. Once the echo of her frustrating died away, she accepted her fate.

"Only for you, Soph." Jaz clenched her fists and relented.

"Okay! Yes, I need help."

Nothing, no response.

"My legs are killing me!" she called out louder. Nothing.

With her mouth tight, her nails dug into her palms, she called one last time,

"Please?"

Jaz glared at Jude, who reappeared in an almost blinding flash just a few inches in front of her. She stumbled back; mouth open, ready to discharge a well-practised insult. Jude, however, placed a finger gently against her lips. She flushed instantly.

"One dirty word and I'll drop you on your arse." He scooped her up quickly and, without warning, hugged her into his chest. His wings unfurled again, humming and bright. Jaz flushed an even brighter scarlet as their skin touched. They rose into the air and sped quickly into the depths of the Kaymakli underground city.

Jude felt the rush of her pulse, the heat of her cheeks against his chest. Amusement returned. It tweaked the corner of his mouth.

"I know. It can't be helped. It's only natural."

"You pig!" Jaz snarled. Jude dipped in the air.

"Argh don't!" she screamed as he let her legs dangle, threatening to drop her.

"You wouldn't?" She clung to his torso for dear life as he sped mesmerisingly fast thought the air.

"Try me!" Jude teased, flying left and right, making her legs dangle more precariously. Despite fuming at his amusement, she relented to his will… again.

"Okay, sorry, just pick me up, please?" Jaz' fingers dug deeper into his skin as her legs brushed against the wall when they took a sharp corner.

Jude scooped Jaz back into his chest and continued their brief journey, whilst Jaz glared up at him. Hate and fury… and something else boiled under her skin.

Chapter Seventeen

"Get up!" A tinny, impatient voice drew back the heavy tide of sleep, immediately allowing confusion to flood in as a replacement.

Something shoved at me from behind as I tried to regain my bearings.

"Get up. It's your birthday, pretty one, and Yeqon is throwing you a party." The owner of the voice snickered weakly. That name brought reality to the forefront of my mind with a punch.

I rolled around quickly, urging my eyes to adjust. Standing over me was the skeletal frame of the Afflicted woman who had brought my food. I dodged just as her foot was swinging back to kick me again. Backing up quickly, my palm aimed in threat, I saw a shadow in the doorway behind her. The Afflicted stood her ground, but no longer tried to touch me.

"Get away!" I felt the edge of the wooden blade by my foot, useless to me for now. I edged it covertly behind me with my heel, so I could find it later.

"Please, make this is easy. He's waiting. It will be better for you, if you just do as you're told." Ben emerged from the shadows. His voice was flat… defeated.

Every muscle tensed, all the fine hairs on my body prickled.

"What's going on, Ben?"

My voice was thick with the hangover of this strange, once a week sleep. Strength flowed back, liquid underneath my skin. My senses cleared whilst I waited for him to answer my question from the safety of the doorway.

"Yeqon is waiting. It's time to open that box you pulled from the river. I've delayed him and his brothers as long as I can." His voice hitched.

"How kind of you to delay my death!" I bit as hard as I could with words as I slapped at the bony woman to get out of my way. Her smell was a nauseating sweetness.

"Back off!" I threatened, and she reached for me again.

She looked at Ben, who had now entered my cell. He nodded silently for her to stand down, slipping her a small vial as she left. He grimaced with disgust at her.

For a moment nothing happened, other than my fists became rock hard as I imagined punching his face in. Ironically, it wasn't necessary, as it appeared someone had recently beaten me to it. He was sporting a fresh array of purple and blue, his white markings glistened beneath new inflammations and swellings.

"Making more friends?" This fresh slice of happy vindictiveness was not me, but it felt so satisfying in the moment. Ben remained quiet, his palm pointing to the exit, waiting for me to just walk on out.

"Bad day at the office, then? So, do I need to bring a plate to my party or just offer a vein?" I snapped, wondering if I could flick my shiv up quickly enough.

He ignored me as I was trying to delay, to think of something, anything, that could help me out. My toes felt around for the shiv, it was buried somewhere behind me. All I had were my wits. The two secret scrolls burned more intensely against my leg. I shifted so that the crinkling sound they made didn't give away their presence.

I cursed inwardly that I'd not had the chance to conceal myself again before the sleep overtook me. *It's not over till your heart stops beating, Soph.*

So, pull it together, I thought as Ben invited me out with another impatient wave of his hand.

Shit, crap, shit! I normally didn't swear, but I was thinking of all the worst curses. Jaz would be proud. I was madly hoping a search party was nearby. Lorcan had found me once before, when I'd accidentally transferred myself back to Australia. Hopefully, he would find me here, wherever that was.

So, despite my imminent mortal death awaiting, I walked past Ben into the dingy corridor with as much dignity as I could muster. I deliberately shoved my shoulder hard into him as I walked by, wondering if my death was going to hurt, and how they were going to do it. Could I avoid helping them and die, my knowledge and skills going with me? That would leave everyone stranded, but giving into these monsters could allow for something much, much worse for everyone.

I hurried past the vile hollering coming from within the other cells. My skin crawled with their insults and suggestions. Ben slammed the outer door shut, just as I heard a phlegmy suggestion.

"I'd like to spread you on my bread, ah, ha, ha, ha!"

It caused raucous laughter from all the residents.

Ben chose not to cut down anyone else for their offensiveness, and pointed for me to move on into the dark, ascending tunnel.

"This way," he said.

I moved slowly, knowing I had no other option at this point. As I followed him out, he maintained guard at the rear. I picked and fussed over every fissure and bump, trying to delay, just in case an opportunity or light bulb moment occurred.

He didn't bind me. There was no point. There was also a witness to his actions as the Afflicted woman kept a detail on us a few paces behind. It felt bizarre that I just followed along like a puppy dog, restraining my innate desire to fight and flee. My heart did flip-flops, my chest hurt with fear. *Where are you Koi, Brennan, anyone?*

The weight of Ben's own worries was heavy in the glare I could feel behind me. He was in a world of pain. His pulse raced. I heard him gasp through every breath. His fresh injuries had him weakened. *I could fight him*, I thought, but then there was still the Afflicted out back and what would I do if I took him down? I could fight her, that I was sure of, but I was one hundred percent lost in this steaming labyrinth. As I journeyed on, hands free, I made a move before I could think.

Jumping over a meter-wide fissure, I pretended to fall, seeing a decent-looking shard of stone up ahead. When Ben made it to my side, waiting for me to get up, I kicked out at his legs, bringing him down.

The woman screeched and rushed me. I pulled the point of rock and slashed across her arms as she reached for me, opening a wide gash on both. She recoiled, horrified by her own blood loss. She hugged her arms close, seemed to be trying to hold the sparkling fluid in. She fell backwards, lighting up her hands, quickly cauterising the wounds. Ben had a tight grip around my ankle by then.

"What are you doing?" he hissed.

"What I was taught." My heel connected with his forehead, snapping his head back. He yelled and yanked my leg harder. His wings opened up, elevating his weakened body and dragging me along the punishing ground. Intense pain seared across my back.

"Stop it!" he growled.

"Never!" I screamed as I flipped onto my stomach and yanked free of him.

I ran, weapon in hand, bloody and desperate. Dodging, jumping and weaving lava and heat vents, I raced along the unfamiliar terrain. The lazy flap of Ben's wings was right behind me.

Rounding a few turns, I felt like I might have a chance, and I pumped my legs harder.

He was still nearby, but I was forging determinedly forward, and fast. I rounded another corner and stopped suddenly short, careening forward onto my toes.

Ben was waiting for me. Battered, bruised, bloody, and with a face as dark as sin. He'd transferred ahead of me. I was fuming at the unfairness of it all. Without a second thought, I lunged with the weapon still in my hand. Aiming at his chest, I screamed, "Traitor!"

He easily overcame me, grabbing my arm and spinning me around. He held me tight into his chest, one hand twisted behind, the other secured against my stomach under his other arm.

His ragged breath warmed my ear as I struggled. He clung ever tighter until I settled, realising I was stuck.

After a tense silence, he hissed louder, "I'm trying to help you."

I could have sworn he nuzzled into my neck.

"What?"

"Yeqon will have your head if you kill her, Nik'ael!" The crusty Afflicted woman was back with an equally vile expression, having healed the wounds I'd inflicted.

Ben barked an order at her.

"Go tell him we will be there shortly… and do not address me by my name!"

She flinched and quickly disappeared without question.

Ben's heavy, hot breaths sent shivers down my body. I struggled again.

"What are you playing at?" I turned my face away from his, concentrating on the orange glow beneath my feet.

"Do what I say. Keep quiet. Don't speak unless Yeqon asks you to."

Frustrated, I responded, "And I should trust you because?"

"Because, believe it or not, I'm your only ally here."

"I thought you made it pretty clear I was nothing!" I wriggled again until his grip was so tight my hands began to numb.

"You are everything, and you will never understand what that means," he said, then snapped nastily, "Try that again and I'll rip your limbs from their sockets!"

The Afflicted woman had reappeared just ahead, her eyes dilated, her hands excessively fidgety. He seemed to put on a show for her. Was he really on my side? I was so confused.

"Hurry up Master. He is killing Rogues in frustration!" Her voice was scratchy and panicked.

"He might start on us soon!" she worried.

That didn't sound too promising, and my pulse raced even faster. I quickly took the opportunity to study the Afflicted's ghostly appearance again, cementing her in my memory. *You'll come in handy, lady, if I have long enough.*

Hastened by Yeqon's deadly actions, Ben unravelled me and pulled me into a run. The ascent steepened quickly until we burst out into an open cavern, not unlike the one hidden beneath my old backyard shed back in the Dandenong Ranges. When I say not unlike, I mean in size, certainly not ambience. There weren't any beautiful murals or homely Keeper spirits. The air here smelled of pain.

Red and orange flames licked the walls from gruesome bone sconces. A malevolence pressed upon me. I could taste it, sour and rotten. A giant light orb kept the darkness away. It hovered above a red, pulsing Zythros stone shrouded by garish spectres zipping in, around and through it. Behind the glowing portal was a platform of sorts, which housed the owner of the voice that pierced through me with two deep, rumbling words.

"Welcome Soph'ael." Yeqon reclined casually. A beautiful, God-like creature rubbing his hands along the armrests of his stone seat. Ben let go, pushing me forward.

I winced inwardly, trying to maintain an outer strength, no matter how see through my feigned bravado may have been. I grabbed my opal necklace for support, wishing for a vision from my grandmother, Elizabeth Woodville. None came, yet the sparkling gem seemed to warm and hum against my fingers. I quietly apologised to I'el for being disrespectful and brash, hoping for a thread of help from somewhere.

The soul stone in my bracelet matched the rhythmic pulse of the pendant, as though the two were connected. In that fleeting moment, I felt that somehow, somewhere, someone was watching over me. I thanked whoever or whatever it may have been, if anything at all.

Since the bracelet was a gift from Enl'iel, her kind face was in my thoughts as Ben guided me slowly around the massive red stone as though he too were scared and hesitant on the inside. His outward demeanour was the complete opposite. A scowl had returned to his face. His tight-lipped expression stressed the injuries on his skin. The cut where my boot connected with his head had blossomed into a nice big lump. All the while, a feeling of doom emanated from Ben. It had my guts twisting harder. The big question in my mind, given his erratic behaviour, was how insane he actually was? As each unwilling footstep across the gravel dug mercilessly into my feet, time slowed down as I came closer and closer to the anti-me.

Two sharp claps of Yeqon's hands startled me into a clearer awareness as I found myself at the foot of a craggy stone dais. It was backlit by more hideous wall flames that cast shadows across six tall chairs. All but one was occupied.

The largest throne hugged the immense, horned figure of Yeqon. Never would I forget that face. He stood immediately, clapped his hands again, rubbing them together in delighted anticipation. He looked happy, calm even. His movements relaxed and smooth as he took a few small steps towards me, glancing back victoriously at his brothers, who sat eagerly forward in their own seats.

"Just shut your mouth, Soph, and play it cool," Ben whispered covertly through the side of his mouth. I yanked my arm roughly away from him, repulsed by the feel of his breath in my ear. Just for a moment, I shut my eyes.

Deep breath in, deep breath out, repeat.

I defiantly met Yeqon's eyes as he descended the platform melodramatically; sauntering, swaggering, taking his time with a smug expression. The other beautiful beasts remained glued to their seats, yet they regarded me with the heaviness of hate and delight intertwined.

"About time, Nik'ael. You've played your ridiculous game long enough." Yeqon shook his head but continued to smile.

"I assure it was not a game. I was merely trying to get the most information from her I could," he lied, and I wondered why.

Ben moved to ascend the stairs as though to join them. A quick shot of light burst from Yeqon's palm. Foul black smoke erupted from Ben's leg. I gasped as he collapsed to his knees. Ben grabbed at this fresh injury, looking up at Yeqon with open disdain. It was a tense moment waiting for Yeqon to aim at me, too.

Yeqon laughed a little, his smile waning quickly.

"You will stay there, dog. You no longer deserve a place amongst your brothers for your continual betrayal."

Ben tried to defend his position. The pain straining his voice.

"I've brought her to you, haven't I?"

"You hid her!" Yeqon bellowed.

Another shot and Ben was flung back again, just as he was recovering from the first assault.

Now I was terrified. For me, and for Ben, which was utterly ridiculous.

"Stop, you're hurting him!" I cried.

"That, my dear, is the point," Yeqon said, and to emphasise this, he floored Ben a third time with a shot to his chest. Ben grabbed at his heart and groaned; he writhed on the ground. Despite everything, despite how I hated who he was, my lashes flooded at the scene.

"You cry for him? A monster, a Daimon, a betrayer? No wonder you were so easily caught. Foolish girl!"

The happiness in Yeqon's face was now shadowed by the true Daimon that he was. Darkness deepened under his eyes; his jaw clenched with an eager, delighted malice.

Ben or Nik'ael, or whoever he was, stood again, and he stumbled away. He fell to his knees at the bottom step, but not before glancing back at me, a desperate conflict in his dark eyes. He then hung his head, defeated. Was he sorry, regretful? What did it matter? Here I was, and it was all his fault, and still he was messing with me? I looked away from him just in time to see the sizzling spittle of the other Daimon splat to the ground as they all spat in Ben's direction.

"Ooh, I can think of a more deserving punishment, my love." Lilith slithered her way in from behind the thrones, licking her bee-stung lips as she eyed off Ben, like a starving beast.

"Not now, my queen. But you make take Nik'ael's seat as your own," Yeqon said. With a trill of laughter, Lilith slunk delightedly into the chair, the size of which made her look smaller, thinner, and more unreal than she already did. She crossed her long legs and sucked on her little finger seductively.

My attention flickered between Lilith, Ben, and Yeqon. Yeqon seemed calm once more. He looked me up and down.

"So, we finally meet properly." His stare was heavy, his eyes flickering a dozen different colours like Ben's did, between what he was and what he may once have been.

"How have you found your accommodations?" he asked. Gravelly laughter erupted from the four Daimon behind him, followed by a trill snicker from Lilith. I didn't answer, just kept watch, trying to look innocuous whilst madly scrambling for survival ideas. I didn't want to provoke this particular snake into biting too soon.

"Lost your voice? Perhaps it was the food?" Yeqon arched his ashen brows.

"Apologies. We can only seem to grow leeks and onions here. Surprisingly, though, Lilith is a dab hand at growing the most amazing apples!"

Lilith blew him a provocative kiss.

"Eve came in handy for at least one thing, my love." She winked and licked her lips.

Yeqon smiled, but there wasn't a cell of warmth in those eyes.

"Well, as luck would have it, today is your birthday, so let's see if we can't do a little better." Sarcasm oozed from Yeqon like the slow leak of lava that slid down the walls.

He looked back to Lilith and the others. They laughed at their own little inside joke as Yeqon clapped his hands loudly again.

"Let's celebrate! Guards, bring in the entertainment… and a feast!" He clapped his hands multiple times to hasten everyone into action.

My birthday? This was not the party I'd been hoping for. I recalled Enl'iel talking about twenty-one being the age that Eudaimonian children fully matured, the age at which I was to awaken into my truest form. Thanks to Cael, I had *quickened,* pushed to awaken rapidly in the most painful of ways, so much so, that the physical and emotional shock still lingered. Why would Yeqon toy with me like this? Could he really be that vindictive, rather than just killing me and getting on with it? The answer was a big, horrifying yes, as a procession of foul Rogues in various states of re-animated decay appeared, laden with platters of food and drink.

"Lilith, sing for Soph'ael," Yeqon demanded. The other Daimon groaned and seemed to squirm in their seats. Lilith cast a death glare in their direction for the insult.

A cacophony ensued as even more Rogues entered, heavy with food for a party for one. Spectral beings flew in erratically, screeching with an ever-increasing fervour as Lilith sang. A forlorn looking Afflicted male played a harp made of bone. I didn't dare guess what the strings were made of.

I didn't know where to look. It was so awfully creepy. A Tim Burton movie come to life. I snuck a quick look back at Ben, who seemed as confused as me. He caught my eye just as I swivelled my attention back to Yeqon, unsure of what his next move would be. Almost intuitively knowing I was monitoring Ben, Yeqon made a move and took my hand and pulled me further away.

Revulsion swept through me. The nausea from his touch hit me like a truck. My face and back burned. This instinctive survival mechanism stopped at just that. I could not, in this hellish place, draw out my power. It was frustratingly stuck somewhere deep inside.

"Come now Soph'ael, a young woman as important as yourself must celebrate their final Right of Sevens. Don't be coy. You are of age now, even you deserve to celebrate that… before we get down to business." He smirked cruelly. His calloused hand squeezed tighter, hinting at his true intentions. He drew me up to the foot of his throne and forced me to sit at the base.

Rogues with platters surrounded me. They almost fell over themselves to offer me what they had. In fact, some literally did as the odd limb just fell off. I groaned with disgust, refusing their offerings.

Lilith began a second, surprisingly melodic song. Her voice was smooth and child-like, like a siren of the oceans. Beautiful, yet deadly. It made me briefly wonder why Yeqon's brothers cringed. Perhaps it wasn't her voice that revolted them, but something else?

As I pushed away the oncoming platters, Yeqon forced my hand open.

"Refusing your last meal is terrible luck. Were you never taught manners?" he growled, and shoved a shiny red apple into my palm. The Rogues growled and gurgled along with him. The one who carried the apples glared at me with her one eye that seemed to hover precariously in its socket.

"Show respect to your hosts and eat," Yeqon commanded, pushing my hand to my mouth. I glared hatefully at Ben. He dared not look at me; his head remained downcast. Yeqon laughed deeply.

"He can't help you know, young one. He can't even help himself!" Yeqon laughed deeply.

Lilith increased the intensity and pitch of her strange song. My quivering hand betrayed my stoic demeanour. The apple weighed heavily in my palm. It felt as poisonous as anything could. I must have hesitated too long; the room fell to an immediate silence. I glanced up from the untrustworthy fruit to find everyone's attention on me.

Crap, I thought.

Deep breath in, deep breath out, repeat.

Every iridescent, black-rimmed eye bored into me, following my hand as I raised it slowly. Hesitantly taking a bite, the crispness of the mouthful seemed too loud, too poignant for such a simple act. I chewed cautiously, waiting for it to constrict my throat or stop my heart. However, I remained perfectly fine, the sweetness of the apple a stark contrast to the bitter situation I was in. Mid chew, the festivities resumed as rapidly as they'd ceased.

Lilith addressed me.

"There, there, now, Petal. That wasn't so hard now, was it? Just like I told Eve!" Lilith cackled like a madwoman at her own joke. She resumed her repertoire in an ancient language I understood, despite never having heard it before. She sang of lost love and betrayal, and finding her true soul mate.

Letting my arm flop back to my side, the apple feeling like it weighed a ton, I watched on with incredulity as the horrifying spectacle played out. Atop the altar-like platform, Yeqon and his brothers feasted, laughed and languished across their thrones, eyes constantly darting in my direction. They kept raising their flutes to me in celebration, dragging out their moment of victory, savouring the pleasure of every second. I swatted away the evil smelling Rogues who, though they remained frightening, were annoying me like bush flies as they continued to push food in my face. Lilith remained in her own operatic world as the strummer of the harp grimaced though the blood that dripped from over-worked finger tips.

I felt the pain of Ben. He remained slumped at the base of the steps. His heart pounded. The distinct earthiness of his blood-stained sweat distracted and frightened me further. His fear invaded my thoughts, as though it was my own, in a most unwelcome way. This made it hard to stay focused on the threat right beside me.

As Lilith began a new, slower ballad, there was a whisper in my mind.

You can survive this. You just have to show him your power. He will want your power more than your blood. Trust me. Ben was intruding upon my thoughts. I glanced at him ever so quickly, but his head remained low, not daring to look up at me or anyone. I'd never mastered this mind-speaking business, but I imagined the words I wanted to say out loud to him.

What? Trust you? Bit late to help now, Ben! I have no power here and you know that! I mind shouted back at him, anyway.

Yeqon rose from his seat. He was watching me in a way that made my blood drain. I shuffled back from his intimidating presence.

Look for your power Soph, damn it! I lied. You can use it here, you just have to try harder than normal. Much harder! I gasped as Ben shouted desperately inside my mind. He could hear me! Startled, I immediately feared being caught in this secret act of conspiring with Ben. I brought the apple back to my mouth, took another bite, allowing myself to look as distraught as I could, and that wasn't at all difficult. Hoping this would conceal the secret conversation, I bit some more and averted my assuredly guilty face from Yeqon's glare.

Yet, Yeqon silently studied me with more intrigue as he took a slow gulp of his drink. Belching loudly, he shoved a Rogue with a platter out of his line of sight. Yeqon paced around his seat, moving to Lilith, planting a lingering kiss on her pasty arm as she cooed through her song. He lounged across an arm rest. He chatted and laughed with a Daimon who deftly twirled a huge, threatening axe. Their merriment suggested they were comfortable, that I was cornered and done for.

Why are you in my head? Get out!" I responded finally to Ben.

Just do what I say, if you want to live.

Why should I trust you? There's the minor fact that you brought me here!

A lengthy silence ensued.

It's complicated. Just do as I say. Please, Soph. We can get out of this. Yeqon loves power over everything. He might re-think slitting your throat if you can offer him something more.

I gulped at the image I conjured of blood spurting from my sliced open neck.

More? What more than my life could I possibly offer? I took a pretend bite of the fruit, eyes glued to the partying Daimon.

Your power. If he believes he can control you, he controls your power, and that gives him an edge if he ever opens the portal. He knows he needs much more than he's got if he wants to invade A'vean. He needs a powerful army once that portal is reconnected.

How do I find my power then? I asked.

Look at me for just a moment, as though you hate me.

I do hate you.

Look at me! he hissed.

I glanced up quickly. Ben's head remained down, but his fingers were rubbing across the angry rash on his wrist.

What? I asked, confused.

Your bracelet, use it. For the love of I'el! Didn't Enl'iel teach you anything? Your soul stone will contain the E'lan that has surrounded you from the day you were born. The more you draw it out, the stronger it will become.

I held my breath, dizzy at the potential of freedom. The scrolls burned more furiously in my pocket, as though they too, were excited by the possibility.

I slid my hand covertly over my bracelet just as there was a loud bang, making me jump in fright.

"Drink up!" Yeqon smashed his goblet against another's. He leaned towards me, offering his disgusting brew.

"Refreshment? Can't have you dying of thirst now, can I? Where would the fun in that be?"

The others roared with a gruesome laughter. One was so thrilled by the joke he cast an arc of energy from his palm, instantly incinerating a nearby Rogue by accident. The tray it had been carrying clattered noisily to the floor. I grasped my wrist tighter; the bracelet warmed.

"Ged'erel, not another one!" the Daimon beside him chided with amusement.

"Argh, that was one of the good ones too! Damn," Ged'erel and the friend beside him roared with laughter. This exchange drew Yeqon's attention long enough that I could glance quickly at the bracelet that Enl'iel had given me. The soul stone glistened within its delicate chromious setting. I grazed my thumb across the white gem. As though I'd tripped an electric fence, an immediate surge permeated my entire body, making me shiver uncontrollably for a moment. Every nerve ending reignited after days of nothingness. This soul stone was fully charged with the energy that was so lacking in this foul place. E'lan was with me. It had been with me the whole time, right under my nose.

I glanced quickly back at Ben. He'd quietly heard my thoughts as his head subtly nodded in approval.

You know what you need to do now, don t you? he asked.

I considered whether I should confide in him, then responded,

Yes, kill him before he kills me, and then you if I get the chance!

Chapter Eighteen

"Come on Jude. You've freaked the human out of her wits! She's enough dead weight as it is. Just babysit her like you promised Sophia and keep her out of the way. She's not a bloody plaything! I've got enough to worry about looking for Sophia and sorting this place out, I don't need to be worrying that you've finally gone barmy!" Lorcan punched Jude in the shoulder hard enough to leave a red mark across the many white markings that neatly shone against Jude's golden skin.

"You're up for another burn shortly. What is it? Fifteen thousand years?" Lorcan punched Jude's markings, then gave his attention to the procession of Watchers, Eudaimonians, and humans descending into the depths of Kaymakli. He acknowledged many of them with a respectful bow.

"Bugger off, Lorcan. That bloody girl and her smart mouth deserved it. Haven't you got a squad to prepare for tonight's scout before you go back to Yeqon's crap-hole?" Jude retorted. He leaned more heavily against the door that contained the foul-mouthed rantings of Jaz within.

"Just listen to her, will you?" Jude uncrossed his arms, elbowing forcefully at the door, hoping the intimidating bang might silence her raving.

"Why do you care about the welfare of this one, brother? You've got it all on for Sophia, or maybe that *is* why you care? Panting over the saviour of all people?"

Lorcan's face reddened, his mark burst into angry life.

"Shut your mouth!"

"Just saying it as I see it. Totally punching above your weight, as usual!" Jude responded smugly, crossing his arms again, enjoying how easily he could rile people up.

Lorcan opened his palm. A small wisp of electrical energy danced across it.

"Go for it, brother." Jude quirked a brow, teasing Lorcan for a fight.

Familiar voices echoed in the distance.

Lorcan used this sobering sound and that of the furniture crashing behind the door to pull himself together. He ran a hand through his shoulder-length, pale hair, dousing the energy he wanted to ram down Jude's smug throat.

Jude elbowed the door again before changing the topic, "So, talking about more important matters, are you prepared for tonight?"

Lorcan bristled a little, grinding his teeth, but swallowed his pride and focused on what was more important than being a smart arse like Jude. He ground his jaw, forced his temper to retreat.

"Pathos, Koi and I fly out at midnight to scan the Empyrean realm. Gedz'iel and the other Eloi are already on the hunt in the usual Daimon ghettos. Brennan is staying here to protect the sanctuary. Koi has placed Kea and Dash in charge, with Kristen and Thomas, to take their infantry to patrol the local town. All you have to do is turn up and keep an eye on things with them."

There was an almighty crash against the door, jolting Jude ever so slightly forward.

"You better let Jaz out before Enl'iel…."

"Before Enl'iel what?" Enl'iel looked them both up and down as Lorcan put his hands up in defence.

"I'm outta here!"

Enl'iel caught hold of Lorcan before he could make his escape.

"Where is Jasmine, Jude? I need to make sure she has eaten to keep her strength up. She is quite fragile at the moment and still recovering from that transfer from Stonehenge." Enl'iel glared expectantly at Jude whilst her fingers dug into Lorcan's arm.

Rolling his eyes, he stepped away from the doorway just as something smashed forcefully against it again from inside.

Enl'iel dropped Lorcan's arm, "What's going on here, Jude?"

Lorcan returned Jude's attitude with a smug smile, like a good smack in the mouth. "Good luck with that, brother. I'll just be out hunting Daimon whilst you explain this to her. Enjoy." Loran blipped out in a quick burst of light.

"Enl'iel? Is that you? Get me outta here!" Jaz screeched desperately from behind the door she was frantically banging on.

"Jude! What in I'el's name are you doing? Have you locked her in there?"

"She's a hothead Enl'iel! She shows no respect. She's nothing but trouble!" Jude crossed his arms, doubled down on his decision.

"A hothead, you say! By I'el, if I could reach, I'd more than clip your wings!" Enl'iel snapped, her usual calm timbre dissolved. "Move out of the way!" She flicked her hands at him. Jude slid to the side without hesitation, merely sighing in annoyance.

"She's a fragile innocent under our protection, not one of your prisoners for interrogation." Enl'iel made quick work unlocking the door, but hesitated for a moment, lowering her voice to a whisper.

"You had one simple job. You made a promise to Sophia. There is something about Jasmine. She quite reminds me of Kristen. I will mind her manners; you will train her to fight. She will be an asset to us, you will see. Show her a little kindness, please. I don't feel that she's seen a lot of that in her life. No more heavy-handedness. Are we in on the same page?"

Jude's shoulders dropped. He pulled his dagger out, habitually tossing it around from one hand to the other.

"Yes, Enl'iel. We are on the same page," Jude acquiesced and he rubbed his eyes as though the entire ordeal gave him a migraine.

"Good. Eilir has returned to us for a while. Apparently, she complained non-stop until she was allowed to join us," Enl'iel said. "I hear she has made a lovely batch of Eccles cakes. Please go fetch some for Jasmine, then I will take her off your hands for a few hours."

"I'd kiss Brennan's feet if that's all it took to get her off my hands for five minutes." Jude grimaced and disappeared as quickly as Lorcan had.

Enl'iel knocked on the door before lightly pushing against the worn planks.

"Jasmine? It's me." Enl'iel moved with a fluid grace, righting an upturned table with barely an effort. She placed the tray of food she'd been carrying upon it.

Recognising her visitor, Jaz slumped to the floor with relief and exhaustion.

Red-rimmed and puffy eyes competed with her flaming cheeks.

"My dear, dear girl, everything will be okay. You will see." Enl'iel knelt next to Jaz, removing her own armour and setting it aside. She opened her arms and Jaz melted into her soft, motherly embrace. Surprised, Enl'iel stroked Jaz' hair gently, noting it had grown considerably. The white streak across the fringe thickening into quite the highlight.

"I know what will make you feel better, dear." Enl'iel smiled to herself. Mothering came so easily to her despite never having her own children. "How about we trim your hair the way you like it and get you some clothes that you feel comfortable in? I know you really don't feel yourself in our attire."

Jaz brightened a little, wiping her eyes.

"You can do that?"

"Of course, why not? Who says you have to wear these drab old things." Enl'iel chuckled, "I always did like your spark and vibrancy. Who are we to dull it?"

Jaz eased back, regaining her composure.

"Why is he so awful to me?"

Enl'iel drew in a long breath. "Well…" she thought about it.

"Jude has been trapped here for a very long time. He was, and is a very decent Watcher who unwittingly made a mistake. Despite being a good and pure soul, he holds a great deal of resentment towards humanity. He could so easily have let the darkness swallow him up and become a Daimon. A lot look up to him for the strength required to continue a very long internment here. I dare say that the strength and character you show challenges his prejudices against humans as being weak and full of fault. He can be prickly with all of us. Try not to take it quite so personally," Enl'iel said.

She gently took Jaz' chin in her hand.

"Work with him. He has always commanded respect from his troops. Your colourful language certainly doesn't help matters. Let him teach you, mind your tongue, and he will train you to be a powerful fighter. Do you want to help find Sophia? To fight along with us?"

"Yes, more than anything!" Jaz' eyes widened with the intensity of her resolve.

"Well, how about you start by referring to him as Jude, not Freak?"
Jaz grimaced.

"Jasmine?"

"Well, he calls me Human!"

"How old are you?" Enl'iel waited patiently through Jaz' pouty silence.

"Okay, I get it. I'll use his name, but we are *so* not friends."

"You are not required to be friends." Enl'iel nodded, "Good, we are in agreeance then. Now, between Koi and I, we shall reign in Jude's ego a little too. If he continues to harass you, Gedz'iel can be called upon."

"He doesn't much like me either," Jaz mumbled.

"Gedz'iel is not one to bother with the warm fuzzies of life. His only mindset is to protect and guide us to freedom. He holds no grudge against you. He just worries about anything that might jeopardise our mission."

"I won't jeopardise anything. I want Soph back as much as anyone."

"Of course you do. So, you will soften that temper and tongue?" Enl'iel didn't wait for an answer, merely hugged Jaz again before pushing the plate of food towards her. Jaz began to pick at the plate.

"Good girl, eat up. You will need your strength. Jude will train you hard, but train you well. Along with Brennan, Lorcan, and Koi, he has trained all of our human kindred. You will not find a finer or more passionate instructor. There now." Enl'iel passed her the glass of iced tea. "Drink up." she smiled as she watched Jaz devour the meal with gusto.

Wiping her mouth on the back of her hand, Jaz inquired hopefully, "Why can't one of the others teach me? Obviously, Jude and I don't gel."

Enl'iel scooped a handful of hazelnuts from the plate, eating one thoughtfully before she answered.

"We all have our place in this difficult existence. Lorcan is our primary tracker and will depart to the edge of the Daimon realm this evening with Koi, Gedz'iel and the Eloi to scout for signs of Sophia. Brennan always oversees deployment of our human warriors and must protect us here. Kea and Dash are to mind the safety of the local townsfolk, an obligation that remains from the beginning of our time on Earth, no matter what else is going on. Koi must be present for everyone; he is really next in line to Gedz'iel so he will flit between here and there if need be. Jude is excellent at reconnaissance, weapons, and fighting skills. He secures all of our sanctuaries from infiltration by Daimon and Rogues and whatever else is out there; *and* he has always overseen the training of our human kindred. Have you not seen the strength of Kristen?"

Jaz sighed, "Fine."

"Good. Now I will show you around to a nicer room and see to that awful mess of hair."

Chapter
Nineteen

The macabre celebrations continued as I tried to suppress the thrill of discovering that E'lan existed in the wedge of my soul stone. I was itching to keep my hand on it to absorb the beautiful energy. It was like a door had suddenly swung wide open and freedom was within sight. Self-preservation tempered my excitement as I sensibly kept my arms limp at my sides, lest I draw Yeqon's attention to this escape route he'd clearly overlooked. The two scrolls, always in a strange unison with my mood, seemed to hum in silent acknowledgment of the secret power pressing against my wrist.

In the midst of my covert joy, a thunderous clap from Yeqon brought the party to an immediate standstill. He leaned forward, hissed through his perfect, white teeth for the Rogues to disappear. They obeyed without hesitation. Platters and goblets scattered as they rushed to disappear.

"You! Bring me the damned box," he growled at the bloodied Afflicted playing the harp, which was the only thing that brought a stop to Lilith's self-absorbed stage show. The emaciated leftover-of-a-man disappeared immediately into a tunnel behind the thrones.

"Ah, the moment approaches." Yeqon sniffed the air like an animal in search of prey. The others seemed unsettled in their seats as Yeqon paced around, taking in every aspect of the room. He threw his arms wide and looked at the ceiling.

"Soon, I bring this all to you, I'el! Ready yourself, for you will face my wrath and sink to the depths of Tartarus! You shall suffer as we have!" Yeqon screamed and bared his teeth. His neck muscles stretched; his veins pulsed with rage. Recovering through angry gasps, he glanced around at all present. His psychotic eyes feverishly landing upon the other Daimon.

"Brothers, can you smell it?" Yeqon sucked air deep through his flared nostrils. He turned his attention back to me. In two swift paces, he loomed tall and foreboding. The redness of rage drained from his face; a softness settled upon his mouth. He seemed relaxed and resigned to his success. Yeqon leaned into my face.

"Vengeance!" he whispered smoothly. His breath was not ugly or rancid, it was warm and sweet. His ugliness was not tangible at all; it was a feeling that buried itself under my skin. It was his spirit.

I swallowed hard as the four other males suddenly stood, twirling their weapons in excited anticipation.

The swirl of sword and axe, the gentle sizzle of a light orb on a palm, and the glow of a bow, six arrows full, brought the tension of the situation to a head.

"Get on with it then! Spill her blood now!" one of them muttered impatiently.

"Asbel, another few moments won't kill you; we need Enoch's damned box after all," another said, and I was grateful for it.

Asbel grumbled and slammed his weapon into the ground. Yeqon paid no heed to him, his wicked smile trained intently on me. He twirled a piece of my hair. Sweat drizzled down my cheeks. He rubbed it away, smelled the salt of my fear on his skin.

"Shame. You *are* so pretty." Yeqon trailed a finger across my facial mark. I pulled back, feeling a burn crawl up my back, and a sting in my veins. My body was responding to the E'lan that I'd unlocked. I had to keep my cool until the right moment, whenever that might be. He pushed my face back roughly, my chin snared between his fingers. I grit my teeth as my nostrils flared with anger and the effort of keeping everything calm. The last thing I needed right now was to have a wing explosion and show my hand too quickly. I was already proficient at not having control. This was the one time I needed to pull it all together. What I did do though, was look defiantly into his clear, mad eyes.

"Still feisty as you face your fate. I am impressed." He tipped my chin this way and that.

"Killing her won't work. I've told you that before," Ben said behind me. Yeqon abruptly dropped his hand; spun on Ben, his back heaved, a rabid growl rumbled from him.

"Silence, you insolent half-breed!" Asbel yelled, pointing his weapon-laden hand in Ben's discretion. The others glared accusingly at Ben as well.

Lilith then slithered her way around Yeqon's torso again, looking me up and down. She blew me a kiss as she trailed her fingers across Yeqon's chest. There was something altogether more frightening about her.

"No Asbel, let us hear him out while we await the prize. We have a few moments to spare, so let us be entertained with Nik'ael's fabrications," Yeqon roughly pushed Lilith away and walked down a step closer to Ben. Lilith looked somewhat hurt, but quickly regained her composure, holding her head high as though she were in control. For me, there was immediate relief. The nauseating feeling Yeqon elicited eased as distance came between us.

Yeqon crossed his arms. The cords of his biceps twitched as he questioned Ben, who now dared to raise his head.

"Well, boy? What is your solution?"

Ben's anxiety was palpable. With careful consideration, he slowed his breaths, choosing the right words to answer. He snuck a quick glance my way before gingerly standing, boldly facing his apparent former ally. He clutched his abdomen. Purple and black, with a red sheen, dressed most of his skin. He'd allowed his eyes to return to the solid, sickening black that made him look so frightening.

"Whatever is within that box, I don't believe it is the complete artefact. I'm sure of it. I heard her read Enoch's verse in the caves of their Library," Ben paused, winced, took a fresh breath, "It insisted that there was something more, that even perhaps there are others unknown to us also after the Kaladai as well. If you kill her now, just to open the box, you may have played us into an eternity of damnation. I think the Watchers are right. She doesn't need to die, at least not yet."

I felt the verbal slap of those final words. *Not yet.* My fingers clenched. Power burned under my skin. Those words reaffirmed the traitor Ben was. I had begun to waiver a little whilst he had defended me, but his words, his actions, between Yeqon and myself… nothing was consistent. Buying me time certainly didn't atone for what he had done, not by a long shot… and trust was not something I imagined I could ever equate with him again.

"He lies, Yeqon. He is in love with her. He lies to save her for himself," Pineme said.

Ben growled at the accusation.

"Pineme is correct," the one named Ged'erel interjected. "He pines for her; I can smell the lust on him."

My heart quickened; my face flushed.

"My own feelings are irrelevant. You must believe me. My intel on the inside has determined they have more knowledge, insights that we do not have. They insist that if her blood is spilled in anger or by force, then the Kaladai will never work, or even be found.

It was his spy! He knows who the spy is! My mind raced through everyone I knew, but could find no fault in anyone. If I had the chance, I promised myself I was would squeeze that name out of Ben, in any way I could. I glared accusingly at him as he continued to be barraged by the Daimon surrounding us.

"He lies still," Lilith said, licking her noticeably paler lips. Her face appeared strangely and abruptly drawn. She looked older.

"Her life force runs in Soph'ael's veins. It is long known that it is this force that will save you, my love." Lilith trickled her nails down Yeqon's arm again. "Her blood will open the gate, whether she pricks her finger or you carve her to pieces. What does it matter how it flows?" She smiled at the thought.

"Quiet woman!" Yeqon growled. Lilith feigned disinterest in his dismissive attitude, attempting to portray a dignity clearly not afforded to her. She climbed the steps, repositioned herself in the stone chair with a regal sweep. Lilith snapped her fingers whilst Yeqon kept an eagle eye on me and Ben. He seemed to be weighing up what to believe. I could sense his uncertainty. That was a big positive.

"You, come here!" Lilith called to a random Rogue that was frothing at the mouth noisily. "Bring me something to eat or I'll eat you!" Lilith gnashed her teeth at him. The obscene creature rubbed worriedly at his pasty neck. He made a hasty retreat just as the Afflicted harpist reappeared, arms laden heavily with a cloth covered object. I instinctively felt Enoch's treasure enter the space. Apparently, so did everyone else, as all attention fell to the Afflicted who tentatively approached Yeqon.

"Put it down. At her feet." Yeqon pointed to me, immediately agitated, clenching his fists and jaw. The object landed heavily, puffing up a plume of dust. A corner was exposed from under the ragged cloth, just touching the edge of my bare foot. The hum was familiar.

The room was knife-edge tense.

"Open it! Your way or my way!" Despite his calm tone, Yeqon's celebratory demeanour was gone. He retrieved a huge weapon from behind his throne. Raising and lowering the trident slowly, he banged it rhythmically on the floor. He waved it around until the points faced my direction. He grazed his fingertips along its length. The weapon glowed red hot along its three nasty points. I gulped, flaring my fingers. My mind raced between rebellion and submission a million times in a matter of seconds.

"No," I muttered quietly.

"Speak up Soph'ael. I do not think we all heard you."

Terrified, I clasped my hand over the soul stone, drawing on its positivity.

"I won't open it for you." The quiver in my voice gave away the fear I was trying to suppress. Keeping my eyes glued to his every move, I watched and waited as he absorbed my rebuff. He seemed surprised, stepped within a foot of me, taking care not to touch the box. Ben was yelling in my head, telling me to do what I was told. The box was increasing the intensity of its strange thrumming, and Yeqon was breathing down my neck, holding the hot trident inches from my face.

"You defy me in my own realm?"

Deep breath in, deep breath out, repeat.

What the hell was I thinking?

"I defy you in every realm!" I jutted my chin out, feigned bravado, all the while my heart thrashed wildly. I felt faint, the air pressed in, I could hardly breathe.

A collective gasp of surprise circled the cavern. Lilith stood up, licking her lips. She clapped her hands with the anticipation of action.

Soph, don't push him, Ben screamed desperately.

I wouldn't be here but for you. Get out of my head! I snapped back.

Almost frozen to the spot, I surveyed Yeqon's expression, which seemed jammed between confused and amused. His eyes narrowed to slits as he contemplated his next move. Ben must have got to him. Yeqon set his trident back on the ground.

The standoff didn't appear to affect Lilith's routine as the Rogue she'd ordered away abruptly returned with a platter of perfectly shiny apples, and another, smaller female Afflicted. I watched Lilith out of the corner of my eye.

"Ah, delightful! Main and dessert." Lilith stepped back, smacking her lips with appetite. "You are a most thoughtful dead thing." She shooed the Rogue away from the trembling, vacant-eyed girl. Lilith lunged at her as quick as lightning, biting into her neck and sucking so hard that her cheeks hollowed with the effort of her greed. It was disgusting. As she drew the life or death from the Afflicted girl, rosiness returned to Lilith's cheeks and the fine lines on her face disappeared. A small, screeching flash of ghostly light emerged from the girl's limp body. It floated to the back of the cavern, disappearing through a dark fissure. The morose holler of her soul clung to me… it was pain, it was fear, it was obliteration in a single howl.

"Well, she didn't hang around to chat, now did she?" Lilith laughed as she threw the limp body to the ground. The freshness of youth shimmered across her cruel expression.

"I do like dessert first. Here, boy, scraps," Lilith giggled. She then crunched into an apple, daintily dabbing blood dribble from her chin with her little finger and sucking on it seductively. The Rogue fell at her feet, greedily and noisily finishing the last of whatever was left of the corpse. Lilith nonchalantly settled back into a throne. She ate her apple contentedly, and she watched the feast. When the Rogue was done, the body of the girl burst into a bright blue flame that burnt out as quickly as it had begun. A diamond skeleton remained behind. No one but me seemed shocked at the easiness of this murder.

"Oh, don't mind me. Carry on!" she commanded with a wave of her hand, surprised that the standoff between Yeqon and I continued throughout her little show.

"Lilith, will you stop eating our own kind?" Ged'erel asked. Even he sounded disgusted.

"What do you care? Really?" She took another bite of her fruit.

In the mere minute this all took place, Yeqon hadn't made a move until now.

"Perhaps my queen has the right idea. A little blood flow might get things moving along?" Yeqon side swiped me across the face with the trident. The hard, hot metal split my lip. I seriously saw stars and just barely kept myself upright as I tried to not let him out of my sight. Ben grimaced; his pained voice echoed in my mind.

Bastard, I'll kill him.

Yeqon moved quickly to the diamond skeleton, and as Andr'eal had done, he snapped off a piece of rib and fashioned it into a crude, much less beautiful, diamond dagger than the one I'd lost.

An earthy tang filled my mouth as blood coated my tongue. Yeqon made his way back to me. I'd dropped to my hands and knees trying to regain my strength, to clear my still-clouded vision. Anger seethed beneath my skin like the flow of lava in the surrounding rocks. I let my secret power slowly build.

Yeqon grabbed me, pulled me roughly to my feet. He kicked at Enoch's box to reveal it from beneath the cloth. He pushed my head forward so that my blood dripped into the creases of the artefact. I felt the heaviness of the other Daimon as they drew closer with anticipation. Yeqon's fingers dug into my neck. He throttled me, urging more blood out. Ben's screams in my mind were inaudible.

When he was satisfied with the bloodletting, Yeqon threw me aside. I landed on the step just above Ben. Everything hurt. I could still feel Yeqon's touch on my skin. I couldn't seem to shake it off.

Ben desperately tapped at my mind. I ignored him as I pulled myself upright and prodded gently at my lips. The burn intensified along my spine and fanned out a little. My pterugia, my wings of light, were aching to emerge. *Not now, I'm not ready.* I told them.

Tension coiled in the room as the Daimon milled about the box.

After poking at it with their weapons, Yeqon looked up.

"Why is it not working?" He glared dangerously at me.

"Make it open, Soph'ael!" Yeqon pointed his crystalline dagger at the box.

I was swallowing back my power that more urgently sought to release when a reprieve came via Ben.

"Her blood cannot be spilled by another; she must open it of her own free will. That much I know to be absolute. You can see that your way does not work," Ben said.

The Daimon glared viciously at Ben. Yeqon bore down on me, mouth tight, jaws clenching.

"Your *own* will? I see. Well then, if it's motivation you need, it's motivation you shall have. Nik'ael, retrieve the boy and be damned quick about it!" Yeqon snapped. Ben pushed himself up, took a step towards Yeqon. Concern darkened Ben's face.

"You want to play this card now, Yeqon?"

"Oh, I've wanted to play this card for a very long time." Yeqon pointed sharply to one of the tunnels, "Now go get him!"

Ben inclined his head obediently and disappeared from the room without looking back.

Despite the fact he was my enemy, despite everything he had done, when Ben left that room, I felt more vulnerable than ever. It took all my willpower to continue to stand up to Yeqon.

"I'll never help you."

They all took a step closer toward me.

Enoch's crimson-stained box hummed louder.

My veins screamed.

"Well, we will just wait and see about that," Yeqon replied ominously.

Chapter
Twenty

The time-weary underground space swelled like a roaring ocean with the sounds and movements of hundreds of bodies training for battle. In neat and orderly groups, their metallic clangs echoed around the smooth earthen walls. Much like the Katoika training room, the Kaymakli amphitheatre was now generously stocked with thousands of years, and many battles worth of armoury and weapons. Gold tipped chromious swords, daggers, quivers full of bows and axe heads, cut smoothly through the air with the well-practised movements of an earthly and unearthly army.

Red orbs flew harmoniously through the air, chasing down trainee warriors with regular stings to their backsides. Wings emerged and disappeared as youngsters wobbled through the air, getting used to their new appendages.

Alchemae huddled here and there, tending to wounds with glowing palms along with sweet-smelling herbs and tonics. The air was aromatic with lavender and cedar, which burned constantly to ward off the unwelcome.

Jaz' face pinched with focus, her eyes and mouth narrow as she practised the purple belt level of karate. Koi had instructed Kristen and Thomas to give her a crash course.

As she finally pulled off a smooth round-house kick without wobbling over, Jaz threw her arms in the air victoriously.

"Finally! Yes!" Her smile swelled with satisfaction.

"Ha! I love this new you! Full of energy and focus. She does well, Thomas. No?"

"She's doing okay." He looked Jaz up and down whilst swigging his water bottle.

"Don't lather on the praise there, man." Jaz raised an unamused brow. Her smile waned. She bent forward to stretch out her hamstrings, grazing her fingers along the ground in front.

"If anything, you'll at least distract the enemy with everything that's hanging out of your… um…" Thomas took another gulp as Jaz straightened up, dusting down her outfit. A devious smile spread across her face.

"Bit of a prude, eh Tom? It has the Enl'iel seal of approval, so suck it up!" Jaz winked at him.

"I like it. I really do," Kristen commented as she enviously ran a finger along the thick belt that topped the mid-thigh khaki layered skirt Jaz had swapped for the regular battle attire.

"This belt is very 'andy for weapons. I must talk to Enl'iel. I'm a little jealous actually," Kristen smiled wistfully. Jaz peered down at the cream t-shirt decorated with an intricately embroidered reproduction mark of A'vean. The dark brown belt, thick with decorative engraving, cinched her waist in just the way she liked it. It hung heavily with several small satchels. One long scabbard cocooned Sophia's diamond dagger. Jaz made sure it remained close. She liked the weight and feel of it, and of course, its connection to her best friend.

"Thanks, Kristen. I work better in my own kinda gear. Have to say, Enl'iel kinda surprised me. I wasn't expecting this." She ran her hands down her sides, only wishing she'd received the stilettos she'd asked for, not the black combat boots.

"And your pixie cut, magnifique! Ninja fairy. I like it!" Kristen's laugh trilled amongst the clanging swords nearby.

"Get on with it, ladies. This isn't the catwalk!" Jude appeared, not bothering to hide his disdain.

"Okay, okay, Jude. Relax. She's doing very well," Kristen said.

"You'd better be." Jude looked Jaz' outfit up and down and shook his head. "You're not going to a night club. You're heading out into the real world tonight, Human… er, Jasmine."

Thomas patted Jude from behind. "That must have stung man! Well done, my friend," Thomas laughed. Jude gave him a death stare.

"Run her through all the katas until she sweats to my satisfaction. And make sure she covers up. It's snowing outside," Jude instructed Thomas.

Jaz' face fell with the news that the training was to continue for longer. She shook out her weary arms and legs.

"You're enjoying this, aren't you? Torturing me?" she accused him.

"Jasmine, very little amuses me, yet watching you squirm does." Jude's mouth quirked up slightly. He turned away, leaving before she could get another word in.

Jaz was on the floor before she could blink. Thomas brought her down with a swift kick to the back of her knees.

"Hey! I thought it was kata, not sparring? Your brother is an arse-hat, Kristen!" Jaz wiped a dribble of blood where she'd bitten her own lip.

"Consider it poetic licence. Now, show me what you can do!" Thomas challenged. Kristen smiled, knowing her brother would do Jude proud. He would refocus Jaz' strong will into something useful.

Jaz spent more time on her backside than her feet, but gave nearly as good as she got. In one surprising manoeuvre, she managed an impressive uppercut that split Thomas' chin, causing Kristen to clap in delight.

"Ma soeur, de quel cote es tu?" He shot an incredulous glare at his sister as he wiped away the blood striping it down his shirt. "You're meant to be on my side, sis!"

"Not on your team at the moment!" Kristen held her stomach as she laughed. Whilst Thomas was pondering his sister's hysterics, Jaz took the opportunity and swiped a foot under him, bringing him crashing down.

"Never take your eye off the enemy! I'm pretty sure that's standard!" Jaz smirked as she looked down at the now completely pissed Thomas. Kristen had tears in her eyes.

"If Papa could see you now, e'd clip your ears for the arrogance, Thomas!" She clutched her stomach with both hands as the tide of laughter swept over her. Lorcan's unexpected arrival brought the trio's antics to a stop, causing them to shield their eyes.

"A little warning next time? Doesn't that blind regular people?" Jaz demanded, accusingly.

"Yes, and you are most certainly very…regular," Lorcan smirked.

"Thanks for caring," Jaz snapped.

"You're welcome," he replied with a smile and a bow, reminiscent of his brother, Brennan.

"Aren't you all smart arses today?" Jaz responded with a middle finger.

Kristen grabbed her hand, her face amused and alarmed. "Uh, uh Mademoiselle. Enough now. Lorcan would never cause us injury."

"Hmmm, still feisty, isn't she? Jude's been round, huh?" Lorcan asked, looking about the room that was slowly emptying of people.

"He's always in my face," Jaz grumbled.

"Better him than a Daimon, Jaz. I caught that last move as I was transferring in. Your moves are looking brill," Lorcan nodded.

"Really?" She seemed genuinely surprised by the compliment.

"True. And sorry. I'll try not to '*nearly blind you*' again. I can dial down my spectacular entrances."

"Yeah, you do that," Jaz smiled, trying not to look too amused as she shook out her arms, rubbing down extensive bruising. She glanced to Thomas.

"Sorry man, you know, for your face." She offered him a hand. He hesitated a moment, then shook it.

"No problem, part of the service." Thomas smiled a little as Jaz laughed again, her mood lighter than usual. Thomas laughed despite himself; all the tension melted away.

"Good, now we're all on the same team. Bit more of a sense of humour and who knows, we might actually have a chance at being half decent," Lorcan complimented the trio as he ran a glowing palm over Jaz' visible bruising, lingering a little longer at her thighs.

"Hurry it up down there, buddy!" Jaz glowered at him, unamused.

"Interesting clothing choice," Lorcan responded. He stopped the healing before the bruising had completely faded, his cheeks slightly more blushed than before, "It's a bit cold outside, you know. As in, snowing. You might want to cover up a little more."

"Ugh, you sound just like Freak boy!"

"Lorcan, did you ask Jaz' permission to heal her?" Jude growled disapprovingly. He appeared out of nowhere, as he did so well, "And I heard that…. Human!"

Jaz rolled her eyes.

"I was just helping her, Jude. She doesn't know to ask to be healed," Lorcan responded.

"There are standards, especially with her lot. Teach her Lorcan, and you definitely know to seek permission first, regardless of her ignorance."

"Thomas, would you like me to heal your injury," Jude tilted his head towards Thomas' split chin.

"Sure, thanks," Thomas replied.

With a swift movement, Thomas healed, leaving no mark to evidence a wound had ever occurred.

"You're a handy mobile ER, if nothing else!" Thomas joked as Jude swatted him over the head.

"Ouch!"

"I've got worse if you want it. Now get out of here," Jude ordered. He turned back to Jaz.

"Jasmine, would you like the rest of your wounds healed?" Jude asked, his voice even as he cast a reproving glare at Lorcan.

Caught off guard, Jaz stammered.

"Um, yeah… nah… I'm good. I'll grab one of Enl'iel's tasty potions." She held her palm out, keeping the distance between them.

"Your choice, then, to endure your wounds." Jude shook his head, as though perplexed at her refusal.

"Let's move out. It's time for our meal before we rest and head out at midnight." Jude transferred away without another word, followed by Lorcan. It made Jaz jump; she wasn't used to it yet.

"What the hell is wrong with the door?" Jaz asked as she massaged the bruising on her thighs.

"Oh, don't knock it Jaz. That little trick 'as saved me more than once. Do you remember the last time, Thomas? You know, I was nearly a Rogue entrée when I slipped on the rail track! Where was it? Ah, Calais, that's it. Remember, we were 'unting Rogues, trying to cross the tunnel into England?"

"Last January. It was bloody freezing down there! I remember!" Thomas nodded whilst he packed up.

"Well, Jude, 'e just popped out of nowhere between me and this ugly Rogue. That thing was ashes at my feet, just as it was about to strike. Their magic might save you one day too, Jaz." Kristen smiled. She gathered Jaz, arm in arm, her quiver and bow slung over the other shoulder. They left with the flow of other exhausted warriors, who had put down their weapons and headed out the door, en masse for food and rest.

"Quiet down, please," Koi called, and the room immediately stilled. He took in the crowd, each and every person an equal in his eyes. He smiled broadly; his face glowed softly. The tendrils of his mark coiled around his cheek, highlighting the angles of his face. His hair had lengthened somewhat. He'd given no thought to keeping it the unusual short trim he preferred. Koi's hair was a mark of respect to Gedz'iel, who kept his own hair a few bare millimetres long. Koi felt bound to honour him for the authority and forgiveness the leader had bestowed upon him, a Watcher who had betrayed his duty, along with the rest of them. However, times called for more important things than appearances. All the souls in front of him needed his strength and guidance more than ever. He rolled his hands together. The words tattooed across his fingers shimmered. *Love and hate.* How easily things could have been so different for him, too.

A thousand eyes waited patiently for him to begin.

"By the grace of I'el, it is pleasing to see you have all arrived safely. Derinkuyu, unfortunately, was not as secure as we hoped. Kaymakli is old, I know, and not as well serviced, but we are safe here. There is no record of a Daimon ever having set foot anywhere near this location. I trust that we shall remain secure here," Koi said.

The room murmured in collective relief.

Jaz shuffled in her seat, picking at the hem of her skirt, whilst Kristen twirled small plaits into her own hair as she snuggled next to Thomas. He was polishing the chromious tips on the quiver of arrows wedged between his feet as he listened, glancing up periodically.

Lorcan and Jude stood behind Jaz, Kristen and Thomas, arms crossed, faces taught in concentration.

"Unfortunately, our numbers are down as many of our young have begun their transition into the third Rite of Sevens. This means their families must stay close to them, further reducing our available warriors. It is only a few hands, but each pair of eyes, ears and pterugia we have right now are essential to not only finding Sophia, but preserving our own safety. That said, it means that soon we will have fresh young warriors to train and that is always a great joy." Koi glanced around before continuing, accepting a drink from Enl'iel, who hovered nearby.

"Unless otherwise ordered, no one is to leave the safety of the lowest levels of Kaymakli. We have all the provisions required for a long internment. There are still plenty of eyes and ears on the outside, should anything be needed," Koi instructed. Another round of murmured acknowledgment ensued before he continued.

"I have consulted extensively with Gedz'iel and Jude. We have assigned everyone present to a group appropriate to your level of expertise and experience. As it stands, Gedz'iel, the Eloi and their trackers will patrol the boundaries of the Empyrean realm in search of Sophia…"

At that moment, a buzz filled the air as Gedz'iel and the five Eloi transferred in next to Koi, who didn't bat an eyelid and continued speaking, "The trackers will search for any energy signature left by Sophia or Ben, and potential cracks in the borders of the Yeqon's lair that can be penetrated for an offensive."

When Sophia's name was mentioned, Jaz immediately stopped biting her nails and gave her full attention.

"Jude will oversee our younger warriors on the ground. They will patrol Derinkuyu, the Fairy Chimneys, and the upper Cappadocian Mountains. To our less experienced and human kindred, we ask you to oversee the towns in and around Nevşehir. This is most likely the safest place, and you will blend in easily to be our valuable eyes and ears. Jude, Kea and Dash will be nearby with a handful of Watchers, just in case there is any trouble. All reports so far from Ahmet and Elmas, is that Nevşehir has been quiet for decades. Consider this a training exercise." Koi nodded as he looked over the crowd.

A few teens in the front row fist pumped with the excitement of their first foray into the real world.

"That is us, we will go to Nevşehir." Kristen lightly elbowed Jaz, who acknowledged her with a quick nod as she hung on Koi's every word.

"Everyone will leave in staggered groups. Full armoury is required under your concealment. Watchers will ensure that everyone is glamoured to blend in. Koi pointed directly towards the human warriors, who nodded, striking their weapons across their armour in gratitude. "Do not put yourselves at unnecessary risk. With my heart and soul, I wish you all a safe and speedy return before dawn and that we shall succeed in finding Sophia. It has already been nearly two weeks. The longer she is missing, the more dire the situation becomes.

I have faith she remains alive, though. If Yeqon had any measure of success, there would have been a definitive movement out of the Empyrean realm. I believe Sophia is stronger than even she understands. She will resist him to the best of her ability," Koi said, a hand over his heart.

At that, weapons and armour were clanged with the anticipation of success. Shots of electrical pulses flew to the ceiling in comradery, exploding in a mini-fireworks show.

The tut-tutting of Eilir could be heard down the back as she fussed to cover her table of refreshments from the falling embers. Her elderly frame more bent than before, yet she remained as feisty as ever. Dash hovered about her, helping her out as he always did when he had the chance. Her face was always brighter for it.

"Go now. Be ever vigilant, and remain in contact with your squad leaders at all times. No one is to venture out on their own. No unnecessary heroics, please?" Koi nodded at the crowd; they returned the gesture.

Koi released his wings, called to Lorcan, and nodded to Gedz'iel. Lorcan jogged over and joined Pathos, as did four other trackers. They partnered up with the remaining Eloi, who kept the same, ever-silent and dignified presence. The leaders of this underground army fired up their A'vean marks. Their wings to unfurled to their widest, and they transferred out in one massive blast of white light.

"Well, you gotta give it to them. They really know how to put on a show," Jaz quipped as she looked up from behind her hands once the energy had dissipated. The remaining static tugged at her hair. Jaz smoothed it down, grabbed herself an Eccles cake. She took a big bite and followed Jude, Kristen, and Thomas back to the training rooms to prepare for their trip into Nevşehir.

Chapter
Twenty-One

Still standing my ground under the terrifying presence of Yeqon, I picked up the sound of footsteps in the distance. They were getting closer by the second. *What now?* My attention, though, was firmly hooked between Yeqon and the box. This silver container, that apparently meant everything, had caused only death and destruction. I hated it in that moment as it gleamed up at me in all its prettiness. To me, it had become ugly and dangerous, and I wanted to run from it.

"Open it yourself!" I snapped, surprising and scaring myself. Immediately, I worried if this precarious balance between defensive and complicit was going to get me in more trouble than I could anticipate. After all, I hadn't done too well with Ben. I wondered if I should I just show my hand, get it over with as my power screamed for release. Trying to keep my wings under wraps, I was breaking a thicker sweat. I supposed I could just fight to my absolute best right then, or go along with Yeqon, waiting for a more opportune moment to escape, rebel… whatever. I'd missed the class on *'Saviour Angel 101.'* Only instinct drove me, minute to minute. Perhaps that was what I was supposed to do, let my instincts take over? Now that I could call on some of my power, and hopefully effectively, perhaps this inner angelic Soph might just pull something out of the bag? *Use all your resources.* That's what Koi had drummed into me.

Yeqon appeared genuinely surprised by my tenacity. He smiled snidely at my rebuttal. His brothers chuckled behind him. Apparently, this was as amusing as it was deadly serious.

Yeqon growled, "You defy me? Stupid girl." He circled me like a shark. "You think if I could touch that damned box, I would have allowed you to live to this point? I would have drained your blood and sated the Rogues if I could open it myself. Enoch protects you from eons past, damn him!" Yeqon spat to the ground. The earth rumbled again. A vent of steam hissed overhead.

Yeqon shoved the box with the staff of his trident until it slid right up against my feet. His diamond dagger waved back and forth in front of me. His maniacal expression distorted more grotesquely through its blade.

"Open it!" Yeqon's nostrils flared, his knuckles whitened around his weapons.

Before I had a chance to make a decision as to what to do next, I noticed Ben return. He came up behind Yeqon, dragging someone behind him. It must have been his footsteps I'd heard. That someone appeared wholly unwilling to follow, by the way his head hung low and his feet lagged.

A man, a boy…no, a young man with long white hair. He came to a stop behind Yeqon. He wore nothing but pauper-like weathered pants and had bare, bloodied feet. His well-developed torso was hatched with countless scars, not the neat tattoo-like ones of the Watchers. They looked like they resulted from vicious wounds.

"Ah, Leverage. You have arrived." Yeqon's shoulders relaxed immediately, and he appeared to be visibly lighter. He struck his trident hard into the ground. He really seemed to enjoy doing that.

"Finally, after all this time you can repay your debt and fulfil your true purpose." Yeqon grabbed the young man by the scruff of his neck, shoving him in my direction. His unkempt hair swayed back and forth, hiding his facial features. This unwilling newcomer came to a stop right in front of me. For some reason, his proximity caused every hair on my body to prickle, and my skin felt the sweep of anxiety rush across it. The secret scrolls hummed in my pocket. The pendant pulsed stronger; air sucked from my lungs. There was an intense increase in the barely hidden surge of my returning power. It slid hotter through my veins. My heart raced anew, and I didn't know why.

"Look at her!" Yeqon grabbed the stranger's chin, forced his face upwards, pulling at a fistful of his hair to ensure he had no choice but to look at me. The poor young man kept his eyes closed tight.

I don't know what you're going to do now, Soph, Ben whispered.

Leave me alone! I screamed as I stared at the face barely two feet from mine.

My mouth slackened as I studied this face. It was like looking at myself in male form. He refused to make eye contact initially. Yeqon shook him roughly.

"Look at her!" Yeqon growled into his ear and the young man opened his eyes unwillingly. Initially, he averted them to the ground, but I saw it immediately. It was like a slap in the face, a punch in the guts. The shape of his nose, the oval face, the full lips and his Mark of A'vean… all identical to mine. My guts churned.

"No!" I whispered to myself.

"Oh yes, young one. Yes, yes, yes!" Yeqon swelled his chest out with self-satisfaction. A victorious smile, wide and confident; his eyes glittered all the more vividly. The others chortled with amusement in the background.

Yeqon shoved the fiery points of his trident into the boy's back, "I said, *look* at her!" The mirror image of me flinched from the weapon. His breaths hastened. I could smell his fear, see it run down his chest.

Without looking at them, I sensed the other Daimon moving closer. I dared not look away. I was entranced, horrified; lost in the most unexpected of moments. The unwilling male clenched his fists, bravely shoving back at Yeqon as he slowly allowed his eyes to finally meet mine.

I don't know how long it had been since I'd taken a breath, or even moved, for that matter. Sparkling blue eyes, beautiful… yet vacant of emotion, stared at me. A clenched jaw and taught body, he struggled against Yeqon, who maintained pressure with the trident at his back. Copper tainted the air; the blood was fresh.

"You ugly beast," I hissed at Yeqon.

Yeqon snarled with pleasure.

"Close your mouth, Sweetie. It's so unlady-like to gawk!" Lilith meandered back into the scene. She pointed between the two of us.

"Soph'ael meet Boy. Boy meet… your sister!" Lilith cooed with pleasure and clapped her hands gleefully. She raised her eyebrows and hands in expectation, as though there should be some warm reunion hug with tears of joy. Obviously disappointed that we both remained frozen in place, Lilith babbled on.

"I raised him like one of my own… sans the blood lust, of course. He only eats vegetables, most inconvenient," she sighed, stroking the length of his hair. My brother only barely hid the need to pull from her touch. Revulsion rolled from him like an incoming tide. His jaw feathered as her spindly fingers raked harder through his hair. They slid down his arm and finally into his hand. Hate bubbled inside me as he flinched ever so slightly when she placed a gentle, yet threatening kiss against his neck. She let her lips linger a few seconds longer than necessary.

"So handsome, don't you think?" Lilith looked expectantly at me. I had no response as my twin and I tentatively studied each other for the very first time. I couldn't help it when my mark glowed. His hand shone weakly, like a reflex in recognition of one another.

"Told you, Yeqon, her power emerges despite us. Get on with it!" Ged'erel challenged impatiently. Lilith, however, fought to maintain the limelight for the moment.

"What, no hugs?" She tried to push us together. I held my ground with firmly planted feet, as did he. I'el himself could not have known the workings of my brother's mind, such was his pained, tortured expression.

"Well, this *is* disappointing," Lilith's voice was beginning to sound like nails down a chalkboard. She shoved my brother towards me. We were now only inches apart. I could feel his warmth, hear his breaths, sense the panic within him. I felt an immediate and intense connection and wondered if the feeling was mutual. Tears welled in my eyes, not his.

What now, Ben, damn you? I thought.

You should have just opened the box. It's checkmate, he replied flatly.

I must have shown some kind of reaction to Ben's comment. Yeqon was glaring back and forth between the two of us. He suspected something.

Shit, shit, shit.

"Get out Nik'ael, now, before I rip your pterugia from your spine! Place one cell of yourself back in my realm, and I'll grind your bones to feed the Afflicted!" Yeqon yelled. An intense explosion of pulsing light flew from Yeqon's palm, but Ben's wings were already wide, his hands up in defence as the ammunition fell just short of him.

"Go back to where I found you, alone and pathetic. Your purpose here is done!" Yeqon drew his arm back again, a fiery orb poised, ready to discharge. Ben disappeared in a flash of white before the orb found its target. It smashed against the wall beyond with a sharp crack.

He deserted me! He actually deserted me!

Obviously, saving his own butt was more important. I'd almost believed he was going to help. Fooled again, naïve me! Stupid me. I snapped out of these fleeting thoughts as Yeqon yelled in my face.

"Open… the box!"

My attention wavered between Yeqon, my brother, and the others practically breathing down my neck. I fumbled for an out. Despite Ben's betrayal and desertion, my courage seemed to slowly creep upwards. Despite everything, the strength that was quietly building up inside emboldened me. It may have been stupid, but I had to let instinct run the show.

Folding my arms, I looked down at the rectangle of silver at my feet, then up to Yeqon's beastly face. Then I turned away, giving him nothing more than the sight of my back and utter silence.

He roared. I flinched, but I refused to face him, despite every cell telling me it was not a good idea to have my enemy behind me.

An agonised yelp had my attention instantly back on this devil of a creature. My brother dangled by the scruff of his neck in Yeqon's grasp.

"Open the box, or I start here." Yeqon reproduced the deadly sharp dagger, ran the flat side down the rigid arm of my brother.

I hesitated too long. Without a second thought, Yeqon plunged the tip deep into my brother's biceps. The blood-curdling scream brought me to my knees.

"Stop!" I screamed, immediately knowing my back was against the wall. My weakness had played its hand already.

"Stop? Why? I'm just beginning." Yeqon grimaced and slashed several times, quickly and decisively, across the already scarred chest. Thin red lines opened; a slow, constant ooze drizzled into the waistband of my brother's filthy pants. The strained sounds of stifled screams tore at my heart. I, too, felt each cut.

"You beast! Stop it!" I yelled, allowing my mark to come out full force, not a reflex, a deliberate warning this time. My wings began to unfurl; my body was alight with fire, inside and out. I took a step back, noticing the others bristling with the anticipation of a fight. Their wings flickered with excitement. By harnessing the positivity swirling in the soul stone, I drew upon its power. Albeit limited, it was sufficient. I took another step away from the box. I raised my arm threateningly, veins bioluminescent with pent up energy, ready to explode. An orb began to manifest upon my hand.

"Let… him… go!"

Yeqon's eyes widened with delight. He seemed pleased, and to my horror, it spurned him. He slashed again until my beleaguered brother's chest was stained entirely red.

"Sister, please?" The very core of my soul broke at the sound of his sweet, defeated voice. The first time I'd heard his voice had been through his agony. My anger and resolve were slashed into weakness, just like his body. To hear him beg me for mercy cut me just as deep. I couldn't ride this teetering roller-coaster of emotion. I didn't know how to navigate myself to a place of constant strength, because I was always diverting down the alleyways and side streets of compassion, indecision, and in my own mind; failure. Those pleading eyes had me throw my orb uselessly into the air. It exploded, sending a rain of debris from the ceiling. As the rubble pelted me, I gave in again.

"Stop Yeqon, just stop!" I put my hands up in surrender, "I'll open your precious, damn box, just let him go."

Yeqon's mark lit up, his expression victorious. His eyes glowered in my direction. With the bloodied dagger still in hand, and my brother in the other, he bellowed impatiently.

"Do it. Do it now!" He pointed the dagger at the box. I edged back towards it. Spittle pooled disgustingly in the corners of Yeqon's desperate grimace. I looked morosely at my brother, his body limp, his head hung. Blood now striped to his feet. I swallowed a sob.

"I'm sorry… brother."

"No more delays, we've had our fun. Get it done now!" Yeqon demanded.

The weight of failure pushed me to my knees. With a trembling hand, I wiped dirt from the top of the box, exposing the now crusted brown remains of my own blood in its crevices. Lifting it unwillingly into my lap, I thought of all those who had suffered so that I could protect this, protect them, and now here I was, as weak as the scrolls had predicted. I was about to deliver victory to the Daimon. Peering up at my broken brother once more, I wanted to say something, anything, but sorry was not going to make a sliver of a difference now. Yeqon pushed him to his knees where he remained hunched over, out of the way, like a piece of rubbish. I had never in my life had the urge to kill, but in that moment, I wanted to rip Yeqon's head from his shoulders. As if knowing my thoughts, reading the hatred in my expression, he kicked my brother, pointed the dagger at him again.

"Time ticks on…"

I bit my lip, ran my glowing hands across the lid of the box. The metal vibrated gently under my touch. I could feel my brother's gasps of pain, smell the degradation wafting from his beaten body. I needed to stop his torture. I pressed on the lid, felt around the box until there was a click. A hidden latch opened in recognition of who and what I was.

"Well? Open it up! Give me the Kaladai!" Yeqon dropped the dagger. It tinkered like glass on the ground. His hands reached out, ready for delivery.

My hesitation angered him further.

"Give it to me!"

I was surrounded now, on all sides, by Yeqon and his brothers. Lilith cooed her strange mutterings in the background. I slowly and regretfully opened the lid.

I gasped.

"Oh, my God!"

Chapter Twenty-Two

A foot pounded into my chest. The force rolled me down the rough stairs, away from Enoch's box. Yeqon had moved so quickly, I hadn't even registered his desperation to see what I'd seen. I righted myself, ready for the next assault. After what I'd just seen in the box, nothing good could be coming.

He poked around the inside, the staff of his weapon scraping the ancient wooden base. He let out an almighty roar of rage, pointing that frightful trident in my face.

"What is this trickery? Where is it?"

The trident was quickly pressed against my throat, forcing me to back down the rest of the steps, away from its fiery points. Yeqon followed me, teeth gnashing, eyes reddening by the second. He never allowed my skin relief from the sharp heat. Blood trickled down my chest. I fleetingly glanced towards my beleaguered twin as my back hit a wall. He was no help to me; he was used and broken.

Yeqon's eyes bore into me.

"What have you done with it?"

"I don't know what you're talking about!" I cried under the sharp pressure.

"You tampered with it before you took it from the river, didn't you? Damned Gedz'iel told you to do it, didn't he? He and that cursed Uriel have known all along. I damn them to lowest pits of Tartarus and back, and I'll damn you too! Tell me, where is the Kaladai?" Yeqon's spit sprayed across my face as he screamed.

I shook my head in terrified denial, but he wasn't in any state to hear the truth.

"Liar!" He grabbed my arm, yanked me back up the steps.

"Don't you dare fool with me, girl. I can have fun with your brother again, if that is your wish?"

The diamond dagger flung through the air from someone's hands. Yeqon caught it with expert and eager precision. "I'll slice him in two, and the memory of that pain will haunt him endlessly, long after his soul leaves his flesh."

My nameless sibling tensed, rigid. He curled up into a protective huddle. His face paled a deathly grey. He knew what could, and would, come his way. Normally, I would give in seeing someone in danger, but now, I had nothing to give. I knew nothing and was beyond helpless to protect my own flesh and blood. I was outnumbered anyway. The chips were down, and I had none to bargain with as the dice were rolled.

So, I did the only thing I could…I let myself explode.

My wings unfurled in an instant. Burning energy poured from my spine, the feeling an instant relief. The room was luminous with my light. I glared at Yeqon. All but he, took a step backwards. Lilith hid behind one of the thrones, this time not at all enjoying the show.

"I *don't* know what you want, Yeqon! I haven't opened it before today. I never had the chance because I had the misfortune of bumping straight into you!" I pointed a white-hot finger towards him. He glared daggers at me. My wings flexed, whipping up dust. The tension in my body replaced with strength. My feet raised a little from the ground, I floated towards Yeqon. Surprise lightened the darkness of his glare.

"As for the others? Gedz'iel has told me barely anything, and Uriel, well, I haven't had the pleasure. I swear on my life *and yours*, I don't know what was supposed to be in there!" I threw a small bolt of energy at the box, angry at the emptiness of it, furious that I'd been through all of this for literally nothing. Yeqon glared ominously at me. I felt the weight of his hate, and I hoped he felt the avalanche of mine.

I don't think either of us knew what the other might do next. Every second I was intimately aware of the safety of my brother, and wondered how long I could pull off this offensive towards them.

"I've tired of this, Yeqon. Just kill her, keep a vial of her blood and we will hunt down the Kaladai ourselves. Let's get on with it. These power games and your ego are tiresome." Pineme pushed forward. I recognised him from the attack at the shed, the time that I'd accidentally transferred myself from England to Australia. Pineme brandished his multi-arrowed cross bow, very ready to use it.

"A little bolder than the last time we met, aren't you?" Pineme questioned with a lustful grimace. He bit his lip, "I like that in a lover!" His cheek twitched.

I moved my other palm to face him too, one hand towards each of them.

"I'll warn you only once to stay away from me!" My pulse raced impossibly faster with the double threat. They knew I was unsure of myself, yet they were smart enough to keep a safe distance, just in case. They were playing with me as much as I was trying to threaten them.

"Stand down, Pineme. You heard Nik'ael; we can't spill her blood… unfortunately. We have been misled and our egos clouded the truth," the one with an aged voice, yet youthful face, seemed almost a ray of light for a brief moment.

"Kasadya is right, Pineme. Nik'ael has no reason to lie about that. He wishes to return to A'vean for the vengeance of his beloved as much as we all do. He brought her to us in the end. We will find another way," Yeqon answered as he glared at my brother.

Both Yeqon and Pineme circled me, and I moved with them, turning and watching their every move. They, too, opened their wings as though in threat of a duel. The others kept their distance. Lilith re-emerged, this display obviously more to her liking now.

"Indeed, we can kill her after the portal to A'vean has opened," Kasadya added with a gut-wrenching chuckle. "She's made us wait long enough for her arrival. That's the least fun we can have," he concluded. I couldn't feel more chilled to the bone.

In a sudden change of pace, there was swift movement amongst them all. Lilith now circled with them, my brother prone beside Kasadya's feet. A long black sword dangled loosely, like a pendulum over him.

"God, you're all animals," I stammered. Tears pooled above my top lip. An arc of frustration burst from my palm, hitting Pineme in the shoulder. He roared and reacted, not towards me, but my brother. His bow now also aimed at my sibling. My brother groaned under Kasadya's boot.

"Soph'ael," Yeqon sighed. "Surely you can see poor Kasadya is weary. I don't know how long he can hold that heavy sword aloft." Yeqon's face remained sinister, despite his voice softening. He pushed the box back towards me.

"Work it out. Where… are… the… contents? It's quite simple, really. Why don't you help her out, Lilith, my love? Soph'ael seems unsure of her choices."

Lilith smiled wildly; old blood still clotted between her teeth. She kneeled at my brother's side, licking her lips, desperate hunger in her amber eyes.

"Please, just give me an excuse to taste him?" She scratched his neck with a long nail, threatening to dive right in. The fire in my palms burned harder, yet my resolve weakened. I had nothing, I thought I had nothing, but right there on the floor, under threat of an excruciating death, I had something. And I couldn't let that go.

Watching the precariousness of that giant sword, and Lilith's ruby lips glistening with anticipation, I made a quick decision. I would make it look like I was trying. They were as unsure of me as I was of them, but I certainly didn't have the upper hand at all. I couldn't be responsible for the mortal death of a brother I'd only just found. Kneeling to the ground, I sniffed back those bloody tears.

I recalled my wings, calmed my energy to a dull hum. "Okay, I'll try." I lowered my eyes in false submission. The scrolls protested covertly; they crackled a little more ferociously in my pockets. I looked at the box, gathered my thoughts, then picked it up.

I played a million ideas through my head, but came up with nothing that I thought could delay what was coming; utter failure. I'd wondered briefly if I should have risked that deal with the Asmodai back in Ben's cave. I quickly corrected myself. There *had* to be a way. I had something Yeqon wanted. I just had to work out how to hold him off whilst I dangled that carrot in front of him. But then, there was my brother, prone underneath two very dangerous weapons.

"Get your filthy hands off him first!" I hissed, sounding as far from myself as ever.

"When you give, so shall we," Yeqon responded.

"Ugh!" I screamed in frustration and looked Yeqon straight in the eyes.

"You will regret this!" My voice was low and threatening.

"Kasadya?"

Kasadya lowered his sword. It swept across my brother's torso. His skin peeled open, he screamed, his back arched. Lilith salivated, her fingers clawed into her palms, her tongue swept over her rich lips. My brother groaned, faded into the palest shade of white, almost to the point of passing out. I wished he would, so he was unaware of the torment.

"Stop! God damn it, stop!" I had to play this and quickly. I was back to pleading, but I was certainly not going to give them what they wanted. I would not help them. I just needed to buy some time for us both.

Hastily, I yanked the box back onto my lap. It hummed against my skin, along with those scrolls. *I hate you all,* I thought ridiculously at the inanimate objects.

"A wise choice, pretty one." Kasadya pulled the sword back a little. Lilith drew threatening circles against my brother's neck.

Opening the lid, it was clear the stupid thing remained empty. What was I supposed to do other than pretend to look like I was doing something? My mind raced for ideas. I glanced up at Kasadya, whose white tipped black hair swung in pendulum motion with his sword, precariously close to skin again. Why didn't my brother at least try to defend himself? Was he that beaten down? Had he been so abused that he complied like someone with Stockholm syndrome?

A growl from Yeqon had me scanning inside the box again.

What to do. What to do?

The wood inside the box showed signs of water damage where it attached to the metal casing. I could feel that the edges were swollen and soft. I ran my fingers along the base. Again, it hummed, as though the thing were alive and recognised me. *Well, bloody help me then, you stupid box!* I released the remaining energy in my hands; it flowed into the metal. The box glowed momentarily. Nothing! There was nothing there. Nothing to work with, nothing to manipulate, nothing to fool them long enough to escape… to help my brother.

Tears welled again. Failure, I was a failure. I stared at my useless hands; thought on the power I'd seen in myself, which now failed me. All I could see were the scars on my hands. The scars from when I'd pricked my skin to open locks and chambers and graves. A shiver ran through me.

I stared at these hands; my eyes widened.

"What are you doing?" Yeqon demanded impatiently.

"Give me that dagger!" I demanded back of him.

"Bold child," someone from behind said as they shoved me. I turned, "Get off me!" I shoved back at Asbel. A shot of hot energy exploded from my palm, landing at his feet. They chuckled like this was all some dark inside joke.

"Just give me the dagger, if you want me to help. I have an idea, that's all. I don't know what was in there or where it is. If you don't at least let me try, then you'll just have to kill us both and be done with it." I called Yeqon's bluff. I wriggled my fingers expectantly, allowing my mark to glow brighter, trying to exude some confidence once again.

"One wrong move and you both most certainly *will* be dead." Yeqon cautiously palmed me the crude weapon. He glared at the others. They took a step back, all except the hungry Lilith, who teetered close to the raging carotid pulse of my brother, just hanging on the climax, like it was a daytime soap opera.

With the dagger lying in my palm, I focused on its clear edge, studying it intently. I glanced at my brother who remained prone, bleeding, defeated.

"I'm sorry if I disappoint you, brother." With that, I pressed the knife deep into my thumb, let my blood ooze into the base of the box. Lilith slapped her lips. She jumped up from her position, drawn like a disgusting blowfly to meat. Luckily, she was unceremoniously shoved onto her backside by Yeqon.

As I watched the blood dribble out, my mind quickened, racing for ideas and answers, hoping something useful would come of this. I smeared my iridescent blood over the entire base of the box until it took on the look of just-polished mahogany.

"What are you doing?" Yeqon demanded, ever more impatient. His presence was heavy, too close behind me.

I stemmed the last of the bleeding with a quick glow from my other hand, easing the unpleasant sting immediately.

"By the power of Tartarus, she most definitely has her power," caution shadowed Pineme's deep timbre. "Be careful, Yeqon."

"Of course, she has it. She's always had it," Asbel said. "Are you that stupid, Pineme or just vastly ill-informed?" Asbel asked sarcastically. Pineme raised his bow in warning. These fools seemed barely united; I wondered what it would take to split their loyalties.

I studied the box with deflating hope as the Daimon continued to argue.

"You said she wouldn't know how to use her power once she got here," Ged'erel snapped.

"She wasn't meant to know," Pineme answered.

"She's reached her maturity; she's worked it out herself, you fool!" Asbel retorted impatiently. Clearly, they hadn't picked up Ben's covert messages.

"Shut up, all of you!" I snapped. Something caught my attention inside the box.

"What is it?" Yeqon leaned in too close. He smelled like ashes and spice. All those years, Ben had smelled like the Daimon that he was, and I'd been in love with it. I was such a fool.

"I don't know yet, so back off and I might be able to see better," I said, shrugging his presence away. Yeqon complied, as though he believed I was onto something.

"Know it quickly then." Yeqon stepped back further, avoiding getting too close to the box. I briefly wondered what it would do if I threw it at him? But then again, there was only one box and four more of them to deal with.

I ignited my palm, let it illuminate the base of the box. The blood was almost dry, crusting and clotting in the corners. Something, however, was taking shape within the drying fluid, slowly evolving within the macabre mess. When Jaz and I were kids, we made secret messages using lemon juice on paper, then added a lit match underneath to reveal the words. Just like that, with the energy from my blood, the heat from my palm, swirls and strokes bloomed across the base of Enoch's box. Words, a sentence, neatly etched into the wood. It was written in Italian.

Seguimi, il discepolo di insegnamento. Svegliame

One of the scrolls burned fiercely against my leg. I spoke the words to myself.

"Follow me, the Disciple of Learning. Wake me."

Twenty-Three

"So, what's your story?" Kristen asked in a whisper as she leaned into the shadows of the old stone building. The overcrowded development on the hill of Nevşehir made for a great many places to hide when you were sequestered on a stakeout. Jaz looked suspiciously back at the pretty dark blonde. Midnight light cast a shadow across the soft angles of Kristen's face; their silhouettes stretched across the bakery wall they were squatting behind. Rats scuttled around a bin for scraps, leaving a trail of bread crumbs in their wake. The silence was deafening as Jaz studied Kristen a moment, mulling over whether she was going to answer, whether she could trust her. Kristen waited for her response patiently, eyes trained on the corners, on every shadow that moved.

A rusted downpipe creaked behind Kristen as she repositioned herself. They both froze, assessing the situation, ready to run, or attack. They listened, covered the white plumes of their breath with their hands, staying as invisible as possible. After a short moment, that felt excruciatingly long, they conceded that they remained safe. Both relaxed again, shook the tension from their limbs and settled back down. Their position remained secret, as did all the others who were stationed quite specifically around the hilly township. Watcher-trained humans, ready to take the offensive if anything otherworldly, dead or otherwise, showed its face.

Kristen relaxed back against the building, and began polishing the tips of the large arrows that were almost always slung around her shoulders.

"So?" She encouraged Jaz.

"What?" Jaz questioned back, a suspicious furrow above her nose.

"Come on Jaz, don't play games." Kristen smiled. "Tell me your story."

"I don't have a story," Jaz replied as nicely as she could muster. She busied herself re-checking her belt, heavy with Sophia's dagger, an extra soul stone Enl'iel insisted she carry, a sheaf of lavender to '*smell away*' the Rogues, and a handful of high energy biscuits Eilir had baked. She took a bite of one.

"Oh please, everyone 'as a story. Don't be shy," Kristen kicked out playfully at her. "We are friends, no? You are learning our secrets, isn't it time you share some of your own? You can't shock me, Jaz. I may be young, but believe me, I've seen and 'eard it all!" Kristen smiled. "Well, I 'ope I 'ave anyway!"

"I'd rather have not seen or heard any of this." Jaz pointed at Kristen's quiver. "You really like those things?"

"They're very precious, you know, made of chromious. I must salvage every single one I use, if at all possible. There was only ever a finite amount of this precious element brought to Earth from A'vean."

Jaz knelt forwards and ran the tip of her finger across the top of one. It glinted in the slits of moonlight that clawed around the corner into the alleyway.

"Lethal!" Jaz nodded admiringly, "I saw you use them in Tewkesbury. They literally set those creatures on fire." Her eyes widened at the memory.

"Afflicted? Yes. They die like Rogues, except they burn blue, not orange since Afflicted still have some goodness left inside. Chromious is a repellent to negative energy. Since it's from A'vean it is full of positive energy, like the E'lan. Those that live on A'vean absorb E'lan.

They turn literally into a living, conscious energy. It's very powerful. Can you imagine, floating around like a ghost, immortal, powerful and just - wow!" Kristen's attention wandered for a moment, as she stopped polishing, lost in thought.

"Yeah, nah. I'm happy having a body actually right here on solid ground. Thanks anyway." Jaz patted her thigh for effect.

"Oh, me too. I'm not ready to die, trust me. But I feel so connected to the Watchers, I don't fear mortal death. I know there is definitely a better place for us… that is if we are good and kind inside and out. Like you Jaz."

"Me?" Jaz gawped in genuine surprise. "I'm a total bitch! Don't know who you've been talking to?"

They both smiled.

"We all 'ave our moments, but its's what's in your 'eart that matters. Death measures your soul, and I'm afraid Jaz, yours is 'eavy with love. You will 'ave to float around with me one day. That is if we ever get this portal open." Kristen polished up the last arrow head and slid it back in the quiver.

"You know you sound a little left of centre, Kristen. Floating and hearts and love."

"Perhaps, but doesn't weird keep good company? Who's sitting right next to me?" Kristen smiled.

"You got me there," Jaz conceded with a shake of her head.

"It was a fire," Jaz' voice was suddenly solemn.

"What was?" Kristen slung the weight of arrows across her back before giving Jaz her full attention.

"My parents were freaks, like serious run away to the circus, read your tarot, ghost-busting, drunken weirdos!" Jaz glanced up at Kristen, waiting for judgement, but only found another girl her own age who maintained an expression of compassion. There wasn't the derision with which she was bombarded with as a youngster.

"Yeah, they drank. Always one drink short of unconscious. Mum told me only once it was to chase away the demons, whatever the hell that meant!" Jaz grimaced with the disgust of the memory. She poked at the ground with a stick, harder and harder as the memories flooded back. "Now I wonder, perhaps how sane she actually might have been?" Jaz bit her lip, blinked a little harder to quell the burn in her eyes.

"We were constantly on the move. Mum thought she was a medium, always talking to shadows. It scared the crap out of me. Dad was a magician," Jaz rolled her eyes and looked away, "And fire breather. Yeah, I know. Its crazy right?" Jaz' fingers, red with cold, were crusting with ice as she circled the white ground. The twig snapped.

Jaz slowly revealed a small piece of herself, a hidden piece that even Sophia knew nothing of. Kristen moved not a muscle, hugging her knees, totally enwrapped in Jaz' every word. A bird cawed in the distance. Unusual for this time of night, Kristen put up her hand to pause Jaz. She did a quick check around the corner, tucking her long lavender-threaded hair behind her ear. She nodded for Jaz to continue.

"Well, one day I came home from school number five, I think, and Mum and dad were arguing as usual about having to move again. Mum was convinced she was being stalked by a poltergeist. She was taking all kinds of pills, so who knew what she was imagining. The argument got worse and worse. I got scared and hid in my room. I was curled my bed, covering my ears like always, when there was an explosion. It shook the entire house. I thought it was a bloody earthquake. Mum was screaming… like really screaming. I remember the sound so clearly…" Jaz' eyes glazed; moistened at the edges. "Sounded like she was being murdered," she whispered. Kristen's fingers curled in, her arm moved forwards, about to reach a hand out to Jaz, when a gust of cold wind whipped by, it snapped Jaz' emotions away. Jaz blinked, back to her usual hard-to-crack shell. Kristen pulled her hands subtly back.

"I snuck down the corridor and peeked into the kitchen. Mum was on the floor with a knife in her chest… blood was everywhere. Dad was slapping at her with a tea-towel because she was also on fire. He was screaming. God, I remember that smell!" Jaz gulped, pinched her nose and grimaced. Kristen didn't take a moment's attention from her.

"I thought one of his tricks had gone wrong. I literally peed my pants in fright. Mum eventually stopped screaming. The last words I heard her say were, "I told you!" It was then I realised the entire house was on fire. I ran back to my room and shut the door, which was pretty dumb. I was choking on smoke so quickly. It poured under the door and filled my room until it was almost black. I tried to get out through the window, but the dump we lived in had the windows nailed shut. It was deep in the bush; I don't know how far from town we lived… probably an hour. No one was going to see us in time. I thought I was going die. I hit the window with a Christmas angel I'd kept on my bed from the previous year's tree. I banged so hard with that damned thing, calling for help, trying to crack the glass. I remember the burn in my throat, then I blacked out. The next thing I remember was the sound of smashing glass and someone scooping me up. That was Ben." Jaz' mouth tightened at the mention of his name.

"Ben rescued you?"

"Yes." Jaz' cheeks flushed, despite the cold.

"He took me in. I've really only vague memories of the first few years with him. We had foster parents, but then they died. I really can't remember them at all. He always looked after me. And now…" Jaz managed to pale even in the bitter winter night, "He's such a lying bastard!"

Kristen shook her head. "Ben's betrayal, it is unforgivable. I understand your anger." She nodded in sympathy and placed a gentle hand on Jaz' knee.

"No one could possibly under…" Jaz stopped as Kristen suddenly shoved her back behind her, deeper into the shadows of the back alley. A mist began rolling in over the snow-peppered ground.

"Stay very quiet," Kristen whispered with a finger to her lips.

Footsteps on gravel echoed in the distance, piercing the silence. People were suddenly moving in every direction.

"Why are they 'ere?" Kristen whispered to herself.

"We 'ave to move." Kristen muffled a cough in her elbow as a foul stench filled the air. She pulled a small bottle from under her thick coat and splashed it over herself then passed it to Jaz, who looked confused.

"Lavender concentrate, it won't keep the Rogues away for long, but it may give us just us enough time to drive an arrow through them. Or run." Kristen nodded at Jaz to hurry up and take the bottle.

Jaz was wide-eyed and bathing herself haphazardly in the clear liquid without a second thought. She mumbled nervously, "God, I smell like an old lady now!" She didn't hold back, splashing every part of herself with the floral aroma. They slowly retreated away from the direction the thick grey mist was rolling in from.

"It's coming from out of town. At least that means they are not on their way to the sanctuary, I 'ope. Come, let's find Jude. I want to get to the top of this town. We can fire down at them from above when they show themselves."

"I thought there wasn't much chance of anything happening here. Isn't that why Jude brought us here? Because it was safe?" Jaz whispered as they moved stealthily along the back streets.

"Well," Kristen checked around a corner before motioning for Jaz to follow. "Times are stranger than ever right now. We must expect the unexpected." Kristen wriggled her fingers more urgently, "Come."

They ran hastily and silently, keeping an eye on the main street through the gaps of the alleyways, watching the mist slowly ascend the main road.

Approaching a dumpster behind the coffee shop they'd visited a few days before, they found Thomas and a few others; a tightly huddled group.

"You guys okay?" Thomas whisper-shouted to Kristen as she approached. He gave her a brief hug, "Jaz, you too?" Jaz nodded she was fine and gave a thumbs up, but the whip of her heart in her chest betrayed her lie. Jaz clenched her jaw, curled her hands into fists; tried to look as brave as the others

"We're fine. How many?" Kristen asked.

"Not sure. They still haven't shown themselves in the town. They seem to be hiding outside of town. For now, at least, but definitely headed this way by the smell. Xavier made a hell of a dash up to inform us." Thomas gestured towards a stocky young man leaning on his knees, plumes of frigid breath coiled above him as he gasped through the recovery of his effort to alert everyone.

In a Yorkshire accent, Xavier shared what he'd seen, "It was quiet, dead, not a sound. They appeared outta nowhere. Their stealth was better than I've ever seen. We were about ten clicks outta Kaymakli." He sniffed, wiped crystalised sweat from his upper lip, his nose and cheeks bright red. "Lorcan had just checked in on us before returning to the Eloi to hunt for Sophia," Xavier said and took a few more breaths and a sip from his water canteen. "Lorcan said he'd scouted the immediate area and it was clear, said that we wouldn't have any trouble. I swear, within a bloody minute of him disappearing, these bastards started showing up! Think I seen at least ten or so back on the flats. There's not much lead time ahead of that stinking fog though!"

Thomas tapped his head, slid his finger through the snow, drawing a map. "Right, I think we should take the back streets up to the old citadel. We can pick the Rogues off from up there." Thomas pointed to a rise on the snow map. "The street lights will give us enough sight. Keep as quiet as possible. We don't want the locals coming out and turning into a midnight feast." His lips were tight at the macabre thought. Thomas waved everyone on, immediately leading the small group away. They picked their way carefully up the rise of the town, towards the ancient Ottoman relic.

Climbing the jagged mountainside, they used the trunks of walnut trees as intermittent shields, to meld with the shadows, looking out for danger. About half way up the hill, Jude landed with a heavy thud from the branches above.

"Mother fucker! Why are you up a tree?" Thomas held his hand up, everyone stopped behind him.

Jude put a hand up to silence them as a few other Eudaimonians and Watchers joined him, dropping from the branches of the surrounding trees. No glowing faces, no pterugia, just fully loaded with weapons and armour, like the humans. Jude put a finger to his lips, pointed the group to follow him, and they did so without sound or question. Jaz attempted to ask what was going on, but Kristen shook her head, finger to her lips, just like Jude.

The fog thickened and chased them up the rough terrain, blanketing up to their waists in minutes. The moon and its generous smudge of stars were obliterated by rich clouds blowing in on a foul wind. Pitch blackness invited the group into the remains of the old Ottoman fortress. They scrambled into its shadows and bunkered down.

Jaz fiddled nervously with her belt, edging closer to Jude without realising it. Her fingers tightened around the pocket containing Sophia's dagger. Jude finally spoke in an urgent whisper.

"It appears we have a problem. A big one."

As the moon reappeared, the hard line of his face reflected the gravity of the situation.

"Daimon are roaming the outskirts of the city. Not only do we have Rogues on the move, it appears she has brought Afflicted with her. I'm not sure if the Rogues are hers as they are moving separately to her."

"She? Who is she?" Dash asked.

"I have my suspicions, but it would be strange for anyone to take the chance using an Afflicted army, rather than the easier to control Rogues," Jude responded.

"Bloody hell!" Xavier exclaimed, "Rogues are enough to bloody deal with! Afflicted are too unpredictable."

"They follow whoever feeds their addiction, Xavier, and that could make them predictable enough," Dash explained.

There were murmurs of discontent. Jude let them release their tension, albeit in whispers. His gaze swept constantly over Jaz. She stubbornly averted hers every time their eyes met. Without a word, he took her arm and pulled her behind his position, next to Dash who smiled warmly at her. Jude looked over his shoulder.

"You will stay with me." His voice and face softened ever so slightly before he added harshly, "So you don't get any one killed." Jude turned his back on Jaz, avoiding her indignant expression.

"It's far from ideal to spill the blood of the Afflicted. They are or were, one of us in the past. Something is amiss tonight. However, we are soldiers of A'vean, and we face whatever comes our way without prejudice. I expect you to do whatever it takes to protect our security and the locals of this province." Jude's command was met immediately by eager nods from all.

Trees rustled; rocks tumbled below. They all froze as rapid footsteps crunched in the snow. The fog now three quarters the way up the hillside, Jude instinctually tucked Jaz further into the shadows. The soft footfalls had everyone with their weapons drawn, until there was an unexpected and relieved whispered laugh from Dash and Jude.

"You nearly scared me to death, Kea. We thought you were an Afflicted!" Dash chided her with a hug as she emerged from the darkness below.

"How insulting! I'll try not to be offended." Kea flashed a mock look of reproach. "Sorry guys, you're not that easy to find when you're under the radar. I had to wait until I was close enough to have a little mind chat!" She winked at Dash. "Steep hill!" Kea smiled and caught her breath.

"Sorry I'm late. Koi called on me to double check the security of the sanctuary before I joined you. Glad I did from the looks of things. He told me they'd seen Rogues spill out of the Empyrean realm through the fracture over Mexico. These are strong ones that Lilith has kept alive, so to speak. Need to be careful with these; they're smarter than usual. They're at the bottom of the main road, under the bridge. About twenty or so, and they look nasty. Nothing we can't sort out, though. The problem is, there's also been a sighting of a group of Afflicted as well. It's incredibly strange for this territory." Kea frowned, and they all nodded in agreement.

"We've already spotted them," Jude muttered, his mind clearly working on piecing together the strange events.

"Something unprecedented is going on, Jude," Kea said. "I've sent out another group to check what that's all about. We've got some time up our sleeve with the Rogues though, while they're stationary." She waved her hand at Jude. "Don't mind me, keep going. I'll catch up with your plans. I felt that Daimon was female too, but I didn't see who it was."

"Having Afflicted brought into this mess changes the ball game slightly. We were just discussing the issue of the Afflicted when you snuck up on us. Not a good reflection on any of us, to be honest." Jude shook his head. A wry smile broke the hard edges of his face. "Keep an eye on her for me will you, Kea?" Jude pulled Jaz from the shadows and pushed her towards Kea.

"Hands off, will you?" Jaz yanked away from him, "You could just ask nicely, ya know!"

Jude's smile stayed put. "I don't ask Jaz, I order." He waited for a retort that never arrived.

"It's nice to see you two still getting along so well. Come here, hon. Stick with me." Kea pulled Jaz into her side. "Nice outfit, my friend!"

Jaz frowned, but still managed to straighten out her top and look somewhat impressed with the compliment.

"Enough!" Jude rolled his eyes. Without the need of his wings, with pure strength alone, Jude launched the seven-foot jump onto the overhead turret. He peered across a stormy horizon, waved back down.

"Front and centre, Dash. We need eyes," Jude called quietly. Dash obliged, jumping up with the same smooth, feline ease. He took up a sentry post in a craggy corner, the swords hugging his hips glowed in the moonlight.

"We were discussing the Afflicted," Jude reminded everyone as he landed softly back on the ground with just the slightest clang of his armour.

"So, how are they bribing the Afflicted? Surely, they prefer to stay underground in their ghettos with their drugs?" Xavier asked.

"Good question. Could they have run so low that they'd risk fighting?" Kea asked.

"It appears to have begun in Tewkesbury, when they first attacked and kidnapped Ben. We weren't expecting that. We know now that was all Nik'ael's doing. A set up." Darkness couldn't hide the stain of Jude's anger at the mention of Ben. "Afflicted rarely come out and have only ever shown aggression if cornered, or desperate for their next hit. He clearly had what they wanted. Remnants of Thanratos were found in the back alley by the barges. Anyone heard any different?" Jude asked.

"They always keep to themselves. I've rarely seen them apart from a quick scavenge after a battle looking for remains to grind down," Dash called from above.

"Thanratos must have run severely low for them then, as Kea suggested. They're so desperate now, it appears they're taking blood payment from Yeqon. He must be paying them in dust." Jude glowered. "They can't help themselves." His fists whitened. "They will do as they're told as long as they are fed…. that makes them so very unpredictable and dangerous."

"Who's Yeqon's lady lackey then?" Xavier asked.

"I don't know. He's the ultimate misogynist," Jude replied. "It's usually Lilith slithering by his side, but she never ventures far without him." Jude scratched his head. "Never the less, no matter who or what is controlling the Afflicted, we must be extra cautious."

"Like us, if Afflicted don't draw on their power, they are almost impossible to detect, unlike the Rogues," Thomas explained to a confused-looking Jaz. It changed to the pallor of fear quickly, as she processed what she'd just learned.

"That's why they've recruited the Afflicted," Jude surmised. "We don't notice them until they're too close. They also retain immense strength, despite appearances. Don't be fooled by how weak they look. They can sneak up, just like Kea did. They leave the same energy signature as us, that's why we must remain on foot and in blackout. The Rogues can sense us too, don't forget," Jude added, bringing those who were on their first mission up to speed.

"So, why are they in the town? Wouldn't they be more interested in attacking Kaymakli?" A raven-haired female asked from the back of the group.

"I'm not sure, just yet. They could just be hungry, but it's most likely a diversion; a way to divide and reduce us to smaller groups. The problem is, yet again, how did they know we were here?" Jude growled to himself, flipped his favourite dagger up and down whilst he thought on the issue. "What I know is that each of you is to stick with at least one other person. No one is to go off alone. I'm going to deploy groups of three to various points around the town's perimeter. One human with two of us." Jude pointed to Jaz, "Keep out of sight and you might just live through the night."

Jaz hid the shiver that struck her, clenched her hands, jutted her chin forwards. "I've survived worse monsters than you'd care to imagine."

Kea pulled Jaz in close as a shadow flickered through Jude's eyes.

"You want her to stick with me?" Kea asked.

"Yes," Jude nodded. He turned away and paired up all the human fighters with the A'vean warriors.

"The less experienced will patrol the centre of these ruins. You'll have to stay here too, Kea." Jude looked Jaz up and down one last time. She flipped him the bird. Kea grabbed her hand quickly.

"He's just as dangerous as a Rogue, Missy!" Kea moved away with Jaz, hoisting her up in a scramble to the highest point of what remained of the parapet. Xavier joined them both, along with Dash; the four of them bunkered down, waiting and watching.

Jude edged back down the slope with the rest of the warrior groups. His shoulders tensed when he glanced back up at those he'd left behind. He sighed, rubbed the stubble on his chin. Jaz' spiky hair poked over the top of the ruins. He bit his lip, shook his head. "You idiot," he grumbled to himself and disappeared into the murky fog that swallowed the hill.

Chapter
Twenty-Four

The room erupted into a volcanic anger. The ambient temperature rose by degrees as frustration rolled from my enemies. Yeqon threw his trident across the room. It sailed over my head and embedded deep into a wall.

"Don't dare tell me again you don't know what it means!" Yeqon kicked towards Enoch's cryptic chest. He drew himself up as menacingly as possible, grabbed me around the neck. I gasped, pulled at the iron grip of his fingers. I was simultaneously trying to keep one eye on my slumped, exsanguinating brother. My energy burned, my back ached, I felt like I might burst inside out.

I drew on that calming waterfall in the depths of my mind, beckoning it to contain the surging power ripping through my veins. Whilst my brother lay there, whilst they believed I had something they wanted, I had a point of power over them that gave me a renewed hope to not give in, or blow it all in an uncontrolled emotional rage. I had a chance to string them along if I could just protect my brother, if I could just get out of Yeqon's clutches. I needed to make them believe I was as clueless as I felt about the inscription in the box. Yeqon was at the point of murderous frustration now, the way his jaw ceaseless clenched, the way he spoke through gritted teeth. I was truly dicing with the Devil.

"I'll have no regrets in plucking your brother's limbs off, one by one. On the death of I'el, I'll even chase down Nik'ael and pull his soul from his chest right in front of you." Yeqon's smile deepened, his breath hot in my face. I couldn't pull away. "We aren't under any illusions here that your heart skips an extra beat when he is near. Are we?" Yeqon tilted his head and smiled, his top lip peeled back. "Truth hurt?"

"I… hate… him," I spluttered. His grip tightened; my eyes felt like they might explode.

"Well then, I'll help you out and bring him down with absolute pleasure. Perhaps we can murder him together?" Yeqon smiled when I flinched. "As for your brother, though, that might hurt a little more. Pineme, grab the boy!" Yeqon's breath was fire, and it ignited my heart into action.

Just as I thought I might have the upper hand; I was beaten to the punch; my hand forced. Yeqon squeezed tighter and my air was completely cut off. I was yet to understand how I didn't need oxygen, so my body reacted as a human body would. The image of my brother faded, pressure filled my head, blackness seeped into my peripheral vision. This forced something subconscious to ignite my power and purge it out in self-defence. I let it; I couldn't fight it. My wings peeled open again, the burn of my face seared as I tried to take myself to a calm, happy place while my consciousness continued to fade.

"Yeqon!" someone warned. It sounded dreamily far away.

"Stay back!" Yeqon responded with a slow growl.

My vision faded quickly, my blood and bone and flesh just couldn't trust in the supernatural me fully… not yet. It was in this moment, seconds short of collapse, that I focused on that swim under water in the Avon River. I recalled the freezing current, the urge to breathe when I'd searched for the silver chest. I forced forward that memory of not needing a single breath. It was my humanness, my normal upbringing, that was fooling me into weakness. That nagging desire to be ordinary had tricked my flesh, my lungs… the Sophia part of Soph'ael, that being deprived of air would weaken me, when in fact I could survive off the power of the E'lan. With that clarity, I drew a breath, not from my airways, but from within. My chest expanded as though the air was actually rushing in. Empowered with this revelation, I flapped my wings so damn hard in my mind that those things actually followed suit, perfectly powerful for the first time. The soul stone thrummed wildly against my skin. I grabbed Yeqon's biceps, dug my nails in hard, and let out everything I had. An intense, pulsing flash lit the room. There was bellowing, growls and the definitive screech of Lilith. In the confusion and the haze of it all, I heard the Daimon warning each other to stay away from me. As my vision cleared, I found them dusting themselves off, searching for their weapons, looking a whole lot more warily in my direction. The stone seats they'd recently occupied glowed red with heat, sparks, and smoke coiled up into the darkness above.

Yeqon was flat on his back across the top step, much like Gedz'iel had been the first time I'd met him. He roused quickly and voraciously, rising into the air, his murky wings spanned wide and terrifying. I backed up with a gentle flap. A satisfied smirk on my face, yet my guts were jelly. What had I just done?

"You!" Yeqon pointed at me. Rage shook his hand. The whites of his eyes glowed. My guts were now watery, and I quickly scooped up my brother. I placed him gently down behind me.

Searching for words, Yeqon struggled to contain his anger, desperate to explode. His cheeks twitched. He glared at his hoard of Daimon. Clenched jaw and quivering lips found no words, a flash of fear most definitely washed across that anger. As he glanced nervously between me and the other Daimon, I seized the opportunity of his indecisiveness again.

"What, Yeqon? What is it you want to say?" Holding my hands aloft, allowing them to burn bright, I challenged him with as much bravado plastered on my expression as I could muster. It was time to stop this ridiculous pendulum of *'will I or wont I?'* I had to stand up to him, no matter what. Whether I was meek and submissive, or an all-out raging angelic bitch, Yeqon was never going to give in. I knew then that I had to rule less with my heart and more with my head. So far, I'd completely stuffed this balance right up, big time. But no more.

Yeqon swooped, hand ready to throttle me again, but he hesitated and stopped just an arm's length from me. His breath in my face, the smell of him, the heat of him all too close. He wreaked of death, of hate; of outright terror.

My hands lit brighter. "Just try me, Yeqon!"

Yeqon laughed, nervously at first, his eyes wary on me. Dark black coals searched my body, but then he laughed hard. They all did. Lilith trilled in the background. I wanted to burn the smile from her face.

"You think you know me? You think you understand what you are up against? Well, let me tell you this, young one," He drew in a long slow breath, nostrils flared, the indecision and fear in his face evaporated. Yeqon retracted his wings and floated gently to the ground. I followed suit, wanting to keep pace with his every movement. An uncomfortable calmness overcame him. He spoke gently and methodically, utilising each word with care.

"I have more control over you than you realise. You see me," he pointed to himself, then the others. "You see us, momentarily affected by your little power display, and you think you've won? Well, my dear, power runs much deeper than what you can do with the elements. Power over the mind and the will of others has seen me to many a victory." Yeqon wagged a finger at me. "*That* is where you will fail. You can play your little game; I have a game I can play, too." He leaned close, pushing my hands aside and tossed a piece of my hair over my shoulder. He whispered into my face, allowing his cheek to brush mine. Our marks touched briefly. It was like being assaulted; the resultant feeling had my stomach upside down. He inhaled deeply, enjoying the intimacy of the unwelcome contact.

"Ahh, yes. You smell of power and purity. So deliciously innocent. Too weak to control such immense power, too scared and flimsy to utilise your resources to their full potential. *That* is what will see you undone!" He reached for my hair again, I recoiled, he dropped his hand.

Despite holding my ground, I felt unsure, not knowing where he was going next. I concentrated on keeping my brother behind me, he noticed.

"Boy, get up!"

I grabbed for my brother, holding him back, but he sniffed back the drool and blood from his nose and pushed past me. He stood behind Yeqon like a terrified animal, shaking, bruised and caked in flakes of blood.

"Brother, no. Stay with me!" I reached out my hand. He didn't respond, his eyes downcast.

"Exactly, my dear. *This* is power Soph'ael, a dog so terrified, yet he still obeys his master. I've had enough of this. You have until the rise of the sun to work out that little puzzle in the box, or your sibling will be just a brief memory. Boy, closer." Yeqon drew the dagger again.

"Offer me your neck," he commanded. To my horror, my brother leaned his head to one side, allowing Yeqon the open invitation to slit his throat. He quivered uncontrollably, yet seemed unable to stop himself from offering his body for sacrifice.

"No!" I threw a warning shot at Yeqon's feet. He looked up, surprised.

"Oh yes! And you'll have to do much better than that!" Yeqon boasted through a broad smile of gritted teeth.

"What have you done to him?" Tears slipped into my mouth, salty and useless.

"Only what needed to be done. And before you think of trying anymore little tricks, just remember, I have eyes on the inside too." He pointed down, as though indicating the real world. More threats, and they seemed to be aimed at the rest of my family and friends.

The traitor? Who was it? Had Ben returned to continue his subterfuge?

I cursed at I'el on the inside. At every turn, something new was thrown in my face. I sighed, dropping my arms, not in defeat, but in recognition that I had to bide my time… wait and hope the others would be coming. Or could I still somehow save myself?

"Take her back to her cell." Yeqon pointed to an Afflicted nearby. "One night, pretty one. One night!" Yeqon joined the others, dragging my brother by the scruff of the neck. He didn't look back. An Afflicted male along with a particularly hideous Rogue, took me by the arms and pulled me away. I struggled, craning my head to see what they were doing. My brother was pushed inside their huddle. I could no longer see him. As I rounded a corner, it sounded as though the group had erupted into a heated discussion, Lilith cackling in the background in maniacal glee.

Chapter
Twenty-Five

The heavy door slammed shut with an echo that reverberated through my bones. The noise roused the foul creatures that were my cellmates. Their screeching was muffled, but I could hear it well enough, and it grated on my frayed nerves. I screamed, not in fear or pain, but in pure frustration. Long and loud, fists clenched, tense and shaking; just like Yeqon. I flung my head back and let it all out.

"What do you want of me?" I yelled through my teeth. I cursed at I'el, the designer of this sick game.

"Just tell me how to fix this! Damn you!" I kicked out at nothing before sinking to my knees. Agitated, my fingers worked at the filthy remnants of my pants until I allowed myself to calm, slowing my thoughts, letting the coil of frustration unwind. I was a mess, literally.

A damp chill wicked up from the inky pool. It drew my attention from the simmering anger. I stared at the sorry looking face reflecting back at me. The image made me realise just how alone I was.

You have to get yourself out of this.

Deep breath in, deep breath out, repeat.

This old, comfortable mantra helped me calm to the point that I could start threading some sensible thoughts back together. I looked deep into myself. I couldn't rely on anyone else. If I wallowed in pity,

I was dead; death was the only outcome. I just *had* to escape. There was no question of allowing myself to remain a prisoner at Yeqon's beck and call to toy with. I had no idea what the damn box was saying. It couldn't have been more ridiculous had a monkey written it. I didn't know how far Yeqon was going to go. Would he really kill my brother or the others back home? Yes, I knew he would. Look what he had done to my dear to Esme. Never had there been a less threatening soul, yet she was slaughtered by his minion. I bit my lip, blinked a hot tear away. My fingers clawed my thighs.

The problem was, how could I escape and take my brother with me? I couldn't just save myself. The possibility that I might have to face that as a choice was dawning very heavily on me.

Your heart is your weakness.

I had understood this all my life, not just since I was railroaded into this new existence. I had to face this weakness head on, and it would not be easy, perhaps not even possible. Rescuing my brother would mean I would at least be able to fight back, because they would no longer have anything to hold over me to keep me in check. Ben was gone; good riddance too. The only thing to do was escape, or die trying, and with or without my brother. I had to convince myself to look at the bigger picture. Would I ever be able to sacrifice one life for the greater good? I shuddered at the thought of it and my fingers dug a little harder.

It felt like hours passed, drawing ideas in the dirt, trying to reform an escape plan. That damned box and its stupid cryptic clue interrupted my thoughts over and over; it infuriated me. '*Disciple of Learning!*' What was that supposed to mean? My forefinger scrawled the words into the ground a dozen times, illuminated a sickly blood-red from the beastly energy beams that locked me inside. Circling around and around the words almost mindlessly, I was only drawn from the haze by the faint burn and hum from the scrolls in my pocket.

I sat bolt upright. Almost ripping my pocket completely off. I scrounged quickly inside it. I carefully pulled Elizabeth's scroll out with trembling hands, unrolling it at my feet. Scanning through, my breath caught immediately. "Oh my God!" There was the same reference to this disciple person in my grandmother's scroll!

The kaldai is your key to be bathed in your purity,
Thrice created, hence scattered in pieces by the disciple of learning.

This 'disciple of learning' must be a person, a real person. But who and where were they? If Elizabeth referred to them, then the odds weren't looking in my favour. She was a queen who lived over 500 years ago. Perhaps, though, if I dug more into her life, I may find out who this stranger was? Of course, at this point, it wasn't looking like I was going to see anyone, ever.

Yes. Yes, you are, Soph.

"C'mon Granny, can't you send me another dream? Tell me who this is?" Clearly speaking to myself and lost in thought, I didn't notice the door open until I heard it slam shut again. There was a thud in the dark recesses of my prison. I spun around, scanned the area, and tucked myself closer to the wall behind the water pool. My right hand lit up and protectively shielded my chest. Was there a shadow? I squinted. No, my eyes were playing tricks on me. Then I saw the source of the thud. A plate with more stale bread and a shiny red apple lay in the darkness a few feet away.

Uninterested in food, I gazed back into the mirror of the water pool. After thinking some more about this strange new twist in the game, I decided to return to concealing myself again. Disguising myself seemed the only probable way I could escape. There was no way I'd be waltzing out in my natural state, not without one hell of a fight. They didn't know about my little party trick, so I'd use it to my best advantage.

Squeezing my eyes shut, I recalled as much detail as I could of that Afflicted woman who'd tended me in the cell. I easily morphed in and out of her numerous times, only breaking a sweat after change ten or so. Clearly, I'd reached some new milestone since my twenty-first birthday ticked over. Previously, the effort of this new skill was much more intense. It now came with much greater ease, almost feeling as simple as taking a breath. This realisation pumped my confidence, which, quite frankly, needed a boost. I stopped to rest awhile. My thoughts turning to how I would overcome the scrawny gate keeper so that I could take her place and escape. I hunted around for the shiv I'd made earlier. As I was rummaging along the ground, imagining the quickest and quietest stealth mugging that I could, there was shuffling behind me. I spun dizzily, narrowing my eyes and focusing deep into the shadows. A silhouette of someone huddled in a corner. Its outline slowly sharpened. I sucked in a quiet breath. Moving ever so carefully, I reversed on hand and knee until I was backed right up against the opposite wall. The drip, drip of water from the steaming rooftop was suddenly much louder.

"Who's there?" I demanded in a shaky voice with as much authority as I could muster.

Coughing and more shuffling.

"Who are you? I can see you there."

A thin, haunted voice answered.

"Sister?"

Startled, I ignited my palm. Its soft light spilled across the darkness.

A grubby pair of feet appeared first. I guided my palm slowly upwards until I'd illuminated the tattered form of my brother. He shielded his eyes as his face was brought into view.

"Brother?"

I tentatively crawled his way. Mud oozed between my fingers, seeped deeper into my clothes. My pulse raced, a rapid whoosh in my temples.

"Brother?" I whispered again. He cowered, and I halted.

"It's okay. I won't hurt you," I soothed. His arms fell from his face to his knees. He huddled into a tight ball.

"May I come closer?" I asked softly.

After blinking rapidly for a few seconds as though adjusting his sight, his haunted blue eyes sparkled, and he nodded his head sharply.

I made my way to within a foot of him. I sat; mimicked his same huddled position. The scrolls were going wild in my pocket. My pendant hummed softly against my chest. I took it as a sign that their energies recognised a kindred spirit.

For a few moments, we sat in silence. I studied him with a heavy heart. Battered and crusted over with scabs from the torture inflicted by Yeqon, he was the sorriest of sights. My blood ran more angrily through my veins. My brother was equally as massive as any Watcher or Daimon, yet his energy seemed weak. It made no sense that he gave himself back to that beast earlier. I knew all too well the power of the mind over body, and he had seemed absolutely beaten down, unable to resist Yeqon's orders.

He appeared agitated. He looked back and forth between me and the ground.

"You're badly injured," I said softly. "Why do you not heal yourself?"

He considered this, then held out his hands with a questioning expression.

"You don't know how to heal yourself?"

He looked back at the ground.

My heart flipped in empathy for him.

"May I heal you?"

His eyes dared to look directly at me, flitting here and there, as though assessing the risk.

"I won't hurt you; I promise." I nodded my head encouragingly.

He tilted his head side to side, still looking me up and down, considering the offer. I wondered if he had ever experienced a positive touch, or if this was the only life he knew. How long had he been here? I backed away a little, and he seemed to let out a held breath.

"How about you tell me when you feel comfortable and we can try then?"

He nodded; his eyes softened. *Slowly does it, Soph.*

I shuffled back. The dripping had quieted, but the muffled screams of the horrid things outside reminded me of exactly where I was. A quick glance behind reassured me that for now, we were alone.

"What is your name?"

He looked quizzically at me.

"What do they call you?"

"Boy," he answered in a coarse whisper.

"Boy? You don't have a proper name?"

He shrugged his shoulders.

Stripped of freedom and his family, he was also stripped of his identity. A tear precariously sat on my lashes again. I blinked it away.

"Well, that's just not good enough. You must have a name. I don't know what our parents named you, but I do know our father's name. How about we name you after him, at least for now, until we discover your real name?" I smiled.

He arched an eyebrow.

"I remember." He sounded parched for water.

"Remember what?"

"Him."

"Our father?"

He nodded.

I was overwhelmed by an immense rush of jealously and had to check myself back to reality. How ridiculous to be jealous of him. Just looking at him pulled my head right back to where it should have been.

"You remember him? What was he like?"

He shrugged his shoulders, looking away again. "Brave," he whispered.

Brave! Well, that was something new and precious that I immediately locked in my heart.

"So, you must remember his name, Rik'ael?"

He nodded.

"May I call you that?"

He nodded again.

He adjusted his position and winced.

"Are you in pain?"

Another nod.

"Would you let me heal you?"

His eyes widened. He appeared to become agitated again. His fingers fidgeted up and down the seam of his pants, if that's what you could call the tatters barely covering him.

"Don't be afraid. I've healed people all my life. Well, since I was twelve that is. That's the first time I was allowed to, if you don't include all the animals I brought home. Oh, God, I'm babbling. Sorry." I ran my palms over my face and took a breath. My pulse was racing.

"Yes," he answered quickly, decisively. Rik'ael looked away again, as though thinking upon it too much might make him change his mind.

"Okay," I smiled again, trying to maintain the thin thread of trust.

I shuffled forward. An immense scream suddenly rumbled through the walls. I held my breath and froze. A few more screams were followed by a loud crack. Immediate silence ensued. I watched the door behind me, just waiting for someone to enter. The silence continued long enough that I relaxed, as much as was possible in the current situation. They weren't coming for me yet. That was something. I calculated I must still have a few hours before sunrise. Turning back to Rik'ael, I noticed he, too, seemed more tense.

"It's okay, Rik'ael. I think we're okay for now."

The pallor of his face noticeably brightened, and his shoulders slackened when I used that name. I smiled again. I felt connected to him instantly.

Shuffling as close as I dared, I slowly opened my palms out to him.

"Has someone healed you before?"

A shake of the head. Those blue eyes felt glued to me.

"Healing doesn't hurt. You will feel stronger afterwards. I will have to place my hands over the injuries, though. Is that okay?"

A long pause followed. He looked down at himself, prodding gently at the ghastly gashes, wincing here and there.

He nodded again.

I was more nervous about this than any other healing. I didn't want to frighten him. He seemed so small in that moment. I wondered if he knew his own potential strength.

"Okay, may I start now?"

A quick nod and he averted his gaze.

I tentatively scuttled right up to him, smiled nervously. As I inspected the wounds with a gentle touch, he spoke more than a single word, surprising me.

"You… you look… like me," he whispered with a weak smile. My heart could have burst. I wanted to throw myself at him and hug him forever. I didn't obviously, that would have completely freaked him out, so I smiled more broadly and nodded.

"Yes, I noticed that. It's kind of strange seeing yourself in another person's face," I said.

"I have… dreamed of… meeting you." They were weak and slow, but his words flowed, and I loved each soft syllable.

That damned tear again. I didn't dare tell him I had never known or dreamed about him, thinking it would wound him even more so. I allowed myself a little white lie.

"Me too, Rik'ael."

He smiled wide enough to reveal pearl white teeth. The mark on his face glowed ever so slightly.

"Do you use your elemental power?"

He held up his thumb and forefinger, indicating *'a little'*. This was good to know. Emboldened by this, I rubbed my hands together, ready to help him.

"May I place my hands on your chest?"

"Yes," his voice now a little stronger. He was relaxing.

As I rested both palms across the multitude of ghastly gashes and swellings, I received an unexpectedly huge energy jolt from him, only just managing to keep my hands in contact.

He must have felt it too. He released a massive sigh.

"Are you okay?" I asked.

He nodded through a groan. "Feel… better,' he breathed through the words.

"Oh, I haven't healed you yet. If you feel better though, that's good!" I smiled again, a little confused. I didn't know what that sucker punch had been. It hadn't felt good to me.

"Alright, shall we do this?" I asked.

Another nod.

Deep breath in, deep breath out, repeat.

The burn and heat travelled quickly and easily up my spine, coursing down into my arms. Closing my eyes, I curled my fingers in slightly and drew back gently at first, then more forcefully at the horrendous amount of damage. The negative energy was almost overwhelming. Nausea engulfed me immediately, yet I didn't falter. It wasn't surprising to me that my brother, a captive of Yeqon, was literally infected with his foul signature. Rik'ael groaned. I opened one eye a crack to see his head lolling to the side, mouth tight in a grimace. The intense light that had bloomed between us showed all too terribly the extent of his injuries. All manner of green and purple hues created a macabre backdrop to the fresh gashes across his torso. His face slackened; it was all too much for him. I put all I had into the healing. Minutes of personal discomfort went by as I bit back the bilious taste that burned my throat. Slowly, the nausea ebbed away, and I knew it was time to give him a rapid injection of good energy. Opening my eyes again, I couldn't suppress my smile. His skin was now beautiful, scarred, but healthy and healed. Rik'ael relaxed, the tension in his muscles gone. I sent a last pulse through his chest, making him jolt and sit upright.

Tucking my hair behind my ears, I sat patiently and watched him. He inspected himself, running his hands in awe across the golden tone of his arms and stomach. He looked at me with a somewhat suspicious expression. I smiled, but wondered at the feeling he'd given me as I'd healed him. The stomach rolling nausea was the same I'd experienced with Ben, but how? He was abused, beaten into submission, and he was my brother. It had to be that. He was a victim and his depressed energy must have reflected onto me.

"Thank you," Rik'ael's smoother, healed voice was followed by a much brighter smile.

"You're welcome, brother." Saying that word tripped something in my brain. Despite the obvious distrust he had of probably everyone, I couldn't help myself. Without warning, I flung myself into his chest and held him tight, offering my new-found sibling a lifetime's worth of hugs and love. He stiffened and didn't return it, but I held on anyway. I wanted him to know that there was something good left, despite how jaded he most certainly must be. As though the sheer force of a strong embrace could infuse him with hope and healing, I held on for as long as I could. I'm not sure he even took a breath, yet neither did he pull away. Despite the hangover of negativity that his proximity gave me, I didn't want to let go, not just for him, but for myself. It seemed so long since I'd felt security. The feeling of his warmth and innocence against my chest repaired some of the self confidence that had crumbled away. I had something else to be strong for, to fight for, and I absolutely wasn't going to surrender to fear anymore. What I would surrender to was my destiny. Finally, I released my grip and sat back. He didn't look as shocked as I'd expected. Probably shyer, to be honest.

"Sorry," I said and smiled meekly. After a moment of studying me even more intensely, he responded, his voice quiet and cautious.

"Do not be sorry." His body relaxed. There was a new sparkle in his refreshed eyes. As uncomfortable as touch must be for him, from the right person, for the right reason, I felt that he now knew it was as healing to him as it was to me.

A small, nearly-comfortable pause passed between us. I glanced between the door and Rik'ael. I was torn between imminent escape and relishing this moment with him. The stone-cold reality of this situation was rammed straight back into the forefront of my mind when I noticed that it had become very quiet outside the door. A skin-prickling silence that gave me zero comfort. It was time to fast forward this information gathering opportunity and get moving as quickly as possible.

"Do you know where our father is?" I nodded my head, encouraging him. Rik'ael squirmed a little, pulling his knees back up to his chest. My face fell with disappointment.

"Sorry, I shouldn't have asked that. I got a little over-excited about maybe finding him. You don't even know me." I looked down, embarrassed and fiddled with my necklace. I'd been too pushy, too quickly. The pressure to get away was overwhelming. I was about to reassure Rik'ael that he could keep his silence when he spoke.

"No, I can talk of him. It is just that no one has asked about him in a long time."

My mouth dropped. The sadness rolling from him made the air seem thicker. His despair felt as rich as though it were my own. I supposed it was; he was my brother, and this was our lost father we were discussing.

"I have not seen him for a long time. I cannot remember his face." He looked away into the shadows, picking habitually at the frayed wisps along the seams of his pants. I wondered on how long since he had bathed or been cared for.

"How did you get here?"

He drew himself up and edged slightly closer to me. I was surprised when he reached forward and tentatively stroked a lock of my hair that hung over my shoulder. He inspected it thoughtfully, rubbing the hair between thumb and finger as though it were something of great interest. I didn't dare move. I held my breath, as though he were an injured bird I didn't want to frighten. He let it drop, sitting back again. He spoke more fluidly, his deep voice a little child-like.

"Father and I were always moving. He told me we were looking for you, but I think he was actually hunting him." Rik'ael nodded his head towards the door and grimaced. This was good to see. There was still passion underneath all that broken-down spirit. His lips curled back, his complexion paled, as he stared at the barrier between us and them. Rik'ael was a conflicted soul, much like myself, but wholly more betrayed and wounded than I could ever imagine.

"We travelled a lot. We met scary creatures in bad places. Father paid them whatever he could for information. One day, he asked the wrong person… creature…" Rik'ael's eyes became glassy, the sparkling blue suddenly cool and resentful.

"Before we knew what was happening, the place we had been living in was attacked. I remember the smell of ashes, black eyes and… and… there was white hair." His eyes narrowed as he recalled the memory.

He was troubled by it, and so was I. Daimon seemed to have dark hair. Watchers and Eudaimonians had white.

"White hair… As in a Watcher?"

"Yes." The flash of pain in his eyes told me he already knew the answer.

"You sure it wasn't our father's hair? Perhaps you saw it in the struggle?" I asked.

"No, we kept our hair short to blend in with humans."

The inference that a Watcher was working for Yeqon was a dreadful one, yet Gedz'iel had hinted that he suspected as much. Immediately, my mind raced with the possibilities. *But who could it be?*

"That's a terrible memory. I'm sorry."

He sniffed, pulling a whole thread out and opening a new hole above his knee. The piece of cotton was well and truly suffocated inside his trembling fist.

"Yes, but not as bad as when we were brought here." Rik'ael's fingers worked more frantically now at the hole by his knee, as though ripping at the threads plucked away his unpleasant memories. I had to sit on my hands; I could barely restrain myself from reaching out to him again.

"I have not seen father since that day. I do not know what happened to him."

My heart shattered into pieces. I don't know if what they say about twins is true, but I felt every pain, anger and regret that my brother felt in that moment. I didn't have the words to comfort him, so as though having its own mind, my hand reached for his. Unsurprisingly, he pulled away as though stung by my touch.

Enough Soph, give him space! One hug at a time!

My hands remained firmly clasped in my lap from then.

"What happened to you here?" I asked as gently as I could.

"Nothing you want to know about." He looked away again. I'd asked for too much, so I left it at that.

"Is there a way out of here?"

The blue of his eyes lightened; the haze of memories seemed to lift with the change of topic.

"I tried running a few times, years ago, but as you can see, I had no success. I stopped trying because the punishment each time was too painful." He pointed to a cluster of silvery scars that marred his torso. My heart filled with guilt and rage. A new purpose blossomed; vengeance. For him, for Esme, for all who had been wronged.

My God, I sound like one of them!

"Can we do what you have tried in the past, do you think? To escape, that is?"

"I would say not. I do not know *how* to get out. I know where they leave, but not how."

"Where is that?" Hope whipped my heart a little faster.

"The standing stones at the base of the son of Tartarus. Though," his eyes lit up. "I have heard whispers that there are other ways to leave." Rik'ael looked wistful, then without warning he stood, seemed anxious, pacing back and forth.

"There is a rumour I have heard." He ran his hands through long grimy hair and paced around some more.

"The guards talk a lot. They are loyal but only through fear. If they were able, they would also escape. They whisper that there is a way out through the Pits." He stopped and stared at me; through me. The sparkle left his eyes and his shoulders fell.

"But you would not want to try that, not unless you were sure. It is a bad place, a very bad place."

"What are the Pits?" I was intrigued and stood up as well. The proverbial cup suddenly felt more half full than half empty.

"It is where the worst of the Daimon are sent for punishment along with all the bad human souls. I have seen them dig around in there for tortured spirits to create Rogues. I suppose you have not seen many Rogues?" He seemed to pale at the memory, and he glanced around for danger, a habit I noticed he did frequently. Distracted, he reached down, retrieving something from the ground. It was the crude shiv I'd made.

"I've seen my share recently," I said.

He looked up, surprised, then back to his prize. He turned the weapon over in his hands before sliding it snugly into the back of his pants.

"Are you sure it's not worth a try?" I kept him on topic as he looked around the floor some more. Perhaps he was hoping for a cache of weaponry.

"They say it is Hell down there. I think it is Hell up here. I am not sure that I am brave enough to try a worse Hell than this, not unless I really am sure it is a way out," he answered, giving up his search.

"Okay then, let's focus on the standing stones. How do we get there?"

"I do not know how to make them work."

"Don't worry about that for now. If we can get there, I'm sure I can work it out." I actually felt sure of this because of Stonehenge.

"We must escape this place. I know how to get out of the tunnels, but how we get past all the guards with you, I do not know." Rik'ael shrugged. I waved my hand at that, flinging away his doubt. My thoughts were in an excitable overdrive.

"Let me worry about that. So, you definitely know how to get from here to the stones?"

"Yes." He nodded cautiously.

"Good." I clasped my hands, cracking my knuckles to release the excited tension. I went back to the pool of water, one ear on the door, listening to make sure there were no sounds of footsteps coming our way. I glanced back at Rik, motioned for him to join me. He hesitated, wiped his hands down his pants, then settled next to me. He checked out his own reflection.

"I saw what you did when they put me in here with you."

I raised an eyebrow.

"I saw you change your face. How did you do that?" He continued to look at his own image as the slow drip of its secret source pin-pricked the quiet.

"It kind of happened by accident. The others... the people who are the same as us, do it all the time to blend, as well as to hide. I'm still working on it."

"You are good at it. You looked just like Spider."

"Like who?" I narrowed my eyes, confused.

"The one who feeds you. She also feeds me."

"Her name is Spider?"

"I don't know her name; it is just what I call her. The side of his mouth quirked up a little, like a mischievous child.

"Why do you call her that?"

He looked back into the water. "It is the way she moves. Her long arms and legs and big eyes remind me of a spider. I hate spiders."

I laughed a little.

"What?" His eyes narrowed at me, almost offended.

I raised my hands in surrender.

"Oh, you are *so* my brother! I'm terrified of spiders! One day I'll tell you about the spiders where I grew up," I giggled as I recalled the evil shed.

"You're right though. When I think about it, she is a bit spindly and creepy. Most definitely creepy!"

He smiled again and I returned the gesture.

"Sister, if you can make yourself look like Spider again, I know we can at least get out of here. She takes me everywhere he wants me to go. It is a good plan."

"Please, call me Sophia?" I asked.

"Sophia, it is a good plan."

My heart melted a little.

"Okay, then. We at least have something to start with. I'm just not sure how long I can keep the charade up. We will have to keep a quick pace once we get out. I've been practicing since Ben kidnapped me, but haven't had a chance to test how long I can maintain it."

"Ben? Who is Ben?"

"The lying scumbag who brought me here." My teeth clenched.

"Oh, you mean Nik'ael? Is that what he called himself in the other realm, Ben Scumbag?"

I nearly choked back a giggle. He seemed so innocent.

"Yes!" I quickly regained my composure and realised how profoundly weird it was that he knew Ben.

"You know him?"

"A long time."

"How do you know him? I mean, did he hurt you, too?"

"No! He protected me from Yeqon. He was my only friend. I wish he had not left us."

To say I was shocked was the absolute least. My betrayer was my brother's saviour, of sorts.

"What do you mean by that? How did he protect you?"

"Nik'ael would distract him so I was beaten less. He brought me things from the other realms to play with. He hid them for me. He was like a brother."

I bit down on a rage that was emerging for a very different reason. How dare Ben have that with my brother? How dare he ingratiate himself into his wretched world and leave my brother remembering him so fondly, whilst I was left feeling gutted. I was fuming with betrayal and jealousy. He must have noticed.

"You are not friends?"

"No. We are not!"

He left it at that. He was not as pushy as I was, and right then, I appreciated it.

I pointed back to the pool of water. A singular drop of water rippled the surface.

"I'll change to look like Spider then, okay?" I nodded at him, making sure he was listening. He nodded back.

"We just need to make sure that next time she turns up that we can knock her out long enough to get out. I'm pretty sure we can manage that between the two of us, as long as she is alone." *Cut me some slack for once, I'el,* I thought quickly.

"Will it take long to get out of here? Are we far from the entrance?" I asked as I waited for the water to settle back to stillness.

"It is not far. We cannot rush, though. Spider never hurries. You must look like you are taking me somewhere. You will need to hold me by my hair and push me."

"She sounds nice!" I grimaced.

"She is not nice!" His eyebrows were tight, his face paler again.

"Okay then. We knock her out. I do what you say and you guide us out? Right?"

His sparkle returned, those eyes brightened a few shades, his complexion pinked up. My brother was excited, hopeful even. It was infectious and my pulse quickened. We had a chance, as long as no one else came in before Spider. *Did you hear that I'el?*

I edged as close as I could to the red beams and listened. Silence.

"If we do this, we do it now and wait. Hopefully she'll be back soon and we can get out of here," I said, kneeling back at the water. Rik joined me, hanging on my every move.

I looked deep into the blackness of the liquid and hoped to hell that this would work.

Deep breath in, deep breath out, repeat.

Closing my eyes, I imagined Spider but was immediately interrupted by Rik, my concentration lost.

"Will you teach me how to do this, if we are successful and escape?"

"Rik, if we get outta here, I'll teach you everything. There's a beauty out there that will take your breath away." I patted his hand softly; he didn't pull away.

His eyes cooled, becoming distant for the briefest time before he responded, his face lighting up again.

"I want to have what you have too," he said. The smile drained from his eyes. A little taken aback by his strange reaction, it took a few moments to relax again, finding the E'lan and drawing it in. Rolling my palm over the soul stone brought the energy flooding back. Tingling goose bumps coursed up my arms and into the back of my neck.

I let my body relax and continued to chat with him.

"Can you use any of your powers?" I asked in a sleepy tone.

"Not really, I have had no one to teach me," he answered. Again, there was an edge to the statement that was unsettling, but I remained in my moment of calm and my heart beat in sync with the energy.

"I set Asbel's hair on fire once. He scared me so much that lightning came out of my hand by accident."

He giggled and I heard him do the same. I cracked one eye, saw his smile was once more a boyish one.

"I wish I'd seen that. Well, at least we know it's in there somewhere. Keep an ear on that door. Koi will teach you as he did me."

"Koi?"

"The best teacher you could ask for, now watch that door, I'm about to change."

Eyes tight, breath held, the E'lan had reached its peak. Every cell in my body burned. I breathed out slowly, Spider's face solidly plastered in my mind.

A shiver washed through me. My muscles contracted and relaxed numerous times until a stillness returned. It wasn't painful, but I'd liken it to getting the drill at the dentist. Even when you're numb, it's still wholeheartedly disgusting, but the ends justified the means.

I felt lighter, like I might float away. My hands patted over my face and chest. Taught skin and high cheekbones, protruding ribs and dry skin. I leaned forward to see the results of my efforts. The watery mirror rewarded me with the image of a skin and bone Afflicted woman, complete with Spider's hazy grey eyes, sallow complexion and sparse unkempt silvery hair.

"What magic you do!" Rik sidled closer. He placed his hand on my cheek and I felt the excitement in his heart.

"Well, what do you think?" My voice was a thin, unsettling murmur.

"I want to do that too!" Rik'ael's face was alight with awe.

"Well, you will one day too, Rik." I put my hand on his and smiled with my strange new mouth.

Rik and I mulled for hours over the best way to overcome Spider. There were many unanswered *what ifs?'*

What if she arrives with another?

What if she doesn't return?

What if Yeqon is the one to come for me?

What if we both just panic and freeze?

I sighed, bony hands under my chin.

"Well, it is what it is, and we have no choice but to deal with whatever comes through that door." I found my strange voice disconcerting.

"And that could be anything," Rik'ael replied ominously.

"By now brother, I realise that is a distinct and likely possibility." The scrolls had been unusually active since I concealed myself as Spider. They tingled and sparked against my legs. I moved frequently to gain some comfort.

Are you trying to get my attention? As I wriggled in, Rik questioned me.

"Is something worrying you, sister?"

"Please call me Sophia. Do you mind if I call you Rik?"

He nodded, "That is fine."

"Are you alright, Sophia?"

"That's better," I smiled, "And no, nothing's wrong. It's just..." The scrolls were burning my leg now. I wriggled a little more.

"What is it?" Rik's head tilted in question.

Without thinking, I unbuttoned the pocket and pulled the two scrolls gently out. They crackled in my palm like static filled laundry. I showed Rik and quickly explained what they were.

His face darkened as he studied the curled-up parchments.

I suddenly felt stupidly exposed.

"This is what he wants?" Rik asked after a very uncomfortable silence. He licked and bit his lower lip. The pulse in his neck stretched the little spot of skin in and out. He glowered at me. The air was thicker, the joy of reunion suddenly squashed.

"Are you going to answer my question, Sophia?"

"Ah, well I..."

It occurred to me in an instant that I didn't know him at all. Not a thing about him, other than the coincidental fact that we shared genes. I worried with an intense immediacy that I might have already said too much, so I tried to give him something but nothing at once.

"We haven't found everything yet. We don't know the answers and these are just meaningless words from a long dead person I know nothing about." I rolled the scrolls tight and went to put them back in my pocket. Rik lunged forward and snatched them from me, his face aglow, brighter than ever.

"What are you doing?" My reflexes were pathetically ineffectual as he dashed away, turning the scrolls about as though they were the Holy Grail.

"Give them back. Yeqon doesn't know I've got them."

"You said they were meaningless, so why does it matter if he knows?"

My pulse hammered in panic. What was he doing?

"Give them back!" I demanded.

He held them aloft as I reached for them, his height eclipsed mine. I could barely reach his hand.

"What are you doing? They could help us; they could help you."

His eyes seemed suddenly greedy. He pushed me back.

"This piece of rubbish is what has kept me here and you have it hidden inside your clothing?" His voice was stronger, his words more purposeful.

The accusation stung.

"I …" I was taken aback by the sudden and aggressive change in his behaviour. His tone was darker. Rik held the scrolls cautiously by the tips of his fingers, as though they were both life and death to him. Pushing past me, he paced, tapping them against his forehead, eyebrows tightly knit; he mumbled incoherently to himself.

He reminded me of a broody Ben. That reminded me of Ben's deception, and that thought sent chills through me. If someone I'd known most of my life could deceive me, what of someone I'd met mere hours ago? It was then that I realised with horror that despite the genetic connection, Rik had no loyalty to me, he owed me nothing.

"Rik, you're scaring me. Please give them back?" I was so worried by this erratic behaviour that I drew some heat into my hand, ready for anything, now choosing my thoughts and words more carefully. As though the tension in the cell permeated through the walls, the howls from the other prisoners reignited, only adding to the anxiety I was suffocating under.

Rik's face darkened by the second. The insidious glow from the cell beams cast deeper shadows across his scarred torso. Shadows highlighted the curves and depths of his strong musculature, and I worried if he really did know how strong he actually was.

I felt sick. I felt threatened. I felt that same confusion with him that seemed to plague me of late. He turned away from me, revealing the fern pattern across his spine that blossomed with a million scars from unimaginable tortures. His energy glowed from within, the little slits along his spine lit up, hinting that his wings were there and wanting release. The scrolls crackled in the now tight grip he coveted them in. His head fell back. I froze as he drew in a breath and let out the most heart-wrenching scream that silenced all those outside. The sound was desperate, destitute in its heartache and depth.

My eyes welled with both apprehension and compassion. I felt his pain, his anger, and betrayal. My guts churned with the overwhelming hurt. Normally, the usual good old Soph would rush to the side of someone in so much angst, but I took a self-preserving step back this time. Something primal told me that this was something to keep at a distance.

My pendant hummed approvingly with this decision and I grabbed it for reassurance.

The earth rumbled as though joining Rik in his emotional eruption. Debris rained down on us as he calmed to silence, letting his shoulders slump and his arms relax by his sides. He stood in silence for some time whilst I waited, ready for anything. The light glimmering from his back died down and the tension in the room seemed to settle a little.

His left arm raised up as he held the two scrolls out. His voice remained flat and cold.

"You sit here with these?" His fist crunched into the delicate artefacts, making me wince. I didn't think to photocopy them!

"I've lived a thousand deaths at his hands, and you have what he wants right under my nose?" Rik turned slowly. I retreated into the darkest shadows, palm hot and still at the ready. I didn't want to hurt him, but I would if I had to.

Rik's eyes blazed, not like a Daimon's, but like a man at odds with whether to kill or show mercy.

"Rik, they're just… it's more than those scrolls. They are mere clues yet to be deciphered. I'm so sorry, Rik, for all that you've endured."

"Don't call me that!" he snapped

"Sorry?"

The howling had recommenced outside as the ground shuddered with another tremor. Boiling steam vents spewed from the roof and a faster trickle of water ran into the pool, spoiling its smoothness.

"My name is Boy."

My heart cracked, "No! No, it isn't! That's what that monster calls you. You're not his, no matter what has happened. You're one of us. You're my brother. Please see that?"

His eyes were red, lower lids heavy with moisture.

He held the scrolls out, pointing them at me.

"What I see, is that my sister…" his lips trembled, "My sister has what could set me free! Why did you not give this to him?" He waved them about. A diamond tear trickled down his cheek. A tear of the betrayal he felt.

For reasons I still cannot explain, I stepped out of the shadows and knelt down in front of him, under the scrolls that he still pointed accusingly at me. I lowered my head and raised my palms up to him.

"Forgive me brother. Please forgive me for the life I have led and for the one you have endured?" I was at his absolute mercy, felt like I owed him that.

Tension rose again and I had to fight my instincts to back off. The pedant rebelled against my decision and buzzed more furiously. The soul stone burned in warning as I felt a wet droplet hit the back of my hand and then a thud in front of me. Only then did I look up. Rik kneeled in front of me, tears streaming down his face. I finally let the power pulsing along my arms dissipate and my hands fall to my sides.

Reaching tentatively, I wiped his tears away with a gentle sweep of my fingers.

Pointing at the scrolls still in his hand, I spoke softly.

"Those won't help you, brother. They merely sent me in the right direction. You saw yourself that he wants the secret of the chest, and I don't have that. Not yet." I implored him to believe me.

Rik threw the scrolls at my knees; he leaned into my hand that continued to wipe away his desperate tears. I quickly scooped the scrolls, shoving them into my pocket, immensely relieved.

"I wasn't hiding anything from you, I promise," I soothed, although I secretly thought that perhaps I should have kept more to myself than I had.

He reached up, wiping his own face clear with the back of his hand, sniffing and clearing his eyes.

"You have lived a good life?" he asked.

"Until recently, yes. A very good one."

He thought on this a while. The guilt I felt was almost unbearable.

"Good. At least one of us can have a clear head then, to do what needs to be done."

I tilted my head in question.

"What's that?"

He moved forward, and I stiffened, calling on my power to be on standby again.

Instead of what I was fearing, he took my hand in his and attempted to kiss away the car crash of emotions swirling across his face. His beautiful blue eyes sparkled beneath the moisture that still besieged them.

"I wish to escape this place, to descend Yeqon into the deepest pits of Tartarus where he deserves to suffer eternally."

Rik growled, and he pulled me into his trembling chest. He hugged me hard and desperately, so close that we seemed inseparable.

This amazing connection lasted a mere few seconds. A deep bang outside, followed by a gurgled scream, pulled us apart. We recoiled from each other, startled. Rik backed away into the shadows, my shiv in his hand. I hid to the side of the door, waiting, hoping my concealment lasted. Footsteps moved back and forth. Metal ground against metal as someone yanked noisily at the locks. The red beams of energy sealing us in the cell disappeared with a snap.

I beckoned Rik forward with my pale arms, needing him to be ready.

"Quick," I called in a husky whisper. I could smell the salty sweat of fear on him. Instinct at least seemed to switch on his under-utilised energy; his mark glowed in faint sputters.

He took up a position on the opposite side of the door, the shiv glancing from one palm to the other. He played with that weapon in a way that told me he was perhaps more than he seemed, as was everyone in my life. My face and hands lit on fire, ready to attack. The veins in my arms glowed like rivers of light as they brought forth the energy to the centre of my palms.

I was ready. The door creaked open just a smidge, not enough to see who was entering. There was whispered arguing, then the door pulled shut again with a thud. The bolt slid back into place and the evil red beams shot back down. I only just got out of the way before having an ear singed off. Surprised, I edged as close as I dared to the pulsing bars, and put my ear near the door.

"Not now. He wants her at sunrise," a gruff voice barked, followed by the crash of something clattering to the ground.

"But…" it was Spider's surprised voice.

"Do not second-guess me, pig. You will leave her until morning. She is not to be fed again. Tend to the other prisoners until then. Bring her no later than when the sun sits upon the horizon, or you shall suffer as she will. It is midnight. Go to Lilith. She is thirsty. You look plenty full enough to keep her sated a while longer."

There was a smug laugh, followed by hollering and hooting of the other prisoners. Footsteps faded, and we were alone again. That didn't instil much hope in me, but at least now I had an idea of when someone would come for me, and it seemed that it would be Spider at dawn. I would, we would, be prepared.

"Sister, what is it?"

"They will be back at sunrise." I sat back down, letting myself relax back into the real me.

"We wait all night, then?"

"Yes brother. We wait."

Twenty-Six

az shadowed Kea and Dash as they surveyed down the slope of the ruins for danger.

The slumbering town of Nevşehir remained blanketed in a heavy, putrid fog. Its cumulus tendrils now lapped the base of the ruins.

"See anything, Dash?" Kea whispered over Jaz' shoulder.

"No, but it's the calm before the storm. Agreed?" Dash said.

"Agreed. I can barely open my mouth for the stink. The Rogues must be in the town now. How you going, kid?" Kea looked down at Jaz, who also covered her nose from the foul smell.

"Those things need to stay frigging dead," Jaz coughed through the last word, choking on the freezing but foul air.

"I wish Jude would give us an update about what's going on down there. Look!" Dash pointed towards the bottom of the hill where the buildings were completely shrouded. Kea and Jaz followed his line of sight.

"Shit, this isn't how I was planning my night." The smooth metallic ring of Kea's sword being drawn had Jaz' eyes wider with anxiety.

"What's that supposed to mean?" Jaz peered further over the ledge, not seeing what their sharper eyes saw. Her hands played nervously with the clip that secured Sophia's diamond dagger.

"It means do as your told, kid, or you'll be a midnight snack for a Rogue!" Kea rolled her eyes in frustration. "Sorry, Jaz. I shouldn't have said that. Just nerves, Hon." Kea patted Jaz on the back.

Jaz waved her off.

"I've heard worse. I wouldn't have thought you guys would get nervous though, with all the power and stuff." Jaz flicked the black and white strands of her scruffy fringe out of her eyes. A feistier breeze picked up, dusting them with a soft fall of snow.

"Believe me, kid, I never feel warm and fuzzy before a battle. Besides, I've got you to look after. Jude would literally ascend me if you got hurt!"

Jaz scrunched her brows, narrowed her eyes.

"Why the hell would Freak-boy care?"

"To be perfectly honest, I'm not actually sure with the way you speak to him." Kea tucked Jaz behind her as they moved cautiously along the crumbling ledge, carefully stepping over gaps underfoot.

"The fact is, kid, he cares. We all do. Jude's really a teddy bear under all those weapons and snide remarks. Kind of like you!" Kea chuckled to herself, "Isn't that true, Dash?"

"He was nice to me once, I think?" Dash smirked, winking at Jaz who he shadowed closely. They reached the edge of the only intact turret and stopped.

"A teddy bear? More like a freaking grizzly bear!" Jaz stopped, sandwiched snuggly between the two Watchers as they tracked murky shadows slinking through the town below.

"You just haven't got to know his warm and squishy side yet," Kea said, and motioned for Jaz to kneel, out of view.

"I'm happy *not* to know!" Jaz muttered as she squatted, noticing her bracelet for the first time in a while. She fidgeted with it.

"C'mon, Soph. Find your way back," Jaz sighed as her thumb rolled over the small wedge of white stone. A loud bang made her jump. Almost falling backwards off the ledge, Jaz only just regained her balance when she caught the back of Kea's armour. Jaz gasped with the shock and peered back over the ledge. She couldn't see anything.

Feeling a hand on her head, Jaz resisted with futile cursing whilst Kea shoved her down again.

"Don't move, kid, I mean it!" Kea lifted her sword. The steely ping of Dash doing the same had Jaz' heart racing and her hand back over the hidden dagger on her hip. As the moon hung high in the sky, Jaz glimpsed her elongated reflection in Kea's sword. She shook her head, prodding her face as though trying to convince herself she wasn't dreaming.

"Dash, over there!" Kea pointed with her sword. They looked down across to the east of the town.

A neon blue glow illuminated across the flat-roofed buildings. A solid beam of blue and white light shot up towards the heavens. It stretched out long and thin, then snapped back on itself. It disappeared in a nanosecond of brightness. Shouts ensued in the distance but quickly stopped. Discomforting silence hung in the air.

"Oh no!" Kea gasped.

"This is not a good sign, Kea." Dash flipped his sword, the silver of it flashed in Jaz' face. His mark burned brightly.

"What? What's going on?" Jaz asked, panic edged her tone up a notch. She scrambled to stand, but Kea shoved her back out of sight.

"Someone has ascended," explained Dash. He swiped his free hand across his iridescent mark, raised his palm to the sky. Kea repeated the reverent gesture.

Frustration and fear in her voice, Jaz forced her way back up, swatting away Kea's hand, taking advantage of the Watcher's moment of distraction.

"What's that supposed to mean?" Jaz' nose poked over the ledge of the turret. Waning moonlight struck paleness across Jaz' already pasty skin. Her mouth dropped silently as she took in the scene below. Multitudes of sloth-like shadows coalesced all over the town. The decomposing stench thickened, rich and putrid. Dark shapes slithered through the streets and alleyways, and that was just in the areas that the Watchers could see.

"Ascending, Jaz, is when a Watcher or hybrid has had their mortal body destroyed by one of those Rogues lurking down there. Their soul has been forced to ascend to their original essence… or, in human terms, they die," Dash answered solemnly.

"Well fuck!" Jaz pushed back from the edge, bumping into Dash. His arm cocooned her, and she sunk gratefully into it.

"I don't want to see those things again," Jaz said.

"I know, kid, but one of us has been attacked which means that we are probably outnumbered down there. We have to help them." Kea looked at Jaz with a grim, sorrowful expression.

"Shit, no!" Jaz' eyes bulged; she paled impossibly whiter.

"What if it was Sophia down there?" Dash asked.

Jaz' expression changed; her cheeks now flushed with anger. "Well, that's different. She's my best friend." Her hand tightened on Dash's arm. She pulled herself up to peer back over the ledge.

"And are they not our friends and family?" Kea asked. "Not to mention the innocent local population unknowingly in bed and at risk. Sophia, in fact, has more chance of saving herself than most of us. One of us has been overwhelmed, which is highly unusual. Rogues are generally unable to fight with any level of sophistication. If there are Rogues down there that have the slightest ability to plan and work as a team, then our warriors will definitely need our help, Jaz. Every one that we lose leaves us at a disadvantage. Daimon relentlessly churn out Rogues, but we can't replenish Watchers or hybrids the same way. We can't return once we've ascended, just like humans. So, every mortal life, both human and A'vean, is precious. Until we unlock this portal, wherever it is, we don't get to see our loved ones and friends again in this realm," Kea explained.

Jaz sighed, "Well, when you put it like that, I sound like a cold-hearted bitch."

"No, you just don't see the world as we do. Now you can," Kea said, grabbed Jaz' hand and motioned for them to retreat down from the parapet.

Another huge explosion sent tremors up the hill, crumbling the outer edges of the fortress. The three of them held tight as the Citadel rocked under the impact.

There were distant cries of panic and confusion as the townsfolk awoke. They began emerging from their homes to see what all the noise was about.

"Damn it! Now we will *have* to look after the locals as well!" Kea was uncharacteristically sharp and frustrated.

"As if we don't have enough to worry about. You'd think they're doing this on purpose." Dash rammed the tip of his sword into the rubble as they crept along the edge of the ruins.

"I think you're right. They're trying to keep us busy, out of the way. Rogues shouldn't be here, or anywhere, for that matter. There's nothing in this town for them. Something is going down. I bet it's because Koi and the others are causing a whole lot of crap for Yeqon in the Empyrean realm. They've probably broken through. These bastards are here to keep reinforcements away." Kea stopped, held up a hand for them to halt. She listened for anything swarming through the thick fog they were now enveloped in.

"Why don't you guys just go blow up some shit and be done with those filthy things?" Jaz asked. "Seems simple."

Kea smiled.

"Anywhere else, kid, and I'd happily *'blow some shit up'*, but our mandate remains that we cause no harm to humans. We serve and protect them as discretely as possible. You should know by now that we can't use our full power near them unless absolutely necessary. It's lethal to them." Kea peered around a corner, snapping quickly back. "Only I'el knows how *you* survived that transfer with just that scar to your hair. We all thought you were a goner." Kea flicked Jaz' white bangs. "The more elemental power we use in the open, the more we attract the enemy, as well. Not really what we want, kid. Less is more, as they say." Kea's smile waned as the fog thickened further. She coughed into her elbow.

Jaz tugged at the white strands of her hair and shoved them behind her ears. She ducked as another explosion vibrated the ruins. This time, three orange lights flashed across the sky.

"Rogues this time," Dash answered Kea's concerned expression.

"Thank I'el for that!" Kea said as she guided Jaz to the lowest ledge. She jumped back to the ground elegantly, almost floating. She reached up for Jaz, encouraging her to jump. Jaz hesitated.

"Come on, Jaz… hurry!" Kea waved impatiently at her.

Jaz stared at the ground, which looked a long way down. She bit her lip, smelled the vile stench of the air; she remembered the Rogue she decapitated as the fog climbed ever closer.

"Fuck me…" Jaz cuddled her arms into her chest and jumped, landing snuggly in Kea's arms.

"Wasn't so bad?" Kea set her down.

"Too easy," Jaz lied, still shaking.

Dash joined quickly after and they made their way out of the heart of the ruins. Thick, elderly trees took on a menacing presence with the skirt of fog around their trunks. A haven of shadows for all things sinister. Jaz walked twice the pace to keep up with Kea, her eyes wide, body shivering and ready for literally anything.

"Seems kinda crap. You've got all this power you can't use!" Jaz muttered, one hand on her belt, one reaching for a fistful of Kea's shirt, only to slide across Kea's armoured chest plate.

"Here," Kea said and reached out her hand. Jaz took it gratefully.

"We use plenty of power, kid. It's just not all about lightning bolts. Now, keep that motor mouth quiet for a bit, okay?"

Jaz grimaced, but nodded and clamped her mouth into a thin line.

"I'll head towards the bridge at the town entrance. You go that way." Dash pointed to where the first explosion had occurred. Kea nodded.

"I'll hunt down Jude," Dash said and drew a curved dagger into his other hand, the moonlight giving it a magical, silver glow. "Meet up back here when we're done?" he asked.

Kea nodded, her mark glowed faintly, and they shared a K'ufili.

"Take extra care, Kea. Eilir would miss you too much," Dash said and disappeared into the pea soup.

Jaz chattered with cold as Kea drew her quickly along, their bodies swallowed by the stinking mist. Jaz held her breath, covered her nose, knew that smell all too well; pungent decomposing flesh…dead things.

A haunted moor would have felt more welcoming. Jaz placed her footfalls carefully behind Kea's as they neared the town below. Muffled groans, thuds and the odd scream punctuated the night's pained silence. Small explosions broke that quiet every few minutes. So far, it had been several orange flashes lighting the sky. This reassured Jaz that yet another Rogue was toasted, but she shadowed Kea as close as she could.

A rush of air had Jaz jump right into Kea's side. Kea's arm enveloped her. They paused as dark shadows moved in the mist. Sailing by like ghost ships bobbing on a dead sea. Jaz held her breath, worried the mere act of breathing would give them away.

Kea whispered into Jaz' ear.

"Don't move. Don't make a sound. They aren't looking for you. They're sniffing out *us*. I've turned my switch off, so we will be okay if we stay very still and very quiet," Kea said and held her sword front and centre, just in case. Her dagger was hidden flat against Jaz' back, pressed into her thick winter coat.

Gurgling breaths, sucking phlegm and oozing fluids bubbled mere feet away. *Thud, ker-thud.* Mangled limbs dragged across the frozen ground. One shadow deepened into focus; way too close. So near that its undead breaths plumed through the fog, ragged and putrid. It paused, sniffed at the air, and turned in their direction. Kea's arm started to slide out from behind Jaz as the Rogue took a step forward. Its shape sharpened, yet its features remained hazy. Jaz swallowed back a silent retch at the smell.

Kea gripped her tighter. "Shh." Her breath warm and reassuring as Jaz' eyes glued to the creature. Kea placed her dagger-clad hand across Jaz' chattering teeth, the smallest sound needing to be extinguished.

The fearsome shape was joined by four more. Misty silhouettes of dread. Collectively, they sniffed the air. Wet snorts, grunting between themselves as though communicating like pack animals. The two women remained statue still.

Something touched the back of Jaz' knee and she let out an involuntary yelp of fear. The Rogues hesitated, sniffed the air more noisily, then all five shadows slunk towards them. Jaz attempted to run, but Kea held her firm.

"Don't … move… a muscle," she whispered again. Jaz bit her quivering lip behind Kea's palm. She tasted blood. Tears froze on her lashes, her eyes burned with fear.

The creatures took terrifying, detailed shape, emerging within a foot of them. Three women and two men. Not one had all of their body parts. All were naked and frostbitten, or rotten, or both. They gurgled and cocked their heads as they considered their next move. One leaned in, taking a particularly long sniff of Kea, her mouth drooping lopsidedly. Black drool spilled down her chest. Something bumped into Jaz again and then zoomed out from behind her. As quick as a flash, a small fallow deer ran for its life, the movement taking the Rogues with it, heady for a chase.

Only after the Rogues had dragged themselves after the poor creature, did Jaz lean forward to her knees to catch her breath, to stave off the wave of dizziness threatening to drag her to unconsciousness.

"What the fuck, Kea?" Jaz gasped.

"They weren't after us. We weren't bleeding, I had my energy hidden. They're looking for energised Watchers or injured things to feed on. That poor deer was hurt. They were sniffing him out, not us."

Jaz swallowed the blood. "Well, you coulda told me they weren't after us!" Jaz glared at Kea, then regretted it. "Sorry, Kea, thanks."

"You're welcome. Come on, kid. Let's keep moving. If we run into anything else, just keep a lid on it, okay?"

Jaz nodded, happy to comply.

The unpleasant yelps and clanging of combat increased. It was now mixed with the confused cries of locals emerging onto the main street of Nevşehir. A lone man stood in the middle of the street, rugged in a heavy coat and boots. He craned his neck, trying to find the source of disturbance. A few others called out from their doorways further down, looking for reassurance.

With a finger pressed to her lips, Kea tucked Jaz behind her once more and slunk silently up behind the man who continued to look this way and that, shovel in hand, ready for trouble. As she approached, Kea reached her hand down, in line with the man's skull. She pulsed a soft, white light into the base of his head. He slumped immediately. Kea caught him before he hit the ground.

With fluid motion, Kea hoisted the slumbering body over her shoulder. Jaz' expression a hybrid of surprise and hero worship.

"What can't you do?"

"A lot, kid. A lot. Now, I just have to find him a safe place to sleep it off," Kea answered as she ducked down a quiet alley lit by a sub-adequate single globe.

A freshly painted door attracted Kea's attention, and after peering through the windows and listening intently at the door, she had Jaz unlatch it. They walked into darkness. A small bed lay fully made under one of four fogged out windows. With the skill of a mother tucking a newborn to bed, Kea settled the stocky man in.

"Right, this one's safe for now. He'll sleep till morning. Come on, stick close." Kea guided Jaz back out and locked the door.

Sidling along the buildings, hugging tight to the shadows, Kea brandished her sword out front, her other hand still behind Jaz, keeping her safely in place. Jaz hesitated a few times as that familiar gurgling sound echoed in the streets nearby.

"You have a plan, don't you?" Jaz asked.

"Nope. Only to keep anyone in danger safe and take out whatever comes our way until we find the others."

"It's the *'whatever'* I'm worried about! Can't you like, talk in your head to them and find out where they are?"

"In normal circumstances, yes, but it's all a bit garbled like static at the moment. Everyone is talking at once. But I can hear that Jude isn't too far down there." Kea pointed across the main street, still studded with locals, who nervously peered outside their doors.

"He's somewhere down one of those alleyways, and up there," Kea pointed towards the top of town. "There's a couple of squads moving down this way. So, whatever is left should hopefully be cut off in both directions." She flashed a reassuring smile at Jaz.

They made their way through a number of small alleys that turned off the main street, not coming across any of their companions.

"In there." Kea pointed to a recessed doorway lit by a small sliver of moonlight.

She turned Jaz around, unclipped the pouch that sat just behind her right hip.

"I know Jude doesn't trust you with anything sharper than your fists yet, but this situation calls for breaking the rules." Kea turned Jaz back around.

"Here. Only if you really need it, okay?" Kea's deep blue eyes pierced Jaz'.

The glass-like dagger glittered in Jaz' palm, her eyes dazzled by the sight. She turned it over a couple of times, admiring its lethal edge. She touched the tip, drawing a small drop of blood on her finger tip.

Kea groaned inwardly; grabbed Jaz' wrist, "Bloody hell Jaz! It's not a toy. Don't do that! You want a Rogue to sniff you out? They're like blood hounds, literally!" Kea whispered angrily. She quickly cauterised the small droplet of blood away with the lightest pulse of light from her palm.

"Sorry!" Jaz clenched her jaw, annoyed with herself.

"Walk with it pointed to the ground so you don't stab yourself!" Kea pointed Jaz' dagger-wielding hand towards the ground.

"Me and this baby will be just…"

Kea shushed Jaz, tipped her head side to side, listening.

Another explosion, they both ducked.

Kea motioned for Jaz to run across the street to the adjacent alley.

"Jude is close; back over there. I can hear him now. The Rogues are retreating out of town. He wants us to meet him so we can make sure all the locals are safe, then get straight back to Kymakli. Lorcan is meeting us back at the sanctuary. That's either a good or bad sign."

"Why?" Jaz asked, holding the dagger with two hands now.

"Either he's found Soph, or something is going down back there. Let's go, kid."

Jaz nodded, mouth thin, courage a little thicker as the dagger warmed in her palms. Her nerves felt dulled by its exquisite deadliness.

Still curtained in the now dissipating fog, they made their way across the street, spotting a local closing their front door, their curiosity satisfied. Two unmoving shadows formed at the corner they were heading towards.

"Heads up, kid, and keep that handy," Kea eyed the dagger. "Don't react, unless I say so."

As they approached, Kea breathed out in relief. "Thank I'el. It's one of our own."

No sooner had the words been uttered, one of the shadows slumped heavily to the ground. An anguished cry followed.

"No!"

The sound of weapons clattering to the ground had the two of them cross the rest of the distance at a sprint.

Just inside a tight, rubbish-strewn alley, Thomas knelt across Kristen, his hands stemming a gush of blood from her neck. He looked up to Kea, eyes red and streaming.

"Please, help me!"

Kea ran a glowing palm across Kristen's punctured neck. The bite marks were deep. Long gashes that had luckily stopped just short of her windpipe. Her cheeks were flayed, her arms covered in fresh defensive wounds. She was still, her lips a dusky blue.

Jaz was instantly in nurse mode, clearing Kristen's airway, helping where she could, as Kea attended to the mortal neck wound.

"Give me your shirt, Thomas." Jaz held her hand out. He pulled it off without question from under his blood-soaked japara. Using the diamond blade, Jaz ripped the shirt into makeshift bandages and wound them around the wounds on Kristen's arms, stemming the non-lethal bleeding as best she could. Kea's energy sealed off the neck haemorrhage. Jaz felt Kristen's pulse. It was rapid and thready. Jaz bit her lip, knowing this wasn't good.

"Will she be okay?" A sobbing Thomas asked.

"I hope so, honey. She's lost a lot of blood. What happened?" Kea pulsed a little brighter, Kristen's neck muscles glistened as they knit together to seal the worst of the bleeding.

"We were tailing Jude at the base of the fortress hill. The Rogues were gathering there," Thomas sniffed, wiped his eyes. "Dash arrived and both he and Jude drove them down towards the town perimeter. We stayed with Xavier and Am'iel to keep the locals safe. The fog was receding; we must have felt too safe, let our guards down when a deer ran past us, tripping up Kristen." Thomas clutched Kristen's hand. "It was followed by four or five Rogues that came out of nowhere. I don't think they would have bothered us, but Xavier was bleeding. They must have smelt his blood. It was a frenzy. Am'iel tried to protect us all, but they jumped on her at once and… it's too horrible to tell. She didn't make it," Thomas cried and lowered his head; his tears fell onto Kristen's hand.

Kea bowed her head. "Oh no," she sighed deeply. "Am'iel was a trusted friend."

Thomas looked back up. Anger dried his tears, reddened his eyes more deeply.

"We chased them down through the streets, taking out three. One ran off by itself, the other was determined to fight. I swear it didn't matter how many arrows we put in it, it just kept coming at us." Thomas' face hardened, yet his lips betrayed his distress. "We ran out of arrows; we only had our daggers. I don't know how we were overcome by just one. It jumped onto Kristen. Oh, Mon Dieu, I've failed her!" He held her limp hand to his cheek.

"Forgive me, sister." Fresh tears spilled.

Kea, having stemmed all the bleeding, placed her hand over Kristen's head and heart and injected a series of light bursts into her body. Kristen flinched with each pulse, yet remained unconscious. Kea then put a hand on Thomas's shoulder.

"She's stable for now. We need to get her to Enl'iel and the Alchemae immediately. You've done well, Thomas." Her voice was hypnotic, soothing, like an angel.

"I've called for Jude and he's on his way. The Rogues seem to have gone now," she said.

Kea carefully scooped Kristen into her arms. She looked back down at Thomas.

"Try to retrieve your weapons, if you can," Kea said.

"C'mon, I'll help you," Jaz offered Thomas a hand up.

"Merci, mon ange. You are a true friend." He took Jaz' hand, wiping his nose on his coat as heavy footsteps sounded nearby.

"It's just the others," Kea reassured them both as Jude rounded the corner, taking in the situation within seconds. He was splattered in blood, nostrils flaring; a low grumble of displeasure escaped his tight mouth. Sheathing his weapons, he wiped his hands clean against his pants, shaking his head.

"This is not good." Jude rested his hand over Kristen's heart.

"She is weak. You'll need to transfer with her, Kea. She's too ill to wait. Here," Jude placed a luminous palm under Kristen's slack head.

"She's in the deepest sleep possible now; it should protect her," he said.

"Thanks. You got these guys?" She nodded towards Thomas and Jaz.

He narrowed his eyes at Jaz, slapping a palm on Thomas' shoulder with a nod.

"Both of you, close your eyes," he ordered.

"Get going, Kea. Return immediately, I want as many eyes and ears for the journey back with this lot." Jude pointed to everyone milling behind. Kea nodded.

Kea transferred quickly. Jaz peeked through her fingers, curiosity getting the better of her. The radiant flash was startling, leaving her blinking for minutes. Jude checked her over quickly, grumbling deep in his chest.

"Don't you *ever* listen?" he snapped. Jaz wiped the remaining sting from her eyes, trying, but failing, to stare indignantly back at him.

"Lucky it wasn't you," Jude grumbled, eyes roaming over her for evidence of further injury. The rest of the warriors gathered in the alley, in shock about the unexpected affray.

One followed Thomas to help him retrieve the precious chromious arrows. Jaz tried to help. Jude pulled her back, tipped her face up to his.

"Since it's impossible for you to obey even the simplest order, you will stay with me." He turned her towards the main street. They left the alley, Jaz compliant, still in a little shock. The street cleared of the Rogue fog quickly. The pre-dawn air was crisp and clean, as though nothing unearthly had just swarmed through it at all. Piles of glowing orange ashes dotted the streetscape though. Two diamond skeletons were amongst them.

Jude made his way to them, looked at the remains, and shook his head. He burned them into a glittery ash, then pulled a small satchel from his belt.

Kneeling, a delicate light emanated from his palm. Jaz watched on, intrigued. His power lifted the ashes into a swirling column. When every last molecule was retrieved from the icy road, Jude's gentle hand guided the floating remains into the pouch. The angelic skeletons that had lain there were now tucked away within the safety of Jude's armoured bulk.

Jaz only then realised that Jude had been wounded. Deep scratches gouged across his chest; blood crusted in the grooves of his abdomen.

"You're hurt," she said.

"Not as much as Am'iel and Ty'rael," Jude snapped.

"Fine, if you don't want me to give a damn, I won't."

"I don't care what you give. I care about my family." Jude's eyes were icy. Jaz balled her fists, ready to let all her fear and frustration out in a tirade against this vexatious Watcher. Her glare travelled all the way up to his hardened jawline. She stared straight into his iridescent eyes. Instead of raging at him, she pulled the diamond dagger back from her waist, raising it in a tight fist, her face murderous.

"What the hell are you doing with that? Put it away!" he growled.

Jaz lunged, she screamed and ran towards him.

"What the…" Jude didn't finish. Jaz dodged around him and slammed the dagger hilt-deep into the one remaining Rogue that had snuck up behind Jude.

She stabbed the thing over and over in its skeletal head. Jaz's furious screams were met with a spray of gelatinous blood clots. She only stopped the frenzy when the thing finally expired, bursting into a putrid orange ball of fire. The agonised scream of the beleaguered soul rushed past her on its way to Hell, knocking her to the ground.

Struggling to catch her breath, dagger glued with blood to her palm, she scowled up at Jude.

"You… may not give… a fucking damn… but I do!"

Chapter
Twenty-Seven

Amais dove from great heights towards the loping Rogue, yelling at Koi to get out of the way. Koi transferred quickly from his position, reappearing mid-air, enveloped by his wings. With a fiery orb in one hand and a bloodied sword in the other, Koi surveyed the warring below with a quick sweep of his keen eyes. The explosive heat bursting from Amais' ebony palm penetrated the creature's head, resulting in an instantaneous implosion of rotting flesh. Putrid remnants fluttered to the ground in a haze of orange flame. Koi nodded towards Amais, the smile of victory in Amais' cerulean eyes as he lowered slowly to the ochre earth.

Rogue stench remained, the foul fog that always accompanied them thinning out at least. They were depleting, one by stinking one. The other creatures on this forsaken burning landscape had fled the moment the Watchers had breached the boundaries. Evil little creatures, horrendous hybrids of Daimon boredom and Lilith's need for a constant food supply. It was the Zombies of Yeqon's imagination, left to the offensive.

The Empyrean Mountain rumbled in disgust; ash spewed from its peak. The ground cracked a little more underfoot as the Watchers darted about both on foot and by wing, looking for stragglers.

"Where are you, Yeqon?" Koi bellowed in challenge, as he blasted an unsuspecting Rogue in two in the middle of a sleek, black henge.

Always was a coward, leaving the dirty work to others. Gedz'iel spoke in Koi's mind as he searched from afar, looking for Yeqon as well. Koi growled, acknowledging the truth.

"Behind you!" a voice called to Koi.

Lorcan appeared above Koi in a flash of blood smeared fury. The heat of Lorcan's wings burned the Rogue sneaking up behind Koi into a scrambling skeleton. Koi barraged its putrefied form with a rapid succession of energy bolts. The monster exploded into nothingness; its remains fluttered back down into the depths of the chasm. The rest of the Eloi flew menacingly through the standing stones, picking off stragglers with their deadly accurate, ethereal ammunition. Any creatures on the wrong side of the fight descended alongside a multitude of strangely weak, newly animated Rogues. The obsidian henge was now a stinking graveyard of smouldering detritus.

Koi kicked at a tiny skeleton and shook his head, "This sickens me. A child, a mere human child, degraded like that." Koi looked at his hands, still glowing as though they had committed an atrocity.

Gedz'iel appeared as Lorcan soared back across the burning sky.

"Koi, it was no longer a child, no longer an innocent. Her true soul will be safe in the Middle realm."

"I know." Koi bit his lip, his shoulders slumped, "But seeing them like that it, it is hard to separate the facts from the emotion, from the horror of it." Koi shook his head, his knuckles whitened around his sword.

"Even for myself, this can be difficult too, my friend. But we must see with our souls, not these mortal eyes." Gedz'iel placed a reassuring hand on Koi's shoulder. Koi nodded, and they left it at that.

"The bigger problem, Koi, is that this battle was too easy. They expected us. Those Rogues were vastly untrained cannon fodder." Gedz'iel's face darkened and his blue eyes swirled in anger.

Koi's gaze swept the blazing landscape below. Shadows, large and small, darted haphazardly across the plains, towards the great mountain, terrified of the mighty Watchers.

"Yes, they were a mess; a mere breath from death. Where are the seasoned Rogues then? Where is Yeqon? Hiding behind Lilith, no doubt!" Koi spat, unusually emotive.

"Oh, he *is* here. My gut churns when we share the same realm." Gedz'iel's face was grim, his mouth pressed tight.

"As much as these mortal bodies are appealing, they are far too sensitive. I've retched through this entire battle for the sickness this place draws out!" Gedz'iel said. He scanned the vast plains below for any further aggressors.

The immediate surrounds were quiet, unusually so. The stifling air punctuated only by the last slayings of the foul creatures left to defend the Daimon. Gedz'iel wiped sweat and blood spatter from his eyes, ran his hand over the buzz cut of white hair. He turned back to the group gathering behind, eyes narrowed, mind working.

"I expected more of Yeqon than this. Hiding away, trying to weary us with mere puppets. It's vastly beneath even him, and that's why it is suspicious." Gedz'iel cracked his knuckles. "I'm overdue a one on one with my former friend."

Gedz'iel's face glowed with fury. "This pathetic battle was no accident. This has been a calculated move; a delay, a distraction. Yeqon is here, his eyes are on us, and Sophia is in all the more danger because of this," he said.

As the last of the gurgles of battle died down, the older, most experienced Watchers and Eudaimonians emerged from various points around the henge-like structure, healing their wounds on the move.

Lorcan flew in with a rush, so sudden that he blew up a cloud of dust in his haste to stop. His face was flushed, "I need to go back, Gedz'iel. There is trouble at Kymakli, Brennan's energy is fluctuating. Everything was quiet before I left, but now, something feels… off."

"You sure he's not just flailing over Enl'iel, brother!" Amais laughed smugly. Lorcan's face blazed, sweat beading down his cheeks as the Daimon sun scorched more viciously.

"Shut your ancient mouth, Amais!" Lorcan crooked his elbow as though to throw an orb at Amais. Gedz'iel grabbed his arm, forcing it down.

"Amais, who are you to speak this way? This is beneath you, brother. Get out of my sight until your senses and respect return." Gedz'iel waved the Eloi companion away. Amais grimaced and glided to the back of the group, fuming, yet obedient.

"Lorcan, I need you to continue tracking Sophia as you did before. You are our best…"

Pathos interrupted, "I warred with Lorcan on Satanos. Together we tracked and rescued stolen souls. Let Lorcan return, I can find Sophia. Was I not Lorcan's teacher in the beginning? We are already within the vicinity of her imprisonment. Lorcan found remnants of her energy signature over there." Pathos pointed to a distant cave surrounded by steep hills of shale. "It points us the right way. Lorcan is our strongest tracker. If he is correct, if Brennan is in trouble, then our young may be in harm's way." Pathos' eyes swirled; his wings widened. "Brennan is supposed to be helping Enl'iel protect them after all. Our young are our future, whether we make it home to A'vean or not. If we do not have our young, we have no future anywhere."

They were all quiet a moment.

"I have not seen a good battle for many years. My mouth waters to light up one of the Unseen. Let me continue the search myself, Gedz'iel. I do not fear Yeqon's subterranean gutters," Pathos said and inclined his head respectfully.

Gedz'iel thought on it, "Koi?"

"We are already near Sophia. Lorcan can track the quickest and most accurately. It makes sense that if there is a threat at Kaymakli, he will find it faster than any of us. Pathos is certainly capable enough to track Sophia here. Please take no offense, Pathos." Koi bowed to him

Pathos returned the gesture; the darkness of his skin hid the flush of the slight he felt.

"No offense taken at all," Pathos lied.

"Go then, Lorcan, I bid you find Brennan safe and well. Pathos, head to Yeqon's hellhole. Others shall join you shortly. Keep your wits about you. Neither of you war often and I wish to see you sup at the Throne in good stead." Gedz'iel offered Lorcan and Pathos a K'ufili. They bowed respectfully to him.

Lorcan was gone before the blink of an eye as Pathos swooped away from their lofty meeting point without hesitation. Pathos alighted on top of the largest monolith in the middle of the Daimon henge. He melted seamlessly into it, like water into sand. He disappeared into the depths of Yeqon's lair.

Gedz'iel, it seems deserted down here, Pathos whispered into Gedz'iel's mind.

She is here. Beware the trap they are surely setting. Call on me if you need backup, Gedz'iel responded.

I will manage this. Stay out there where your leadership is most valuable, Pathos answered, and the mind chatter went dead.

Noticing movement below, Gedz'iel, bristled with anger. He called down to the warriors, who hovered throughout the landscape, taking one last look for any stragglers that they could ash to Hell. The soft light of his translucent wings distorted the blazing horizon behind as he waved them gently, keeping aloft, as though held in place by invisible strings. The Watchers looked up to him.

Gedz'iel was a powerful creature of beauty, capable of cutting down anything with the wave of a hand or sword. He sensed their need for leadership, their trepidation in this frightening realm. Gedz'iel swallowed down a blooming anger, such emotion a weakness in his mind. His face glowed, a sign of his power and kinship. The others followed suit, and he immediately sensed the strength that their combined energy infused into them all.

"Warriors, we have broken Yeqon's minor defences. Pathos is through to their dungeons. He has alerted me that it is strangely deserted as he searches for Sophia amongst the tunnels of the damned. This is not good news. It means Yeqon knew we were coming and he will be waiting for us somewhere with his strongest forces. Sophia is here. I feel her energy. I fear that my tracking is not as well-tuned as it should be, however. If it were possible for me to locate her without putting you at risk, I would save you from any potential harm. But we each have our own strengths, and as we have done in the past, we work together as one."

The warriors nodded in agreement as they looked up to Gedz'iel, their marks glowing brighter with comradery.

"I fear there is a trap awaiting us. Yeqon would not leave without Sophia willingly, not now that he has her and part of Enoch's prophecy. Come now." Gedz'iel glided downwards. Everyone trailed him across the landscape of rocks and sporadic steam vents.

Gedz'iel called to them all, "Be on full alert. It is time to call in the reserves. Do not become disarmed, leave your chromious armour on, no matter the heat of this place. I do not want a single one of you ascending."

The pack of glowing warriors followed him towards the shimmering breach they had opened between the human world and the Empyrean realm hours ago.

As they flew, Gedz'iel confided quietly in Koi, "I already regret sending Lorcan back to help Brennan and Jude. Those two are fully capable by themselves. His superior tracking skills would be better utilised here. He insisted on helping his brother though, just as strongly as Pathos insisted he could find Sophia."

Koi nodded, "Pathos did chase down those who kidnapped Rik'ael if you recall. Despite being outnumbered, he was able to track her father. He is old and very wise, Gedz'iel. He…"

"Yes, but he did not retrieve Rik'ael, did he? To this day we know not of the fate of Sophia's father and brother." Gedz'iel ran a hand across his cheeks; wearied. He sighed. "Yet, indeed, he is wise and long served and in need of more than yet another council meeting to satisfy him." Gedz'iel nodded to himself, conceding the decision he was already regretting.

"If for any reason we do not hear from Pathos before the setting of the sun, I will recall Lorcan and we will both go into save them all." Gedz'iel spun around, pointing to another warrior.

"You, call up the reinforcements," Gedz'iel asked a heavily armour-clad female. He pointed into the fissure in the atmosphere below. The rest of the awaiting Eudaimonian warriors waited patiently below a bank of clouds above an aging hotel where a group of humans lay prostrate by their motorbikes. Frozen in sleep, whilst the angelic-demonic war raged in the northern Mexican skies, the humans would never know anything had happened when they awoke.

The female Watcher glowed head to foot with the honour, nodded and transferred, returning within minutes with their younger, less experienced fighters. The grim-faced group followed their leaders back towards the ominous henge, awaiting their orders. Many were wide-eyed, having only ever heard the anecdotes of this almost mythical place; a scary bed-time story from their childhood.

"No Daimon or wretched creature is to leave this realm. Guard this henge and the rip between the dimensions. Enough crawl upon the Earth as it is. Nothing enters or leaves this henge without my permission," Gedz'iel commanded. They all nodded in understanding.

"What of me, Master Gedz'iel?"

A figure glided forward; head bowed in respect. It was the one who had brought the warriors up from below.

"Master, allow me also to track the Saviour. I could not help overhearing your worries about Pathos. Forgive me for eavesdropping. I do, however, have a heightened sense of hearing, especially where people feel fear or worry. Indeed, I feel the worry of Sophia. I am sure of it. There are positive ions here that should not be present. It can only be her energy signature. The vibrations emanating up from the ground are ringing uncomfortably loud in my mind. I feel drawn to it." The stranger put up a hand to stop any interruption, brave indeed in the face of her superiors.

"Before you judge me, I too have warred with Lorcan on Satanos, I have fought the Satans, who as you know, are much, much worse than Yeqon. The Unseen are unworthy even of the term Satan as they so love to refer to themselves. We are all aware they are far from the worst in the universe."

Gedz'iel, Koi and the rest of the Eloi council eyed her with suspicion as the mountain spewed forth again, a foul burst of repugnant gases. The ensuing rush of ash-filled air gusted chaotically, causing all to flap their wings a little harder until the unsettling breeze passed.

Koi coughed away the disgusting taste, Amais spat out the vulgar gases before addressing the stranger.

"How would you know to track her? You have never met her and would not know her energy signature," Amais questioned; eyes narrow.

She bowed again, "With respect, Master Amais, when rumours of her awakening began to circulate, I took it upon myself to track her down, to help. There were many a Daimon sniffing around for her. I thought perhaps I could help. Unfortunately, I arrived in the aftermath of the destruction of the home of her youth. I found her sleeping place which was rich with her energy. I can assure you; she is as powerfully running through my memory as if her own life force were my own." She pulled from her armoured belt a brush, knotted full of rainbow coloured hair strands, "I have kept this token to help myself."

This proof of her story softened Amais' expression somewhat.

"Why have you not come forward until now?" he questioned.

"Seeing the battle remnants in Australia, it felt more prudent to return to the underground to gather whatever intel that I could. Besides, I was not sure where you had gone. Only when I heard the call to action after her abduction did I re-join the warriors. I thought my skills would now be of valuable service." She bowed respectfully.

"Tell me, who are you then, and why do you live in the underground?" Gedz'iel queried, still suspicious. He regarded her as though trying to place her sweet voice.

"Of course, forgive me. I have moved through the underworld since the great flood with my sibling, hunting Lilith's vile offspring." She allowed her face to glow, highlighting extra fine facial features, larger than normal piercing blue eyes that drew Koi's gaze more than once.

"My name is A'glacea and I am most honoured to be in your presence." She bowed deeply.

The others respectfully returned the gesture.

"Many of us remain hidden, some because of shame, others because they seek quiet repentance. Unfortunately, many more have sought the wrong path. Myself, I chose the path of cleansing. I wish to rid the world of all that was not meant to be here. Every Rogue and child of Lilith must be eradicated if it is ever to be the glorious world it was when it was first passed into our hands." A'glacea smiled softly and bowed again. The mountain rumbled.

"And this realm, it should not even exist." A'glacea glanced around, hands on hips, disgust dripped from her at the sight below. "I'el would be horrified" She grimaced, then looked back expectantly at Koi and Gedz'iel. The two conferred covertly.

What of this Gedz'iel?

I have not seen or heard of her before, though indeed there are Cleansers who hunt the children of Lilith with the sanctioning of the Eloi.

She speaks well; thoughtfully. Her energy is strong. She is one of the oldest of us, Koi assessed.

This is why we may have not met her until now, Koi. How many thousands of us descended to the Earth in the beginning? Gedz'iel questioned.

Too many to count, brother. Koi answered.

And after the Fall, we dispersed in a hundred different ways. We must remind ourselves that all who follow our cause are not the entirety of our numbers. Who even knows how many survive in the hidden societies. What of the rumoured Apokathae? The restorers of the Afflicted? Gedz'iel asked.

Indeed. I forget, after so many eons, that we are not the only ones, and our fight is not the only battle, Koi conceded.

We need more, not less in the battle.

Yes, Gedz'iel, you are correct, Koi nodded.

Gedz'iel turned back to A'glacea who waited patiently.

"Kindred, it is agreed. At this point, the more help we have, the better. I can feel Sophia's presence, but I cannot be sure if it is just residual. You seem well prepared with weapons and knowledge, but please take another with you. What lies beneath is as unknown to you as it is to us. I shall inform Pathos you will join him below."

"Agreed and many thanks." A'glacea turned to find a partner, looking no further than a besotted soldier only an arm's length away. A'glacea raised an eyebrow.

"Partners?" The other woman glided forward, wings brightening as she banged her sword across her breast plate.

"Gal'ielle, your bravery is noted. Travel well and return safely, with our other kindred and, most assuredly, Sophia," Gedz'iel said.

Gal'ielle nodded, slipped her hand into A'glacea's. They descended towards the ground, swallowed by the shining monolith as though it devoured them with pleasure.

Twenty-Eight

"She did what?" Dash asked with incredulity after Kea returned from taking Kristen to the safety of Kaymakli.

"She literally stabbed a Rogue to descendance, with Sophia's dagger no less!" Kea beamed with pride. "If Jaz hadn't been paying attention and saved Jude's conceited arse, he would likely have had to crawl to Enl'iel to have a nasty bite, at the minimum, healed. Oh, the irony!" Kea laughed.

"That's a war story Jude won't be recounting, I'm sure!" Dash chuckled, then quickly quieted. "How was Kristen? Sweet girl, I hope she may be saved." His face was grave. Kea's own expression fell into heavy despair.

"So do I. She is one the best of us, A'vean blood or not. The Alchemae took her straight into isolation. She's in the best of care." Kea leaned into Dash's shoulder. "I feel good about her. She's a strong soul." Kea sighed and looked up at Dash.

"How is Eilir, Hon? She was looking a little tired the other day, still feisty, but tired."

It was Dash's turn to pale.

"Her time is almost upon her, Kea. I don't know what I'll do without her."

"Oh, Dash! I'm so sorry. You've kept her so well and happy for so long." She rubbed his arm with a motherly warmth.

"But have I? She has lost so much because of me," Dash lamented.

"No, don't think like that!" Kea squeezed Dash's hand. "Accidentally blinding her wasn't so suave, but I can promise you, I've never met a happier soul. You have both been honourable and content in an impossible situation."

Dash nodded his understanding, but still looked forlorn at the thought of the death of the love he could never truly have.

"Besides, if we sort this bloody portal, all souls will be released and free, and you will see her again, sooner than you realise," Kea said. "Anyway, last I saw, she was still chasing the kids around with tea towels and clipping their ears! I think you will have her a while yet!" She cuddled into his arm. He smiled a little, but Dash's eyes spoke a different emotion.

"Let's get on then. I want to get back and see her," Dash said and perked up as they quickened their pace back to the sanctuary.

The exhausted warriors made their way back towards Kaymakli, Jude leading up ahead in the foulest of moods. Not a soul dared talk with him. Everyone allowed him space to cool his temper. Watchers and hybrids kept a vigilant perimeter around the human troops, a standard formation to protect their more vulnerable comrades.

The moon slipped behind clouds as a bitter wind built. As the A'veans moved in a tighter formation, they emitted a sufficient amount of E'lan energy to radiate warmth among their human warriors. The group travelled in companionable silence for a time, picking their way across a vast and dark landscape, each in their own contemplation about the unexpected assault in Nevşehir.

Jaz, splattered in dried blood, was also unusually quiet. She kept Thomas' company as he followed, heavy-footed, at the back of the group, pale and drawn. He carried Kristen's full quiver and bow almost reverently. Jaz placed a hand on his shoulder.

"She *will* be okay, Thomas, I'm sure of it. I've seen how they can heal. Look at Brennan, he couldn't walk for so long and ta da, we have

the pleasure of his wise-cracking antics all over the place now!" Jaz'
awkward humour was lost on him.

"Thank you, but I think I'd like to be alone for a while," Thomas
responded with a poor attempt at a smile. Normally, Jaz would be
affronted at being blown off, but this time she nodded in
understanding, "If you want to, you know, talk or something later, you
know, you can."

"Thank you, mon ami," Thomas said and let his head hang low.

Jaz glanced back over her shoulder at him before she jogged over
to Kea who travelled with Dash, a few paces back from Jude.

"You're not coming to rub it in, are you?" Kea asked.

"You know; he kinda deserves a good dose of humble pie, but I'm
not giving him the opportunity to bite my head off again. It's quite
satisfying seeing him sulking about it!" Jaz chuckled.

"Sulking, he most certainly is!" Kea responded, enjoying Jude's
tantrum as much as Jaz. "You were very brave, Jaz. You will make a
great warrior if that is what you wish.

"I d wish."

Kea nodded, "Good to hear, kid."

"So, is she going to be okay? Thomas looks like he is about to keel
over himself!" Jaz checked back on him, just making out his silhouette
shuffling along dolefully.

"Well, luckily the blood loss wasn't too bad, but the damage to the
tissues around her neck was substantial," Kea said.

"Was hard not to notice. I actually don't know how she's still alive,"
Jaz responded.

"That she will live, I'm fairly sure of. However, the Alchemae and
Enl'iel have their work cut out for them. Then again, they've done
wonders with Cael. I understand he is now fully conscious and able to
sit up, so fingers crossed. She's strong. Kinda like you, kid."

They passed into a narrow chasm shadowed by two craggy
mountains.

"I'm no stronger than anyone else."

"Don't pretend to be shy about it now, Jaz." Kea grinned wryly. "You saved Fat Head's butt! He's pissed and impressed, but he'll never admit that. Ever!" Kea laughed quietly. "You're strong, and more than just with words, kid. Your heart, your instincts and life force beat as one. It wouldn't surprise me if you end up leading your own regiment."

That silenced Jaz. Contemplation held her tongue.

As the clouds gave way to a slit of moonlight, Jaz looked about at everyone. With each glance, she took in the movement; the weaponry and mystery of the bizarre world she had fallen into. Every little detail about this tight-knit family was what she had wanted of her own family. Strength and solidarity… and love. This realisation bolstered her resolve. She was determined to meld into this new life.

Ahead, the entire group came to a halt as Jude raised a hand. Silence reigned as his head turned this way and that. Jaz noticed Kea stiffen and feel for her weapons. Dash moved along towards Jude, sword singing out of its scabbard.

Jaz fumbled around her belt for the diamond dagger, her skin prickling with a keen fight or flight reaction. The wind whipped a sea of white hair and tugged at Jaz' heavy coat. The metallic chime of swords was overcome by the thrash of her heart.

"What is it?" Jaz asked.

"Shh!" Kea whispered as she also searched the darkness and sniffed the air. She pointed to the right where Dash followed on, knowing exactly the meaning of her hand signals.

Everyone was on edge again. Weapons gleamed an unearthly blue in the moonlight. The group moved through the dark expanse of the narrow valley. Kea tilted her head left and right, as though listening to something. She then mumbled to herself, "But why?"

Just as Jaz was about to ask who she was talking to, Kea's face lit up in a snap of luminescence, her sword high. The glow of Kea's veins ran bright under her skin and Jaz' face suffered immediate sunburn from the proximity.

"You gotta hone your reflexes, kid. You need to anticipate when we light up, keep your eyes down," Kea whispered and pulled Jaz into her side.

"Stay right near me, kid, no matter what. And if I say run, you will bloody well run, okay?"

Wide-eyed and confused, Jaz nodded as the group huddled in an even tighter defensive formation.

"Xavier?" Kea pointed with a nod of her head into the blackness amongst busy rock formations. Jaz followed their line of sight. She had to stand on tiptoe to see past the height of the two Watchers and immediately regretted it. Shadows darted rapidly; silent things slipped around the landscape. These dark forms skittered in and out of the moon-striped scenery; menacing night terrors teasing for attack.

Jaz' nostrils flared; her eyes rolled wildly, trying to find out what exactly was out there. She switched from fear to decisiveness, locked her jaw into a determined grimace. Jaz pulled Sophia's diamond dagger out for a second time that night.

"It's you and me." Jaz kissed the flat edge of the weapon whilst keeping her other hand protectively over her eyes as the angelic energy intensified up to another level. She ducked under Kea's raised arm to get a better look at what she might need to stab.

The wind dropped too suddenly. The surrounds left in an eerie silence, but for the stealthy movements of the tightly bound group.

Kea was nodding at the unseen conversation she was having. Jude glanced back many times at her. Only once did his eyes fall to Jaz, arctic cold and daring her to step out of line. Jaz matched his icy gaze. One brow quirked, lips pouted.

Jaz searched for a telltale fog and foul stench which didn't arise, yet the group remained as tense and ready to spring as though the danger were as deep.

"Kea… Kea?"

"Shh, stay quiet," Xavier whispered, a finger to his lips. Jaz tossed the dagger from right to left nervously, licking her cold, cracked lips.

An immense boom reverberated through the group. The shockwave plucked at the ground. The ensuing flash of white light shuddered through Jaz. She grappled at her chest to make sure there wasn't some gaping wound under her armour.

Kea broke the quiet, "Sorry everyone, we have to go in now. No choice."

Everyone nodded at her secret, all of them seemingly in on the situation at hand, all except Jaz.

"What the hell is going on?" Jaz demanded as both metallic and ethereal weapons intensified in soft white glows. Needing to be pragmatic as usual, Kea kept it plain and simple.

"Afflicted are hunting us. They're trying to break into Kaymakli."

"Those are the things that took Ben! Well, at least pretended too," Jaz scowled.

"Yes," Kea replied sharply and pushed Jaz back under her arm, out of the way.

"Stay in the middle of the pack, Jaz." Kea's back faced Jaz as the group moved in a slow circle, facing outwards at the new and unexpected threat.

"Why are they hunting us? Jesus, can't we cop a fucking break?" Jaz held the dagger higher, the diamond glow quivering in her hand. She saw the warped shape of something in the angled prism of the blade, but there was nothing there when she twisted the dagger to see what it was.

"Why are they hunting us, Kea?" Fear rattled her voice, her wall of bravado weakening in the face of the unknown.

"Yes," Kea blurted out.

"What?" Jaz screwed up her face in confusion, then realised Kea wasn't talking to her at all.

"She's right behind me, and I'm right behind you. So, you can talk to me normally. Let me keep my head clear, Jude!" Kea whispered.

Jude's grumbling tone floated backwards, still inaudible to Jaz.

"No, I wouldn't risk transferring her again." Kea sounded annoyed as she tried to concentrate on the shadows that swelled in number and proximity.

Jaz' knuckles whitened around the dagger. It hovered above her shoulder, ready to plunge into anything that came too close. She became aware of Thomas and Xavier who had sidled up either side of her.

"Stay close and you will be okay," Thomas whispered. Everyone ducked as an ear-shattering thunder exploded overhead. Lightening followed; the landscape lit daylight bright for a few seconds. In that one moment of clarity, they saw exactly what they were up against.

The horizon was peppered with hundreds of Afflicted. They stood high upon the craggy rock formations, littered the ground, statue still. They surrounded the group, shrouded in the veil of midnight shadows. More lightning ensued. The Afflicted flickered in the sinister light and dark. Their ghostly pale figures unmoving, threatening, unnerving.

"Holy mother of I'el!" Xavier exclaimed.

"What the hell is going on?" another cried.

Slack-jawed, Jaz stepped closer to Thomas as she noticed the lightening was actually emanating from the deathly-still Afflicted. They flashed their energy on and off erratically. The landscape looked like the flickering reel of a black and white horror movie. With each flash, they moved closer, just a step, but definitely closer.

Sweetness punctuated the air, like plunging one's head into a vat of honey. The group halted, gathering in a tighter configuration.

"Close your eyes, Jaz," Thomas whispered into her ear.

"What's going on, Kea?" Xavier asked quietly as another flash revealed at least a dozen Afflicted only meters away. Their grey eyes marked their prey.

"Brennan's fighting them off at the sanctuary entrance. I don't know how they know we are here, or why they're bothering us." Kea shook her head. "Nothing makes sense at all." She then responded to someone not present. "Great, is he there yet?"

"Who are you talking about?" Jaz asked, increasingly impatient, increasingly terrified.

"Lorcan is supposed to be on his way to help Brennan, but we all have to get to the sanctuary to protect it, and quickly. We move only on either Jude's word or mine. I've sent Dash in already, so at least he will be a little back up for Brennan," Kea said.

Jaz felt a jolt as she realised the group were moving again. She shuffled quickly, tightly squeezed within their protection. Her eyes remained squinted as their angelic power was released. The glow was hot, like summer at the beach, the effects of which brought out a sweat beneath her heavy coat. If only she hadn't refused one of those useful helmets the other humans wore to protect against the elemental heat. Funnily enough, the issue of 'hat hair' seemed vastly less important now.

She threw off the coat at least, grateful to lose the bulk and have freer movement, the cold air refreshing. Jaz' arm accidentally grazed through someone's wing, singing the skin into a nasty burn. She kept a more life-preserving distance from then on, which wasn't easy in the squished circle of protection.

"Kea," Jude growled.

"I know," Kea answered as she materialised a pulsing orb onto her free palm.

"Get ready," Jude snapped loud enough for them all to hear. Static electricity arced around him, it plucked at Jaz' skin.

A tinny screech ripped across the landscape. Ear-piercing enough that Jaz nicked her cheek with the dagger when she slapped her hands to her ears to dull the horrendous sound. The sky lit up again; they were surrounded by a thick sea of agitated Afflicted. A hundred deranged silhouettes clawed impatiently at their thighs. Silver hair blew wildly. Despairing, sunken eyes with dilated pupils glowed in a collective psychotic stare.

The rapid panting of these desperate creatures made for a terrifying rhythmic undertone to the clanging of weapons and explosive bursts of fire power echoing all the way from Kaymakli. Bright flashes lit the sky just beyond the next turn around the mountainous pass. The closer the Afflicted approached, the sickly sweet tang in the air deepened. Dishevelled, drawn and addicted to Thanratos; Afflicted worked for whoever paid them with the crystalline drug; recent remnants of which glistened on their pale lips. They had been satiated just enough, to keep under control as they awaited whomever pulled their strings, whoever commanded their next move.

"Why don't we just attack them?" Jaz asked impatiently, her fingers white-knuckled around the dagger.

"They outnumber us right now by at least three to one. We aren't in a good position, kid," Kea responded. "Thomas, keep hold of Jaz and get her underground when this all goes down, okay?" Kea said.

"Of course," he answered, stepping closer to Jaz.

"But, why are they…" Jaz didn't finish. There was another inaudible screech. Jaz grabbed her ears again, smearing the old blood across her cheek.

"Ready yourselves," Jude yelled, glancing back. He caught Jaz' attention; his eyes hooked hers intently for a nanosecond.

"Get her out of my sight!" Jude growled as his wings emerged to full width. He raised his sword, luminous energy travelled through the metal, emerging in a threatening maelstrom of lightening. The Afflicted circled faster, bobbing their heads up and down, left and right, as though searching for something or someone.

"She isn't here, if you're looking for the Earth-born. Even you should have heard she was taken by the Unseen!" Jude bellowed.

"Leave us in peace. We don't carry your poison," he hissed viciously.

Jude lunged forwards, challenging anyone of them to do the same. The intense electrical charges sparking from him melted the snow in his wake. The first row of Afflicted cried out hauntingly and in unison. They, too, allowed their power to emerge. The night sky gave way to a brightness that would challenge the midday sun. The human warriors engaged their protective face shields whilst Jaz had to make do with peering uselessly through squinted eyes to avoid instant blindness.

A single voice spoke up in response. Shaky, unsure, like prompted by a hidden earpiece.

"We look not for Thanratos from you."

"Then what is your cause with us?" Jude demanded, lunging closer in challenge. The Afflicted didn't flinch at his threat. They didn't respond immediately either, infuriating Jude further.

Kea interjected, "Stand down. You have one chance. We can help you. We will search for the Great Healer, the Apokethae, and restore you to health. Please don't make us defend ourselves against you?"

The same Afflicted responded after tilting his head this way and that, as though he too was listening to a distant voice.

"We do not wish for your healing."

"If it is not redemption, then what is it you want?" Jude moved closer, orb erupting on one palm, sword spinning in the other.

"What we want is… her!" the spokesperson pointed to the centre of the pack.

They all looked inwards… towards Jaz.

"The fuck you will!" Jaz yelled; her eyes wild. She pointed her weapon threateningly at the offending Afflicted.

"You have no need of this pathetic Earth dweller. Trust me, she is nothing but trouble. I do not wish to fight you, but I will have no reservations if you continue to threaten us. I will not ask you to leave again." Jude pointed the blazing tip of his sword towards the Afflicted, setting his orb free to float in the air. It waited patiently for his command.

"In I'el's name, I command you to tell me, who is your master?" Jude demanded as the orb reacted to a silent directive. It exploded at the feet of the Afflicted, knocking a few unconscious.

They quickly regrouped. The static tension reached fever point as the stand-off continued on. Tendrils of energy snaked through the night. Jude called to the Afflicted one last time.

"Sons and daughters of A'vean, put down your weapons and let us pass."

"We cannot do that." A male stepped forward, answering Jude's demand. He let his energy emerge more fully in sputters and pops. His wings, however, were every bit as powerful and threatening as Jude's. The rest of the Afflicted followed suit, as though arming for detonation.

The wind whipped up in a freezing flurry of snow and rain. It's change of pace accentuated the volatile situation. It howled and swirled through opposing armies in tense preparedness. Feet shuffled nervously; bodies glowed.

The Afflicted suddenly paused their circling, and as one, turned in freakish synchronicity to stare down the pass behind them. Jude and everyone else followed their line of sight. In the distance, atop the tallest of rock formations, stood a lithe silhouette. It lit from behind as enormous wings emerged; the shadow made all the more foreboding by their threatening, rhythmic beat.

"Who the hell is that?" Kea asked Jude.

"I'm not sure." Jude hesitated. In that moment, the Afflicted turned back, en masse, and charged. The roar was deafening, punctuated by the spitting and cracking of electrical missiles.

"Oh fuck!" Jaz screamed as she was yanked backwards by Thomas. Jude, Kea and the others launched in every direction with both sword and elemental firepower. Humans raged with chromious weaponry. Their method was swift, with accurate deadliness. Arrows flew with precision repeatedly, landing front and centre, deep within the chests of the Afflicted. Swords cut from throat to belly in a bloody mess.

They cut down the first two lines of Afflicted with ease. Plumes of blue fire and smoke left diamond skeletons scattered under the melee of rushing feet. A handful of Afflicted stopped with uncontrollable addiction overruling their senses. They knelt to snap bones from their fallen in a cannibalistic fervour. Glistening bone was rammed into tattered pockets. This momentary distraction was enough for Jude's small army to cut down another dozen.

"Fight, you imbeciles!" A feminine scream bellowed down from the tall peak, accompanied by a scorching orb. It throttled towards them in a snapping, fiery howl, and landed in the middle of the chaos, knocking both Afflicted and Watchers alike to the ground.

Dusting herself off, Kea helped Jude to his feet. He swore a dozen four-letter words. He retrieved his sword and quickly cast an orb. It crackled upon his palm; his biceps flexed impatiently to launch it.

"Which way, Kea?" Jude growled as he glared into the distance.

"Over there!" She pointed to the highest Cappadocian fairy chimney as she pulled Xavier up, cauterising a gash to his cheek.

Jude cut down two Afflicted with one bloody slice through their chests, then took up position and aimed for the peak.

"Show yourself, you traitorous bitch!" Jude yelled. His incandescent orb sailed from his hand like the world's best baseball pitch. It exploded above the craggy peak.

For a short time, an apocalyptic glow illuminated the horizon. For the briefest moment, the Watchers and their comrades saw the owner of the voice, the destructive puppeteer of the Afflicted.

Posing like a goddess, was a woman whose wings of light rivalled any of theirs in both beauty and power. Long, dark hair fluttered about her slender frame. She stared down the valley at the chaos she lauded over. Ember-like tatters of energy flittered around her, giving her already ethereal quality an even more surreal appearance. As though basking in the picturesque moment, she threw her head back and laughed. A long, luxurious trill of madness. She pointed towards Jude, nodded her head, then transferred away in a snap of blinding light.

A thunderous roar ensued as hundreds more Afflicted emerged from the shadows. They descended upon the group in a sea of lightning strikes and slashing of weapons. The woman from the stone pedestal appeared again, silhouetted high in thunderous clouds. She watched and waited, haloed by coils of orange static.

Kea screamed, "Was that her? For real?" She blasted a half dozen less proficient Afflicted into ash and bone, jumping and dodging the onslaught, saving several own warriors as she went. Many fell, though. The night sky lit over and over with vertical beams of a sombre blue hue, angelic energy leaving their mortal forms. The much smaller, white spectres of human souls ascended into the farthest reaches of the sky, towards the Middle Realm.

"It's her," Jude cried and flew upwards to avoid a group attack, blasting Afflicted from above. He sent dozens wounded and scattering back into the rocks that dotted the mountainous pass they were now trapped in. Yet, despite Jude and Kea's merciless assault, they were outnumbered as more and more Afflicted appeared, baying for blood, and for Jaz.

Jaz, still in Thomas' shadow, looked like a bobble-head doll as her head swung back and forth, trying to keep up with everything. Thomas and the others remained in the tight circle as they protected Jaz and themselves. Their weapons slashed at anything that came near. Just like Rogues, the Afflicted had no apparent care for their own personal safety, they threw themselves literally into battle.

One surged close enough to grab a girl near Thomas. Saved initially by her armour, the creature's grip slid from the chromious. It retched in response to the metals' effect. The young warrior jabbed expertly forward, deep into its chest just to the left of the sternum. The Afflicted male, still nauseated, fell to its knees. It looked dolefully up at her as she searched out another weapon, her group all the while inching further away towards Kaymakli.

The wounded aggressor looked down at its flail chest. It dripped iridescent blood and slowly withdrew the sword with a sickening, sucking sound. As he did so, he met the eyes of the retreating girl, who now brandished a shorter sickle. The Afflicted flung the bloodied sword to the ground. It smiled a crimson mouthful of teeth. Zero humour and a war full of hate. He raised himself up with a flap of his wings, healing himself with a quick swipe of a spindly hand. Without warning, an energy pulse exploded in the warrior girl's direction. She was launched into the air before she crashed to the ground with a metallic thud. Screams from her comrades ensued, but they did not change their manoeuvre. Their strict training meant that no matter what, they followed through an order to its conclusion, and that order was to protect Jaz. The Afflicted male hovered towards the fallen girl, lowered to the ground and kicked her over onto her back. She groaned in agony. He shook his head, and he pressed a bare, muddied foot to her chest.

"But for you," he accused as he pressed his foot down harder and harder, the metal collapsing under his foot, until it gave way to her delicate frame. Only when he heard her rib cage crack, her screams cease, and her body go limp, did he release the pressure. He roared like a wild animal in the direction of the others. His eyes glowed ever brighter. Rain pelted his face, sparks crackled from his palms. More Afflicted appeared behind him. They seemed to garner a new strength from his. Like a sea of electrified zombies, they washed in like a tide, advancing and retreating, slowly getting closer to their mark.

Jude and Kea, along with the other A'veans, attacked from above, protecting the retreating humans. They marked their targets like birds of prey. They attacked the Afflicted without mercy.

"Get her the hell outta here!" Jude screamed through his teeth. "Get her underground now!"

"For fuck's sake, let's listen to the Freak for once!" Jaz screamed and fumbled with the diamond dagger. Her hands shook uncontrollably as she kept it aloft, teeth bared, eyes wide. Sweat poured across her flushed face, despite the freezing sleet and wind.

"Why the fuck are they after me? Isn't one kidnapping a month enough?" Jaz screeched fearfully. Thomas let a flurry of arrows loose, the last in his quiver. He dropped it to the ground before pulling out a set of slim swords that criss-crossed his back.

"Does it matter?" Thomas yelled through the effort of slaying two Afflicted at once.

"But...." He thrust forwards as a new onslaught emerged. He could see they were losing the war of numbers as their dead and wounded mounted up. Little time allowed the A'vean's to heal themselves, to replenish their numbers. He launched one sword like a javelin, ascending an oncoming woman.

"But... I think..." Thomas threw his remaining sword the same way; the weapon pierced the eye socket of another woman who had scorched his arm to blisters with a fiery blast. Thomas frantically dabbed at the flames of his fighting gear. Jaz helped as well, slapping a hand full of snow onto the seared fabric and pained flesh.

Thomas finally finished his sentence as their airborne fighters regrouped and charged forward, a mass of fury and firepower towards the un-ending threat.

"Now, I think we run Jaz! Go, go, go, go, everyone!" Thomas yelled. Deplete of weapons and hopelessly outnumbered, the humans turned and ran… literally for their lives. Thomas screamed for them to double back around the outside of the pass, away from the rocks where surely more Afflicted were lying in wait.

"Faster!" Thomas screamed as they took the longer route back to Kaymakli. Slipping and tripping across the cold and uneven ground, the entire group faltered in the panic of retreat. They were quickly spotted by the enemy as they rounded the outer face of the closest mountain.

Kea flew in above them. "Run for your lives! I'll hold them off as long as I can. Underground…now!" she yelled. Kea spun around; the heat of her powerful wings accidentally singed them in the panic. Thomas waved his arms frantically. "Hurry!" He led the terrified group into darkness, through gaps around the mountainside as they ran faster from the battle. The screams of attack, of horror, pain and death echoed ever more loudly behind them.

Chapter
Twenty-Nine

"Quick!" I called in a whisper to Rik. The snapping retreat of the red bars brought me out of a vague stare. He, too, had retreated into whatever messed up world his mind dwelled in. I motioned frantically at him. His glazed eyes brightened, and he returned from wherever he'd been.

His face glowed. I didn't know whether by instinct or design. He backed up to the wall on the other side of the door, pulling my make-shift shiv from the waist of his pants. He tossed it from hand to hand as though he were a member of an underground fight club. For a flicker of a second, I wondered if he really was a lot more than the abused pawn that he seemed. Or, perhaps, he'd picked up on whatever he'd observed, secret survival skills? Everyone in my life seemed to have secrets. Why not him? I narrowed my eyes in thought as I considered his sudden change from a speechless dribbling mess to a more powerful presence; an A'vean, looking ready to cut down anyone in his way.

He caught me staring, so I quickly nodded encouragingly at him. He responded with a short sharp tilt of his head towards the door, which was being noisily unbolted from the outside. Rik and I seemed complicit and in sync with our plan, which bolstered my courage. The complaining whine of the door had me conjure a sizzling orb, ready for whatever came through. *Please don't be Yeqon?*

A quick glance down reassured me that I'd successfully regained my concealment as Spider. Plucking at my necklace, I gave it a quick kiss. "Be with me now Gran," I whispered to myself, hoping for a little otherworldly assistance from my long dead grandmother, the regent Queen Elizabeth. Gran must have been busy though, because it was just me and Rik as the door screeched wider. It was like a nightmare, where scary things happened in extra scary slow motion.

Wriggling my fingers, as Koi had taught me, I teased out the light from my skin. It filled my palm with a swirling, burning weapon, ready to bite. With my arm raised, I was ready to launch. The air had a sudden sweet aroma, which told me there was at least one Afflicted on the other side of those few inches of gnarly wood. Rik retreated into the nearest shadow, only the glow of the intricate mark across his face evidence that he was present. The moans of the beings outside were strangely absent. This didn't bode well. It sent a chill up and down my spine, which was already aching to set my wings free. The thought that the other prisoners might have been disposed of, or worse, set loose, made my stomach flip.

A deep voice growled, not too far behind the door. The bony fingers of an Afflicted grasped around its edge.

"Bring her to the Blood Stone when I call on you and make it quick, or you will be Lilith's lunch." It wasn't Yeqon, but it was one of his beastly Daimon.

"Wait with here for the command. We've urgent business to attend to above ground," the voice growled again.

A snap of energy echoed through the underground. I sighed with relief; he'd transferred away. My jaw unclenched. Every other muscle remained tense as Spider entered the cell. With the silence and fluidity of a ghost, she made her way in a few feet before confusion washed over her face. She cocked her head from side to side. She searched the cell.

"Hiding? How ridiculous. Where have you to go in here?" she laughed, but it was nervous and wary. Undoubtedly, the threat of being fed to Lilith weighed heavily on her mind. Her fingers splayed; her eyes narrowed.

"Your fate is sealed. Just deal with it!" Spider quivered with false bravado, then she turned around and our eyes met. Her mouth dropped with the surprise of seeing herself standing in front of her. Her hand shot up to her face, prodding at it in confusion. Before she could try to make sense of it, I pulled my arm back and launched my orb full force. It exploded in the centre of her chest, knocking her against the far wall. She slumped to the ground; her moaning died away slowly as blood pooled in the dip under her neck.

I waited a moment to see if she was going to get up. Although not quite unconscious, she seemed overcome. A burn across her chest left her clothing in cinders, revealing just how emaciated she really was. It was hard not to feel sorry for her. I knelt, covering her modestly with a scrap of fabric that lay intact by her waist. I was not a monster. I just wanted to escape.

I stood, about to tell Rik to follow me out, but he launched onto Spider, stabbing wildly at her with the shiv. Blood sprayed everywhere. The sweet tang of it brought the burn of bile to the back of my throat. For a moment, I was rooted to the spot in shock, not quite believing what I was witnessing. I quickly came to my senses, ran at him, grabbed his arm before he could land another wound in Spider's now very unconscious, nearly dead body.

"Stop! Stop it! What are you doing?" I whisper-screeched at him. We wrestled wildly to the ground. Rik resisted me, his strength surprising. He reached desperately to slice at Spider again, but I managed to wrench the crude weapon from him.

Rik rolled away, caked in filth. He jumped up and turned on me. Eyes peppered red with blood and burst blood vessels, Rik got right up in my face. For a moment we breathed heavily, staring each other down.

"What do you think *you* are doing?" he panted, spittle dribbled from the side of his mouth.

"Rik, calm down. She was out of it; you didn't need to do that!" My voice was screechy and not my own. He continued to glare intimidatingly at me.

"I thought you asked me to help you escape? To help us get out of here?"

"I did, but that… what was that, Rik? Don't do that, it was cold-blooded. It was what they." I caught myself before I continued.

"It was what?" Rik squared his shoulders in threat, pumped his fists together. His eyes dilated; his energy drew goosebumps to my skin. I stepped away.

Already not one hundred percent sure of his mental state, or how much I could trust him, I quickly decided I needed to go in hard and fast. I needed to keep him in line and myself in a safe position. My actions were instinctual, and so very unlike the old Sophia.

I lunged, grabbed the arm he'd used to stab Spider, spun him around so quickly, he didn't have time to react. With his hand crooked behind his back, I held him with just enough force to keep him subdued, but not to hurt him. I hissed in his ear.

"If I ever see you act like a Daimon again, I will ascend you myself, brother. Do you understand?" My voice shook with a mix of emotions. Rik gasped a while longer, struggling fruitlessly, before he relinquished his resistance.

"I don't know what you've been through, but I will *never* be a cold-blooded killer, and I won't allow you to be either. We will defend ourselves and others, but never will I allow you to behave like that again. We are better than that, better than them. You got that?"

Rik quieted; the tension slowly left him. I released the pressure a little as I felt his muscles relax.

"If I can't trust you, I can't take you with me." I paused to let that sink in. "Can I trust you?"

He nodded. I turned him around, wiped the blood from his face, kept it cocooned in my hands.

"I'm here now. We can stick together from now on, okay? But we have to work together, no matter what vengeance you want, and believe me, I know the taste of wanting vengeance." I nodded at him for reassurance that he understood.

"I am sorry," he mumbled.

"Make it right then," I instructed, leaning my forehead against his, then let him go.

Rik kneeled and helped me as I healed Spider. The stab wounds knitted together with perfect precision, making a piece of me heal too, for doing something good whilst surrounded by a whole lot of bad. I placed my hand at the base of her skull, remembering what Brennan had taught me, and infused the deep delta waves of sleep into her brain.

"That should keep her out of the way. Her fate isn't ours to decide." I stood and motioned for Rik to follow me. "C'mon, brother. Show me the way out of this place."

My suspicions were confirmed as Rik and I tentatively stepped out of our prison and moved through to the outer door. The other cells were empty. There were no stinking piles of ash or bodily remnants, so either the other inmates had been taken elsewhere, or let out. The latter thought was not a welcome one.

"This way." Rik pulled me left. We entered the dark, winding tunnel, ascending cautiously. We stopped and listened every so often, hoping beyond hope that we wouldn't come across anything in the dark.

A crushing headache returned the higher to the surface we came. Sounds banged around in my skull, voices in the distance, whispers of my name.

"Do you hear that?" Rik whispered.

"What?"

"Your name. Someone's calling for you."

"You hear that too?" I stopped in surprise.

"Yes, it's not one of *them*. It's… a nice voice. Who is it?" he asked.

I listened harder, and the voice became clearer.

Sophia, are you there? We are here for you.

"That's Koi!" I exclaimed, a little too loud. I slapped my hand over my mouth. My statement echoed up the ascending tunnel all too loudly. Before I remembered I didn't look like myself, I instinctively kneeled to conceal myself in the shadows. I recalled, though, that I should have a safe passage out. I stood again, took Rik's hand.

"Koi is safe?" Rik asked as he pulled me along again.

"Yes, Koi is most definitely safe," I responded, unable to suppress a smile of relief. We moved faster, freedom tapped a little closer.

Chapter Thirty

"Oh shit!" Jaz screamed. She tripped and tumbled in a mad dash for safety.

"Faster, Jaz!" Thomas yelled from behind as he flung a well-aimed dagger into the shoulder of a particularly nasty-looking Afflicted. Their speed was not affected by the drug that held them captive. They seemed to move faster… or those under siege were getting slower with fatigue. The one that Thomas had skewered, at least faltered long enough that they could put a little more distance and shadows between them.

Jaz pumped her legs hard, her fingers cramped around the diamond dagger.

Jumping a boulder, she took a quick look over her shoulder. Thomas was coming up fast behind her, as were the others. Unfortunately, the eerie glow of Afflicted followed as well.

"Don't stop to gawk at them! Run!" Thomas yelled again. Jaz didn't question him. She turned on her heels at the sound of the electric warfare that continued to follow them. Her breaths laboured, sweat stung her eyes.

"Shit… shit!" Jaz' legs screamed in agony; a cramp clenched her left calf. She slowed, limped, and cried through the pain. The sound of her breaths drowned out the noise. Her pulse pounded in her head as she dragged herself to the end of the wide mountain pass. Jaz leaned against a rock, sucked for breath, coughing on the frigid air.

The battle closed in, she pushed herself up, the cramp worsened. "God… fuck!" She limped to the right, disappeared into the shadows of the pass, hoping it was the way to the safety of Kaymakli.

Jaz found herself surrounded by tall, uneven cylindrical columns of rock. She pushed on, one foot scraping through the snow-dusted ground. She heard Thomas.

"Nearly there… faster!" He reached Jaz, pushed her on. "Don't stop, the fairy chimneys are the air vents for the sanctuaries, we are nearly there, keep going," He grabbed her hand, forcing her body to burn more, the cramps to seize one leg completely. Thomas practically dragged her. Jaz glanced over her shoulder.

"Fuck!" she screamed. "Holy fu…" Jaz tripped, lost her grip of Thomas. Crashing heavily, she split her chin, tucked and rolled before forcing herself back up to run. She stopped dead. As blood dribbled from her chin, she held the dagger out, jutting it threateningly into the dark at the shadows that moved quickly around the bases of the fairy chimneys.

"Oh, merde!" Thomas' voice echoed in the darkness as concealed Afflicted surged forwards. With minimal weapons left, the humans backed up to each other, straining their eyes as they stared into the inky surrounds.

"Very clever," Thomas mumbled.

"What's there?" Jaz gasped, eyes bulging at the menace in the shadows.

"The Afflicted. They've dulled their energy so Jude and the others won't sense they've followed us."

"Fuckers!" Jaz' eyes glistened with terror.

"Don't move from my side," Thomas whispered as the shadows emerged to become silhouettes that moved with predatory stealth. A chittering sound bounced from rock to rock. A spine-chilling screechy chatter peculiar to the Afflicted; like nails on a chalkboard.

With only a few swords left to defend themselves, the humans stood their ground, waiting for the enemies' next move. They were surrounded.

It came all too quickly, preceded by a terrifying screech as a handful of Afflicted surged from the shadows. They didn't run. They knew the humans were cornered and exhausted. Grinning and grimacing with the success of their deception, they approached in a casual and cocky manner.

Thomas edged in front of Jaz, ready to defend her. She fisted the back of his shirt, felt the sweat of his exhaustion. Her heart sank. She felt her blood drain to her feet.

The attack was swift and quick. A chorus of screams ushered in the onslaught. Their small group was quickly corralled into a tight circle.

Jaz thrust the translucent dagger at anything and everything. She wouldn't give in, even though she tasted the sourness of defeat. Her knife wielding was perfectly frenzied, but useless. Their group was overwhelmed in an instant.

One by one, the humans were picked off, cut down mercilessly by those who were once their protectors. In mere seconds, most of the A'vean allies were put to rest, either dead or wounded. Thomas, one of the last to stand his ground, slashed and cursed as he desperately protected Jaz, "Run Jaz, run!"

Jaz hesitated as the sky lit bright white.

"Go!" Thomas was fading, his sword pushed down towards him by the bare hand of a huge Afflicted woman. "For I'el's sake… run you fool!" Thomas screamed, then took a blow to the face after slipping in the snow, yet he continued to slash left and right at the fists of the woman. Once upon a time, she could have been considered quite beautiful, but now she challenged the beastliness of a Daimon, both inside and out.

"The… sanctuary… beyond… last chimney," Thomas gasped while attempting to dodge the swipes of his aggressor. This momentary lapse of attention saw him knocked to the ground in a bone crunching thud.

Thomas yelped as he fought away the threat of unconsciousness. With the last of his energy, he kicked out, tripping up the Afflicted woman who fell perfectly across the point of his sword. She screamed, falling limp; skewered through heart and spine. Her body slumped across his. He struggled to roll away, pinned underneath as her body vibrated.

"Get… out… of here!" Thomas yelled as the body burst into a blue fireball that cleansed the flesh and spirit away in seconds. Thomas shoved away a perfectly preserved diamond skeleton, rolled through slush, and jumped back to his feet. This was the change in luck they needed, as the sight and the smell of A'vean infused bone sent the nearby Afflicted into a state of hysteria. Thomas stamped his boot across the bones, releasing the irresistible smell. He reversed, watched, hid in the shadows.

Needing a new hit and having their drug readily at hand usurped any power their master held over them. All Afflicted within sniffing distance fell upon the glistening remnants, crushing it in their bare hands and licking at the hypnotic power with greedy impatience.

Thomas turned from the foul feeding frenzy, coughing up blood, searching for Jaz. He called out to her as he saw her scrambling away through the sleet.

"Faster!" he coughed coarsely. He'd seen one of the Afflicted had notice Jaz fleeing. The male cocked his head, pulled away from the feasting group, narrowed his eyes in Jaz' direction. He wiped his mouth, seemingly satiated as colour returned to his sallow cheeks. His lips sparkled with diamond dust. He distanced himself from the group of addicts and followed Jaz' footsteps in the snow. Thomas' expression went from momentary relief to shock with this strangely unpredictable behaviour.

"It's coming after you!" his breath was too hoarse to be heard, his energy depleted. Thomas punched at the ground; blood pooled in the snow around him.

Jaz didn't look back. She heard the quickening footsteps all too clearly.

"Fuck, fuck, fuck!" she screamed to herself. "I'm gonna fucking die!"

She felt the vibrations of her pursuer's footfalls, heard the rasp of his breaths and the chuckle of his gloating. Tripping over with fatigue, Sophia's dagger went flying out of her grasp, spinning away across the slippery ground.

"Shit!"

With her last burst of energy, Jaz scrambled up and ran for her life. She was slow and fumbling with panic, her cramp worsened. Yet, through exhaustive breaths, she could hear her name being called.

The urgency of the familiar voice gave her a renewed vigour, and she dragged herself faster. Tears pooled in her lashes, blinding the way ahead.

"Brennan?" she screamed; thickening sleet added to her disorientation. "Where are you? Help me!" her voice thin and dry. She stumbled every few feet; the veil of defeat descending swiftly.

"Here, straight ahead. Hurry!" Brennan's comforting voice drew Jaz to the right, towards a cluster of tall rocks. A pale dawn hue cut through the veil of night. Its aqua light haloed the horizon. The breath of day blew the last of the snow south. Jaz swung her head sharply over her shoulder. The pursuer, whoever it had been, seemed gone. With the soft glow of morning, her eyes cleared. She took a relieved breath, leaned against the rock and gasped for air.

Once her breath was caught, Jaz delved deeper into the rocky retreat.

"Brennan, where are you?"

"Here," he called.

Jaz rounded a large squat stone; her coiled; aching muscles relaxed.

She let out an exhausted cry of relief as she made her way to Brennan, who was only a few feet away, his arms open.

"Come with me, I'll get you out of here," he said.

Jaz fell into him. He held her tight. Jaz clung tighter.

"I thought I was a gonna, Bren. I really thought I'd be worm food," Jaz spluttered.

Brennan patted her head.

"I would never let that happen to you; you're way too valuable."

"Have they gone?" Jaz buried her face into his chest, not wanting to look back.

"Who do you speak of?" he asked, his voice seemed strange.

She pushed back and looked up.

"Those freaks who attacked us? Isn't that why you're here? Helping us?"

"Of course," he replied. He smiled in a strange way.

Jaz' eyes widened. She let go, pushed completely away from him.

"Why the hell do you look so clean?" A quiver returned to her voice as she backed up, assessing Brennan from head to toe.

"I don't like getting dirty, Jasmine. I prefer others to fight for me, if at all possible." His smile broadened. "Come now, let us go somewhere much more suitable for a young lady?" Brennan's voice inched an octave higher, his eyes looked odd. Jaz' heart raced again; her mouth dried.

"You never call me Jasmine, you always call me Mini Princess, you annoying shit!" She backed off further.

Jaz checked behind her, seeking the quickest escape.

"Where are you going? I've been waiting for you," Brennan's voice now held a distinct feminine edge to it. Jaz pointed to him with a shaky, accusing finger.

"I don't know what the hell you are, but stay the fuck away from me!"

Brennan tutted, clucked his tongue and shook his head.

"My, my! Such language from one so pretty." He took a step forward as his body began to glow and shimmer, blurring around the edges.

Jaz spun on her heels, only to smack face first into one of the rocks. Crashing to the ground in a daze, she coughed on her own blood, but remained alert enough to crawl around and keep her enemy in sight.

Jaz spat blood, sniffed it back up her burning nose.

"Get the fuck away from me!" Jaz held her hand up in warning, searching the ground for anything she could use as a weapon. She dared not let her gaze wander too long from the rapidly changing form in front of her. Brennan's face faded out, his shoulders narrowed, his waist thinned, and his long white hair grew dark with white streaks. The glossy hair shimmered in the rapidly rising sun.

"Who the fuck are you?" Jaz screeched through gritted teeth. The veil of defeat was heavy; she could no longer stand.

"Oh, a friend my dear. That is, if you choose to help me. If not… well…" The woman picked at her fingernails a moment. "Things can get a little dicey when I feel that people are not on my team, as you mortals like to phrase it." She threw her head back in laughter; a sweet angelic trill.

"I'm not going *anywhere* with you, lady!"

"Oh, that makes Anjou'elle most unhappy." She shook her head, her finger waggled back and forth as she lazily approached. Jaz scrambling hastily backwards, her body utterly spent. Anjou'elle knelt, stared at Jaz with black-ringed, sparkling blue eyes.

"Come now, we can be friends. You have an enviable fire in your soul." Anjou'elle titled Jaz' face with a slender finger, tenderly wiping away fresh blood from Jaz' swelling nose.

"I have enough friends, thanks!" Jaz spat a mouth full of blood into Anjou'elle's face, stunning her.

Anjou'elle winced. The soft edges of her face tightened into hardness; her eyes blackened with the insult.

She rose, calmly patted down her clothes that were now spotted red.

"Well, we can play it your way then, little brat." Anjou'elle clicked her fingers. Jaz heard shuffling; she didn't wait to find out what it was. She sprang up and tried to run again.

Her legs were useless, weak and unable to find purchase on the sloppy ground. She scrambled exhaustively to the tune of Anjou'elle's laughter.

"I am most bored now. Take her. I want to get back to my sister. You know how Neph'reus frets without me. If you wish to have your filthy drug, get on with it!" Anjou'elle snapped at the Afflicted that cowered at her feet.

Jaz froze, her vision distorted with panic. She could no longer see who or what was around her, but she knew she was out-gunned. On her hands and knees, head low to the ground, Jaz screamed.

"You won't get away with this, bitch!" Jaz collapsed. Fingers curled around her ankles, Anjou'elle slid Jaz away along the freezing, rocky ground.

With barely an ounce of energy left, Jaz screamed long and loud.

"Jude!"

Thomas crawled in the direction he last saw Jaz, a blood trail behind him. Everything now eerily quiet. The Afflicted had disappeared along with the skeletal remnants. No more weapons clanging, no more ethereal warfare, only the odd groan from an injured fighter coming around in the after-math. Shaking his head to gather his senses, he made his way towards a faint glow just ahead.

Yes! he thought. They'd found them and made it to Jaz in time.

He moved quicker and managed to rise to his feet. Limping as fast as he could, he coughed repeatedly and spluttered blood as he went. The glow turned into shapes. The shapes became familiar.

Kea came into view, her wings low but bright enough that Thomas still had to shield his vision.

He called out as he approached, "Jaz? Jaz? Is she okay?"

They turned to him. A forlorn expression devoured their faces. A tear slipped down Kea's cheek.

Thomas pushed his way into the middle of the group, where he found Jude kneeling. "Jude?" Thomas questioned, noticing the smear of fresh blood across the ground.

"Oh no! I failed her too!" Thomas whispered; his face ashen.

Jude slowly raised his eyes to Thomas. His face as dark as a Daimon's. His jaw clenched; his eyes wild with fury. In his hands, he cradled the diamond dagger as gently as if it were a baby. He held it up and looked at the sky.

"No Thomas, it is I who have failed."

Thirty-One

Like a liquid nightmare, everything felt like slow motion. I waded through the foul, thick atmosphere as we carefully made our way along the creepy corridor. Rik and I made quick but careful work of jumping around the ebb and flow of lava that threatened to erupt beneath us at any given moment.

The whisper of Koi's voice became clearer and louder the further we went. Rik stopped every now and then to double check the right tunnels to take. The comforting calls of Koi, along with Rik's determination, gave me hope that we'd have safe passage home.

My heart swelled to know they'd come looking for me. Despite frantically calling back to Koi in my mind, he wasn't responding. I kept calling anyway, hoping he would hear at least an echo of my voice. Now that I had done this with Ben, I knew I could mind-speak. I wasn't going to forego any opportunity to garner help and a way out. I listened more intently to Koi's calls, hoping that following the clarity of his voice would lead me straight to him.

"Once we reach a certain point, you will have to hold onto me like a prisoner, sister," Rik whispered.

I acknowledged the unpleasant thought with a solemn nod. As I was processing this, we came literally to a fork in the road. Two arched and dark options loomed ahead of us. The vague orange flicker of a wall sconce in the distance was the only light to guide us.

"Are you sure this is the right way?" I asked him as he immediately headed to the left.

"We take this one. It heads to the chamber under the Thyros." When I looked at him questioningly, he explained,

"Thyros is the circle of stones, the doorway in and out. Yeqon altered the energy to make it difficult for intruders to breach. Only those who know the right frequency can enter without being harmed. It is controlled by the Blood Stone in Yeqon's throne room."

I nodded in understanding, recalling that this must be what the Zythros stone's function was. Not only to communicate but also to facilitate entry into a secure, secret world.

"You know the code?" I asked.

Rik nodded. I stopped, looked at the tunnel to the right.

"That goes to the throne room, where we were before." Rik looked to the ground, I felt the fear rolling from him. The torture I'd witnessed him receive at Yeqon's hands was unbearable for me to recall, and that's why it was difficult for me say what I did next.

"We need go to the Throne room first," I said as he attempted to guide me further to the left.

"What? Why? Are we not getting out of here?" He looked confused and slightly pale. His mark lit; his hand tremored in mine.

"Yes, we're getting out of here, but I need Enoch's box. I can't leave it here."

The mountain roared above with as much disapproval as was splashed across Rik's face.

"Even the son of Tartarus believes that is a bad idea," Rik said, pulling a little harder for me to follow.

"Firstly, we can't make decisions based on a volcano. Trust me, it isn't my ideal destination either, but as I'm in disguise, I should be able to sneak in to grab it. Something's going on. The prisoners are gone, Koi is nearby, and it feels strangely deserted. Can't you feel it?"

Rik nodded.

"I'll bet they're all out defending themselves. I'm pretty sure it will be the only good chance we've got." I wasn't convinced it was a particularly smart idea, but I needed Enoch's box.

Shadows flickered across Rik's face. His fingers untwined from mine.

"Your logic makes sense. You have come so far, but I can't go in there. I can't, sister. Please don't make me?" Rik backed away.

Frustration welled up, but I pushed it away. I needed a clear head, and it was beyond reasonable he wouldn't want to return to a place of torture.

"Fair enough. You stay here, and I mean literally right here." I even pointed to a specific spot by the edge of the archway where shadows afforded a little camouflage. I didn't want to lose him.

"If anyone comes by, keep out of sight. I'll go on my own and meet you back here, then we'll get outta here, okay?" I nodded at him. He hesitated. He looked so very pained. He ground his teeth, but then nodded.

"How far is it from here?" I glanced into the depths of the right tunnel, immediately feeling vastly less brave.

"A few minutes." Rik studied the tunnel anxiously, as if waiting for something horrendous to emerge. This was a real and distinct possibility. A shudder ran down my spine. I studied my palm and created a small orb. I placed it gently in his hand. He took it reverently, eyes wide.

"If something happens, if I'm caught or I'm not back by the time this orb dies down, the story is that I overwhelmed you and escaped on my own. Got it?"

"Yes, I understand." He nodded solemnly.

I placed my hands on his shoulders and squeezed.

"It'll be alright, I'm sure of it. Koi is so close; he sounds almost like he's right above us." I smiled encouragingly. Rik didn't return it. He was so messed up; I couldn't blame him. I gave him a quick hug, which he didn't return either.

Don't read into it, Soph. Be patient.

"Right, do I still look like Spider?"

"Horribly so!" he grimaced.

"Good." I took a deep breath, hoping this crazy plan would play out just right.

"Okay, stay put unless you need to protect yourself. I'll *hopefully* be back soon." I kissed him on the forehead. Rik unexpectedly grabbed my hand, held it tight and ran his thumb across the base of my hand.

"Be careful, please, sister?"

I nodded. "Especially for you, brother." I held his hand until he pulled away.

He's with me, I thought. *Underneath all that hurt, he's with me.*

Before I could change my mind, I took the right-hand tunnel.

Deep breath in, deep breath out, repeat.

Hand on my necklace, I prayed lady luck was finally on my side.

Rik was stiff and awkward as he stood guard, awaiting Sophia's return. He fiddled nervously, picking at pieces of crumbling wall. Every few seconds he glanced cautiously around, eyes wide, staring down the length of the dark passageways.

Sounds began echoing up from the Thyros chamber. Immediately, sweat beaded more profusely down his face, pooling above his lips. He pushed a long piece of hair out of his face, his attention drawn to the mouth of the left tunnel. Raised voices caught his attention, voices he had not heard before. They were not getting closer, though. He bit his thumbnail, wondering why someone would transfer in and remain in the receiving chamber. Running his hands through his hair, he argued with himself about whether it was help arriving.

"You do not know these voices. They must be help," he whispered. He clutched his face in frustration and paced indecisively.

Perhaps they were help, and they were lost? Of course! How would they know where to go? He should show them the way. Then both he and Sophia could be free from this place. It could be her friend, Koi, he thought

Back and forth, he paced, completely at odds with himself. The voices were louder now, but still not any closer. He decided they must be Sophia's friends. He peered deeper into the left tunnel, letting his rigid hands fall from his face.

Sister will succeed. I will find the help and be here when she returns. I will bring the help to her. She will be proud of me.

Rik padded stealthily down the familiar pathway towards the voices. The closer he came, the more it seemed they were voices of anger, like an argument was going on. Nerves caused his face to light up. He swallowed hard, took some deep breaths to calm himself, the glow dimmed a little. He kept one hand over his mark to cover the light that remained.

"Who are you?" A male voice bellowed.

Rik froze for a moment.

"I could ask you the same question?" A female retorted.

Rik moved on, edged closer to where the amber light of a dozen wall sconces warmed the Thyros chamber. He held his breath and stuck his head ever so slightly around the corner.

Two Watchers faced off. The body of another lay crumpled at their feet.

"Why are you not injured, yet I am?" The female questioned with acidic accusation.

She was actively healing blisters and scorch marks across her arms.

"Why did you kill the girl?" The male retorted as he kicked at the body that was smouldering as it prepared to ascend.

"She was practically dead anyway. There was some kind of trap set here. I did her a favour. I'm lucky *I'm* still standing! Not that you seem to care, oh Great One!" Sarcasm dripped from her words as she bowed in jest. Something shifted in the male's expression.

"You seem familiar?' he murmured suspiciously, then grabbed her wrist. She wrenched it from his grasp. Her other arm dangled, as though broken.

"Well, *you* seem like a traitor! How could you pass through in one piece?" She challenged, her face alight with anger. "Look at me! Broken and burnt. I stink like a corpse!" She continued her self-healing as they backed away from each other, keeping a safe distance.

"I am of the Eloi council, you fool. *Who* are you?" he demanded more forcefully.

"I already told you who I am," she sneered.

"No, you have not. I have never heard of anyone called A'glacea." Ambient light picked up the sweat beading down the Eloi's ebony skin, his broad chest heaved a little deeper in the stifling heat. The white of his hair and glint of his eyes seemed suddenly familiar. Rik licked his lips nervously as he watched on from the shadows.

The two of them didn't give any ground. Rik was confused. They clearly weren't of this realm, but they were fighting each other, not trusting each other at all. He gulped when blue flames finally engulfed the body on the ground, leaving nothing but crystal bones behind. He imagined it could have been him. A heavier sweat erupted under his arms.

"One thing I do know, oh Great One of the Eloi," A'glacea rolled her eyes. "Is that we need to hide these remains. They are a dead giveaway that security has been breached." She looked at the diamond skeleton, no emotion in her eyes.

"Indeed. Over there for now." the Eloi pointed to a darkened corner.

A'glacea dragged the delicate skeleton away and crushed the bones into dust.

"You do that all too easily, woman. By the name of I'el, who are you?" He circled her, his eyes swirled brighter, something dawned in their glow.

"Your name, it isn't a name. It is an ancient word for Daimon." The Eloi's eyes widened at the revelation, he summoned an orb to his palm.

A'glacea faced him, smiling wide, no fear or care for the might of an Eloi.

"Oh, put your big scary orb away!" She chuckled. She shimmered, her body faded and blurred at the edges. Her shape snapped in and out of a hundred different images, as though searching for just the right one.

The Eloi, who seemed somehow familiar to Rik, moulded the orb larger. He stepped back, his face scrunched in anger, not fear. Rik sunk even farther away into the shadows, wishing his pulse would stop raging so loud. The slowly evolving woman spoke with various voices, both male and female. She sounded like one who was possessed with a dark entity. The only part of her that was clear were her eyes, and they were dark and hateful.

"Oh well, I suppose it was a risk." A'glacea ran an arm along the length of her new body. It lengthened and shortened, almost set in its new shape.

"I'll just have to hope plan B works! Thank I'el, bless him, for teaching us about plan B's. After all, wasn't that miserable flood His plan B for all us bad, bad, angels in the middle of this forsaken planet?" She tipped her head back and laughed. "Hang on, that wasn't such a good plan B, was it? Only took out a few thousand. He forgot about the rest of the world!" She laughed again. "Luckily my plan is a real kicker!" Her laugh deepened into a more menacing threat. Rik gulped; glad he knew how to get by without taking a breath.

A'glacea kept teasing the Eloi. She sauntered around him, not in the slightest bit affronted by the threatening weapon sizzling upon his hand. The Eloi watched her cautiously, eyes narrowed.

"I just wanted to get out a bit, you know? See how the plebs get along and all." She laughed again as her body finally morphed into a completely different visage.

The pretty young woman was replaced with a resplendent beauty. Ebony locks feathered her thighs, streaked white like a Daimon. Plump red lips pouted playfully in the Eloi's direction. She batted her eyes at him. His jaw clenched; anger flashed across his eyes.

"Neph'reus!" he ground out her name.

"You remember! I'm flattered." Neph'reus' hand fluttered over her heart.

"What are you doing here? I thought you…"

Neph'reus cut him off, "Ascended? Oh, sweetheart, you think so very little of me! Am I at least not as old as you? Perhaps a little more resilient, too. After all, sis and I take such good care of each other. Always have each-other's backs. You know how it is with siblings? We always stick together."

That statement felt like a needle in Rik's chest. He swallowed away the hurt and kept listening, hooked on the conversation.

Neph'reus arched her brows and finished healing her broken arm. The snap of it knitting together echoed through the chamber. She rubbed it, flexed it, smiled at it, and wriggled her fingers. "Better!"

The Eloi dulled the orb a little, moved closer.

"We all had hoped you and your conniving sister were mere memories," he said.

"So sorry to disappoint. Well, now that the cat is out of the bag, I best find that sister of mine and get back to business." Neph'reus waved her hand, her soft wings emerged.

"And what business is that?" he growled.

"Oh darling, my business, your business, isn't it all really the same? I want power, you want power, damned I'el wants power!" Neph'reus smirked. "Greedy little Watchers, aren't we?"

"You *do not* know what I want!" The Eloi's white hair fluttered in the breeze of her wings. Rik's heart hammered.

"Well, who's not being quite truthful now?" Neph'reus transferred away in a mesmerising flash. The Eloi screamed in rage, punching a nearby wall as the mountain rumbled above. He too disappeared, leaving Rik more confused than he had ever been.

Chapter Thirty-Two

An unusual chaos reigned within the depths of Kaymakli sanctuary. Unexpected wounded were rushed in by the dozens. Bodies glowed and sputtered in uncontrolled bursts of elemental energy. They writhed in pain, unable to heal themselves. Sheaves of herbs smouldered where they hung from the ceiling, a heady smoke coated to the room. Lavender-laden Alchemae healers moved with a determined poise to bring calm and relief as they assisted Enl'iel in triaging the wounded. Humans were sequestered to one area, those of A'vean heritage to another. Both required completely different healing techniques. The floor was slippery with blood. Hurried footprints smeared through it. Bandages, emulsions and soul stones were brought in by the basket load and applied to the neediest first. Teens tended to cleaning and restocking. They expertly threaded the hair of the unconscious with protective herbs until all who lay in a bed wore a halo of sweet-smelling purple halos.

Enl'iel directed where to send the overflow of injured that didn't fit into the available recovery beds. Her face furrowed with the heavy worry of the situation.

"Clear out the dining hall. We will use that as a temporary first aid area. Take the least wounded there. You," Enl'iel pointed to a teen, their arms heavy with herb baskets.

"Take that lot to the dining hall. We've enough here for now." She waved the girl hurriedly away. The teen acknowledged the order with a quick bow before she ran off to the task.

The argument erupting from within the intensive care area was getting out of control. Enl'iel had glanced in that direction a couple of times, trying to ignore it, but it was now carrying out to where it was very clear for anyone to hear. Amidst triaging the injured, everyone took turns sneaking peeks in the direction of Jude and Brennan's shouting match. Enl'iel took a calming breath, ran her hands down her sides, yet her face flushed scarlet as she made her way through the white veil of energy that protected the most gravely ill.

Inside the chromious-lined room, an even thicker, cedar-wood smoke hugged the ceiling. She glared reprovingly at the Jude and Brennan. Lorcan shadowed his brother. He gently caressed Kristen's hand with his healing, glowing one. Kristen lay in a deep coma, her upper torso and neck smothered in herbs, bandages and crystals of all varieties.

For a few moments, Enl'iel watched and listened to the two alphas rip each other to shreds. Luckily, only with words.

"And your solution was what? Leave her here just so she could sneak out and be killed anyway?" Spittle sprayed from Jude into Brennan's face.

"If you'd let us talk some sense into her, she would have stayed, you moron! She's a smart kid!" Brennan retorted, wiping his face with the back of his hand. "Soph will be devastated!" His fists clenched; the knuckles cracked.

"Smart? That girl is reckless and impulsive. She would have given the sanctuary's position away trying to be something she's not. Something she will never be! It was best to keep her exactly where I could see her." Jude's face raged, his eyes shadowed like a thundercloud.

"Well, great job you did with that! Where the hell is she now, Jude?" Brennan shrugged.

"And what did you do? Tell me Brennan? Were you out there being ambushed? No, as usual you were safely tucked away playing house!" Jude glanced towards Enl'iel with a sneer.

Enl'iel sucked a sharp breath of offence. Brennan swung a fist, collecting Jude's jaw and snapping his head back. Jude didn't move a muscle, solidly standing his ground. He regained his focus, licked the blood that sprouted on his lips. He readjusted the dislocation of his jaw with a click. Jude glared at Brennan; his mark nuclear.

"I have been protecting our young, Jude! Did you not hear how many Afflicted I cut down on my own before Dash arrived to help? I was protecting our next generation, just like I watched over Soph with Cael all those years. You want me out there in the thick of it? Fine, I'd love to go. I breathe war and death." Brennan exaggerated a deep breath. His eyes glimmered with anger. His fingers clenched as though they ached for more contact with Jude's face. Brennan smiled, kept prodding Jude's limits.

"I love the smell of Rogue smeared all over my sword! Send *me* out and *you* stay in with your apron on. You play house and look after the kids!" Brennan laughed, shook his head. "But no, you want to be the big man, the one who calls the shots, the one claiming to protect us all. You know what? I'm sick of the debt you're collecting on. It was a long time ago. Let it go! I didn't mean for you to be banished. It happened before we knew I'el's opinion, on free love and all that!" Brennan wiggled his hands mockingly. "It's about time you got over your ego and precious hurt feelings and moved on. It didn't only happen to you! How long do you need before you can forgive me?" Brennan jutted his chin out accusingly, along with a finger just short of poking Jude's chest.

Jude snorted, clenched Brennan's finger until it turned white and pushed it away.

Jude opened his mouth, but was cut off by Enl'iel.

"Jude," her voice was soft. "This bitterness is only dividing us. Please, look past this? Both of you?" She glared at Brennan, "It is no one's fault that Jaz was kidnapped. No one was expecting Nevşehir to be attacked by Rogues. This was supposed to be a routine sweep, something done a thousand times over. As for the appearance of Afflicted, that, in my opinion, seems to be separate all together. It appears either Yeqon is throwing everything he has at us to disorient and deplete us, or, even more worrying, is that we have more than one enemy. Jude says he saw a female directing the Afflicted. That is not at all like Yeqon. He has never liked the difficulty of using Afflicted, or women for that matter. The Afflicted are only loyal for as long as you supply Thanratos. That is an inconvenience Yeqon doesn't have the patience to worry about. The Rogues, however, just do as their maker tells them. Do not get me started on how he treats women." She pursed her lips on that subject. "I'm positive it wasn't only his influence tonight."

Brennan and Jude kept quiet, both still heaving with anger.

"I think you're right, Enl'iel," Lorcan said, joining the conversation whilst remaining by Kristen's side.

"I was tricked into leaving, Koi. I thought I heard Brennan in trouble. You *were* in trouble, but I was lured the wrong way. I thought you were just past the fairy chimneys, but when I arrived, there was merely the scent of a Daimon and blood in the snow. I can't believe I was so fooled." Lorcan's face flushed; he tightened his mouth. "Someone was obviously concealing themselves as you to cause some form of confusion. Whoever it was is not young, because I truly thought it was you, Brennan. I heard you as clear as day. Who do we know that could, or would do this so convincingly, and why?" Lorcan shook his head, disappointment clouded his eyes.

"Lorcs, I did call for help, but that was right near the entrance to the sanctuary, not where you were." Brennan plucked his lips, his brows pinned. "Dash arrived; we sorted the lurkers pretty quick, then re-glamoured the entrance," Brennan said, his face as shaded as Lorcan's.

"So, who could be so convincing? Clearly there's Ben, but he hasn't been seen since Stonehenge," Enl'iel said and readjusted some herbs around Kristen's neck. "I'm convinced he wouldn't risk a return, not yet, at least. He would know we could sniff him out this time." Enl'iel clasped her hands under her nose. She peered at Brennan, Lorcan and back to Kristen. "And why would he want Jaz?" she mumbled more to herself.

The tension between Jude and Brennan died away as the discussion veered more toward who the imposter was. An Alchemae snuck in to check on Kristen, changing the crystals that glowed atop her shoulders. New, more vibrant ones glimmered bright along the bandaging.

"I know who would and could conceal that well," Jude grumbled. "But I haven't seen them in a long time. No one has. I assumed they'd descended, but I'm sure it was one of them that I saw tonight."

"Who?' Enl'iel asked, plucking at her necklace.

"It couldn't be? Surely not? What in I'el's name would they want after all this time?" Brennan said, his eyes brighter, fingers curled into fists.

"Who?" Enl'iel asked a little more impatiently.

Jude answered, "Neph'reus and her sister, Anjou'elle. They've been trouble-makers since they were first born. They were banished from Satanos and sent here to keep out of trouble because they showed too much of a liking for the Satans. They were a pain in the arse for a long time, a pain in *my* arse to be exact… until they disappeared around five hundred years ago."

"Ah, yes, I remember the stories." Enl'iel adjusted a piece of errant hair away from Kristen's face.

"They fraternised with mortals, interfered in human affairs, basically caused a shitload of trouble." Jude shook his head. "Attention-seekers, never content to just watch on. They always needed to interfere for their own amusement, despite it more often than not causing injury or insult to unsuspecting humans. Where do you think the word 'nefarious' came from? The abominable and depraved Neph'reus of course. They had a taste for possessing kings and queens, sending them mad purely for the fun of it." Jude cracked his shredded knuckles.

Enl'iel's shook her head, "We were just talking recently how decent King Richard III had been until something strange happened to him."

Enl'iel nodded to herself, "Neph'reus and Anjou'elle disappeared not too long after. They were caught up in whatever happened to Sophia's grandparents."

"Yes," Jude responded. "The timing is slightly suspicious, don't you think? Considering the last time they were seen."

"Do they work for Yeqon?" Enl'iel asked, twisting her pendant again.

"Never. They would sooner ascend than deal with him. Despite their behaviour being exactly like that of a Daimon, they never identified as one. They were freelance, I suppose. Everything was for those two alone. They stopped answering to I'el, the Eloi council, or anyone but themselves long ago. I was hoping they'd just shrivelled up somewhere." Jude sat on a stool, leaning his face into his hands. His shoulders sagged. Enl'iel ran her hand across his back.

"So, it appears there may be two factions at work. One, we know what they are after, the other is a conundrum. All the more reason you two need to put an end to this ridiculous feud. We must work together, now more than ever. We now need to find both Sophia and Jaz," Enl'iel said. "Why on earth would they take Jaz? It just makes no sense."

Lorcan kissed Kristen's hand and left her side. He paced.

"I think…" He stopped.

"What is it bro?" Brennan asked.

"The timing is clearly not coincidental, as Jude has pointed out. They were last seen sniffing around Sophia's grandparents, King Edward IV and Queen Elizabeth. Kind Edward died mysteriously, Richard went bonkers and tried to kill his brother's two boys, one of whom was Sophia's dad." Lorcan wrapped one hand over a clenched fist. His eyes thinned as his mind worked.

They all had a glint of understanding glean across their expressions. Enl'iel tightened her grip on her pendent.

"They disappear for half a millennium until now, until Sophia is born? Do you see the connection?" Lorcan asked with a wide sweep of his arms.

"Those two bitches want our Soph as well? Why?" Brennan glowered.

Quiet reigned for a few moments other than the gentle sound of Kristen's breaths.

"They want the Kaladai as well," Jude said, looking up from his hands, weariness cast grey crescents under his eyes. "I don't know what they want it for, but why else would Jaz be taken? Just as she was snatched at the hospital, to be used as a pawn to get to Sophia and to get to the Kaladai. Somehow, they've managed to work out Jaz' worth and snatch her too," Jude surmised through clenched teeth.

"Poor Mini Princess. She didn't ask for any of this." Brennan's lashes glistened as he looked down at Kristen and patted her pale hand.

"None of us asked for this!" Jude snapped.

Enl'iel glared his way, her face flared with disapproval.

"Alright Enl'iel, back off." Jude waved her off and stood back up. He ran hands through his hair, still matted and bloodied from battle. Jude wiped himself clear of the gore and took charge.

"Obviously, we've got a new and very big problem. I don't know what their agenda is. We need to find Sophia, but I want to be out looking for Jaz as soon as things settle down here. There is no way Sophia will hold up if she returns to find Jaz missing. That damned pain in my arse will be dangled at Sophia like a carrot." Jude licked his lips, flipped his favourite dagger in his hand.

"I'm worried Sophia will take the bait." He pointed to Lorcan. "We need to get in contact with Koi. Go back to the Empyrean realm, inform Koi about what's going down here. Hopefully, they've found Sophia by now. Take Kea with you, help him in any way you can." Jude grimaced, jerked his head at Brennan. "You and I are going to find Jaz. I've got some contacts in the underground. Grab Dash and organise a search party. We'll leave in an hour."

Chapter
Thirty-Three

To say I was scared out of my wits was an understatement. It took every ounce of strength and focus to maintain my disguise. I eased through the dim and stinking surroundings. I must have frozen and held my breath a dozen times, straining to hear for anyone, or anything, that might have been following me. The cracks and sizzles of geothermal activity sounded like footsteps and whispers, holding me in a heightened state of anxiety.

With one hand grasping its way along the wall, the other burning with an orb, I made my way as quickly as I dared through the shadows. The heat was insufferable. I didn't understand how the Daimon could bear it. Then again, I suppose their choices were taken away when they'd turned to the dark side, so to speak. More than once, I blinked away the sting of sweat. I hoped, beyond hope, that Rik had stayed put. There was something very unstable about him. I was gambling on how much he wanted to escape, hoping it would keep him following my lead.

The ground vibrated with a new tremor. I wobbled out of the way as steam spewed through small fissures overhead. The sulphuric odour made me gag, the vapour drenched my hair into a knotted frizz. Up ahead, the tunnel appeared to widen, the wall sconces increased in frequency. Darkness receded; yet illumination did nothing to dwindle the horror of the place. Dark smears smudged the walls. They didn't at all appear to be natural variations of the stone; more like bloodied finger prints. I slowed my pace, took a calming breath. Intuitively, I felt something was around the next bend, and it certainly was when I poked my head around the corner.

Scattered platters and food scraps littered the floor around the base of the ominous thrones. A dark pool of congealed blood stained the earthen floor where Lilith had feasted on the unfortunate Afflicted creature earlier. An eerie disquiet thickened with tension. I stepped carefully through the mess; nerves on a razor-sharp edge, just waiting for unwelcome company.

I searched desperately for Enoch's box.

As if they'd just leave it out ready for you! I thought and made my way tentatively up the steps towards the six stone seats. An animal pelt adorned each one. Grooves had worn into the armrests. I ran my hand across the one Yeqon had sat in. Even this inanimate object felt evil. I yanked my hand away quickly, rubbing it free of the feeling. Through another rumble, I was ever so sure I heard a scream or two. I picked up my pace and searched on. The orb reabsorbed into my palm, so I had both hands to sift through the mess. They weren't the best housekeepers, for sure. Old wooden crates were stacked a dozen high behind the thrones. The odd rotting apple and onion glued to the floor, thick with green and blue mould. Discarded drinking flutes of horn, bone, and wood lay scattered here and there.

In the back of my mind, there was another call from Koi.

Sophia, are you here? If you can get to the surface, we are here for you. His voice faded to static, replaced by the crack and clang of elemental and metal weapons clashing.

"They know I'm here," I whispered to myself.

"Who knows you're here?"

I froze. It wasn't the kind of voice I wanted to hear right now, or ever.

I clasped my hands tight into my chest, preparing to draw out a new orb. I slowly turned to find, of all people, Lilith. She stood behind me, twirling a coil of dark hair. Her amber eyes flared as she puckered her plump lips in my direction, awaiting an answer.

"Who are you talking about, slave?" she demanded. I stumbled backwards, bumping into the crates, sending a few toppling over my head. Her dagger-pointed stilettos clicked as she made her way closer. The red velvet of her boots glowed in the ambient light, clung tight to the length of her legs. She looked like a runway model who'd gone off tap. For a moment, I'd forgotten I was concealed, but quickly regained my rhythm and pretended to be the victim.

"I…I… no one," my scratchy voice responded.

"You lie. Would a little bloodletting draw the truth from you?" Lilith licked her lips suggestively.

"I'll have no traitors here! Yeqon feeds and houses you, treats you with your drug. You *owe* him your life!" She leaned into my face and sniffed.

"What are you up to?" Lilith wrapped her fingers around my chin, turning my face left and right, boring her amber stare into me.

"I come to clean for my master," I stammered, subtly aware that she continued to smell me through her delicately flared nostrils. She seemed to try to work out what meal I might be. She glanced around at the cluttered chamber and snorted.

"I see little very cleaning. You lie!" she spat through gritted, pearly teeth.

"We are under attack, slave. Are you hiding? Have you sided with the enemy? Hoping for rescue? *They* will give you no protection. *They* despise your kind. You know that, do you not?" Lilith softened her eyes, slid her arm about my shoulders, almost motherly. This was even more threatening.

"Come, tell me your troubles. Mother Lilith can help you. I've counselled many a babe. Let me ease your mind." Smiling maliciously, she pushed me down into one of the thrones. She turned away a moment and seemed to chat to herself, before spinning back on her heels and picking at her fingernails.

"Now, who knows you are here, my dear? Do you fear someone? Is someone after you? Are you feeling threatened? Do they know where you are?" Lilith barraged me with questions.

Hell yes, I felt threatened! I had to keep the charade up. If I lost it now, I'd jeopardise Rik, Enoch's Box, and my chance of escape.

"Come now, speak up." She leaned closer, running her red, talon-like nails gently across my cheek. "Do not be shy. Tell me, and I shall keep you out of Yeqon's way when he returns."

"I am merely here to clean." I tried to sound more convincing, but it was hard to meet her terrifying eyes. I was sure she could see right through me.

"Hmph!" She raked her fingers through my hair, twirling a few knotted strands around those nails, just as she'd done with her own. I noticed silvery letters tattooed across her fingers in the warm glow of the firelight. *L. O. V. E.* In a flash, I could see no more as her grip tightened on my hair. She pulled it hard. *Were had I seen those letters before?*

"You do not smell sweet like you should. You smell of salt. Of fear!" Her eyes glowed unnaturally, like a raging inferno. Lines deepened at the edge of her widening smile.

"Do you know how old I am, Dear? How much I have seen and learned over my extraordinary lifetime?"

Sweat beaded down my back more furiously than before, and this time it wasn't from the heat. My heart hammered as I felt a tingling rush across my skin.

Oh no, not now. Hold it together, Soph. I needed to keep all my cards close, to keep control until I absolutely needed to let my power unravel. The element of surprise *must* be my friend until I truly had a grip on controlling my powers properly.

She sniffed again, right up into my neck. "I do not believe you." Lilith's breath was hot and bitter.

The burn tingled teasingly up my spine; my mark begged to glow in the face of such danger. I could have just exploded right then, dealt with her. I was sure I could overcome her, even with my less than perfect technique. But what if that attracted someone? I knew I wasn't strong enough to encounter too much at once. So far, my powers had been more reactive than proactive. I had to be cautious if Rik and I were to stand a chance, and I needed the box.

"I assure you, Ma'am, I am just here to clean."

"Ma'am! Assure me! Since when does an Afflicted speak like this? You are not what you appear, are you?" Lilith pulled ever harder on my hair, forcing my head down. Her other hand closed around my neck and she squeezed. The surprise move had me gasping like a fish as she yanked a larger fistful of my hair.

"You clever girl! But you're not clever enough for Lilith. You may have taken the image of a slave, but I see you in there, Earth-born; I smell you. Come out, come out, wherever you are!" Lilith cooed melodiously whilst her hand squeezed ever-tighter.

I relinquished control and forced my head up, met her steely glare. I let the burn soar. The transformation back to myself felt almost instantaneous. Lilith lost her grip when my wings burned through. The heat forced her backwards. She teetered on her stilettos to stay upright. I launched towards her; she came back at me. Her strength was a surprise. We toppled backwards, rolling behind the thrones. We were a ball of light and fists and razor-sharp teeth. Lilith screeched foul insults between gasping breaths and gnashing those teeth. The ground rumbled; a fresh burst of foul steam clouded the air. Koi called frantically in the back of my mind again. It drew a new strength from somewhere, and I let my instincts take over.

Energy arced from my hands towards Lilith. She screeched as the electric zaps bit into her, yet she refused to give in. She tightened her grip, clutching fistfuls of my hair, nails digging into my scalp, holding onto whatever she could. Despite fighting like an amateur, she was a powerful one. Her principal weapon was her acidic threats. She tried to sink her teeth into any part of me she could. Her incisors sliced my upper arms several times. We continued to roll and struggle against one another.

"You!" she panted; her eyes were wide with thrill as she licked hungrily at my blood on her full lips. "You could make me even more powerful again!" Her mouth widened, a ghastly, unnatural yawn as she lunged forward and bit into my shoulder. I screamed as the pain seared down my arm. She drew a few gulps before I yanked her head away and booted her off me. I was up in an instant, an orb poised to strike.

"You have one chance, Lilith. One chance, or that was your last disgusting snack!" I held the orb aloft as I spied Rik out of the corner of my eye, stalking the entrance. *Crap, no!*

Quickly averting my eyes from him, I launched the orb at Lilith's feet. The blowback threw her into the crates and they came toppling down on her. For a moment, I wondered if she was out cold because there was no sound or movement, other than the hiss of steam and crack of new fissures in the cavern. The volcanic activity increased in fervour, as though the confrontation was driving the mountain into a frenzy.

Completely drenched in blood, sweat and sulphurous mud, I took a few breaths to calm myself. I eased away from the thrones; assessed the situation, all the while aware of Rik's presence. My shoulder burned with pain. I lit my opposite hand and healed the ripped flesh, immediately feeling the relief.

I sighed. The comfort of my skin held its own strength. Rik slid further into the chamber and was thankfully keeping to the shadows. He approached cautiously, his back firmly against the far wall. I put a finger to my lips as I eased further away from where Lilith lay.

Like the Wicked Witch of the East, Lilith's red boots poked out lifelessly from under the pyramid of wooden debris. She wasn't lifeless, though; the rush of her blood was all too loud to my keen hearing. Her heart pumped rapidly with life. She was stirring. I took the opportunity while I had it to search for the box.

Scanning the entire room, there was no sign of it. Yeqon would have taken it with him; he was ancient and cunning, and wouldn't be careless with such a precious artefact; surely?

Despite me waving him away, Rik approached, his eyes glued to where Lilith slowly roused.

"We cannot stay here, sister. She will alert him!"

"I thought I told you to stay put? I have to find the box, Rik, otherwise it's all pointless and everything will have been for nothing. He will have all the cards in his deck. Please, Rik, my destiny can't be wasted because we're scared," I said.

He nodded slowly, "I'm sorry, I'm trying to understand."

Well, that made me feel like a heartless bitch. I approached him. "No, I'm sorry. You've been dragged into something horrific just like me, but you've had a much worse start than me. I'm sorry for expecting too much when you've been given so little." I reached for his hand. His fingers curled into mine for a beautiful moment, then slipped away.

"It's okay. I would just like to get out of here," he said.

"Well then, let's find that box and be dust in the wind," I said and he half smiled.

"Okay, since you're here, go look over there." I pointed along the craggy steps to where there seemed to be wide cracks in the walls.

"Look in those, but please be careful."

Rik moved with caution along the stairs. As he did so, I was rammed into the ground, the wind knocked from my lungs. Another razor bite plunged into the back of my neck. I screamed as Lilith sucked hard and fast from my jugular.

She groaned with pleasure as my blood pooled on the ground, soaking into my cheeks. Her gulps were guttural, animalistic. She pressed my face harder to the ground as she had her fill of me.

"Sister!' Rik cried.

"Back off, you piece of filth!" Lilith stopped, pulled my head back by the hair so I could see Rik, pale-faced.

"Is this the thanks you give your mother? Treason?"

"You are not my mother!" Rik's lips peeled back in disgust. His face glowed with a rage so passionate he seemed to blossom into a new person.

"Get… out of… here," I stammered. I struggled as Lilith pulled my head up higher and then rammed it hard into the ground. I saw stars.

"Get off her!" Rik growled. My clouded sense of consciousness made his voice more liquid and far away. I let myself go limp, called upon my senses, which quickly returned. I played possum, listening all the while to the exchange between the pair.

"You always were a disappointment, Boy. After all I gave to you!" Lilith snarled.

Rik retorted in a strained voice. "Gave me? You and him? You stole my life from me. My father too, and now look; you stole the chance for me to know my sister. Get off her now!" I felt him move closer, smelled the salt of his fear, the spark of his anger prick my skin.

"Hmph, you always were ungrateful. You could have ended up like your father. You could have descended in the pits. Such a lack of gratitude, you vile cockroach of a son!"

"I am not your son!"

Rik's footsteps felt closer. It took all of my willpower to remain still. I let the burn build again. I knew what was coming. Lilith didn't.

"One step closer and I'll rip her throat out. I can and I will. You know it, Boy."

My head was yanked back again. I opened one eye a sliver, Rik immediately seeing that I was perfectly aware. He took a step back.

"That's the smartest decision you have made, Boy. Behave yourself and I might protect you. This one's blood surpasses even Yeqon's. With her power, I will live forever and be stronger than I could ever have imagined. She drank from me again. One sharp gulp before she dragged me by the hair back behind the thrones. Lilith rolled me behind her, keeping one stilettoed heel on my neck.

"By the power of I'el, I could be the one to lead, to rule. Imagine it, Boy? No longer begging for blood to keep me young. Walk by my side and we could take our own path." Lilith laughed hysterically. "Could you imagine the power of the children I could birth with her blood in my veins? And an entire planet of food just walking around for the taking! Such bliss awaits me!"

"He will kill you if he hears you speak such treason," Rik responded calmly.

"The way I feel right now, I'el Himself could not descend me!" she cackled like a witch. I scanned the darkness as she pushed harder with her boot. The tip of the heal bit hard as I searched for another way out, once I executed my plan.

Rik kept her talking whilst I built my energy. He seemed to know instinctively how to distract her. I closed my eyes tight in preparation.

Deep breath, deep breath out, repeat.

As I opened my eyes, I nearly let out a gasp. A small glint of silver flickered within a gap in the crushed crates. Under the toppled boxes, Enoch's box lay upturned and waiting for me.

That was all it took. I was ready to get out of this cesspit.

One deep breath in, and I let my wings burst free. Energy snapped wildly from my palms in every direction. I rose into the air, toppling a shocked Lilith to the ground.

"Bitch!" she screamed and launched herself my way, nails and teeth bared.

Hovering high above her, I shot a dozen arcs of light straight into the centre of her chest. She flew, spread-eagled over the thrones and toppled down the stairs.

I glided above her, albeit it very wobbly. She was charred and blistered. Blood seeped from a gash in her head, whilst my blood stained her mouth, leaving her looking like a gruesome clown.

"She isn't dead," I answered Rik's unspoken question as he glared warily in her direction. "Watch her, I've found the box."

Rik moved cautiously, sniffing around her unmoving form, before placing his foot on her throat. He winced.

I glided quickly back behind the thrones, landing fairly smoothly, this time leaving my wings out, just in case.

With a surprising strength that grew by the day, I threw the debris out of the way in seconds. Underneath, my prize was revealed. It was the most beautiful thing I'd ever seen. The stunning box was back in my arms, and my hopes spiked.

"I've got it, Rik!" I called excitedly, but stopped as a groan echoed around the cavern. With the heavy chest tight in my arms, I turned to the sound of a new voice.

Kicking Lilith's limp body out of the way, standing with that same horrid dagger to Rik's throat, was Yeqon.

Chapter Thirty-Four

The ground had opened without warning. Hordes of demonic detritus hauled out of the pits and tunnels of Tartarus. The mountain in the distance roared, spewing lava and rocks high into the air. Smoke haze blotted the strange sun into a blinding smear against the horizon.

Koi, Gedz'iel, the Eloi, and the rest of the A'vean army rained down a savage barrage of firepower, setting alight the barely-there collection of flesh and bones.

Humanoid and nightmarish creatures crawled from the fissures with mindless determination. Zombies, in every sense of the word, threw themselves without a care into the burning might of the Watchers, who cut them down with ease.

"They're a distraction, that's all!" Serail yelled over the cacophony, as he beheaded three Rogues with one swipe of his long sword. Koi watched his back as he used extra-large red orbs to ash a troop of fleshless skeletons as they heaved themselves up from the depths. Bone fragments rained like hailstones over the onslaught that spewed relentlessly from the underground.

"Agreed… a vile, waste of time distraction!" Koi yelled back. He swooped from a great height to hover back-to-back with Serail and

Gedz'iel. They had fought a thousand battles together and mirrored each other without a thought.

"We are close to Sophia; this is panic on Yeqon's part. Clearly, he has lost his battle smarts if this is all he sends to stall us," Gedz'iel growled as his keen eyes scanned below. He checked the rest of the Eloi, who deftly cut down the creatures, barely breaking a sweat.

"He never was that smart!" Serail laughed deeply as he sent electric pulses into creatures that salivated like rabid dogs. Hair and flesh sizzled as they yelped out of existence.

"The problem is…." Koi doubled back, took out a hoard of sandy little creatures. The sneaky monsters camouflaged themselves amongst turrets of rock. They climbed quickly to the highest point before hurling themselves towards a regiment of younger Watchers. They had caught the less battle-experienced fighters by surprise. The younger warriors had not seen or heard of Asmodai before. The crusty little devils exploded and blew away in the breeze under Koi's powerful blasts.

Thanks were shouted out from afar; the young warriors thudded their weapons against their armour in gratitude.

"The problem is, this is distracting enough to give him time to hide her elsewhere… or worse!" Koi grunted.

Koi and Serail flew in a well-practiced formation, back and forth across the main fissure, slicing away anything coming through. Gedz'iel called in another fifty Watchers from beyond the mountain. They had chased down a band of lesser Daimon. The Watchers now combined to become a huge, efficient, offensive team. Like fighter jets in pattern, the Earthbound Watchers pulsed white hot munitions in a constant and effective stream. The sound pinged and exploded in a rhythmic death tune.

"Do you think Pathos will find her? He has not tracked in a long time. We've not heard a word yet." Serail asked Koi as the two of them kept close, watching each other's back, picking off the quickly depleting hordes. Serail patted away some of the stinking demonic fluid that blackened his armour. It splattered the deep tone of his immense arms, made him sick to the stomach. His long white hair was caked with the sticky, ashy residue, he pulsed it away with a short fiery burst.

"I can only hope Pathos has found her," Koi answered. As if on cue, Pathos materialised before them, orbs and sword at the ready.

"Pathos! You're alone?" Disappointment blended with fear in Koi's voice. "Where is Sophia? A'glacea? The other young warrior?"

Joining seamlessly into the fight, Pathos called out in his baritone voice.

"There was trouble. We were ambushed the moment we made foot fall. There was a party awaiting us," he lied with ease.

Gedz'iel swooped to his side.

"Who ambushed you?" Gedz'iel asked. "How many were there that you could not protect yourself and two others? What of the others who went with you?"

"They ascended. Forgive me, there were more than I could count awaiting us. It took all I had to retreat to come back to warn you. I could not find Sophia, or save the others," Pathos growled as he speared a Rogue trying to jump across to him from atop the branches of a long dead tree.

The number of attackers dwindled. The Watchers drew into a tighter formation.

Koi swiped his palm across his forehead and raised it to the fiery sky, "May I'el accept their souls back."

Gedz'iel acknowledged the reverent gesture, then he pointed skyward, "We need not waste any more energy on this lot."

They ascended high into the bilious sky, where the foul creatures had no chance of reaching them. Eventually, with no ability to think for themselves, the creatures slunk back into the cracks from which they came.

"Koi!"

They all turned to see Lorcan return with Kea.

"Is all well at Kaymakli?" Koi questioned as he sailed along the upper air current.

"I'm afraid not." Lorcan panted, acknowledging Gedz'iel with an airborne bow. Lorcan shook his head. Kea's eyes glistened with tears. For a moment, Lorcan left them in suspense as he searched for the right words.

"Speak, Lorcan. What is it?" Gedz'iel demanded impatiently.

Tensing every muscle, Lorcan looked up, his eyes ringed red. His wings increased their momentum as the anger within him released.

"There were two attacks on Jude's patrol. One in Nevşehir, and then again as they retreated to Kaymakli."

"What? In the village? Who was it? Are there any casualties?" Koi asked earnestly as he glided closer to Lorcan. Pathos' face darkened; he crossed his arms. Gedz'iel and rest of the Eloi flew forward to listen more carefully to the terrible news.

"Rogues attacked within the boundaries of the town. Kristen was severely injured," Lorcan explained.

"No!" Koi clutched his face.

"Then, when the Rogues retreated and everyone was headed back to Kaymakli…"

"What is it Lorcan?" Gedz'iel glared worriedly between Lorcan and Kea.

"Tell us," Pathos interrupted impatiently.

Amais glided forward, placing a reassuring hand on Lorcan's shoulder, "We are here, brother, sister. Tell us."

Lorcan shook his head.

"Soph will be gutted," Kea whispered.

"What is it?" Koi demanded, "Will one of you speak up?"

Lorcan ran his hands roughly through his filthy hair.

"Jaz was taken."

"What? Again? By Rogues?" Koi's face tightened as he made worried eye contact with Gedz'iel, Pathos, Serail, Amais, Theus and Matias.

"No. By Afflicted, and under the direction of Neph'reus and Anjou'elle," Kea answered. There was a general cry of alarm and surprise across the group. The mountain rumbled as if it thought it funny.

Gedz'iel ran one hand over a tight fist, deep in thought.

"It was so unexpected," Lorcan added, guilt wavered his voice. "I was fooled into going back.

"This makes no sense. Why have those two surfaced now?" Troubled, Koi rubbed his temples. Darkness shadowed his fine eyes. He turned and stared off into the distance, towards the angry mountain, eyes glazed, deep in thought. He did not trouble Gedz'iel, who was churning the information over quietly to himself.

Pathos interjected. "They were always trouble those two. Perhaps they're just looking for a new plaything. They wearied of entertainment so easily in the past. I say it's a coincidence, an unfortunate one for the girl, but merely a coincidence." Pathos squinted and scanned the horizon, also searching for something.

"We may not have just Yeqon to worry about, after all," Gedz'iel said as he scanned the corpse-strewn ground below.

"There is an ugly possibility we have more than one enemy at play," Koi surmised distractedly. He rubbed the tattoo across his fingers, hovering over the word '*hate*'.

Lorcan zoomed away to blast a singular Rogue that was emerging from a rip in the ground. He hit it with such force that its ashes literally vaporised. As he flew back to the floating infantry, he spoke with un-checked rage.

"I was lured by one of them pretending to be Brennan." Lorcan slammed a fist into his hand over and over. "I'm such a fool!"

"Anjou'elle and Neph'reus can do it to the best of us." Pathos smiled, out of character, and out of line.

Gedz'iel growled, "Pathos, be quiet!"

Pathos bowed his head, hiding the scorn that darkened his eyes.

Koi returned from his deep thoughts, "Now we must find Jaz too, and eliminate this new enemy."

"But we're supposed to be concentrating on Sophia. She's the most important person in all of this. Remember?" Lorcan looked around the group; his face flushed. "I like Jaz, I do and I'll blast those sisters arses myself, but we can't be distracted. If someone else is sticking their nose into this, I want to take them out and as soon as possible, but only as long as Sophia is at the forefront of our minds." Lorcan's hands ran roughly across his face.

"She's down there. Can't you feel her presence, Koi? Master Gedz'iel?" Lorcan said earnestly.

"Calm down, brother. We are all on the same team. You're right, Sophia is definitely the most important person." Serail glided to Lorcan, put his arm around his shoulders, carefully avoiding the raw, newly tattooed white line down his shoulder blade.

"Another millennium already?" Serail asked.

"Yeah. Bren and I did them before I came back. It was quick, so it's a little crooked," Lorcan responded.

The mountain rumbled. They all looked about to find no enemy in sight, for now.

"Well, you've nearly caught up to Koi and I, young one." Serail ruffled his hair as he retreated back to hover with Gedz'iel.

"There will be no more millennial markings for any of us, no more passing of the years. We will find Sophia, we will find the Kaladai, and we will leave this planet." Gedz'iel narrowed his supernova eyes, the normal warmth replaced with stony ambition.

"We must not lose sight of our path, but we must also salvage Jasmine if at all possible. Certainly, for Sophia, but also for the mere fact, Lorcan, that she will assuredly be used against us. You," Gedz'iel pointed to a male hovering at the edges of the pack, "Go back to Kaymakli immediately and inform Jude that I approve a search party for Jasmine. Dash knows where to look for Afflicted. He spent hundreds of years in the ghettos, trying fruitlessly to help them. Dash knows how to pay them to spill what they know," Gedz'iel nodded at the young Watcher. He saluted and disappeared through the hazy amber atmosphere that separated the Daimon realm from the human world.

"Now we need to work out why the hell those two witches have come out of hiding, and why they want Sophia? That is the only reason I can imagine they would take Jasmine. So, the question is, are they working for Yeqon or for themselves?" Koi asked.

"If they are in this for another reason, then we had better up our game," Gedz'iel responded. He raised his sword.

"Weapons ready, here they come again."

Chapter
Thirty-Five

Was I ever going to cop a break? This was getting ridiculous. I manage to take out the mother of vampires, and now the King of Hell shows up. There I was, arm wrapped tight around Enoch's box and ready to make a run for it… but no, there had to be yet another obstacle! I swore obscenely in my head; foul words ghosted across my lips.

Predictably, at the site of Yeqon, Rik had reverted to a blubbering wreck, such was the psychological paralysis this monster induced in him. He backed away from Lilith, quivering uncontrollably.

"And here we are once more, pretty one." Yeqon casually reached up to sharpen the dagger against one of his horns. The grating echoed as he slid the sharp edge teasingly against the curve of the devilish feature. Never taking his dark gaze from me, he half smiled. In another time, another realm, with a clean heart, he would have been obscenely gorgeous. To me, though, he was pure ugliness.

"You are such trouble, and now poor Boy here must suffer once more… because of you." Yeqon licked the edge of the dagger. He turned, advanced on Rik and jabbed the newly sharpened point into Rik's neck. My brother groaned, rivulets of blood streamed down his arm, dripping from his fingertips. His skin paled to stone.

Fight back, Rik, damn you!

Yet, instinct had me hold my ground. I held even tighter to the Enoch's precious prize, not moving a muscle to help my brother.

"So, have you had time to discover where that damned box is to lead us? Tick-tock, my sweet. Your rescue team is causing all sorts of trouble upstairs and I am now very much pressed for time." Yeqon bared his perfect teeth, the knife dug deeper. Rik groaned. His face glowed a little, as did one of his palms. Yeqon noticed and yanked Rik's hair.

"Been learning from big sister, I see?" He arched Rik's neck further. "Well, don't!" Yeqon sliced across Rik's torso. Rik's eyes rolled back in his head; his body shuddered.

"You bastard! Stop it!" I screamed. About to doubt my resolve, something passed through Rik's eyes. They cleared; their colour intense once more, a blush returned to his cheeks. It told me to hold off, to not give into this animal. Despite the torture, he was trying to be strong, too.

Rik, brother, you can do it!

I clutched the box tighter again, looked around the empty room, and smiled.

"Looks like you've been deserted by your cronies, Yeqon. It's just you and me, is it?" A strength blossomed in my gut, and it seemed to get stronger with each challenge I faced. My wings expanded once more; heat scorched across my face in warning. Yeqon bristled, his smile faded.

"You want to challenge me single-handed, Girl?" His smile flattened into a grimace; his lips twitched. Pulling Rik's hair harder, he widened his murky wings and pointed the dagger towards me.

I breathed in deeply, controlling the involuntary shiver that his presence elicited.

I knew I had to get past these threats that so easily brought me undone. My heart could no longer be my weakness, despite what Enoch and my grandmother had prophesised. I would and could prove them wrong. I'd been so crippled by fear, for myself and for others, that it had brought me to my knees repeatedly. So, I surrendered to the fear rather than letting it drown me. That took away fear's power. I stood taller, hooked the box behind my back, and drew a fiery orb to my palm.

"I can do just fine on my own, Yeqon. Let… him… go!" I snarled.

"You and me it is then!" Yeqon laughed low and deep, a vindictive smile glistened in his inky eyes.

"All it will take is a few more screams from dearest brother." Yeqon cocked his head towards Rik, sank the blade into Rik's flesh again. "I *know* you, child. Young and weak and foolish. You, Soph'ael, were put here for no other purpose than sacrificing your blood for *our* vengeance!" The conviction in his tone, the belief in his eyes, was as cold as ice.

I must have shown a flicker of emotion. Yeqon honed in on it like an attack dog. He squeezed more blood from Rik, each drop hit the ground like thunder. Yeqon's twisted grimace had me back away. I bumped into one of the thrones.

"Yes. Purely meat for the slaughter, despite what everyone says. You were born to die, dear Soph'ael. Born to die… for our chance at revenge!"

I shivered; rage stirred in me. Each drop of Rik's blood like a slice to my own flesh.

"That's not true, and you know it. If you kill me, my blood will do nothing. The prophecy says my blood can't be forcibly taken. Are you *that* stupid? If you kill me, you will never find the key to the portal, because the clues will ascend with me, and you *know* it, Yeqon. You're a thug full of hot air and empty threats. You're nothing but an angel gone bad. You…are… nothing!"

I eased behind the thrones. Lilith groaned, still rousing. Gaining a little more space between us kept my bravery at the forefront. Rik blinked, ever so slightly nodded his head, encouraging me to stand my ground. His own energy grew, his face brightened, whilst Yeqon's darkened with rage.

Yeqon roared. The walls rumbled. The burn of his anger permeated the cavern, as sharp as a slap. He shoved Rik to the ground and made his way towards me. A maniacal grin split Yeqon's face. He waved the bloodied dagger back and forth.

"You would make an excellent queen; your spirit excites me. Perhaps we can come to an agreeable arrangement?" He cocked his head, his brows arched as though he actually expected me to consider his vile offer. That prospect churned my stomach.

Rik recovered quickly in the background, healing himself, pulling himself up.

"I'd rather disembowel myself!" I answered, and threw an orb in Yeqon's direction. Rik took the opportunity to let his wings unravel. The orb masked Rik's light from Yeqon, whose attention was focused solely on me.

Lilith rolled over, rousing further. Her threat would be back all too soon. As I threw another arc of light and flapped my wings, I wobbled a few feet in the air. I clenched my jaw, groaned inwardly as he saw my lack of competence. I flapped harder, lurched to the left, away from Lilith, a new orb forming.

Yeqon's voice and expression softened. His eyes changed from fully black to a sparkling blue. He stopped moving, held his hands out, tucked the dagger into his belt.

"Let me teach you. Join with me. Bleed for me, beautiful one, and I will worship you. We can take the worlds for our own."

The orb left my palm. He dodged it with ease. I sank to the ground, feeling more stable on foot.

"Again… I'd rather skin myself, Yeqon!" I backed away until I hit the wall behind the fallen crates. I threw another orb.

His face darkened again, so very easily his mood switched from kitten to death adder. Yeqon countered my weaponry with a casualness that undermined my newly birthed confidence. His orbs obliterated mine before they met their mark. His face lit with delight.

"You are an amateur, no match for me, *never* a match for me." He ascended the stairs, the kitten in him glimmered to the surface again. "But together, can you imagine it? You could sit on the Throne of

A'vean. You and I together, forever." He wet his lips. The sight of his tongue sweeping across them made me sick.

I kept an eye on Lilith. She could possibly come in handy.

Yeqon held out his hand, invitingly.

"Come, Earth-born. Envisage us storming A'vean, taking down those despots, and controlling everything as we see fit? I'll even give you this forsaken planet to rule for yourself, if you wish? We would be invincible!" Yeqon had made it to within a foot of me. Energy arced around my body protectively, yet he merely reached through and caressed my cheek. My stomach lurched; I turned my face away.

"You are indeed a beauty unequalled. I believe I would rather ravish you, than destroy you." The softness, the sudden gentleness in his voice, dripped with lust.

"Over my dead body, you freak!" I released the energy I'd been building. A blinding white blast. The explosion thrust him backwards, tumbling down the stairs. The noise fully roused Lilith. She pulled herself up along the back of a throne.

"You pig! You want her?" Lilith screamed. She ran at Yeqon, her nails aimed for his face, her jealousy a bloodied tang on the air.

Rolling to his feet, Yeqon blasted Lilith aside. She was once again left moaning on the ground, arms and legs askew. He roared, launched himself my way as I made a run for the tunnel we had come in from. Rik shielded me from behind, groaning as he took a multitude of hits. I tripped on fallen debris, but my wings righted my balance. I grabbed Rik by the hand and flew. Yeqon was in the air, chasing us down the tunnels. The practiced beat of his wings drowned out the renewed screams of the vilified Lilith.

Rik's fingers dug into my skin, my grip on him iron. I wouldn't let him go. We ducked and weaved through blinding steam, trying to find a way out. Everything looked the same. Rocks, dirt, steam, and heat. Corner after corner, a mirror image of the next.

"Which way, Rik?" I yelled in desperation.

"I'm not sure. You've gone a different way!"

"Shit!" I lurched to the left, the smell of Yeqon too close. "Where's the Thyros chamber?" I screamed. Yeqon's roar echoed behind us.

"I don't know where we are. Just keep going. He's right behind us!" Rik was trying to throw his weak arcs at Yeqon. It wasn't much, but damn if he wasn't trying his best, and it pushed my determination.

Yeqon was so close, I felt the seething of his rage as though he already had a grip on me. Shot after shot, his power grazed us both enough to draw blood, but not enough to stop me. Rik was getting heavier though, the further into the depths of this vile place I dove. The heat was insufferable; the walls glowed a brighter orange. Lava flowed fast underneath the skin of the rock.

I could no longer hear Koi, this fact diminished my confidence, but not my will to overcome Yeqon.

"Rik, hold on, *tight!*"

I straightened and flapped hard into a sudden stop, then dropped onto my feet. This unexpected move saw Yeqon zoom past. It gave me the opportunity to fly back in the other direction, hopefully towards to surface.

I flew hard, but I was tiring quickly. I banged into the walls and corners, my skin ripped, pain took hold, but I forged ahead, knowing how much worse it could get. Yeqon made a furious beeline back after us. Rounding another two corners, all went quiet. We seemed suddenly alone. The biting orbs ceased to light the tunnels. After a few more twists and turns, I tentatively pulled up by a dwindling wall sconce, listening through my ragged breaths.

Rik and I looked at each other hopefully. His fingers curled tight around my arm.

"Do you think we have lost him?" Rik asked as he peered up and down the dark passages.

"I don't know. You okay?"

He nodded. I flapped my wings a little harder. We grappled to keep each other steady whilst I tried to work out the next move to make. Rik was both innocent and wizened to the evils of the world. He stared hopefully up at me, his wings flapped uselessly. But they were nevertheless, beautiful.

"Sorry I cannot fly. I burden you." His face was slack with despondence. I pulled him up closer with a grunt. Despite my fatigue, I smiled.

"Don't worry. Hell, I'm only just pulling it together my…" I didn't finish. Despite the inferno, my blood ran instantly cold.

"Stupid girl!" The growl was like a rabid animal.

I winced and turned. There he was, waiting up ahead, fingers twitching. Yeqon glided forward and back, teasing, nothing but death in his black eyes. He smirked with satisfaction as he flapped his wings slowly, showing the ease with which he could catch and hold us without breaking the sweat of effort.

I gathered Rik and the box closer into my body. Rik was rigid with fear, yet I felt a rage swirling through his veins as his fingers clung angrily into the small of my back. Rik was coming around; his confidence would hopefully soon see him rain vengeance upon Yeqon.

Yeqon retrieved his dagger. Rik flinched. Yeqon dipped it into rivulets of lava running down the wall beside him, heating the blade red hot. He balanced an orb atop his other hand.

"Your time ends here, Earth-born." The dagger swept rapidly through the air, my eyes following its every move as the heat of it left swirls of red glowing in its wake.

"So, I gather you don't want to get it on anymore?" I couldn't believe I'd just blurted that out.

"Oh, sweet one. I will get whatever I want from you. You just lost your free pass to live through it!"

I glided back, hitting the searing wall.

"You think you can run from me? In my own realm? You forget transference, but then you've been raised a pathetic human," Yeqon spat in disgust. His phlegm sizzled as it hit the boiling rocks.

"Enough now. Give me the box and surrender. This is your last chance." He flung the orb at my feet. The explosion disoriented me. I flapped hard to move quickly out of his way. Yeqon lunged with the burning dagger. There seemed nowhere to go. He was relentless. We circled around and around as though in a in a duel, except he was the only one with the weapons. I carried the baggage of Rik and the box, which left me at a great disadvantage.

What to do, what to do?

I didn't want to let go of Rik. I didn't want to let go of the box. I didn't want to let go of anything.

"Hold on, Rik!" I whispered. He took the box from my grasp and quickly scrambled around into somewhat of a lopsided piggy back. His body hindered my wings, but it was the best I could do. This freed up my hands at least.

"Don't let go, no matter what." I felt Rik nod against my back as a fresh orb formed in my palm. I raised it towards the gloating laughter of Yeqon. His outrageous conceit prevented him from noticing the approach of another presence. I felt it, and it was all too familiar. A heart hammered wildly, strong and reassuring, deep within the tunnel behind Yeqon.

"Back off, Yeqon!" I warned.

"Your choice is made then? That was your last chance, Earth-born. My patience done." Yeqon rushed towards me, pulling up to a rapid halt as a voice boomed from behind him.

"Actually, this is *your* last chance, brother!"

The familiar voice rang out from the shadows, a blinding flash followed. Yeqon lurched forwards, collapsing at my feet. Charred skin bubbled across his back, cancelling out his wings. He was motionless. Red cuffs of elemental energy bound his hands behind his back.

The owner of the knock-out attack emerged from the shadows. Retrieving the dagger from Yeqon's reach, he jabbed it into the wall nearby.

I lowered myself to the ground and hugged Rik close.

I locked eyes with my saviour.

It was Ben.

Chapter Thirty-Six

"Until we have Sophia in our arms, there remains no option. We must all head underground. Since Pathos was ambushed, clearly, they must have her below ground," Gedz'iel surmised. "I expected to meet Yeqon in person the moment we breached their perimeter. I thought he ached for confrontation; he disappoints me." Gedz'iel shook his head.

Whilst their attention was held with the new plans, Pathos silently moved to the back of the group and transferred away without anyone noticing.

"I'm going in first. I'll find Soph. I did it before. Her energy signature is so strong. I'll always be able to find her." Lorcan's face burned with conviction, and something more, but he was held back by Koi.

"Calm down… don't let emotion cloud your judgement," Koi said.

"I'll keep him company, Koi. You know I can keep his head on straight." Kea blew Lorcan a kiss. He scowled at her.

"We will all go in. No more separating in singles or pairs, it's not safe. We will take Yeqon's dungeons in large groups. There are plenty of us. I don't want to lose another brother or sister," Gedz'iel instructed. They all nodded in agreement.

"If we can, we must retrieve the remains of the fallen for return to the Cavern of Souls," Koi added as he grouped the younger Watchers in order of experience.

Amais glided forward, "Where is brother Pathos?"

All heads snapped up. A deathly quiet had fallen, even the mountain had settled.

The breezeless vacuum of the atmosphere changed. The metallic ring of drawn swords echoed around the Watchers. Their wings expanded; their faces glowed blindingly. They twisted and turned, eyes wide, searching.

"Something is very much amiss, brothers." Gedz'iel hovered higher than them all, like a protective deity watching over his flock. He scanned the horizon, haloed by his immense power.

The air changed from nothingness as it came alive. Snaps and crackles of red and orange licked at the atmosphere and encircled the Watchers. They spun in surprise.

Gedz'iel drew out every ounce of his energy until even the whites of his eyes glowed. He cast forward a protective barrier of light across those below him. The thin shield, barely visible, wobbled like a bubble around them.

Bilious green clouds drifted overhead in a windless sky. They blotted out the angry sun. Five winged shadows emerged from within the stormy mass. They were followed by a larger group of Daimon shadowing them. The five glided ahead of their army. They were all too familiar, despite for so very long being unseen. Staring down the Watchers were the Unseen Satans.

One held a sword as long as he was tall, one an orb burning to explode, another wielded an axe of razor-sharp diamond, and the fourth, a bow loaded with six bolts of energy aimed directly at Koi. The fifth rose higher than the others, two red orbs angrily burning atop his palms. His ebony skin made his blue eyes seem fluorescent until they turned as black as night.

The Watchers collectively bristled at the sight. Growls and bellows of disgust spewed from Gedz'iel's army.

Kea screamed, "Traitor!" She pointed her sword at the heart of the one who only moments ago, was fighting alongside her.

"You will pay eternally, brother." Gedz'iel's eyes swirled angrily.

Koi, ever the head of reason and empathy, sighed. He shook his head in dismay. "Oh no!" He rubbed his temples, then narrowed his eyes towards the traitor.

Koi's wings expanded, nearly as glorious in size and beauty as Gedz'iel's. Every muscle in his chest flexed, he glided forwards, pushing through Gedz'iel's force field. His expression turned vicious; he held his sword aloft. Koi's voice was calculated.

"Pathos…. May I'el strike you down!"

The attack began without warning. No niceties or explanation, just a full throttle melee. The Daimon penetrated Gedz'iel's protective barrier with a collective explosion of fire power. The clouds vaporised, revealing the fiery sun once more. Pathos struck the first blow to Koi, who tumbled through the air, only righting himself seconds from crashing to the ground.

Theus, Amais, Serail and Matias roared at the betrayal. They honed in upon Pathos like vultures. Circling, then swooping after him, fire power times four, they each landed shots to Pathos' torso, enough to knock him off course, but not enough to bring him down. The Daimon horde divided the remaining Eloi with targeted attacks, allowing Pathos to retreat from his former allies.

Arcs of elemental weaponry; orbs, arrows, and swords slashed and exploded as Watcher and Daimon crashed together. Lorcan howled wildly as he hurled his ammunition with supreme accuracy. This made little difference though, as the Daimon transferred and darted within the atmosphere. Their speed and precision in their own realm such that they may as well have been a force triple their size.

As though they'd trained for this moment for thousands of years, Ged'erel, Pineme, Asbel and Kasadya fought in a well-practiced formation. They danced through the motions of death blows as they dispatched Watcher after Watcher, whose ascending blue lights breached the highest borders of the Empyrean realm. Their diamond remains fell to the ground and smashed into Thanratos.

"Where is Yeqon?" Gedz'iel bellowed. He scanned the skies as he slashed someone in two. Orange flames erupted. The corpse fluttered into ash and diamond dust, blowing away, nothingness in the dank emptiness of the Empyrean sky.

Serail and Lorcan moved in unison, with Kea circling above. The three of them pushed hard to spread and divide the mighty demonic force. Daimon after Daimon rushed at them. They tried without success to overwhelm the aggressors with a torrent of firepower.

Lorcan took a painful hit in the shoulder for Kea, pushing her out of the way. She tumbled through the air and bumped into Amais, who pulled her upright.

"I owe you one, Hon." She planted a kiss on his cheek and their marks glowed with comradery. Kea re-immersed herself into the bloodshed.

She bee-lined through the foul volcanic sky with forceful beats of her wings, straight back to Lorcan. She reached his side just as he quite literally cut down two Daimon. The stark reality, for all, was that many of the Daimon were painfully familiar. Brothers and sisters who had long ago allowed their hearts and souls to blacken. Their bodies fell one by one, erupting in flames before the distant crunch of their bones reverberated back.

"That was…"

"I know." Lorcan cut Theus off. Seeing old friends turned bad was almost too much. The strength seemed to drain from Theus. For a moment, it was too much. His normally level head gave way to seething anger.

"I'el!" Theus screamed until his voice was hoarse. No one paid heed to the normally blasphemous act. The feeling, after so many years, was more mutual than most would acknowledge. The Eloi were not known to show emotion, and Lorcan was concerned that Theus' sudden eruption of emotion might engulf him. It was a dangerous state of mind, particularly mid-battle.

Theus was rigid. Clenching both fists, he flew high above the fighting, eyes glazed. Lorcan, Serail and Kea followed protectively. Kea healed Lorcan's still gaping wound as they circled Theus, who remained unnervingly silent. They kept a close eye on the battle below.

"Come, brother. Do not lose yourself?" Serail asked of Theus.

"We need you. They were lost to us long ago. But we are not lost. We need you, as do they." Kea pointed below. Thunder rumbled, the sun seared through their wings, expanding the glow exponentially. Theus looked downwards; his eyes cleared. He took in the carnage, watched Gedz'iel fight without falter. Koi repeatedly saved their own whilst eluding the onslaught of the traitorous Pathos. Theus bristled at the sight of this so-called brother. Even the young ones fought bravely. The sight of their determination and loyalty brought Theus back from the brink of desolation.

"Forgive me. Time has not been kind. I see now though, there are many more to stay strong for." Theus took a deep breath, raised his arms, arcs of light licked along his raven skin to form snapping, red orbs upon each palm.

"He's back!" Lorcan fist pumped, "Let's get back to it. I want this sorted. I've got to find Sophia. You good now, brother?" Lorcan slapped his shoulder. Theus nodded, diving straight back down, firing with deadly accuracy at anything demonic in his way. Kea followed on, backing him up.

Lightning crackled across the sky, an eerie flicker of light and dark. Screams and grunts peeled across the landscape. The mountain came back to life and spewed its displeasure.

"Looks like the battle is evening out," Lorcan yelled. "Let's get back to it, we got this brother." he winked at Serail.

Lorcan seemed distracted, though, as he soared towards the midst of battle. His face beetroot red, his bloodied lips clamped between his teeth. He scanned the ground far below where the battle raged on foot.

Every crack and crevice, every mountain range and elevation, he searched for any sign of Sophia. Kea re-joined him, Serail close behind.

"Lorcan? You coming back down. Theus is right back on his game."

"She's down there somewhere," Lorcan's voice was tight.

"We can all sense her. This is a good thing. It means she still lives," Serail said. "We need to take care of this before we can help her, though."

"We'll get her. Don't worry, I'll make sure of it, or die trying." Kea patted Lorcan on the back.

"I can *feel* her brother, not just sense her, I *feel* her heartbeat, her emotions. She's scared," Lorcan said and held a hand over his heart. He drew in a deep breath.

"That is an exemplary connection, Lorcan," Serail said. "Come, help me burn some Daimon flesh, then we will retrieve her." Serail pulled on Lorcan's arm, however Lorcan pulled away, not taking his eyes from a ground that shimmered through the mirage of heat. Thunder raged around them; sheet lightning blanketed the sky. Lorcan's hair bristled with the static, his eyes narrowed. The wind picked up, tossing them about.

"Lorcan, come now. We need you, just as you told brother Theus," Serail said.

"Soph needs me more, though. You've got this, man!" Lorcan banged his sword against Serail's armour in farewell. "Tell Koi and Gedz'iel I will return, and I will have Sophia with me." Lorcan disappeared so quickly, a mere jet stream was left in his wake, a pure white streak across the murky sky.

"I'el be with you, brother," Serail said and shook his head.

"I got this. Go help Koi; it looks like that bastard, Pathos, is giving him trouble." Kea tapped her sword against Serail's armour, then she disappeared to follow Lorcan's trail.

Kea arrived at the Standing Stones. She melted into them, where Lorcan had done so only seconds before. Lorcan was as strong and experienced as she was, yet he had lived long amongst humanity and she knew how easily he could fall prey to his emotions. This is where she respected the Eloi. As much as she loved them, mortals were weak and often leached that weakness onto A'veans. This is why the Eloi remained so removed from them.

As Kea wandered through the Thyros chamber, she knew she had to back up Lorcan. He was their finest tracker and she wouldn't allow Lorcan's heartstrings to cause his ascension. She flew cautiously through the stinking tunnels, smiled to herself as she realised how ironically alike both Lorcan and Sophia were. Perhaps that's why he felt so connected to her.

Pathos had marked Koi for his own prize. He chased him mercilessly across the Empyrean skies.

Koi, smart and fast, old and wise, out-manoeuvred Pathos at every turn. He matched red orb for red orb. Each hit to Koi was returned, doubled in force. Pathos relished the rage that seethed from the normally calm Koi. Pathos charged and rammed his huge body into Koi. They fell, spiralling rapidly. Both grappled and punched as their wings burned through the atmosphere. They came to an explosive crash, sliding along the sharp ground, leaving a bloodied crater.

As the fireworks of combat raged overhead, Pathos and Koi battled to the death. It was far from general warfare; it was personnel.

Koi rolled out of the ditch that smouldered from the friction of the impact, covered in cuts and abrasions. His cropped hair thickly reddened by blood and dust. He launched at Pathos, grabbed his throat, and rammed him back into the ground.

"Traitor!" Spittle sprayed from Koi; veins bulged in his temples. His blazing eyes were thin and red-rimmed.

Pathos grabbed the sides of Koi's face, dug his fingers in, drew blood that sparkled in the strange hazy light.

"I am no traitor. I'el is the traitor, and you are his pathetic pawn," Pathos growled between exhausted gasps. Koi rammed Pathos' head repeatedly into the ground, but the impossibly old Watcher was not so easily overcome. He crooked a foot underneath Koi's leg and flipped him over. With the upper hand, Pathos pummelled Koi with punches, breaking his nose, splitting his lips. As Koi choked on his own blood, Pathos' ancient ego got in his way.

"It has been a trial putting up with you lot," he growled, breathing rapidly, flaring his nostrils as he chose his words carefully. His blackened eyes regained a little of their bright blue, but maintained the telltale demonic black ring around the iris.

Pathos sat astride Koi, rested his hands on his hips triumphantly. He looked up at the overhead battle.

"How long have you been one of them?" Koi spluttered under the weight of Pathos.

"What does it matter, brother?" Pathos grinned through bloodied teeth.

"I suppose it doesn't matter at all," Koi responded. Pathos shifted, kneeling into Koi's hands, further immobilising him.

"It won't be long before they're done up there." Pathos glanced briefly skyward, then back to Koi. "Yeqon won't be far away, and with Sophia underfoot, they'll do whatever he says. Am I correct?" He leaned in close. His maniacal grin told Koi he was completely unhinged.

Koi remained still, let Pathos have his moment.

"Have you always been on their side, brother?"

"No," Pathos sniffed and coughed. "But I became bored a long time ago of this place. You must remember, I was here long before you, Koi." Pathos relaxed and stretched out his hands, cracking his bloodied knuckles.

"I saw the first human rise from the swamps. Give me some credit for my patience. I'el has not, that is for damned sure." Pathos relaxed a little more. Koi bided his time as he quietly regained his strength.

"So, after all this time, you were the one feeding information to Yeqon?"

"Yes, and Nik'ael. It has been a whole lot more difficult since he disappeared, though." Pathos pinched his nose and blew a large blood out of one nostril.

Koi wriggled, but Pathos' hand came back to his neck. It heated in warning.

"You mean to kill me?"

"Yes, of course." Pathos' smile widened, a crazed look in his eyes.

"Well, get on with it then so I may join my kindred in the Cavern of Souls," Koi said nonchalantly, and let his body relax.

"You do not care to fight for yourself?"

"I am but one in this battle. Sophia is strong, as are the others. They will be victorious, with or without me."

"Oh, so humble, yet so stupid." Pathos drew an orb, held it close to Koi's heart, enough to blister Koi's skin.

"You were always kind to me, brother, so I will give you the mercy of making it as painless as possible."

Koi defiantly looked Pathos straight in the eyes, awaiting the death blow. The gesture caught Pathos slightly off-guard. A flicker of conflict shadowed his eyes, and for the briefest of moments, Pathos' eyes shone perfect blue once more. To clear the confusion, he shook his head. He raised his arm to thrust the orb into Koi's heart, but there was a cracking noise behind him. He faltered, turned, and growled impatiently.

"What are you doing here? Get back to the Pits before Yeqon descends you!"

"I've had enough of being told what to do and when," the gravelly voice hissed. Koi craned his neck to see, of all people, the beaten down figure of Belial.

He tossed the broken remains of his last horn up and down in his hand. He appeared vastly less evil without the Daimon adornment. Wind surged around his imposing size, sand devils swirled, and the ground cracked beneath them.

"It takes a traitor to recognise a traitor, and I wish to be one no more!" Belial said as he took a step forward.

"What do you think you are up to?" Pathos turned, ready to throw the orb meant for Koi, straight at Belial. Underestimating the long-abused Daimon pawn, Pathos was suddenly and spectacularly outmanoeuvred.

Without warning, Belial flapped his wings hard, just once. This hurled him forward, and he thrust the point of his horn deep into Pathos' neck. Pathos rolled from Koi, thrashing across the ground. He twisted, convulsing and gurgling. He grappled uselessly at the impaled horn. Arterial blood sprayed from his body. Koi jumped up, finished Pathos off with a barrage of electrical blasts until he burst into flames.

Heavy with disbelief, Koi stared into the burning remnants with a mixture of sadness and anger. He glanced up at Belial; confused, angry and annoyingly grateful. The two glared at each other as Koi reflexively produced an orb with Belial's name on it. Koi's body alight, instinctively ready to attack. He raised his weaponised hands.

"Keep your distance!" Koi snarled, taking a step towards the Daimon. Belial was smeared crimson, both fresh and old wounds gouged across his once regal features. The whites of Belial's eyes shone from within the bloodied mess. It made him appear all the more threatening. Koi's offensive stance saw the Daimon's body slump. Belial let his weary head hang low and fell to his knees. With a sorrowful moan, Belial lay prostrate at Koi's feet, mumbling into the dry earth.

"I ask only for a quick death, and one day, perhaps the forgiveness of my daughter," he pleaded humbly.

Taken aback, Koi stared open-mouthed at Belial. He quickly healed himself with the remnant energy of the orb that was reabsorbing within his palm. Koi breathed out a resigned sigh.

"I'el, give me strength to forgive and to be forgiven. Only those without deficiency may judge."

Belial dared to look up, eyes wide in surprise. The blackness was gone, replaced with a regretful, sparkling blue look of confusion.

"I ask you to join me in battle, brother. Come, we've Daimon to kill." Koi offered Belial a hand up and they rose in unison, flying skyward to the war above.

Chapter
Thirty-Seven

"Nik'ael!" Rik ran to him, wrapping his arms tight around Nik'ael's black and blue waist. "You are alive! I thought they must have killed you. What happened? Where have you been?" He hugged into Ben's chest with such familiarity. I bristled inwardly at the sight and bit the inside of my cheek. Too many emotions flooded my mind. Why did my heart have to trip a little faster?

Nik'ael hugged Rik back, patting his back in that manly kind of way. The warmth of this reunion stuck in my throat; anger re-surged into every nerve ending.

"Yes, where have you been, *Nik'ael?*" I said as acidly as possible. Ben raised his gaze. His pained blue eyes struggled to match my angry glare. He held Rik away, looked at his adoring face instead.

"Don't call me Nik'ael any longer, little brother. I am more Ben than the Nik'ael you have always known." Ben glanced my way briefly, as if to measure my reaction. When I huffed in disgust, he returned his attention to Rik.

"And you have a name now, I hear. Much better. You are Rik and I am Ben." Ben half smiled. Rik just seemed confused.

Ben seemed to chew on his own thoughts for a moment, then he set Rik aside and turned his attention to the prone Yeqon.

"Help me get him back to the cavern, little brother."

Rik readily bounced at his heels like a lapdog. Dark, broken, and withdrawn with me, Rik was an apparent ray of sunshine with Ben.

"What's going on?" I stepped closer. My pendant sprung to life, pulsing aggressively against my chest as though it too was troubled by the scene before me. I picked up the box where Rik had dropped it. I hugged Enoch's damned box ever tighter. Electrical wisps flickered out of the tips of my fingers, ready for anything. I burned; my spine, my face, my heart.

"What am I doing, Soph? I'm giving us the slimmest chance of getting out of here." Ben finally acknowledged me.

"Hold his hands tighter behind his back," he ordered Rik, who obliged with a scowl aimed at the unconscious Yeqon. Ben's hands glowed white and then a fluorescent red. He shackled snaky red wisps of energy all the way up Yeqon's arms.

Unsure what was going on, I watched suspiciously as Ben bound Yeqon. Holding one foot each, they dragged Yeqon along the floor into the darkness of the forward tunnel. The thump and bang of Yeqon's body trailing along the uneven ground gave me an uncomfortable sense of satisfaction.

I stayed put, confused. My feet seemed immovable. The drip of condensation atop my head may as well have been a hammer. Everything in that moment was an insult to my sense of reality.

My vision clouded through angry, conflicted tears. I focused on the shimmering pulse pumping through the veins in my arms, trying to understand each unexpected twist and turn.

"Are you coming, Soph, or are you going to wait there for something else to find you and eat you for dinner?"

"Ugh!" I stamped my foot. Fury wanted to scream. Self-preservation kept my mouth shut. I moved forwards, once more in the presence of Ben. Conflict consumed me. Despite everything, I had to follow him. I had to protect Rik, my brother, no matter how chummy they seemed, no matter how much I didn't trust Ben. I needed to get this box back to the others. I needed to not fail. Twirling my pendant a little faster, I followed along in the darkness.

I marched ahead with absolute prejudice, wings shimmering, my entire body encased in a crackling shield of lightening… just in case. Static tugged my hair, plucked at my skin, but my energy lit the way ahead like glaring street lights.

Keeping my distance, I quietly scoffed inside at Rik, who clearly didn't know the devil he was fawning over. *Or did he?* Then again, he'd said that Ben had been his only friend, the only one to ever show him kindness. That thought just didn't make sense in light of what I knew of Ben. I bit my lip in frustration. As we came to a final turn, jealousy bristled within me as I listened to them chat like best mates.

The heavy scrape of Yeqon's body thudding along punctuated their whispers. It pulled my mind back from self-pity. I cautiously entered the Throne room once more, to the sight of them shackling Yeqon to Lilith, who thankfully remained unconscious.

Ben leaned over them both, placing a palm behind each of their heads. His hand glowed. Rik looked on in awe.

"This won't keep him out for long, but hopefully long enough for us to get away," Ben explained as Rik hovered over him.

"Kill him! Kill him now!" Rik bounced on his toes.

"You don't know how much that would please me, little brother. But that's not how I fight, not anymore."

"You have to, Ben. *Please,* kill him?"

Ben caught Rik's arms as he lunged towards the two comatose bodies that lay at the foot of the thrones.

"It's this bitterness you feel that got *me* into this mess in the first place. I won't let you follow my dark path. Your soul is well enough broken; I won't let it blacken like mine did. His day will come, but we won't descend someone who can't fight back. Trust me, little brother," Ben glanced my way. "I've lost way too much in pursuit of vengeance, and the main thing I lost was myself."

Rik struggled a little longer before giving in. I was shocked by Ben's admission. He looked my way.

"I know I will never deserve your trust, but if you will at least trust in your brother, follow me. I can get you both out of here."

Ben was right. How could I ever trust him? Jaz, Esme… Oh, poor Esme. Could this be an elaborate ruse? Why wouldn't he kill Yeqon? He was there for the taking. Yeqon wouldn't think twice about ripping us to shreds. But then, I had said the same about Spider, hadn't I? Ben sat impatiently on the steps, keeping a keen eye on Yeqon while he waited for me.

The box was getting heavy. My options were two-fold. Blow him off, take Rik and run, or, allow myself to follow him against my better judgment.

Over a matter of seconds, I ran through all the scenarios which ultimately ended up with one realisation. I had no idea how to get out of this realm, and it certainly didn't look like Rik was going to leave Ben's side.

"Rik, Ben is the one who betrayed me. How can you trust him? People have died because of him. People close to me," I pleaded to Rik's conscience because my own was scrambled.

He looked between Ben and I, assessing us both. The chamber rumbled more furiously than before; debris pelted us. I pulled the box into my chest and it hummed louder.

Ben went rigid and put a finger to his lips. He pulled a dagger from his waistband. "Someone's coming. Make your choice, Soph," he whispered.

"Is it true what she says?" Rik asked Ben.

Ben looked down at him, shame as clear as day flooded his complexion.

"Yes, little brother. I'm guilty of all that she says. Regret will never atone for what I've done. What I do know, is that my mind is clear for the first time in a thousand years. I will pay for my sins, but not before I make right that which I have wronged."

Ben opened his palms out, like baring his soul for judgement. The dagger teetered across one of them. "Please Soph? Come with me, time is running out." His voice strained for me to relent. Ben backed away, towards the rear of the thrones.

Rik shook his head, trying to clear his own thoughts. He'd been through a lot these past few days, not to mention his entire miserable life.

My name rang again in the distance of my mind. It wasn't Koi. I couldn't quite make out who it was through the increasing cacophony of the furious mountain. I looked frantically for another way out, trying to keep my balance as the earth cracked and shook beneath me. The glow of lava far below cast an even more sinister hue across the room.

"I… I cannot believe these things of you, Nik'ael…err, Ben! You confess these things, but you have always shown me kindness. You have hurt my sister?" Ben grabbed Rik gently by the shoulders, looking down at him with those shameful eyes.

"Yes. I have. Never have I regretted anything more." Ben stared intensely in my direction, eyes glistening with more than just angelic pigmentation.

An explosion erupted plumes of dust back through the tunnel that we arrived from. It bit my skin, clogged my throat. I coughed.

"Soph, please. I'm here to help, for real." Ben reached out his hand to me, desperation in his eyes now.

Yeqon roused. Echoes of wings beating roared from the tunnels like the crash of a wild ocean. The energy felt positive, yet Yeqon's proximity and wakefulness made it impossible to wait to see if my intuition was correct. No one called my name any longer. It could easily be Yeqon's lackeys returning.

Damn it! Wait to see Yeqon rise like the hellish monster that he was, or take the hand of the other monster who broke my heart?

I faltered as I took an uncertain step backward, looking between Rik, Ben and Yeqon, whose eyes were fluttering open. He rolled awkwardly; his horns gouged into the ground. He struggled furiously when he realised he was bound.

Yeqon roared, "You all die!"

"Shit!" Ben exclaimed, "I told you I didn't know how long I could keep him out. Let's go, now!"

The horrific spectacle of Yeqon made Rik's mind up.

"Sister, Ben is sorry… and I trust him. Please come with us?"

Rik reached out his hand to me, and before I knew it, I'd leapt over a widening fissure as steam exploded from the depths. I grabbed Rik's hand, he grabbed Ben's, and we disappeared through a vertical crack in the back wall behind the thrones. We slipped into a black heat and hopefully, not death.

A strangely beautiful, red crystalline glow punctuated the blackness of the claustrophobic fracture in the rock. Rik pulled hard on my hand in a mad rush, as he was guided quickly along by Ben. There was no possibility of flying in the tight space. I was forced to retract my wings, which seemed to turn off the comforting force field that had protected me. My skin stung against the sharp and claustrophobic walls. The ground was jagged and wet, the stink worse than I could ever have imagined. The atmosphere was dark, and I don't mean the light. A truly palpable nastiness pressed in on us the further we went.

We seemed to travel for miles, twisting and turning, stopping for brief moments only to make sure we weren't followed. The further we travelled, the hotter and redder it all became, until we fell from the mouth of the fissure. We came to a dizzying stop at the precipice of a cavernous drop. The gargantuan hole was blacker than black, and possibly a never-ending fall.

"This is as far as I'm familiar with. Belial said that when we reach Oblivion, we have to call on the one who will help us find the secret portal back to the mortal realm." Ben was pale, frequently scanning back into the fissure we had burst out of. His steely toughness had given way to palpable desperation. He seemed as eager to leave as I did.

"Hang on? What do you mean Belial told you?" It just registered what Ben had said. Just the thought of Belial coated my throat with bile.

"I came searching for him when I left you with Yeqon," Ben said.

I glared at him.

"You're still consorting with the beast that killed Esme?" I bristled and bared my teeth. My entire body lit, "How could you?"

"Stop that! This place feeds off our energy! Do you want horrors just as deadly as Yeqon to find us?" Ben whispered desperately.

"Sister… he's right, stop it, please?" Rik tugged on my arm.

"Why would I *ever* take advice from Belial?" I whispered angrily, pushing Rik's hand away. Flashes of him kicking Esme's limp, beaten body into an abyss brought tears to the edge of my eyes. Power arced across my face as the tears and electricity reacted.

Ben ran his hands impatiently through his slick hair, responding to my angry question. "Because he's trying to put things right. He's done a shit load of bad things, like me, but someone has to put a stop to Yeqon's madness. I've not felt right about any of this for so long, Soph. Since the day you were born, as a matter of fact." Ben wiped sweat from his eyes. "Now isn't the time to hash through this. I owed Belial for treating him like crap. I got him out of the Pits and he's told me what he discovered while he was down here. There's a portal outta here. Either you believe me and take a risk, or we all just wait for Yeqon. He'll find us. Trust me on that, at least."

I clenched my fists, "If you're lying to me, I'll kill you… slowly." I knew it wasn't an empty threat, which shocked and satisfied me all at once.

Ben nodded sharply.

"And for the record, if you ever see Jaz again, I'd make a good guess that she'll try to kill you too," I added, missing her terribly and wishing for some of her acid wit to keep me company.

"So, who or what is supposed to help us?" I asked suspiciously.

"Come here, Rik." I held out my hand, sorry I'd pushed him away. It slid straight back into mine, eased my heart just a little.

"His name is Andromaleus. According to Belial, we are to call his name three times over the Pit of Oblivion and he will appear," Ben answered.

"And he will just help us?" I asked sarcastically.

"No one helps anyone here," Rik said nervously. "Everything here comes with a heavy price," Rik squeezed my hand, an action that didn't incite confidence in me at all.

"You have learnt all too well about that, little brother." Ben shook his head, "And I'm sorry I didn't protect you better from all of this."

"You kept me alive when I wanted to die," Rik said. My heart flipped in my chest.

Ben took an exhausted breath.

"He's right. Nothing comes without a price, Soph. Escape will cost us. I just don't know what it will be, but we have no other choice."

The lack of choices was really starting to piss me off.

"Fine, just do it. Call the thing and let's get out of here," I said.

As if on cue, the floor rumbled. A wide crack opened up between the ledge we stood upon and the Oblivion abyss below. The teetering platform wasn't going to hold on for long and I didn't relish testing the limits of my flying skills whilst tumbling down there.

"Hurry!" I pressed, suddenly desperate for Ben's help.

Ben breathed deep and called the name Andromaleus three times without hesitation.

The name bounced off the walls all the way down into the inky blackness and back again.

The rock cracked further and shifted. We lurched forwards. Rik and I grappled at each other for support. Ben stood on the very edge, unmoving, as he searched the darkness.

"Is it working?" Rik asked.

"Shh," Ben whispered. He held up his hand for us to be quiet.

"I hear something," Rik whispered in my ear. So did I. A scratchy, windy howl gusted up from Oblivion. Ben took a step backwards, his arms wide to protect us behind him. A twirling mass of dust swirled and bounced like a twister, looking for a place to land. It bounced up and down a few times as though testing where best to land. The ferocity of the gust blew grit in my face; I blinked hard not to lose sight of the thing materialising before me.

Ben cursed the foulest words I'd ever heard him utter.

Finally, it touched down right in front of me. It popped in and out of a dozen different shapes before it settled on a small, hunched form.

"No!" I whispered. My shoulders fell in dismay. Now I knew why Ben had sworn. The creature rolled its sandy hands together and grimaced greedily, blinking crusty, dark eyes.

"Hello again, pretty one. What memories do you offer for waking us from our sleep?'

Andromaleus was the evil little Asmodai.

A strange smudge of starlight glimmered across the onyx sky. Red and orange cinders smothered the exhausted A'vean's that fought overhead. The roar of thousands of years of pent-up passion accompanied a drumming thunder. Caked in the remnants of death, the fury of two factions fought for the same prize; no one relented.

Matias bee-lined for Belial's throat the moment he'd seen him ascend to the airborne battle. He barrel-rolled Belial back to the ground in an explosive eruption of crackling energy and fists. The ground cratered with the impact. They slid for metres, coming to rest against an outcropping of blackened tree stumps.

The rest of the Eloi; Amais, Serail and Theus descended towards Belial.

Koi saved him.

Koi pinned his wings flat to maximise his speed, hitting the ground just before Belial was blown into ashes by the Eloi.

"Stop! Brothers, stop!" Koi bellowed as he came to a skidding halt at the foot of the group. Belial was hunched at their feet and refused to fight back, imprisoned on all sides.

Koi pushed into the middle of the group.

"Stop, I said!" Koi put both hands out in warning. The Eloi glared at Koi, anger and confusion shaded the blueness of their eyes.

"Koi, what are you doing? He is a fugitive we have long sought," Serail growled.

"You do not have authority over us, Koi. Tread carefully," Theus threatened, tilting his head, questioning Koi's next move.

"I know this, brothers, but please listen. He saved me from Pathos who meant to ascend me only moments ago." Koi nodded at Belial who looked incredulously at Koi. Only moments before, Koi would absolutely have ripped him to pieces without a thought. Belial leaned wearily into his calloused hands.

The four most ancient Watchers reeled and hissed hearing Pathos' name. Still raw with the shock that one of their own had turned on them, they spat at the ground in unison.

"Belial was in league with that letch. He has put on a show for you to continue his infiltration." Serail stepped threateningly towards Belial. "You know their ways, brother. They deceive and manipulate."

Koi nodded. "Yes, and his hand will be shown quickly if that is the case." Koi stared hard at Belial, "You realise your fate will be sealed in an instant if you lie, Belial?"

Belial nodded into his hands, "I have nothing of myself left. I do not lie, Koi."

Koi looked to the Eloi, "I vow to ash him myself, if he so much as glows the wrong tone of energy, but please, we have no time for this now. Look above, we are pushing them back. It isn't for us to decide his fate when he is unarmed and surrendering. That decision is for Gedz'iel."

"No threat? Did he not steal Sophia's human and murder the innocent seer woman? Those are but two of his many transgressions," Amais accused. Extra wisps of angry power arced threateningly across his broad chest.

"He is guilty of heinous crimes, yes. He has shown his hand to me, however. Belial seeks to be tried and punished. He asked me for death!" Koi responded, exasperated.

"They are right, Koi. Let them annihilate me now. I deserve no stay of execution. I never afforded that to others." Belial slowly rose, one shoulder hanging limp and dislocated, his body as ravaged as their own with fresh battle scars.

The Eloi grimaced and snarled. Each of them glowed even brighter, enhancing the deepness of the skin tone, the age of their own torment. Their wings widened, flapping angrily. The ground joined the emotion as new fissures opened up, steaming flames burst from deep within the earth. Orange light licked at them; putrid gases blew their alabaster hair wildly.

Serail pointed an accusing finger at Belial.

"We were trusted with this planet. We betrayed that trust. You betrayed *our* trust. We have paid with an eternity of enslavement to a sub-species and we have accepted this. We have waited for absolution. *You* chose to circumvent that through your own greed, Belial. Your own needs and wants outweighed the needs of the whole. Your crimes are heinous. What say you that we allow you to leave this realm in one piece?" Serail demanded the correct answer.

Belial's face darkened with shame. He ran a hand across his cracked mouth, seeking the right answers that were clearly non-existent. He shook his head.

"Belial, Serail speaks a dark and blatant truth. You *must* answer if there is any chance I can keep you in one piece," Koi urged him. "Hurry now, we must return to the battle. Ged'erel remains strong!" The fiery reflection of battle mirrored in Koi's eyes as he took in the scene overhead. Ged'erel, larger than most, had powered through ascension after ascension of their kindred. Blue flames burned and fizzled a dozen times. The diamond remains of A'vean warriors rained like hail.

Gedz'iel chased Ged'erel down for miles into the distance. They crashed through mountain tops, set fire to the avenue of dead trees and toppled the pumice altar, raging over and over in a battle so focused and violent that Gedz'iel remained unaware of the confrontation on the ground.

Belial drew in a long breath. His raven irises fought the inner darkness, straining to maintain their opalescent hue. He spoke hastily, feeling the Eloi's patience dwindling as they flexed to get back to fighting.

"I deserve nothing, but I can help you. Nik'ael found me lost in the Pits and talked sense into me. Not before we tried killing each other first." Belial stared at the hastily healed slashes and burns across his torso. He mused with a wry smile at his appearance and the situation he now found himself in. "Nik'ael too repents and has parted ways with Yeqon. He's wanted this for longer than I. He stalled so many opportunities throughout Soph'ael's life, always feeding Yeqon mere morsels, lies, when we both knew there was so much more going on in that earthly world of hers." Belial drew another tired breath. He looked up at all who stood in judgment of him. Suspicion tightened their glowering expressions. The white of their facial marks burned in threat against the darkness of their ageless skin. Belial glanced skyward, marking the time he had left to quickly explain himself.

"Long ago, Nik'ael lost his lust for violence. I was the one fanning the flames. Whilst I suffered in the Pits, I had time to think on everything. All Yeqon's promises were empty… *are* empty. He treated me worse than a dog. I realised my grievance was less with I'el's plan and more with the fact that I failed to protect my own family. I have despised myself for five hundred years. Yeqon took advantage of that, twisting my pain into something else entirely. That's what he does best." Belial hung his head in shame.

The Eloi quietly took in his confession, but remained stony and unforgiving. All but Koi, who nodded for Belial to continue.

"I discovered a way out of this realm that I believe Yeqon is unaware of. A portal burrowed through to the Earthen realm eons ago by lesser Daimon and other vile creatures, so that they could come and go, entertaining themselves in the mortal world. I told Nik'ael how to get Soph'ael out if he found her alive."

The Eloi's eyes widened in surprise.

"Gedz'iel must know of this immediately. Until then, we finish the battle above and then you shall show us this portal," Serail said.

"I concur with Serail. Brothers?" Amais asked of Theus and Matias. They all nodded.

"Until then, Koi, as you wish to honour Belial's newfound yearning for redemption, he shall be bound to you for the duration of our time here." Serail flicked his hand towards Belial. Crackling wisps of energy shot out from his fingertips at Belial, wrapping around his wrist. He repeated the gesture towards Koi, binding Daimon and Watcher together. Serail stepped closer. Belial winced, but maintained a semblance of dignity as Serail grasped his limp arm with his fiery palm. The dislocation healed in seconds. Serail restored Belial's ability to fight, one-armed.

"Koi?" Serail queried, "Can you fight together?"

"It is only fair, since I vouch for one who has long ago lost respect. Yes, we shall war together." Koi nodded and looked down at Belial.

"I do not wish to die strapped to you." Koi narrowed his eyes.

Belial squared his shoulders, allowing a semblance of dignity to return, "I will forever more be at your side, and victorious with you."

The battle-scarred A'veans launched with a sonic boom back into the sky, their war cries followed, with the threat of no mercy.

Chapter Thirty-Nine

ou?" Ben accused acidly.

"We are not happy?" The Asmodai queried, batting its eyes innocently.

"Where is Andromaleus? You are a liar!" Ben lit his hands towards the creature.

"Asmodai cannot lie. The fault lies in the wrong questions being asked, the wrong deals that are struck. Andromaleus lived long ago in the mortal realm. We are all that remains of him." Andromaleus bowed.

Ben glared at the sandy creature that reached only as high as his knees.

"I have seen many of these, Nik'ael. They are dangerous," Rik said, clenching his fists.

"Dangerous? Such lies! We are servants to those in need." Andromaleus tilted its head, surprised by the accusation.

"You are thieves, existing on the emotions of others. You leave wreckage, that's all." Ben pointed accusingly. The Asmodai put a hand to its chest in shock.

"You tried to steal my memories. You can't help us," I said.

"Steal? Payment is fair for services rendered, pretty one." Andromaleus grinned hungrily at me. Ben stepped between us.

"Show us the way out and I won't kill you now!" Ben growled, his dagger pointed in its direction, arcing energy through it like an electrified sword. The sizzling point hung millimetres from the Asmodai's face.

"Kill us? We are long dead. This is but a fraction of our many souls that live eternally in the dust and rocks. Impale us now and realise your folly. You will never find you way out. He is coming, you know!" Andromaleus chuckled to himself, rolling his gnarled hands over, the sound like sandpaper as he stared behind us. "They are stupid, aren't they?" he mumbled to himself, his face wrinkled in annoyance. His beady eyes darted between us.

"Why do you keep saying *we*?" The way it spoke rattled me.

"We are one, but we are also many. Andromaleus is joined a thousand-fold. We talk to ourselves, consult with each other. Our soul melds with thousands of memories. They feed us and we discuss all matters of importance with them, of course," Andromaleus answered as though it were completely obvious.

"What do you want then?" I asked.

Ben looked incredulously in my direction; Rik pulled me back behind him protectively.

"Soph, wrong question," Ben said.

A roar echoed ominously from the fissure. Yeqon's maniacal screams boomed inside my mind.

One…limb…at a time!

The others looked anxious for answers whilst the Asmodai remained serene, if not amused.

"Well, what choice is there, Ben?" God, it was the first time I'd uttered his name out loud for ages, and it felt thick and poisonous.

"What do we do? He's coming!" Rik panicked.

Ben suddenly grabbed Andromaleus by his wrinkled little neck and held him aloft.

"You will take want you want from me!" he demanded.

The creature barely reacted to the physical threat.

"We seek payment according to what is needed most by the whole. We have no use for anger and regret," it responded plainly.

"What is it you want, then?" Ben bellowed in its face; dust sprinkled away like a sandcastle eroding in the breeze.

"Innocence," was his answer.

The explosions grew louder and closer. Panic was setting in.

"Ben, just give it what it wants!" I yelled over the cracking din.

"You see nothing in me?" Ben asked of it.

"We see darkness and pain in you. We have our fill of these things," Andromaleus snapped impatiently.

Ben threw it to the ground in a dusty heap. The ledge lurched again. I toppled towards the edge, grappling to keep hold of the chest, and it nearly cost me a fall into Oblivion.

Ben scooped me up. I felt sick at his touch. He lingered too long, then set me safely back next to Rik.

"Take payment from me!" Rik suddenly offered. "I may have darkness, but I have little experience of the worlds. Does that count for innocence?"

Ben glared at him, but didn't interject.

"Hmmm, come closer? Let us read you." The Asmodai reached for Rik. I followed Rik protectively.

"Be careful, Rik. Shut down all that you wish to keep. He will rape your mind otherwise," Ben warned. I was furious that he would allow Rik to offer himself like a lamb. As though sensing my private thoughts, Rik spoke to us.

"Brother, Sophia, I have nothing left to lose other than both of you. I have never had anything to give of myself. What I can do now is give you a chance," Rik replied solemnly. My heart lurched. He searched my face; I bit back the fearful quiver of my lips.

"I have only known evil for so long. Let me stamp on it by following a different path. Let me be brave for the first time in a long time?" Rik's pride implored me to not stand in his way.

I couldn't speak, but I squeezed his hand in solidarity.

Rik nodded at the nasty extortionist. Andromaleus couldn't hide the gleeful twinkle in its eyes.

Just as Andromaleus reached for Rik, Ben stepped in, held the dagger to its throat.

"You cannot lie?"

"We cannot."

"You will show us how to get to the portal that opens into the human realm as soon as you have what you want?" Ben's fury at having to pander to Andromaleus feathered his jaw.

"The moment we are compensated, we shall divulge all that we know of the portal of Oblivion," Andromaleus said.

Ben reluctantly stood back and nodded at Rik.

The Asmodai took Rik's free hand, closing its eyes in assessment. It nodded, shaking its head and occasionally grimaced. Rik looked pained, as though a migraine clung to his skull.

Ben held the dagger at the ready, in just in case.

"Ahhh! We are most interested in you. But… it is you that we must have!" Andromaleus snarled, and like lightning grabbed my forearm like a clamp.

I screamed and pulled my arm without success. My mind was immediately invaded. My vision disappeared in a violent snap. Andromaleus flicked and poked through my private memories. Stopping and starting, hesitating here and there until he found exactly what he wanted. I screamed in my mind. There was no physical sensation of my body. It was as though I was nothing but memories in a black void.

"No! Not that!"

I heard the Asmodai laughing victoriously.

"We thank you for your reparations, pretty one."

With that, I blacked out, not sure if I'd actually died.

Forty

"Soph, Soph! Come on, wake up!"

The thick voice was annoying, and I swatted it away.

"Soph, wake up."

My head felt cradled into something familiar and warm. I snuggled into it. The voice became more urgent. I felt my body being rocked back and forth inside this beautiful cocoon.

"Yeqon is coming!"

An explosion of panic rocked through my mind. I swam frantically towards consciousness. The voice that continued to call my name remained strange, but that name, Yeqon, yanked me from delirium and reeled me towards wakefulness in a snap.

I found myself cradled in muscular arms. They held me securely into a broad chest. Beneath the warm skin, the muscle and bone, a heart pounded furiously.

The explosions were not only in my subconsciousness. Deep within the cavernous walls, the rumblings of detonations shook the bedrock. A hail of burning debris left us grey, as I scrambled out of this stranger's embrace.

Someone else grabbed hold of my shoulders and I stumbled under the lurching ground.

Blinking into full awareness, I wiped the slimy sediment from my eyelashes. Another grubby face peered into mine, a mirror image of my own, only male. Still confused, I briefly thought how Esme would want to scrub that face clean with a wattle seed and lemon myrtle paste. *Esme! Yeqon!*

Suddenly recalling where I was, I screamed at Rik over the cacophony of eruptions.

"Did he tell us how to get out of here?" I coughed the words out as the ashen air thickened. Whatever was going on behind the walls sounded like a world war, and it was coming fast.

"What happened?" I looked about. The same crumbling ledge of rock smouldered underfoot as it teetered towards Oblivion. Rik sighed with relief as he passed Enoch's box back to me. The other guy, the one who'd been holding me, calling me to wake up; I didn't know him. The dark hair, flecked with white, the intense pained stare he was trying to mask, none of it gave any indication as to his identity.

He called my name again, with a strange familiarity. His pleas smooth and urgent.

"Soph, we have to go now. I know where to find the portal." His hand reached for mine. He urged me to the edge of Oblivion.

Despite the demonic screams reverberating back through the tunnels, I found it hard to drag my attention from this person. He raked a hand through his hair impatiently; it made my heart skip a beat, and I didn't know why. Those strange blue eyes shadowed with darkness intrigued me. I followed him to the ledge.

Plumes of putrid-smelling steam sprayed some of the sludge from my skin as I drew out my wings, knowing I needed to fly, and fast. Rik's wings emerged, flapping with no coordination whatsoever. I understood that feeling all too well. I pulled at Rik to stay close, as both the stranger and I glanced at each other repeatedly, preparing to jump into the terrifying nothingness.

"Who is that, Rik? Does he know me?" I whispered in his ear.

Rik's eyes glared wide in surprise and I didn't understand why.

"Sister, it's Ben!"

Sharing a look between them both, I noted this Ben's look of surprise as well. His expression then darkened.

"We've no time for this, little brother. Let's go or we're all dead," Ben's voice grumbled impatiently.

The ground cracked and dipped. I stumbled and Ben caught me. I clamped the box into my armpit. Ben fleetingly held my eyes in a strangely familiar way, a way that made me immediately uncomfortable. His eyes released mine. I pushed away from him, tucking the box more securely under my arm.

"Thanks…uh…Ben. Did that beast really tell you how to find the portal?"

"You don't remember?" Rik asked.

"All I remember is the Asmodai grabbed your hand, Rik. Whatever he did to you must have knocked me out. I don't know, maybe because we're twins?"

Rik and this Ben character shared some kind of knowing look.

"What is it?" I asked.

Rocks exploded behind us. Yeqon was close enough that I heard him clawing and blasting through the whatever lay between us.

"Nik…ael!" he roared. On the tail of that horrific sound, there was another voice… in my mind.

Soph! Run if you can. I'm here, but run! It sounded like Lorcan.

There was no time left for second-guessing or discussion. I'd get my answers later, if I survived.

This Ben person grabbed me by one arm, and a trembling Rik on the other. He yelled at us both, "Light up, spread your wings. We have to descend into Oblivion."

I was so unsettled by Ben. I knew instinctively he wasn't fully one of us, yet he wasn't fully one of them. Whatever this darkness was about him, he seemed to be helping us, so I let myself trust in him.

Deep breath in, deep breath out, repeat.

I hoped I was going to see the light of day again. I hoped my instincts were tuned into the right frequency.

Ben pulled us both forward. We fell into the deep black pit where sound evaporated like the vacuum of space.

We fell forever… well, it felt like it. Gravity pulled harder, sucking us greedily in. I flapped my wings hard. Rik flailed and Ben, this huge strong stranger, kept all three of us aloft with elegant and deep beats of his immense wingspan. Despite my heightened vision, even with our elemental glow cutting through the darkness, there was nothing to see in the inkiness that seemed to engulf us with pleasure.

The deeper we went; the stranger the atmosphere became. A heaviness pressed in from every angle. After descending for a long while, the darkness came to life.

Colourful light spectrums flickered randomly about. Little lights burst on and off like pinpricks of stars. The air cooled and the rushing sound of water broke the strange tranquillity of the nothingness.

Yeqon seemed not to follow, his vile cursing long lost in the depths.

Feeling his fatigue, I pushed away from Ben.

"I got this. Falling gracefully is my talent!" I scoffed, staying aloft, floating gently beside him with more ease than I expected.

Despite his grimness, Ben shook his head and laughed a little. It made my stomach tighten. I felt colour rush to my cheeks. He seemed to check himself and quickly rebuilt his stony expression. He checked on Rik, who seemed to have settled as well. Rik's wings were more rhythmic now, his lack of practice the only thing holding him back from letting go of Ben.

"Don't get too comfortable. Yeqon will find a way to get to us if we don't keep moving, make no mistake of that. He'll be needing his right-hand men though, just in case he gets scared of anything that goes bump in the night," Ben smirked. "He's never been into Oblivion. He's basically a coward, but he's always happy to throw others down here." Disgust lit Ben's mark. His face was an artwork behind the beautiful swirls. Something about him was comforting, safe, and yet utterly terrifying.

Whilst Rik concentrated on his flying technique, I took the opportunity to ask the obvious.

"Do I know you?"

Ben sucked in a breath. There was an uncomfortable silence.

"We met a long time ago. You don't really know me though," Ben answered in a strained kind of way.

"I think we're almost there." Ben indicated below with a nod of his head, circumventing any more questions about his identity.

"Hold on tight now, and stick together. I have no idea what's down there," Ben instructed as he grabbed for me again and pulled Rik in tighter.

The lower we glided, Ben angled his wings, agitating them to slow our pace. I helped the best I could.

The aurora-like lights became more frequent and luminous. They seemed to try to rise up, however some kind of force from above blew them back down. They tumbled and spun backwards around my legs, tickling like ribbons of nothingness. The little star bursts popped closer to us. Each pop had a vocal clarity that became louder and more disturbing the deeper we descended. Pleas for help sent shivers through me.

"Take us with you."

"Don't leave me."

"Forgive us."

"Save me."

"Ignore them, both of you," Ben said. "They only mean to hitch a ride to where they don't belong."

As he uttered the warning, the calls immediately turned nasty. A cluster of white spots burst into a frenzy around us. The voices, now guttural, screeched instead of pleaded.

"Suck your soul."

"Devour your heart."

"Pluck your eyes from their sockets."

In response, Ben produced a red orb, like Koi's nasty zappers, and flicked it towards the evil lights. They screamed like crackling fireworks exploding into a shower of glittering debris. In the process of scattering the evil entities, Ben lost hold of Rik, who fell, screaming and yelping; a rapidly disappearing splay of appendages. I tried to go after him, but Ben flew down in a white blur, me in tow. He scooped Rik up.

"Gotta work on that flying of yours if we get out of this." Ben leaned his forehead against Rik's, gasping with relief. They both laughed nervously, as did I. These two had some kind of bond. Ben wasn't my brother; I was fairly certain of that. He wasn't Rik's brother, yet he referred to him as *Little Brother*. That was another question for another time.

Below our dangling feet, a light burned brighter by the second. Rushing water became a roar. Redness glimmered beneath, drenching us in a bloody hue.

"What are we heading towards?" I asked, gripping a little tighter to Ben's hand. He flinched. I released my grip and continued untethered.

Ben worked his jaw as he seemed to process our next move.

"Well, that little bastard Asmodai at least told the truth about one thing. He said we were to head to the base of Oblivion, where we would find a river. The Blood River of Souls.

Following Ben's line of sight. I was met with a scene that was as amazing as it was grotesque.

I gasped.

"I'el save us," Rik whispered.

Chapter
Forty-One

Lorcan raced wildly through the Daimon lair. No transference, no finding the easy way in. Anger and determination propelled him to the deepest, most primal energy field. He emerged in a blinding light. The connection with Sophia hissed, a white snake of energy, pulling him along the trail of where she had tread.

"Lorcan, stop!" Kea chased him down, determined to save Sophia, as well as Lorcan, from his own hell-bent passion.

Whilst the Eloi, the Daimon and the others still fought a bloody battle outside, Kea swooped along with Lorcan towards Yeqon's sanctuary.

"You'll ascend yourself, Lorcan… calm down!"

Lorcan burned bright as he pulsed a crater through a wall. Forked zaps exploded from his palms as he dug his way through the steaming rock, leaving rubble in his wake.

The edges of his body developed an orange and blue aura as the whites of his eyes shone.

Knowing what would happen if he allowed himself to heat any further, Kea joined him, producing the most powerful energy she could muster. They both penetrated metres through the earth with an ethereal, unearthly brilliance.

Whilst transferring would take a fraction of a second, the release of this destructive energy seemed to calm Lorcan the deeper he went. It cleared the fog in his mind enough that he finally answered Kea.

"It's okay, I got this!"

Within moments, they both tumbled headfirst into another tunnel. After a quick check that they were alone, Lorcan nodded, "This way."

The two determinedly flew through many more abandoned tunnels. Lorcan now knew exactly where he was going, despite never having been there before. The white snake of Sophia's light pulled him along, taking every turn without hesitation.

"Her energy is everywhere!"

Initially, they ended up back at the cells.

They probed the entire area.

Kea kicked at broken plates and a goblet before hearing a groan in the shadows.

They both summoned orbs, ready for attack, only to find, in the light of their weapons, a rousing Afflicted woman.

"You are too late. She is gone. Probably dead!" she snickered weakly. Her nostrils suddenly flared. She sniffed wildly, pulling herself onto her hands and knees, crawling towards Lorcan.

"Get back! You are warned once only," he growled.

Kea, ever soft-hearted, knelt down to her, "Tell us what you know of the girl who was here, and I will help you." Kea smiled towards the sickly Afflicted whose dilated grey eyes seemed dry and desperate.

"Help you? Sure, of course!" she smiled as she sat back on her bony haunches. "Just give me a taste of what's on your skin, and I will tell you the secrets of the universe," she cackled weakly, holding her belly.

Kea grimaced with disgust, realising she was probably covered in a dusting of the remains of her kindred from the topside battle. The Afflicted licked her dry lips hungrily.

"Argh, I've no time for this," Lorcan turned to leave.

The woman panicked, roared and launched herself at Kea. Her hands splayed like claws, desperate to get to any tiny morsel of Thanratos.

"No!" Kea screamed.

Lorcan turned and rammed an orb into the middle of the Afflicted's chest.

It took her a few seconds to register that her miserable mortal life was over. Her mouth widened grotesquely, her cheeks sunk further inwards and her eyes rolled back into her head. Lorcan threw her aside as she imploded into a ball of sputtering flames. The small chamber filled with sweet smelling smoke as she fizzled into the exact same thing that she herself craved, nothing more than a glittering diamond skeleton.

"Leave those there, Kea. She doesn't deserve any honour," Lorcan spat on the ground, turned, and left.

"Oh, Lorcan." Kea's heart sunk. He seemed so suddenly dark when he had always been so bright. She glanced back at the pitiful sight, widened her wings and trailed after him.

"This way." Lorcan flew lightning fast. They covered dozens of crumbling tunnels in mere minutes, until they came upon the Throne room. Both stopped short as the snake of tracking light snapped out of existence. They carefully took in the scene. A place of dread they'd only ever heard talk of, and there they were, in the central station of Earth's very own Hell.

Disarray greeted them. Scorched walls were overshadowed by fresh and dried blood smears that tracked in all directions across the floor. The pungent stench of death thickened the fetid air. Kea involuntarily placed a hand over her mouth, shaking her head. Crystalline tears clung to her lashes. Lorcan hovered, unmoved and deathly silent, taking the horror in. His bloodshot glare gave each throne equal attention. The tangled plait of his mud-crusted hair billowed up and down the length of his back in the soft breeze, as his wings flapped just enough to keep him still and balanced. Flared nostrils betrayed the strength with which he hid his disgust, as did the fists that clenched anxiously open and closed. He tilted his head, closed his eyes and felt for any positive energy… for Sophia's energy.

Something clattered to the ground behind the farthest throne. Lorcan's head snapped up. Kea drew her sword as they spied tattered red stilettoes slinking away around a corner. Garbled obscenities trailed the fleeing Lilith.

They both hovered silently, high up by the roof line, drenched in the steam. Lilith hadn't noticed them and seemed to be heading off alone. Kea placed a gentle hand on Lorcan's shoulder.

"Don't mind her, Lorcan. Let her go."

Lorcan wasn't even looking Lilith's way. His gaze was glued to the opposite wall, towards a still crumbling fissure that smouldered in the far corner.

"That way! She went that way, and so has that bastard!"

"Yeqon?" Kea questioned as they flew without hesitation towards the gaping crack.

"Yes, but the bastard I was referring to is Ben!"

"Oh hell! C'mon, let's go!" Kea's face was grim. They tucked in their wings and made foot fall at a run.

The screams and bellows of Yeqon made him all too easy to track.

A Daimon-sized hole was freshly worn into the previously narrow passageway. Fresh lava drizzled down the walls, disturbed from its internal bed.

"She's been here not long ago," Lorcan said and ran faster, his face alight with the scent of Sophia's aura.

Kea brought up the rear, all her weapons at the ready to protect Lorcan from any surprises, whilst he worked his tracking magic.

They picked their way quickly, but carefully, towards the ever-increasing explosions.

Lorcan stopped a few times to touch a specific area of the wall, confirming Sophia's presence had been there.

"Not far," he said, as he picked at a sliver of white cotton tethered to a sharp outcropping of rock.

"I don't mean to state the obvious, Honey, but I'd say, if we follow Yeqon, we find her. Sounds like he's just up ahead." Kea pointed forwards and preparedly called an orb to her other palm.

"Thanks for the support," Lorcan joked with a wry smile, the first in a while. Kea winked back at him.

"The second you see her, you grab her. I'll take care of everyone else. Just grab her and get her out of here, got it? No looking back, okay?" Kea instructed.

"I'll never let her go," Lorcan responded. Kea regarded him worriedly, then quickly drew him into an embrace. She placed a K'ufili gently upon him, her cheek on his.

"Be careful of that heart of yours," she said with an extra squeeze.

Lorcan flushed and pushed away. A defensive darkness flashed across his swirling eyes.

"You worry about yourself. Let's go." Lorcan sped off, jumping rivers of orange, cursing under his breath.

Turning this way and that, they came upon a small dusty creature perched atop a molten rock. It preened itself. It seemed to grow right before their eyes. Moving to run past it, the creature called to them.

"We can help you find her. We have told her of the secret exit to the Earthen realm."

They stopped dead, turning pensively.

"What did you say?" Lorcan asked, eyes narrowing at the strange rocky creature.

"Who are you?" Kea asked curiously.

"Careful Kea, you can't trust anything down here."

"Not trust us? We helped the Earth-born find a way out with her companions. She flees the evil one as we speak. He knows not how or where to follow unless we tell him." It smiled vindictively.

Lorcan leaped forward, grabbing the creature by the neck.

"Are you threatening us? Is blackmail your currency? Well, it won't work, you piece of filth!" Lorcan threw the Asmodai to the ground. Andromaleus recovered quickly, dusting himself down and strangely growing a little taller again. His features more human-like than before.

The grainy texture of his exterior smoother, like tanned hide. A greedy, intelligent spark glittered in the blackness of his eyes.

"Dear Watcher, we deal in information. It is how we survive. Do you begrudge us life?"

"Yes, I do," Lorcan growled. "Let's go, Kea. This is a waste of time."

They turned away. Andromaleus called out, "Just one memory, and you shall know Soph'ael's path. One memory is a small price to pay for such a handsome reward."

Kea faltered.

"Ignore it, Kea. Let's go."

"What if it can help?" she whispered frantically.

"It's less than a Daimon. It's a leftover that thrives on the lives of others. We can't trust it."

Hearing their whispered conversation, the ever more mortal-looking creature threatened them.

"The evil one shall reward us handsomely for what we know! But," Its black irises were shrinking, whiteness beginning to envelop them. "We do not like him so well, and would prefer to help the Watchers. Your memories are more pleasant. We cannot lie, we can only speak the truth… for a price."

"What kind of memory do you want?" Kea asked.

Lorcan grabbed at her, "No! You know it's a trick."

"You've been around a long time, like me, Lorcan. You know as well as I do that sometimes we need to sacrifice things for the greater good. Things don't work the same in this place, and if I have to play by their warped rules for Soph, then I'm prepared to take a chance."

"I won't let you!"

"You won't let me! What are you? A Neanderthal trying to drag your woman back into a cave? Please, don't insult me!" Kea pushed him back. "If it looks like it's doing anything dodgy, just blast it away, okay?" she said. The Asmodai squeaked at the threat as Kea turned to it.

"Tell me what you want first," Kea demanded.

Lorcan grimaced, knowing he could do nothing other than respect Kea's wishes.

"We need to know how to defend ourselves. This is a dangerous home we live in. We wish for a memory about how to fight like a Watcher," Andromaleus said.

Kea glanced questioningly over her shoulder at Lorcan's tight face. "Sounds simple enough?"

"I don't trust him, Kea."

"I'm doing the deal. As soon as this is done, we'll have Soph in our sights." She turned back to Andromaleus. "If you fail to tell us where Sophia is heading, you'll be a pile of dust that I'll happily dance in."

It flinched.

"What do I have to do?" Kea asked.

Andromaleus beamed at the unexpected coup. Two powerful feeds in one day would see him grow immensely. He rubbed his hands in gleeful preparation.

"All we need is to hold your hand, for just a moment." He glanced between Kea and Lorcan in anticipation.

"Fine, here you go!" Kea stepped forward and offered her slender hand.

"This isn't good, Kea."

"Just be ready to annihilate it if it does anything it shouldn't."

The creature grasped Kea's hand with such speed and fervour, there wasn't a chance for second-guessing her decision. In the back of her mind, Kea heard Lorcan's protestations as something filed through her mind. Memories, many millennia worth, flashed across her mind's eye, stopped, started, paused and continued.

Her consciousness faded to black.

Chapter
Forty-Two

The three of us had landed gently on an embankment. Soft white sand felt smooth underfoot. It led to the edge of the source of the roaring sound. A blood red river swirled and rushed in a frenzy. Cautiously, we approached, careful not to touch it. Whilst it sounded like wild rapids, it most certainly wasn't any type of water I'd ever seen.

"What is it?" I said, hand over my mouth, utterly repulsed.

"It is horrendous. Do we really need to cross it?" Rik asked of Ben.

"Cross it?" I studied the viscous swirls of plasma-like energy that snapped and snarled, coursing its way into the distance.

Nasty entities escaped the boiling waves of energy here and there. Most of them were sucked screaming, straight back in.

"Apparently, we need to go straight through to the other side, where a portal exists. I don't like it any more than you two. Ben's eyes furrowed as he studied the horridly unnatural phenomena.

I gulped as things I didn't want to acknowledge swirled and bobbed up and down. Things that looked like limbs and faces clawing for freedom, only to be dragged back beneath the surface.

"Is this Hell?" I asked.

"Pretty much," Ben answered blandly without taking his focus away from the eerie red current. He seemed to be calculating our options as he glanced up and down the shoreline.

Something thudded behind us. We all turned as one; defensive, on edge.

A long silver object lay across the powdery sand. Ben knelt down, touched it, and pulled back quickly as though it stung. He glanced up into the darkness overhead.

"What is it?" Rik asked.

"A sword. It could be anyone's." Ben replied.

"Where did it come from?" I asked worriedly. "Are they catching up to us?"

"I'm not sure. But from the sounds starting to making their way down here, and this," he pointed to the blood-stained weapon. "We best keep moving." Ben turned back towards the river.

A wave crested and a skeletal figure reached for freedom. Its eyeless skull turned in our direction, reaching desperately out to us. A piercing scream from its slack mandible cut me to the core with horror. I muffled a scream as it fell back beneath the greedy waves.

"I do not want to go through that," I said plainly. "Can't we fly over it?"

"No," Ben looked ominous. "The portal is on the river bed, beneath the waves, amongst the lost souls.

"That's what they are? Lost souls?" I asked.

He nodded solemnly. "The Blood River of Souls carries the worst of the condemned, feeding off them. They float on its current eternally, re-living their worst fears and nightmares as punishment for evil deeds. It is a replica of the real Tartarus from our home world," he answered.

"And it's where I belong," Ben mumbled, then moved away before I could question what he meant. Why would anyone think they would belong in Hell?

He kneeled and dipped a finger in the river, then waved his hand through the strange red energy.

"Does it hurt?" Rik asked. Understandably, pain was something he was fearful of.

"No, little brother, it does not hurt. It's just cold." Ben stood back up as a scream echoed from far above. A scream that tore at my heart. Ben glanced up like me. Something resonated with him about it too.

"Do you think the others have found us?" I asked. Rik perked up at the prospect.

"They may have followed Yeqon, but they won't know about the portal either. We have to keep moving forward," Ben said.

I grabbed Rik's hand, "It looks like we have to do this. Don't let go of me, okay?"

"I'll never let go of you, sister."

Ben sniffed and spoke impatiently. "Follow me and stay right behind me. We should keep our energy low, in case the river wants to feed off us. Can you control that, bro?" Ben looked back at Rik.

"I can, I can do it," Rik replied.

We made our way tentatively to the shoreline.

"For love of all things good and pure, give us strength," I whispered.

The first few feet in presented nothing untoward other than a colder than cold rush. The swirling mass was a million pinpricks. Freezing buzzes of dark energy nipped at my skin as my feet sunk into a soft river bed.

Above us was blackness as we moved out of the open cavern of Oblivion. A blackened chamber encased this dreaded current. The deeper we went, the more I was aware of an incessant and increasingly loud chatter within the waves.

It wasn't like chatter over a high tea; it was dark and nasty and desperate.

"New flesh!"

"Mmmmmmm."

"Trust us, we will protect you."

"Come with me, I will take you to safety."

"Let them drown!"

I faltered. Ben halted and turned to me.

"They're just trying to scare you. Whatever you see or hear, it isn't real. Just keep putting one foot in front of the other. You can't drown and it can't hurt you; only scare you. Don't let it get into your head." Ben turned away and his broad shoulders dipped beneath the crimson flow, followed quickly by his head. He was gone!

Rik and I squeezed the circulation clear out of each other's hands.

Surprisingly, he took the lead.

"I trust Ben. He has always looked after me. Now I'll look after you too." Rik pulled me deeper, until we too, sunk fully into the swathe of writhing souls.

The Blood River's current was *'alive'* with things I could never explain. There was a multitude of strangely shaped blobs of energy in various states of composition and decomposition. Some looked merely like jellyfish, others still had the remnants of limbs that grappled for anything as they were pushed mercilessly along the current. Others were horrifically human. Rotting carcasses glared my way as they writhed and struggled. The current didn't affect us, though. Ben was a few feet ahead and responded to my unanswered question.

We are alive, in mortal form. It can only carry the dead of this world. Ben fell forwards, clutched his head and screamed, swatting out in front of himself. He screamed the name Neren'iel!

Darkness then descended upon me.

Although I knew I wasn't alone, I had no awareness of Ben, Rik, or anything; just the suddenly clear red river swirling by. There was a tickle at my feet. I stepped forward, out of its way. The tickling persisted as I felt myself trying to move forward, but my feet seemed stuck. I looked down to see what held me in place, only to be met with nothing less than my own personal nightmare.

The smooth white sand was no longer there. It had given way to a river bed all together very different. What was moments ago soft white grains underfoot was now an endless pathway of tarantula spiders that crawled and tumbled beneath my weight. They arched back, front legs and inch long fangs bared in threat as they crawled up my legs. The soft pads of hundreds of hairy feet overtook my sensibilities. I wanted to cave inside myself and just die. My screams were muted behind my hand however, I dared not open my mouth in case one got in. Kicking and swatting them away made no difference. I was surrounded on all sides. Rik and Ben were nowhere to be seen.

Furry bodies clambered all over me and I froze. I couldn't breathe. My body shook from within until I broke free and ran through the evil current. Arachnids fell onto me as quickly as others fell off. I continued my pointless screams deep inside my frantic mind.

Losing my sense of direction, I was sure I was running in circles, about to spiral down into a horrific grave of legs and fangs; never-ending clusters of eight eyed predators. At the peak of my fear, when I truly believed I was about to be consumed, I remembered Ben had said the river would play on my fears. I frantically began repeating a mantra over and over in my mind.

They aren't real; they aren't real.

I covered my face with one hand, determined not to let go of Enoch's box, despite feeling the sinister crawling all over my arms.

They aren't real; they aren't real!

The writhing slowly died away, the tickling faded and suddenly, thankfully, I was standing alone again on white sand, surrounded by the swirling redness.

Things still felt all kinds of wrong, though. It was silent, too silent. The others were near, but far, calling and screaming in their own agonies. I kept moving forwards when something grabbed my shoulder.

I turned with fright to find Ben smiling down at me. He was clean, glowing with health and strength. His blue eyes sparkled; he reached forwards, cupping my face with his hands.

My skin flamed with a different kind of heat. His touch was like a whip that sent my heart into a frenzy. I was so confused. What was this stranger doing to me, and why did I want it?

He leaned into me. My lips parted. He took advantage of the opportunity and covered my open mouth with his. His lips gently played against mine; his tongue swept them seductively. He pulled me into his body and I felt myself become lost in the touch, the taste, and strangely familiar passion. As his kiss intensified, I wondered why the river would offer me this. This wasn't scary at all. It was amazing. He cradled the small of my back and huskily whispered my name across my lips, "Sophia."

I groaned involuntarily. He grabbed harder and kissed me more hungrily. My breath escaped me as the beautiful warmth in my chest evolved rapidly into a cold and harsh stabbing. His fingers dug deeply until it was no longer pleasure, but pain. I gasped and pulled back. Yes, the river indeed was working its disgusting magic. Ben smiled a grizzly toothy smirk. He grimaced down at me in an altogether hideous way.

"Come on. You know you like a bad boy, Soph," Ben's eyes flickered from blue to black. Curved horns sprouted from his hair. He chuckled deeply as his face fizzled and faded, morphing in and out of other faces. Yeqon, Belial and then the death mask of Esme. Her decomposing face leaned into mine, cackling wildly. The loose flesh jiggled grotesquely.

"Child, I told you 'ol Esme seen the spirits about. Shoulda listened to Esme, Pumpkin!" Her puffed and mangled mouth chortled. Ferociously slapping at her and wriggling away, I fell backwards.

It's not real! You're not real!

Esme's expression sobered, and it faded away, along with the outline of her body. Only the piercing cackle left as it washed away on the swirling current.

When her morbid laughter finally disappeared, it was slowly replaced by the ever-increasing sounds of the rushing of an endless number of souls, flowing and ebbing past. The screams of the damned brought me back to reality, where I found myself once more clasping Rik's hand, standing behind Ben, who himself was as ashen as both of us. Deeply unsettled by my vision of him, I had to force myself to concentrate as he spoke.

"Are you both okay?" he asked.

I nodded wordlessly, unable to stop glaring at him, to not look at his lips, to forget their taste.

"I will be fine," Rik breathed. I dreaded to imagine what he had seen.

"Well, it seems that little freak came through," Ben said, as he stepped aside and guided our line of sight with a wave of his hand.

A few feet in front of him, vertically wedged in the wall of the river bed, was a rectangular doorway of sorts.

No door sealed it closed, there was no lock that needed a key. A blue and green mirror-like opening rippled like the soft ebb of a calm lake.

"What is it?" Rik asked.

"This is the portal back to Earth. Let's get you home," Ben said, his eyes flitting to me more often, as though he, too, had seen what I had seen.

Ben took my hand and all three of us stepped through.

Chapter
Forty-Three

It was one more turn until they found Yeqon heaving his exhausted frame over the ledge of an unstable cluster of fallen rock. Kea had recovered quickly as the Asmodai disappeared into the rocks, cawing with glee. She felt fine. Her senses remained crisp as they came face to face with the embodiment of the term, *'Fallen Angel'*.

Lorcan nodded at her. She returned the gesture, indicating everything seemed okay as they faced their nemesis.

Yeqon turned on them the moment they exited the mouth of the tunnel. The surprise in his bloodshot eyes matched an easy snarl. His bloodied fingers spread along with his wings, readying for attack. He tossed a small dagger up and down in one hand and smirked.

Lorcan launched straight into it.

"So, here's bastard number one! You want to use fists or weapons? Me? I'd rather smash your face in with this!" Lorcan held up a tight knuckled fist as he dropped an orb at the base of Yeqon's feet. The small explosion, a mere warning.

Yeqon roared, spat at their feet.

"This is your last day wearing flesh!" Yeqon launched forwards, his speed and cunning no match for Lorcan.

"I prefer my flesh *on*, you bloody maggot!" Lorcan ducked the slice of the dagger, rolling through the air to face him again. Yeqon rounded for another bout. Lorcan looked down into Oblivion, which he now hovered above. Kea saw the fleeting glance and nodded covertly whilst speaking to his mind.

Go now. He doesn't know where she went. He's merely following her aura. I'll sort him out, Lorcan. Go!

Before Lorcan could respond, Yeqon knocked him clear across the abyss with a mighty orb to the chest, followed by the sting of his dagger which landed in Lorcan's biceps.

Lorcan screamed in rage, pulling the dagger clean out, flinging it back with precision. It landed with a crack in one of Yeqon's thick horns.

Recovering quickly, Lorcan dive-bombed Yeqon, who met him mid-air. The two tumbled and raged. Like a fiery comet, they cut through the darkness and smashed into unseen walls. The snap and crunch of rock falling backed up their clashing. Oblivion sucked the debris away into the immense nothingness below.

Please, Lorcan. Go find Soph! Kea screamed into his head, as she too launched towards the melee, following the raging ball of fists, orbs and lightning strikes. The cavernous space was alight with a primal fight to the death.

Kea rammed between them both, separating Lorcan, and sending Yeqon into a frenzied thump back on the nearly fully collapsed platform.

"Not so impressive on your own, old man!" Lorcan taunted, his eyes wild and red with adrenaline.

In the seconds she had to talk sense into him, Kea grabbed Lorcan hard by both shoulders, forcing him to look at her.

"You can track her like no other. I know him. I can fight him. You know what needs to be done, now go!" She pushed him away.

Lorcan was conflicted as he saw Yeqon rising again. He looked deep into Kea's eyes.

"You got this?"

"Hey, I don't like to talk numbers, but I'm older than you. I got this!" She punched his wounded shoulder, and he winced. "Oh, don't be a sook." Kea turned, looking back briefly.

"Go!" Her face was a determined mask.

She lit up her wings even brighter before he could argue and turned Yeqon's way. Lorcan followed her movements briefly before sinking into Oblivion, the energy signature left by Sophia dragging him down, like he was being reeled in on a fishing line.

Kea rammed Yeqon before he got back to his feet.

Down again, he roared like the mountain that finally shook the stone platform from its haunches, sending it crumbling away. Both Daimon and Watcher hovered out of the way of the falling debris.

"Left his girlfriend to do his dirty work?" Yeqon grimaced, tossing the dagger again.

"Is that all you think about, women? That they are the sidekicks or lovers of men?"

Yeqon smirked some more. He licked the edge of the dagger provocatively.

"We were both on Satanos. Who were the scariest ones of all there? Don't you recall?" Kea toyed, assessing his next move.

"And if only we had more females like that here!" Yeqon's eyes lit with the excitement of the memory.

Yeqon flew straight at her, pummelling Kea back into the tunnel. They rolled to a crashing stop.

She fought him off physically, her strength equal to his. They were in another stand-off, but this time in a confined space, with no flight possible. She tucked in her wings and thrust out a hand, her thoughts turning to the most powerful orb she could summon. Red ones on the forefront of her mind.

To her utter shock, nothing happened. Her face blanched. Flexing her hand repeatedly, Kea urged elemental power from within, but for some strange reason, she couldn't recall how to summon the burning power that coursed within her veins.

Yeqon recognised the realisation and panic in her wide eyes. He let out a deep, rumbling laugh.

Kea drew her long sword out, her hand shaky. Terror and confusion besieged her.

"Well, well. Have you been a naughty Watcher and made a deal with an Asmodai?" Yeqon tut-tutted, waving his finger back and forward in admonishment.

"They are never to be trusted." He glowered victoriously. "It seems you have forgotten how to fight, young one!" Yeqon held his stomach, laughing hard as he enjoyed the moment.

"Shut your mouth, Yeqon! You wouldn't know sacrifice if it hit you straight in your blackened heart!" Kea's sword glinted in the lava light that smeared thicker down the walls.

"Don't talk to me about sacrifice, wench! Look at what I've dwelled in since Lilith chose me over Adam!" He held his arms wide, indicating where they both stood.

Kea groaned in disgust, "You made your own Hell the day you turned your back on us."

He bristled; his torso seemed to swell with anger.

"*They* turned their backs on us! I'el allowed *our* people to judge us! Were we not sent here by *them?* Were we not put on this hole of a planet for a mere sub-species and then punished for entertaining ourselves? I'el sent us to Hell the day he ordered us to watch over these pathetic cretins!" His anger foamed his mouth. Electrical snaps arced and sizzled angrily across his torso, the static raising wisps of his white streaked hair. Kea's aura remained dull; her mortal flesh elementally powerless.

"I'm not arguing with you. What's the point? I've heard it all before. Blah, blah, blah, poor Yeqon! Come on then, let's do this!" Kea leaned forwards, wriggled her fingers.

"Let's." Yeqon nodded, his grimace widened.

Yeqon, the evil predator that he'd become, teasingly took his time playing with the dagger again, a favourite pastime. He cleaned his nails with its tip, then spat on the blade and polished it against his pants.

"You're going to die, you know. And then, so will she." His face pulled back into an even uglier smirk.

Kea ran at Yeqon, the tip of her sword aimed for his heart. Her sword glanced off his tiny dagger, but not before she pierced a decent hole just below his clavicle. He roared. The wound bloomed with dark blood, the chromious turned the surrounding flesh white. He retched with instant nausea.

Yeqon recovered quickly, followed up with a crackling whip of energy so powerful across Kea's chest that she was flung most of the way back towards Oblivion. Her sword sailed from her hand. As she lifted her head from the steaming ground, her gaze followed its path and she screamed with despair. Its smooth length spun over and over before falling away into the depths.

Recovering quickly, dodging an incessant onslaught of explosive orbs and stinging lightning bolts, Kea did all that she could manage with nothing but hand to hand fighting. She rammed Yeqon repeatedly. Bruises and swellings rapidly covered his body, along with a slick cut across his forehead, all thanks to her quick moving fists. Her physical strength matched his as they tumbled over and over. Eventually, though, he got the upper hand and landed on top of her, pinning her hard into the earth. Kea's entire body shook with the effort of holding his dagger laden fist from her throat as he sat astride her. Managing a swift knee to his groin, she turned the tables and pressed him equally aggressively into a sizzling trail of lava. One hand punching him bloody, whilst the other tried to dislodge and retrieve the dagger for herself.

He laughed throughout the entire episode, spitting blood back up in her face as the back of his head roasted atop the oozing primal soup.

"Soon enough you'll tire!"

He played with her confidence, and she knew he was right. Whilst matched in strength, her mortal body would eventually fatigue, whilst he would retain his A'vean firepower.

She screamed in frustration. Desperately, Kea wished and fought her blocked inner mind that prevented her memories of how to use her power.

Yeqon flipped her over again, inflicting a swift deep wound under her armpit. She scuttled from under him, her arm hung limply in pain, bleeding profusely. She couldn't even heal herself.

In that moment, she knew. She took off back towards the Throne room at a run to lead Yeqon away from Sophia and Lorcan. She would give them as long as she could to find each other and escape this realm.

"You can run, but you can't hide, pretty Kea!"

Blood lust obscured Yeqon's understanding of her trick, and he took the bait. Blood poured from her wound; her breaths laboured from the exsanguination. She tripped and stumbled along, but drew Yeqon all the way back to his deserted Throne room. He was close behind.

Once in the middle of the hazy room, Kea turned to face him.

Stumbling, her lips numb and her body shivering, she stood her ground.

"I'd like to say; I'll see you in Hell. But I'll be at I'el's table whilst you'll be wandering the darkest pits of Tartarus!" Kea coughed blood. She fell to her knees, exhausted.

"Oh, I'll be seeing you when I get through that portal and bring down that whole damned kingdom!" Yeqon edged forwards slowly, with all the maliciousness of a predator who had cornered its prey.

"I'll be seeing you, young Kea, as you wait on me hand and foot as *I* sit in I'el's place!" His eyes glinted with the exciting prospect.

"Fine, Yeqon, live your delusion. You always were dumb. Strong, but dumb!" Kea panted for breath, her lips pasty with the pallor of mortal death.

Yeqon closed in and kneeled by her limp frame. She challenged him with the last bit of strength that charged her blue eyes. They sparkled with defiance.

"I forgive you for what you are about to do…"

Yeqon balked momentarily, uneasy with what she said. In that moment of hesitation, Kea landed one last nose-breaking punch across his face, jarring him instantly out of his confusion. Yeqon grabbed her by the throat, shoving her back roughly until she lay helpless below him. He pulled the filthy dagger back out, waving it teasingly across her face.

Kea didn't break eye contact with his sinister glare. She didn't mutter a sound, not a cry or a whimper, as Yeqon leaned in and pressed the blade slowly through her smooth skin until there was nothing more than a hilt sticking out of her chest. Sparkling blood trickled from her mouth. She smiled defiantly, knowing she had given Sophia time. She smiled into the face of evil as she felt her energy sink away, pulling back from this mortal vessel she'd loved for so long. Kea smiled as her sight blurred and faded to black.

Chapter
Forty-Four

We fell. Stepping from the soup of souls through the tingly veil that was the secret portal, I lost my footing immediately.

Encompassed in inky blackness, pin-pricked with glittering stars, I lost hold of Rik. I flailed in a rapid tumble.

I wasn't aware of where Rik and Ben were, as my wings struggled against the tremendous propulsion of the fall. Gravity sucked me harder and faster toward a small light that rapidly became whiter, and brighter, and larger.

The domed outline of the Earth's atmosphere against the blackness of space raced towards me. It was freezing, so freezing. I flopped and rolled, shocked by where I was. A pull stronger than I could imagine fought with the strength of my wings, sucking me down.

The cold rapidly warmed the further I fell. As I crossed from the blackness of space into the white upper atmosphere, the cold turned to a burn. The gravity pull changed slightly, and I was able to wrap my wings around myself, cocooning my body from the fireball of heat that encapsulated my immense descent. The irony that I literally was a falling angel didn't skip my mind.

This heat eclipsed even that of the Daimon realm, and I fought hard to keep myself wrapped in the tight protection.

Every ounce of energy was utilised, until eventually, the heat dissipated as the atmosphere changed once more. Opening my perfectly intact wings, and somewhat impressed by this, I righted myself until I was able to regain a wobbly kind of control. My wings guided me through a rapid, but coordinated descent. I fell and flew, sometimes in charge, often tripped up by a changing updraft.

Tumbling over and over, in the midst of some more impressive gliding moments, I caught glimpses of blues, purples, and reds racing rapidly my way. Realising how quickly I was now cutting through clouds towards the ground, I flapped with everything I had. The cool moisture of the clouds extinguished the remnants of heat from the re-entry burn, leaving me feeling a little more alert and refreshed after this entire ordeal. The change in atmosphere seemed to give my efforts a sudden boost. I managed to halt my descent to a more manageable speed.

Looking about for the others, I wondered where I was. The barren mountainous earth below came closer by the second. Tiny spots emerged into the highest points of mountain ranges. Caps of snow whitened their peaks. The clouds were thick and cold with the icy bite of winter. As I scanned the skies, a distant yelp caught my attention.

Squinting in the glare, I quickly spotted a blur of movement searing through the sky, heading for a definite crash landing. Instinctively, I knew it was Rik. He had no control. The luminosity of his inexperienced wings left a trail of iridescent smoke in their wake.

"Oh no!" I screamed and changed course, banking to my right, heading straight for him. As I weaved through the opaque haze, trying to keep my eyes glued to him, I banged and scraped into a mountain peak concealed within the soupy whiteness of snow-laden clouds. This knocked me off course. I wiped away the injury and quickly corrected myself, continuing on, following his pleas for help.

Increasing my speed, I was terrified Rik was going to hit ground before I made it to him. His image became crisper as I neared, close enough that I caught his terrified expression. Our eyes briefly locked.

Amid his frantic attempts to stay aloft, he pointed towards me and screamed, "Watch out!"

I hadn't noticed until it was too late. Concealed beneath a darker, pre-thunderous fog was a gigantic mountain peak. Rik saw it, I didn't. Slamming into ice and rocks, I came to a sudden and painful stop before I began sliding down the steep icy incline. In all this time, I had held tight to Enoch's box. Through everything, it had remained safe in my arms. This time, though, it slipped away as I grappled to gain my balance. Gravity greedily drew the precious prize away.

I slid down the slush, screaming in frustration as Rik continued his out-of-control descent.

Oh, my God. What do I do? I had to get the box; I needed to save Rik. In seconds that felt like hours, I had to make a choice.

The box or Rik? Rik or the box? I quickly rationalised that he was the same as me, strong, but untrained. He had a chance, a good one. The box, well, it was essential for the safety of two cultures, A'vean and Human. *What if it was destroyed?*

Deep breath in, deep breath out, repeat.

Pushing away from the unforgiving mountainside, I turned my slide into a launch. I breached the mountaintop, away into the air and headed towards the descending box. Chastising myself the entire time, and wondering where Ben was, I knew I needed to bring this precious clue back. I had to pass on the inscription I'd discovered within it. This person, the Disciple of Learning, they could lead us directly to the key that we needed. Yet, as I allowed all these rationalising thoughts pat my ego, I felt a traitor, a failure, for choosing an inanimate object over my brother. *Please Rik, save yourself?*

The tumbling rectangle of silver shone in the morning sun. It glanced off another smaller mountain, sliding and tumbling like a tiny jewel, leaving a gouge in the snowy slush. Closing in, I reached forward. Just a few more seconds....

I caught it just as it was about to propel off an outcropping of rock into the open. I spun through the air, both relieved and besieged with guilt. Immediately, I turned to search for Rik. I called frantically as I headed for the ground, which was still far below. I shook with fear and guilt. There was no answer to my calls.

I searched through the mountain ranges that took on a light brown hue. The more the sun rose above the apricot horizon, the more I saw of this strange place. Coloured orbs rose from the ground, smooth and pretty, followed by a gassy whooshing sound. I hovered briefly within the safety of a small cloud and watched.

Balloons, hot air balloons were making their way across the light breeze, dozens of them. Their colourful bursts against the bland horizon resembled a beautiful postcard.

"Where am I?"

I heard a screech in the distance. "Rik?"

I called his name over and over, following the sound. Over and around another mountain, I found him exhausted and grappling for balance atop a strange looking vertical structure. Many these same craggy structures arose from the ground. Just as I reached Rik, with shame in my heart for the choice I'd made, Ben appeared in a blur of golden skin from somewhere above.

Alighting next to Rik, he scooped him up in his arms. Rik was battered, bloody; he grabbed for Ben eagerly. A pang of jealousy whipped at my heart. He reached for this stranger before me. Shaking such silliness from my thoughts, I breathed a sigh of relief as I hovered, panting with exhaustion and relief just to see Rik safe.

"I thought I'd lost you." I moved to hug Rik, but he turned away, hidden in Ben's chest. He didn't want to look at me.

"Oh, Rik!" My voice hitched.

Ben must have seen the immediate pain in my eyes.

"We all make choices, Sophia; some have difficult consequences. Don't mind him right now, he's quite broken, literally. He needs healing," Ben said quietly. Ben's face softened, as though he felt my pain. "I'll take him to Kaymakli to be healed."

Confused, I furrowed my brows, and he immediately answered.

"It's the most ancient of sanctuaries that dates back to the earliest civilisations. It's the last safe-haven from the Unseen and its where everyone went after… after you were taken." Ben appeared intensely uncomfortable. "Come, I'll show you. You'll be safe there."

"The hell you will!" Lorcan's voice filled the air. Before I knew what was happening, I was scooped up into his strong arms.

Lorcan pulled me tight into his chest.

"I've got you, Soph. I've been looking everywhere for you." His smile pulled dimples into his cheeks as he hugged me impossibly close, kissing the top of my head. His long, white hair blew wildly about, the remnants of his braid rich with lavender and sage. The perfume was comforting, reminding of Esme and Enl'iel. His cheeks suddenly flushed, and he looked away.

"Ben!" Lorcan spat his name like it was poison. "You will never set foot as a free A'vean again. If not for him, you'd have been dead before you could draw another miserable breath!" Lorcan jutted his chin towards Rik, who didn't look up, rather keeping his head buried in Ben's chest.

I felt like I should struggle free of Lorcan's embrace to work out what was going on, yet I felt incredibly tired. His arms were warm and felt safe, relieving my ravaged body and mind for the first time in what felt like forever.

My eyes hooded, and I breathed out languidly. It felt safe to let myself relax, let go of the ball of fear and uncertainty in my chest. With my free hand, I reached across and touched the soul stone in my bracelet, feeling instantly at ease. A weight lifted, at least for now, but the worry of Rik and what was to come gnawed incessantly in the back of my mind. I felt us move off at a gentle glide. Lorcan held me as though I was made of porcelain. My pendant hummed happily against my chest, as though it too knew I was safe. Lorcan whispered,

"Sleep now. You are safe. You'll always be safe with me, Sophia."

With the box safely tucked against my chest once more, Rik rescued by this mysterious Ben and myself in the safety of Lorcan's strength, I let go as psynostris and pure exhaustion overwhelmed me. I was away from Yeqon, I had Enoch's chest, and just for a little while, I could rest. Feeling another kiss planted on my forehead, I drifted off to the soft beat of Lorcan's wings and the calming melodic sound of his heartbeat against my ear.

The two lithe women hovered high above the clouds, observing the display below with delight.

"She has many on her side, sister," Anjou'elle observed.

"And clearly she is powerful enough to evade that dreg, Yeqon," Neph'reus responded with a raised brow.

"You were thinking well ahead to take the human girl. It is not the strength of her physique we must overcome. It is the strength of her heart." Anjou'elle complimented her sister.

"But she did let her brother fall. She *is* becoming stronger." Neph'reus now scowled in consternation.

"Indeed, she did, but how many times can a good girl like that see her beloved suffer?" Anjou'elle questioned supportively with a coy smile.

"What makes you think she will cave in to our wishes?" Neph'reus asked, clicking her long fingernails together.

"Dear sweet sister, once she realises we only want that pretty little box and not her life, she will run willingly to exchange it for the life of another," Anjou'elle replied with confidence.

"Hmmm, perhaps. It's time to send them a little message, let's invite them to our party," Neph'reus winked.

They embraced, giggling like young girls before transferring far away from the warming Turkish skies.

Chapter
Forty-Five

All that separated me from the traitors of the Watchers was an impossibly thin veil of pure energy. Belial in one cell, and Ben in the other.

I'd stood in this same spot day after day, ever since I'd awoken from sleep, surrounded by Enl'iel, Brennan, Lorcan, Cael and little Av'ael, who had insisted on visiting me at least once a day with stories of dreams and pictures she had drawn for me.

I'd learned about Jaz' abduction almost immediately. One thing these Watchers were hopeless at, was keeping a secret. If ever people wore their emotions on their faces, it was them. There was now also another faction at play for Enoch's key, and apparently, they had Jaz. Brennan, Lorcan, Dash and Jude had been searching non-stop in every underground grapevine for talk of Jaz. It was for this reason that I was not allowed to leave the Kaymakli caves until further notice… they knew I'd go looking for her too.

Hearing of Kea's death had knocked the wind from me. I was devastated, in shock, and angry beyond comprehension. I couldn't deal with the fact that another person had died for me. My emotions ebbed and flowed. A tide with an angry current pushed furiously along by Lorcan. He was an almost constant and annoying shadow.

He only gave me space if I was with Brennan or Cael, or if I was in the shower. This left my attitude snarky at best. I knew they were too scared to let me out of their sight, but there was no way I would let up trying to get out to find Jaz. Rik had refused to even look at me after I let him fall. *I'll never let go of you sister*, played constantly in my mind. I had let him go when he would have clung to me. What did that make me? How could I blame him for turning away from me? Saving Enoch's box, over protecting him first, had wounded his already devastated heart even further. I couldn't let Jaz down like that as well.

That damned box hadn't left my side; it went where I went. I even slept with it. It housed the scrolls now, and they were noisier than ever these past few days. I opened and closed it, ran my fingers over it so often. I felt like I knew every molecule it was made of, yet I knew it had more secrets that I needed to discover.

Follow me, the Disciple of Learning, the inscription in its base invaded my every waking and sleeping hour. *Who are you? Where are you?*

"Come on now, darlin'. Don't go beating yourself up any more," Cael's soft, cadence relaxed me a little.

I looked down at him, lapped up his sweet Irish tone. He was his old gorgeous self, sitting contentedly in a wheelchair, his wings a long way from repair. His hair had grown considerably and was now plaited with Daimon repelling herbs, as was the custom. He smelled wonderful; reminding me of Esme and simpler times when Jaz and I worked as nurses together. That seemed a mere fanciful dream now.

"You miss Australia?" I asked him.

"Hell yeah! I miss my bike." He glanced towards Belial's cell. Belial had remained hidden amongst the shadows, refusing to talk or eat.

"A man doesn't mess with another man's wheels!" Cael glowered Belial's way. It was he who had caused Cael's motorcycle crash and subsequent horrific injuries.

I smiled, "You loved that Ducati."

"More than any woman." Cael winked cheekily at me.

I returned my attention to this mysterious Ben that they all whispered about behind my back. I wasn't stupid. It was the one thing

I couldn't wrench out of anyone. Ben was yet to look my way, despite days and days of visits. I sat for hours and mulled over why I was so bothered by him.

Lorcan objected to my visits, of course. To the point that I wanted to punch him. He insisted it wasn't good for me to be near the prisoners. But I wanted answers to gnawing questions that I couldn't even bring to the forefront of my mind. All anyone would give up was that Ben had been the traitor who had blown our cover and brought me to Yeqon. Apparently, he had been watching me my whole life, pretending to help us, pretending to be an ally. It just didn't feel like the whole story.

Nothing made sense. He saved us, both Rik and myself, and fought off Yeqon. He guided us through that disgusting Blood River of Souls and through the portal to home. No one was buying his story though, even when I pleaded that he single handily saved us.

I'd not tried to talk to him. I just watched and waited. Looking in from the other side, he may as well have been a million miles away, like the answers I desperately wanted.

"It's no good doing this to yourself, sweetheart. He made his choice a long time ago," Cael said.

"But why do I feel there's something more, Cael? There's something about him I just can't put my finger on."

Cael shifted a little in his wheelchair.

"Apart from the fact he nearly had you killed?" Cael said.

"You all keep saying that, but even if it's true, he brought me and my brother back. Does that not count for something? For redemption?"

Cael shook his head, "Redemption? That is for I'el to decide. I know what I feel in my soul, but I am unable to absolve him for such great sins. I can forgive him for myself, but not on behalf of us all. Here, eat before Eilir puts a bib on you and feeds you herself. She's going balmy worrying on you, you know?"

He passed up half an Eccles cake, which I took gratefully, despite not feeling the slightest bit hungry. Sweet Eilir, if ever there was a

Welsh version of Esme, it was her. I took a nibble of the flaky currant goodness and felt better for it.

Ben shuffled in his dank cell, turning his body away so all I could see were the scars that ran the length of his back. He had so many.

"Why do you all have those scars? The straight ones, I mean? He has them too."

"Ah, those. Well, it started after the first thousand years we'd been stranded here. Most of us had been in hiding from the shock of being cut off. When we started to emerge, we decided to mark our time here. One line on the right shoulder blade for every millennium, kinda like what you see prisoners chalk onto their cell walls." Cael snorted a small laugh.

I counted. Ben had 12. "He's been here twelve thousand years?"

"He's only young then." Cael shuffled a little to get comfortable. "Count mine," he said.

I did. I gently touched twenty perfectly straight white scars.

"Oh, Cael, how do you stand it?"

"Hon, I'm older again than that. This is just my life on Earth." He smiled, broad and warm, his energy undeniably and perfectly good.

"How will we all get through this?" I grazed my hand across the silvery box. My reflection was clear in the newly polished metal. I looked back down to Cael.

"I dream each night about strange places and voices. I dream that I'm sinking to the bottom of the bluest ocean."

"Be patient, sweet Sophia. It will fall into place for you. Enoch will speak to you, as will I'el. Just keep dreaming and loving and believing," he said.

I returned my attention to Ben. Dreaming, loving and believing. Strange emotions swirled through my heart and pulled at my guts.

"How can you be so sure I'll figure it all out?"

"Because darlin' you're Soph'ael, the Earth-born angel of A'vean."

The End

Thank you for reading Surrender

To continue the A'vean Chronicles,

scan the code below for a link

Allegiance,

book 3 of The A'vean Chronicles.

ACKNOWLEDGMENTS

I want to thank my amazing family yet again, for supporting me as I continue my writing journey.

Writing a second book, and now a second edition of the first two books of The A'vean Chronicles, has been a wonderful journey that I never imagined I might have achieved. I still have the best fan club under my very own roof. Always, my beautiful husband comes first when thanks are due. Writing is not a money-making business, it's a passion and labour of love with no guarantees of success. Chris, you indulge my passion for stories with unwavering support. I literally couldn't publish without your support. Thank you and I love you.

Thank you to my beautiful children, who are always on the receiving end of my endless book epiphanies. I may bore you to death now, but hopefully one day mum's wild ideas may seem interesting!

To my friends Caroline and Yildiz for helping me with French and Turkish translations and pronunciations, thank you so very much. Your help has been invaluable.

To Kat of katartillustrations whose amazing art brings my characters to life. Your concepts are so very beautiful and delight fans of my books. The designer of my original covers, you will always be an artist that I fangirl over and recommend.

To James and Becky of Platform house Publishing who have lovingly re-designed a full set of covers to reinvigorated The A'vean Chronicles series. The new covers are beyond stunning. Thank you for your patience with my appalling time management in sending you my edits to re-format. You have made my books things of utter beauty.

And of course, to my readers, old and new. Thank you for supporting an indie author with big ideas and dreams. I value each and every one of you and strive to continue to bring you stories for years to come. If I have entertained you, my job is done.

ABOUT THE AUTHOR

G.R. Thomas is an Australian indie author. An avid reader since childhood, it has only been well into adulthood that pen was put to paper to capture the stories that have always been her mind.

In between working as a theatre recovery nurse, being mum to three beautiful children, wife to an ever-supporting husband and running a hobby farm, writing is the passion that glues a very busy life together.

Follow me
Please keep up to date with what I'm up to on social media:
Instagram: @grthomas2014.
TikTok: @grthomasindieauthor
Website: www.grthomasbooks.com
Facebook: G.R. Thomas Author

If you enjoyed this or any of my other books, please leave a small review on Amazon, Goodreads, or wherever you prefer to review the books you enjoy. Reviews are the gold dust that make books sparkle and are forever appreciated by authors.
Thank you for reading, Surrender.